The Balance of Fates

Raquel Raelynn

Goldheart Publishing

This book may contain mature and sensitive material. Violence, swearing, sexual content. Mental and physical harm, both self-inflicted and caused by others. (For more in-depth details check rrwrites@raquelraelynn.com content warnings page)

Copyright © 2023 by Goldheart Publishing LLC

All rights reserved.

No portion of this book may be reproduced in any form without written permission from the publisher or author, except as permitted by U.S. copyright law.

This is a work of fiction. Names, characters, places, events, and incidents are the products of the author's imagination. Any resemblance to actual persons, living or dead, or actual events is purely coincidental.

Cover design by Sleepy Fox Studio

Goldheart Publishing LLC appreciates readers, reviewers, and book fans. Thank you for supporting my hard work as an author by buying an authorized edition of my book and for not illegally copying, distributing, or appropriating any part of it without my permission. You're making it possible for me to write more books for you to enjoy. I love and encourage fan fiction with the proper credit. If you would like permission to use material from the book (other than for review purposes), please contact rrwrites@raquelraelynn.com

Contents

Dedication		V
		VII
1.	Under the Midnight Moon	1
2.	Screaming into the Storm	16
3.	A Burger with a Stranger	26
4.	Eggs and Ambush	44
5.	Red Eyes Haunt	54
6.	It Speaks	64
7.	Only a Skull Remains	77
8.	From Memory to Man	88
9.	If the World is Fair	103
10.	With Mouths Closed	110
11.	If All You Do is Fail	119
12.	Things You Find in the Forest	135

13.	Two Things are True	155
14.	What Not to Do at Parties	172
15.	Vampires Can Play Doctor	188
16.	As My Eyesight Began to Fade	200
17.	If You Have to Hate Me	220
18.	A Siren's Love Prophecy	233
19.	Topsy-Turvy Past	248
20.	A Truth and a Lie	259
21.	Sage Advice	271
22.	Servants of Chance	283
23.	Kuai-Yuel	297
24.	Flying Amongst Stars	312
25.	The Balance of Fates	328
26.	The Ties of Death and Love	344
27.	Descent to Madness	370
Acknowledgments		393
About Author		395

I would like to dedicate this book to myself. For believing I could do this and never giving up on my dream. Second, to my family, whom I love more than anything.

The people who have helped me get here:

To my mom, Rebecca, thank you for being an example of a loving and hardworking woman. I love you, and I love how much you love me.

To my twin and other half, Daquan, you are the smartest person I know. I came into this world with you and couldn't imagine a life without you. You have supported me so much on this journey.

To my sister Jomiah, I have always loved and admired you. You are greater than even you realize. Thank you for listening to me ramble.

To my father, Jason, thank you for stepping into my life and always making me laugh. You have bigger dreams for me than I have for myself.

To my Black girls, *I see you.*

Come and fall in love.

Chapter One

Under the Midnight Moon

*T*ICK-TICK-TICK.

The old wooden clock stands tall in the corner of the hall: smooth dark wood; polished gold pieces; a pendulum swinging back and forth, back and forth behind glass. Lucia's nerves tick higher with the old beast. It has been here as long as she can remember, a gift from the head of the Starlight coven to her mother. Hatsia, the Golden Griffin coven head, had it placed beside the kitchens, deep within the halls of the Dol'Auclair manor, because she can't stand the sight of it. Tacky garbage, she called it. Her mother hates anything un-mystic.

Lucia wishes the clock would stop. Every tick brings her closer to her blooming.

Tonight is the blooming ceremony, an important night for young witches, and should be a day of celebration for her, but it is her third ceremony, which is two too many, so that makes it the worst day of her life. Well, at least the third worst day.

That is why Lucia stands outside of the kitchens, amongst a maze of halls, and hiding from her handmaidens, twins Maile and Mila, who are meant to be bathing her so she can be cleansed for the ceremony. She wants to put it off as long as she can so that she may forget about the ceremony altogether. She wishes she didn't have to do it at all. It is humiliating to be rejected by the Mother time and again in front of the entire coven and those who have traveled across Hontaras to watch her bloom.

Over the sound of the clock ticking an hour to midnight, a small voice whispers, "Lady Lucia, the Grand Elder Kaeda has yet to arrive."

Lucia pulls the finger she has been nervously biting away from her mouth as she looks the boy up and down. He has shocking red hair and a smattering of freckles across his cheeks. His apron is stained with food. The boy is the cook's only son, Haru. Their family moved from Whonyia when he was a baab. He was practically raised in the kitchens.

"How do you know?" Lucia asks, trying not to look too interested in the answer.

"When I went to get some air a moment ago, Mila told me so. All of the servants are talking about it. The Grand Elder is late, my lady."

She should feel guilt for the wave of relief that relaxes her stiff shoulders. Lucia shouldn't wish for the Grand Elder to miss the ceremony, but she can never do right in the woman's eyes and this day only brings painful memories for her. Having her grandmother absent will help her frayed nerves.

Each year at midnight on the eve of the autumn equinox, young witches become women. They're paraded on stage in the temple in what Lucia thinks is a humiliating display. Witches from covens all over Hontaras come to witness as they receive their gift from the Mother. It's an age-old tradition dating back to a time when the Mother still walked among witches; Now only her spirit lives, passing gifts and wisdom to the next generation.

In Naprait, the blooming is in autumn, and families make a whole trip out of traveling to the Golden Griffin coven. It sits behind the Ife ring, which keeps them hidden, bordering them from the human towns that sit in the valley below.

The Northwest is quiet; there are only mountains, dense forests, and open fields of grassland, yet witches from all over come to watch their friends, distant family, and coven nobility bloom.

Lucia is of noble birth. The Dol'Auclair are descended from the founder of one of the four major covens. *The first covens.* Many witches will come to watch her bloom—and her younger sister. It will be Gabrielle's first ceremony.

Haru interrupts Lucia's mumbling with the clearing of his throat. His kind face and wide eyes look up at her.

"Milk bread," he says, holding out a white cloth.

Lucia releases an anxious breath, smiling as she takes the treat. It is warm in her hands, fresh from the oven, and soft. It's the only way she likes it. Milk bread is Lucia's favorite treat; it evokes pleasant memories from childhood of sneaking into the kitchens with her sister late at night to eat it hot off the tray. They would get in trouble when they were caught, but they did it anyway.

"Thank you," she says. "You are too kind."

"I figured it would clear your mind, my lady."

Lucia notices the bags under Haru's eyes and wishes she had something to give him in return. He must have been preparing all day for the morning feast. Lucia appreciates it. It is the only part she looks forward to as the ceremony participants aren't allowed to eat the whole day prior and Lucia hates to be denied food.

She slinks away with her prize, disappearing within the many halls with the ghost of a smile on her face and a weight off her shoulders.

Her peace only lasts a short while.

The night chill burns through Lucia like shame as the last dredges of summer sink away.

She is freezing, her skin stinging and rubbed raw by Maile, who had tracked her down and dragged her to the baths where she cleaned every spot of her skin and drenched Lucia in oils made of the last of summer's flowers.

The sky is painted in deep purple hues, and there's music drifting over the clearing, floating above the flickering bonfire and heads of the witches of the Golden Griffin coven.

Despite the good atmosphere, Lucia is not feeling cheery as she grabs her younger sister's hand in the dark. Gabrielle is a rock beside her, her stance confident and her smile wide. Gabrielle is never shaken. Not even when Lucia is trembling beside her like a leaf.

"Come on, you'll be fine," Gabrielle says, squeezing her sister's sweaty fingers. "This ritual is important. Nearly as important as the blooming ceremony, which we couldn't possibly have without honoring the great deities first. No one can sit this out, not even you. Especially not on the night of your blooming."

The ritual ushers out the end of summer. The unwed women over eighteen perform it each year for good health and plentiful food as well as to strengthen the border Ife around Laesbury and keep out negative spirits that thrive in the cold, dreary months.

Lucia blows warmth into her trembling fingers, taking a deep breath of the icy air. She feels guilty, relying on the strength of her younger sister. Just another way in which she is weak. As the eldest and a Dol'Auclair, she should be the one people look to for guidance.

Lucia scans the clearing, her peers are huddled together around the fire wearing their best dresses, sweeping gowns made in town with beautiful fabrics. Clothes they wear for Dai Gemus to please the deities. Still, Lucia feels out of place with her high-frilled neckline and too extravagant in her silks and lace.

Lucia wanted to go for something simpler to blend in, but her mother refused the request. She said Lucia was being too modest for her place, and that it wouldn't do to make herself look lesser for anybody.

When picking out Lucia's ceremonial dress, Hatsia scowled, hands clasped against her chest as Lucia was poked and prodded by the tailor. She had said in her most haughty voice, "A queen does not shrink herself to fit beside the common, so why should you?"

Lucia didn't have a response that wouldn't anger her, something like "I'm not a queen," so she wore the dress.

Now she regrets it.

The other women are staring at her, leaning in close to one another and whispering behind their hands. Whether it's her dress or... other reasons, she can only assume. And given her nature, Lucia imagines the worst.

"Women," the great Priestess of the Naprait temple calls from the shadows of the trees. The coven elders gather in dark robes as they stand by to supervise the ritual. "Gather 'round the late summer flame, and take hands with those beside you. The ceremony is soon to begin."

Lucia shuffles forward; the fire warms her face and casts an orange glow across her dark skin. As they get close, Gabrielle's braid brushes her arm as they stand shoulder to shoulder. Lucia pretends not to notice as the young witch to her left hesitates before grabbing her hand.

The ritual is quick. A hooded figure comes around and pours goat blood over each of the joined hands, and then salt is poured around the circle, the fire jumping twice its height as if reaching for the sky.

Going down the line, they each recite the coven head's words, "Nipas tut, nipas lile. Ainire e oiji nin oru tojj. Mu wa gbara, ayon, bo ulo fera Mother, i pese ilera i ojun si Deipara's yan enyan."—*Through cold, through harsh, despair as the sun in shadow hides. Bring strength, joy, and protection to our dearest Mother, and provide health and food to Deipara's chosen people.*

The goat whose blood was shed for the ritual is tossed into the flames and swallowed instantly as the offering is accepted by the Mother Deipara, the original elder of the witches and the deity the covens have worshipped for centuries since her passing.

The fire dims, shrinking to its original size as the ritual ends, and the salt is broken to release the women from the circle. Lucia lets out a deep breath as she can finally breathe again. The pressure squeezing her lungs and the ringing in her ears fade away. She looks to Gabrielle, who lets go of her hand, all of the women blinking as if in a daze as they try to reorient themselves.

"The ritual is complete," the great Priestess calls. "Now, let us head down to the temple for the blooming ceremony."

They shuffle out of the forest in a line, the coven heads breaking off toward the entrance of the temple while the blooming women go around back to change into their ceremonial clothing.

The wind whistles through thin, barren trees like wind chimes, blowing stiff, cracked golden leaves through the aperture into the small marble room. The large wedge of milk bread begins to expand in Lucia's stomach like a ball of dread as she's ushered into the changing room, where the four women are handed matching garments. Lucia, her sister Gabrielle, and the two other witches blooming tonight—Mairan and Clara.

"Don't be afraid, Lucia," Gabrielle whispers. "Perhaps this will be your year."

Gabrielle is huddled close to Lucia, their voices pitched low like they're passing secrets as the clock ticks down to midnight. Gabrielle's breath warms the side of her older sister's face, their hands rubbing together to heat each other.

"Autumn represents maturity and change. As I become a woman, you will grow into the strength and power I've always seen in you."

Her smile is so sweet and hopeful that Lucia can only mirror it. She doesn't say what she is truly thinking as she remembers her traumatic first blooming. She too had been so excited, watching year after year as other Golden Griffins bloomed, waiting for her turn so she could prove wrong her elders and peers who looked down on her.

Lucia gloomily thinks *Autumn is also decay and death.*

Hontaras counts down to the first day of autumn as the Priestess gives a speech onstage at the Naprait temple to a crowd of awaiting witches. Lucia knows the monotonous speech given each year by heart, inviting in the new season and a new set of blooming witches. Finally, she calls:

"Lucia Dol'Auclair, first daughter of Hatsia Dol'Auclair, and granddaughter of the Grand Elder Kaeda." The woman's voice is cracking, that of an old, wizened woman, her words echoing against ivory marble, plants twisting up the aged pillars.

Lucia makes her way to the center of the stage, followed by Gabrielle, Clara, and Mairan. She keeps her eyes averted from the crowd of witches, the Naprait temple bursting as people sit crowded in the pews on either side of the wide room. As the Golden Griffin is one of the four major covens, no one wants to miss this blooming ceremony, especially not with two of the Grand Elder's granddaughters in participation.

The familiar rug Lucia walks each day of Dai Dimi Dei has been swapped for one red and golden, shaped like a giant tongue. This one is thinner and silken, the cold leaching in through the soles of her feet. She wishes the floor would open and swallow her within as many eyes watch her—a sea of grim faces.

Lucia can imagine they're here to see her fail a third time, or maybe to see her sister follow the same fate. Two noble witches snubbed by the Mother bringing shame to their family and the Golden Griffins.

Lucia can only clench her fists and take a deep breath.

The Golden Griffins are closest to the stage, Hatsia in the front row in a silken headwrap, shining under the moonlight in cool, fetching colors. Blues, whites, and gold color that section, which is a majority of the left half of the room.

On the other side, amongst the visitors, is Hatsia's good friend and Sea Serpent coven head from the Swamps of Swaydan, Linae Devroue. The woman wears a headscarf and a lace face covering that drapes over her mouth and an elegant emerald green dress with buttons up the front. The Serpents favor dark colors: black and green, and deep purples.

Then there are the Black Basilisks, Naprait's flashy northeastern family who live up in the harsh, rocky mountains of Etryae. Eshana Sacrenladre has her face covered by a veil studded with glittering jewels and wears a large red dress with a big fringe. The sight is nearly blinding.

The last major coven is also in attendance; The Starlights from the plains of Whonyia. Amelia Coflar is in a simple dress accompanied by a small party. They are in muted, pastel shades of light greens and pale pink, their clothes a bit weathered and unfinished as they are friendly, hard-working people who don't care much about appearances.

Hatsia's lips are pursed, her figure held taut as long fingers tap a quick pace against the back of her hand. The seat beside her reserved for the Grand Elder is still empty.

Lucia doesn't doubt her grandmother would miss her blooming, as this is her third. The woman is impatient and unforgiving. She doesn't give second chances.

But Gabrielle is in the ceremony this year and she is their grandmother's favorite—the firstborn Kaeda wanted.

Gabrielle is one of those people everyone loves. She's everything Lucia is not—confident, brave, loud, and sociable. She pushes her way into your life, whether you want it or not. Lucia is timid and quiet. They are opposites. Where Lucia is short with a full figure, Gabrielle is tall and slim. Lucia has a plump, round face with big, dark curls and ebony skin, and Gabrielle has light eyes and hair, which she wears most often in long braids around a narrow face.

Gabrielle stands beside Lucia in matching white, yet they look nothing alike. In a way, true sisters. Two sides of a whole.

The four witches stand before the statue of Deipara, who bore magisk into Hontaras centuries before. It is said that Deipara was the originator of magisk, bringing it over from their lost homeland of Ashad Escana.

Deipara had called out to Ig-Akoko, the First Tree, as her people were being slaughtered, and saved them in the battle against the vampires during the War of Mystics. A war that ended the brutality against witches and positioned them at the head of the three Mystic families—the witches, vampires, and wolves—and gained them control of the magisk core.

Lucia's grandmother now holds the title of Eidan. The Orbis Libra's vessel.

A wizened old woman motions for Mairin to come forth, hunched over her cane as the white strings of her hair fall limp at the sides of her face.

As a kid, Lucia joked that the Priestess was immortal. She was old even when her grandmother was young and embodies the essence of the ancient marble temple around them as if she were painted from that time and had come to life.

The ceiling is made of beautiful, stained artwork, and at the center is a clear piece where the moon sits at its highest peak, reflecting down unto the basin of moon water below, the glittering, crystal clear water rippling out toward the sides of the glass as if moved by the moon itself.

Mairan's rosy cheeks are illuminated in the moon's light as skittish green eyes fail to meet the Priestess's. The woman dips her fingers into the basin and presses wet fingers to Mairan's forehead. The iridescent droplets glide down her face, between her eyes.

"Enter Mother, bless your child. Que agba marun i yan."—*From five powers you choose* she says, slipping into ancient Azes. "Bring us a daughter to aid in the protection and nurturing of this great coven."

The Priestess steps back, giving Marian space at the center of the stage, and for a moment, nothing happens.

Marian closes her eyes, letting the moon wash over her, and then a breeze begins swirling the floor at her feet.

Lucia is pushed back, her feet sliding over marble, and Gabrielle grabs her arm to steady her.

The wind gathers in the temple, surrounding Mairan and lifting her off her feet. Red hair whips around the young woman's head, which is thrown back in an arch that points down to the floor.

Mairin opens her eyes, looking down in shock at everyone below. She begins giggling, her face morphing into one of excitement and joy.

Lucia is caught up in it, too, her eyes glued to the floating witch, who seems to have gained the confidence she lacked when she first walked onto the stage, shy and skittish.

This was always Lucia's favorite part of watching the blooming ceremonies—the joy from the chosen and the coven as a collective when someone is given their gift.

Lucia's heart pounds hard against her rib cage, a lump forming in her throat. She has always found magisk beautiful—the versatility of it—the freedom of it.

Lucia has never been able to do magisk. No accidental magisk as a child or the easy cantus learned in first academy. Not even cuma, the coven magisk that most witches can do. *Even the men can.*

That childlike joy Marian is feeling was robbed from Lucia, who now feels small standing before the Mother. The deity's statue casts a long shadow over her. She is lost beneath it, the strength that she had leeched from Gabrielle earlier fleeing.

When Clara scrambles to take Mairan's place beside the Priestess, nearly tripping over her skirts in her excitement, Lucia is reminded of her first blooming ceremony. She had been so happy that she would finally have a gift of her own so that everyone would stop pitying her. Every witch is supposed to provide for the community, and if Lucia can't even do that, then what is she?

In those early years, Lucia grew to hate the smug looks, and the upturned lips of her coven, like she was the joke that sat in the corner of their smiles.

That fateful day in her eighteenth year, Lucia had been so sure she would bloom. So sure that the Mother was saving a special gift just for her.

She had been a devout daughter, hadn't she?

She never missed Dai Dimi Dei, the three holy days of the witches. She attended temple every day, doing charity for the Priestess.

Lucia had been dressed up in her white dress, antsy in the changing room, as she swayed excitedly, a huge smile on her face. Not even Anku and her friends whispering about her across the room had dimmed her shine.

When the Priestess had called the four women out on stage, her eyes went immediately to her grandmother, and her chest swelled with confidence that she would finally make her grandmother proud. She would be called "My moon" and then her grandmother would hug her. Kaeda hadn't hugged Lucia in a long time, growing disappointed when Lucia's magisk never emerged.

Lucia had walked off stage that first year, numb and broken like shattered ice. The temple had filled with whispers, eyes growing wide as they leaned into one another to gossip as if she wasn't right there.

The Grand Elder's face was burnt into Lucia's mind—shame and disappointment.

Gabrielle's warm touch startles Lucia back from those memories, her eyes flitting to her grandmother's empty seat once more.

Turning back to the Priestess, she ignores the curious eyes on her and wipes her sweaty palms on her dress, scrunching the cotton between her fingers. She is terrified, but she can feel the nervous excitement of Gabrielle beside her like a living, breathing thing and it nearly knocks her over. She has to focus hard to block it out.

This is her last year. *Her last.* Most witches don't get a second chance before the Mother, let alone a third. If they don't bloom at their first ceremony, they're sent to one of the minor covens or stuck tending the fields or working their parents' shops. Lucia has only been given this chance due to her family name and everyone knows it.

Clara makes her way back to the line.

Lucia missed the woman's turn, but by the vines and vibrant purple flowers which now climb the stone temple walls, she is a Gaia. Lucia itches to touch her neck, memories of the same gift being used on her.

Gabrielle's warm hand leaves Lucia's back. She bounds over to the Priestess, who halts the eager woman with a shriveled hand.

Gabrielle doesn't look nervous or scared at all. She doesn't fear that Lucia's curse might have passed on to her.

Gabrielle doesn't fear anything.

The woman's bare feet wiggle atop the rug where they peek out from under her dress; she's like a spring, coiled and ready to go off.

Lucia can't help but admire her sister's enthusiasm and beauty. Gabrielle's smile takes up her entire face, alive in a way that conflicts with the hardened and immobile features of the Mother bound in statue beside her, and youthful in the way the Priestess to her other side is no longer.

Lucia feels there is cruelty in that.

Still, she smiles.

Gabrielle's hair is a cherry cloud, her face lit in the prism of color reflected from the moon upon the stained glass above their heads.

Lucia is happy for her sister. That knowledge is a relief. She doesn't think there's anything eviler than a sister's jealousy.

Gabrielle closes her eyes, bending her head back to the sky and her palms facing up the same way. Her eyelids flutter, lips moving silently.

Lucia is desperate to know what she is saying, unable to read her lips.

Slowly, beneath a glow of moon and stars, something begins to gather in Gabrielle's hand. Like water pooling in a stream, light dances along her right palm, filling it up and spilling over in her open hand until there is something sitting in it.

Lucia leans in closer. *It's a golden chain.*

Gabrielle opens her eyes slowly, and a smile spreads wide across her face as she lifts the chain for all to see.

The chain swings from her fingertips, the gleaming surface sending beams of light cutting across the room, a smattering of red and orange across the bridge of their mother's smiling face.

The charm in the middle is a flaming moon.

Gabrielle is a Mallei.

As young girls, the two sisters often played a game where they imagined themselves with one of the four magisk natures. Gaia has earth magisk and breathes life into nature. Mallei conjures and forges matter at will, like the blacksmiths of magisk. Augere can manipulate their bodies in odd and magnificent ways, gaining strength and speed that nearly rivals that of the two other Mystic families—vampire and wolf.

Lastly, there are Sages, the rarest of them all. They can manipulate the mind, a chilling power that makes Lucia shake just thinking of it. She had *never* imagined herself as a Sage in any of their games.

The Priestess calls Lucia over, waving to where she stands beside the basin under a beam of moonlight.

Lucia's about to move when Gabrielle stops her, pressing something into her hand. Lucia's fingers close over the cool metal as she takes a steadying breath. When she opens her eyes, her sister is smiling, and Lucia feels a surge of strength as she moves across the stage.

Standing before the Priestess, Lucia shakes terribly from the chill as her hands are gathered in smaller, weathered ones.

Lucia's eyes close as a cool, wet hand passes over her face, the water falling like teardrops. She feels laid bare on stage before the Mother and all of the gathered witches.

All Lucia wants is a gift. That's all she asks for in this life.

The silence in the room grows long and loud as Lucia gathers herself, trying to find a connection with the Mother. It is said that most witches have a clue of how they will present before their ceremony. Some sort of sign is given by the Mother. Lucia has had no such contact with the deity.

Lucia blinks slowly, the room brightening with every flick of her eyelashes. She feels every eye on her. Judging her. Waiting for her to fail again.

Her movements are stiff as she places her empty hand out before her, shaking as she tries to focus on the curving grooves of her palm and imagines something materializing there as it had for her sister.

She thinks of something easy, an autumn leaf, orange and brittle with five fingers and lobed edges. She pictures it like a scene playing behind her eyes, appearing in her palm so withered and fragile. She remembers how it looked when her sister conjured the necklace, the sparks of light like the glittering of sunlight against a waterfall.

Lucia's heart stutters as she thinks she sees it, the outline of an orange figure as lights burst behind her eyelids.

Then she follows the light up to the moon, shifting lower in the sky, sending a shower of colored glass over her hand. There is no leaf. Nothing besides infinitesimal space within the ivory skin of her palm. Her heart sinks as she lowers her hand and her eyes, her head dropping to her chest in defeat.

She failed.

The truth of Lucia's situation is clear as fantasy washes away with the falling moon. She has been living a lie. Not just these three years attending the blooming ceremony again and again, hoping for a different result each time, but her entire life. She was born thinking she was special, only to arrive at this moment to the crushing truth:

No one is born special. Not even a Dol'Auclair.

A faint, soul-crushing "Poor girl" from the crowd pulls tears forward to cloud Lucia's vision.

Frozen in place, Lucia stands there until a throat clears.

"I am sorry, Lucia Dol'Auclair," the rough, slow voice of the Priestess says for the third time. "You have failed to bloom."

THE BALANCE OF FATES

Terror strikes Lucia's heart with those words. The image of her grandmother appears in her mind and fear freezes her. Round eyes dart to the crowd where the Grand Elder's seat is still empty, and the place where her mother once sat is empty too.

Sweat gathers across Lucia's brow and she trembles as she walks off the stage, the last on the way out as she was first coming in, accompanied by a crushing silence. Lucia can think of nothing but her grandmother's anger when she finally arrives.

She has to get away.

Chapter Two

Screaming into the Storm

Lucia hides behind the statue of Dai, waiting for her chance to slip away. The statue is a larger-than-life boy with a juvenile face and rosy cheeks, his foot nearly the size of Lucia's entire body. He was recorded in coven archives to have been a confidant to the deity Deipara in her life and an active participant in the rebellion against the vampires. He died at a very young age.

There are many statues of him and others carved in that time all around Laesbury and bordering the Merin Korua—the four rings that shelter witches within Naprait, Etryae, Whoynia, and Swaydan.

Lucia leans back against Dai's long leg, having dodged Gabrielle's pitying looks before she gave up and disappeared into the party to celebrate her blooming. Lucia still clutches the object Gabrielle placed in her hand, the hard points digging into her palm.

A buzzing of voices draws her mind back into the room, her name standing out amongst the chatter. She peeks around Dai's legs to see a few of the older women whom she's seen come and go from the manor house on occasion.

"It's a tragedy," one woman says, her wine glass held loftily. "A Dol'Auclair who hasn't bloomed. My daughter's blooming was the same year as hers, and it was unfortunate then; now it's just sad."

Lucia recognizes her now. She's Anku's mother, Lillian. Anku is a cruel girl who tormented Lucia in the lower academy and encouraged her other peers to exclude Lucia from everything. She was very popular and persuasive. The only people who didn't fall under her enchantment were those who got close to Lucia only because of who she is and her family's name. No one wanted to make any true connections with her. *The cursed girl.*

Lillian comes to visit Hatsia often, with some grievance or another. Lucia can expect to see her exiting her mother's office nearly every evening.

Kamila nods along. "I have to agree. At twenty, she should just let it go. She is very pretty, but not very bright. My daughter says she has all sorts of odd ideas. Hatsia's holding on because the girl is her oldest, but I would be embarrassed to parade my daughter before the Mother to be rejected time and again. Once was enough."

The women hum over their glasses, and Lucia's face burns with humiliation. She's used to the teasing from her peers and has long resigned herself to being an outsider, but these are her elders. Coven is supposed to be family. That's what her mother always told her.

Lucia's heart races as she clutches marble with dull nails, the low trill sending a shiver up her spine. None of the women hear it or Lucia's heart breaking, over their laughter and gossip.

"I don't think it's right of Hatsia to send her up there. I tried to warn her against it many times. I'm not sure what it is they're keeping from us, whatever it is the girl did to make the Mother so angry, but it must have been dreadful. Two years ago, on the night before Lucia's first ceremony, I awoke in a sweat from a terrible nightmare. I saw blood and war and..." Melody pitches her voice lower, leaning in toward the other women. "...vampires."

There's a chilled silence for a moment before Lillian titters. "The magisk is fine! My oldest daughter is a strong and talented witch, and my youngest, Mairan, just presented. It's just a sad truth that the long reign of the Dol'Auclairs is coming to an end. Lucia has truly seen to that. No way can a witch without a gift lead the Golden Griffin. *It would be shameful.* And the other covens are just looking for an opportunity to cement our downfall. I mean, look at them."

The woman peeks over her shoulder at the guests milling about and enjoying the feast. "That Escana, such flamboyance," she says through laughter.

"Who cares about politics?" Melody says, her drink sloshing as she waves a hand toward the other two women. "The Mother is angry, and we're only upsetting her further. This could mean trouble for the reign of witches, not just the Golden Griffins!"

There's a dull clack of high heels against stone, a confident stride as Hatsia approaches the prattling women.

"Ladies," she drawls, turning their attention.

Lucia squeezes herself further into Dai, hoping to hide from her mother with her face pressed to the cool stone of the deity's dainty legs. Her nails leave fine scratches on the smooth surface.

"Coven head Hatsia," Lillian says, startled and wide-eyed.

"Everything okay?" Hatsia asks, striding closer, her golden train trailing on the floor behind her as she assesses them. The women bow in sync, clutching the bottoms of their dresses off the floor.

"Yes, madam," they say in unison.

"We were just enjoying the wine and festivities," Kamila says quickly. "We ladies needed to catch up without the children. You know how it is... *I assume.*"

Hatsia meets Lucia's eyes over the bowed heads, all of whom are still unaware of Lucia's presence. Lucia bites her quivering lip but doesn't drop her mother's gaze, her eyes wide and frightened. Hatsia's lip curls with something akin to disgust or disappointment as she turns away, releasing the women to stand.

"Yes, I do," Hatsia says.

As the group trails away, joining Hatsia in conversation, Lucia is left alone once again. Her hand loses purchase against the smooth stone, and she lets herself slide to the floor at Dai's feet, the skirt of her dress blanketing the ground as a sob makes its way up her throat.

The hopelessness fills Lucia as she lets her head fall back, looking up at the lightening sky as the sun rises beyond the temple. Letting her palm fall open, Lucia stares down at the chain resting in her hand, pressed into it earlier by her sister. It's the necklace Gabrielle conjured during her blooming, a half-moon swallowed up by golden flames. Lucia drops her head into her hands, pressing the warm charm into her forehead as silent sobs overtake her.

"Where is she? Where is your sister?" a small, airy voice wonders aloud. "I feel terrible about the blooming. I hope she is okay."

"I'm not sure, Cait," Gabrielle says, the sound of their light footsteps walking past Lucia's place of hiding. "I hope she didn't run off. She likes to explore the forests to clear her head sometimes."

Caitlyn is one of Gabrielle's friends who has also bloomed this year. The westerners hold their ceremony in the summer and she presented as an Augure. Such a surprising gift for such a small, delicate girl.

But their pity only breaks Lucia further, shame and sorrow building within her. As they drift away, she finds her perfect opening. With the distraction of food and wine, Lucia slips away.

Birds chirp in the trees, still unaffected by the encroaching winter up in the mountains where Lucia hides, afraid to face her coven's stares and her grandmother, who should be arriving soon.

She sits in the grass listening to the tinkling of the river with no care of staining her white dress. The heavy outer layer and slippers lie beside her in the grass where she had thrown them off and let her tears fall freely until her chest ached and she had nothing left to give.

It is hopeless. She has let down her coven and her family for the last time.

Lucia's feet dangle into the cool, blue water, sunlight piercing through the cover of trees to heat the side of her face.

The cold night transitioned into a pleasant morning, the remnants of summer not ready to be forgotten. She feels at peace, here alone without a single eye to judge her, leaning her head back to breathe the fresh air.

The last time Lucia came to this clearing amidst a copse of trees deep in the mountain trenches, she wasn't alone. Maybe that's why she loves these forests so much. Her best friend—really the only friend she ever had—was with her.

She can hear the distant ringing of children's laughter bouncing off the trees, an echo of the past imprinted before her eyes. A witch and wolf of five and six, splashing in the water without a care for responsibilities or the pressing weight of their families' disapproval.

When Hetan was still here.

Lucia and Hetan would climb high up into the trees at the edge of the forest surrounding the land that separated the Golden Griffin's territory from the humans at the Ife Ring.

The Ife Ring is also known as the heart ring. The barrier is maintained by the Grand Elder of the witches, Lucia's grandmother, Kaeda.

From their perch holding on tight to a large oak, Lucia and Hetan could see down into the busy human world and would sometimes watch for hours. It was the freest Lucia had ever felt, coming home wet with leaves sticking all over her. Even her mother's anger at her disappearing couldn't squash her joy.

Those gatherings of the witches and wolves were Lucia's fondest memories. She was meant to be sitting in, learning all that she could as the heir, but she and Hetan—future chief of the wolves—would sneak off to play.

Lucia wonders where Hetan is and what he's doing. She wonders if he remembers and would come here now chasing those same memories. She thinks about the wolf a lot. How he is, and whether he's doing better than her. She hopes so. For both of their sakes, he has to be. One of them should be doing well.

He moved away from Naprait when they were children, and she hasn't seen him since. Lucia had her mother send him a letter a few years ago but received no response. To say she was crushed would be an understatement.

Lucia pushes to her feet, staring up at the tallest tree. The branches near the top sway in the wind, reaching out like they can touch the boundary of the Ife Ring. It could reach farther if the heavy winds pushed it far enough to allow escape.

From atop that tree, Lucia used to be able to see the humans in the valley below, the town, and the people. She wonders what they're doing right now.

With that nagging thought, Lucia strides over to her slippers, which have blown close to the edge of the river. She balances on one leg as she shoves her feet back into them, then hesitates beside the tall tree, which stretches so high up into the sky as dark, ashen clouds roll over the sun to set a shadow upon the earth.

It looks bigger now. Lucia thought things were supposed to look smaller as you grew up.

"I can do it," Lucia whispers, clasping Gabrielle's necklace around her throat and tucking it into her dress. She did it all the time as a child, racing Hetan to the top. The wolf used to drag her into whatever mischief he could imagine. Or perhaps she was the one dragging him? It's hard to remember. Time distorts certain memories.

Lucia grabs hold of the lowest branch, using a groove in the trunk to hoist herself up and jump. The branch cuts into her palm, nearly causing her to slip and drop her hold, but she clutches it tight, wrapping both hands around and using all her strength to lift herself up. Her back hits the rough bark as she stops to catch her breath.

Lucia isn't too far, the first branch is only about six feet off the ground. She could jump back down now and go home if she wanted. Forget about this longing for the past— this thing she feels she needs to prove to herself. She could walk back into her home, ignoring her mother's scathing looks and her sister's attempts at cheering her, and pretend like last night never happened. As if she still believed there was some hope, no matter how fragile, that she would receive her gift from the Mother next autumn.

If her mother will even let her participate again.

The wind whistles through the trees, knocking the branches into one another, leaves falling to the ground in a beautiful frenzy like a golden snowfall. Lucia watches two leaves circle each other, spiraling down to the grass and hears the echoing laughter, a glimpse of smiling faces below a hanging branch shrouded in shadow. Two curious children leaning in for a kiss, a first kiss held sacred below a grand fir.

That evening, ten years ago, Lucia had walked home as the sun began to set, having parted ways from Hetan to find her mother waiting for her at the door. Hatsia was rarely ever home, and when she was, she didn't pay much attention to Lucia, either holed up in her office or entertaining guests. But that night Lucia's entire family had been sitting up waiting for her. Gabrielle, only eight at the time, sat on their father's lap on the sofa, her confused face illuminated in the oil lamp and her eyes heavy from being up past her bedtime.

The door closed, and there stood a tall figure, a near mirror of her mother except her face and neck held many more wrinkles, the flaps of skin folding in on each other, and her hair a shocking white. The woman stared down at Lucia without a shred of kindness or light in her eyes. Lucia had turned to her mother and father for comfort or support, and they had both looked away. They were always looking away.

That night Lucia had learned that Hetan was going away. Only minutes before, she had been playing with him, sharing their first fumbled kiss, and then he was headed west to Whoynia that very night.

Lucia screamed and cried, she even tried to pry the door open to run to the place she had last left Hetan. Her grandmother slammed the door shut and looked down at her ten-year-old granddaughter and told her to be strong.

"Dol'Auclairs don't cry," Kaeda said. "Having a fit over a wolf boy. How pathetic."

Kaeda had looked down upon her granddaughter's crying face, eyes red and snot dripping from her nose, with nothing short of contempt. No softness or pity for a young child—her own blood.

"You are a Dol'Auclair. You are a *witch*."

Lucia still didn't get it. Hetan was her friend. None of them understood. Not even Gabrielle. Hetan was her first and only friend. He was everything to her.

Silent tears track down Lucia's cheeks as she blinks away the memory. She gets to her feet, balances on the branch, and begins to climb higher. Her chest is hollow, her heart carved out by clumsy hands and taken while it still beats.

A single tear falls down Lucia's cheek like a raindrop.

She didn't know she had any tears left.

Lucia climbs higher and higher. The air becomes thinner and the wind whips faster, stealing her breath. The ties in her hair come loose, glittering clips lost as they fall to the ground below, and her curls tangle madly around her face.

Many words echo inside her head, raging along with the growing storm. Failure—worthless—she is a stain upon the perfect Dol'Auclair legacy.

As future generations wipe her failure from the great lineage, time will forget her. *Lucia will be erased from history.*

Short, bitten nails dig into rough bark, Lucia's sullied white dress whipping around her ankles trying to trip her up. If Lucia were to scream from up here, her voice would probably get trapped in the current and whisked away by the storm.

She screams.

Lucia's anguish is ripped from her throat and carried off down into the city below, where it'll fade long before it reaches anyone's ears. She screams until her throat is sore and aching.

Lucia falls back against the tree trunk, tired, her hands and heart numb. She has to force herself to keep going, climbing higher into the growing storm and dark, impending rain clouds. All she can think is—*you did this to me.*

Mother, Grandmother, all of those laughing, sneering faces of her coven... they did this.

Whatever this is, she isn't even sure. But the words repeat over and over in her mind until her hands blister and a slipper falls to the ground. Lucia feels unsteady, pushed to the edge of some great horizon. A choice that she can't see yet that will shake the very foundation of who she is.

The sky looks heavy and somber, mirroring Lucia's own heart right now. Like some great Sage is reading her thoughts and casting her emotions into the sky.

She laughs a sad and deranged sound.

Lucia holds no hope of standing at the head of the covens alongside previous Dol'Auclairs, not without magisk.

Lucia was born to take the helm of the Dol'Auclairs. It is all she knows; it's all she has. What is she if she isn't the Dol'Auclair heir? Simple... She is nothing.

Pulling herself up, fighting against nature and the unstable smaller branches that quiver under her feet, Lucia finally reaches the top. Though she's been here before, everything looks so different now.

The sky is angry and yawning, pushing her to and fro. She holds tight, finally able to get her arms all the way around the trunk, her face scratching against the bark as she looks out upon the city behind the faint glimmer of the Ife ring that keeps the Golden Griffin coven hidden from intruders. It's like a pearly scar across the sky; the buildings and lights below are warped.

The sun shines in the distant valley beyond the forest, mountains hidden behind an iridescent cage illuminating a market where people are milling about, unaware of the looming figure watching from afar.

Lucia stretches, reaching out her hand to try and touch it. The bubble distorts, twitching just beyond her fingertips as if it's responding to her presence. She can feel the wave of heat and power emanating from it, an old magisk that was placed in this land by her ancestors long before her time. When the magisk was so strong, you could taste it in the air.

A time when deities spoke.

Lucia sometimes questions whether any of them ever existed at all. Perhaps the statues and stories told about ancient witches are only works of fiction. Tales passed from parent to child like a bedtime story. Lucia can't hear them; the Mother doesn't answer her prayers.

She feels so alone.

Droplets of rain fall onto Lucia's arm, slowly and then all at once, darkening the sleeve of her white dress and making the lacy fabric transparent. Dark skin pales in the sweeping cold. She shivers as the tip of her third finger brushes the silken barrier, which flutters against her touch, and a striking heat races up her arm.

Lucia gasps, her foot slipping as she's startled by this great wave of electric energy; a flood of voices and feelings overwhelm her like a great wave crashing overtop her head.

As she topples backward, the blood from Lucia's palm stains the dark wood. Her nails crack as they scratch hastily to take hold of something. Anything. A branch she catches holds for only a moment before it's pulled free with her weight. She's suspended in space as she pitches back into the tempest, her arms splayed and mouth wide in shock.

Chapter Three

A Burger with a Stranger

Lucia free-falls toward the earth. A sunny patch on the grassy hill she'd been laid out on this morning has now gone gray, and a raging river, which had previously been calm and teeming with fish, all come rushing toward her. She closes her eyes, not wanting the gray clouds streaked with lightning to be the last thing she sees as thunder claps in her ears.

Lucia finds the golden necklace around her throat as it comes loose, wagging in the wind and hovering above her. Her fingers close over the flaming moon, still warm to the touch. Gabrielle's smiling face plays behind her eyelids.

The ground comes racing toward Lucia with lightning speed. She braces for impact, expecting to hit the ground with a deafening crack to shake the mountainside. Her limbs go loose in acceptance, hoping it will be quick, but instead of the harsh impact of the bruising earth, she hits a warm body.

Soft flesh seizes Lucia, an arm wrapping around her shoulders to support her head, and a hand under her legs. For a moment, Lucia fantasizes that it's Hetan and that he truly did come here seeking her.

She's thoroughly mistaken.

"Falling for me already?"

That smooth voice snaps Lucia into the present, cutting through the snapshots of her final moments. She cracks an eye open, stinging rain pelting her face as she blinks up into a pair of brilliant vermillion eyes.

Lucia's heart stutters in her chest, caught by that stare. The woman places her back on her feet and Lucia stumbles. She'd lost a shoe as she climbed, and now her right foot slips over wet grass as her soaked white dress clings to the curves of her body.

Spinning away from the stranger as she realizes how exposed she is, Lucia's arms cross over her chest and hardened nipples poke through the transparent material and red smears across her dress from the wound on her hand.

"You're injured."

Lucia looks down at the shallow cut across her palm from where it scored against a branch. She hadn't noticed the stinging until it was pointed out.

When Lucia looks back up, the woman looms behind her in the water's reflection. Her breath quickens as she watches closely, and she jumps at the hot breath across her ear.

So fast. Lucia hadn't even seen the woman move.

Stumbling forward in fright, she slips into the rushing stream. Her legs nearly buckle from the shot of icy cold; a pair of strong arms come around her waist to catch her before she can be rushed away by the current.

The heat behind Lucia makes her feverish, even through the autumn storm and the layers that separate them. Steaming hands like a vapor leach into the witch's skin, branding her hip in a scorching embrace. She can feel every pass of cotton across her skin like a fiery caress, leaving goosebumps in its wake. She shivers, lips gone pale from the cold, teeth chattering as she tries to blink up at the blurry figure through the torrent of rain.

"Who are you?" Lucia shouts, her voice drowned under the symphony of the storm, and thunderclaps shake the sky above.

"Is that how people say thank you around here?" the woman says, setting Lucia back onto the shore. The voice is both soft and deep, music to Lucia's ears. The voice carries over the storm and it sends a shiver that has nothing to do with the biting rain shooting down her spine.

Though wary of the stranger huddled under a black cloak, Lucia can't help but move closer to the woman's heat. Like standing too close to an open flame in the middle of a snowstorm—she's unsure of which one will bite her first, the cold or the heat.

Lucia's teeth are chattering horribly; they click with every word.

"Thank you," she shouts.

The woman's gaze follows her hand as it pushes against her bosom to still the beating of her heart. The thump, thump, thump is so loud in her ears, they can probably both hear it.

"You're shaking," the woman says. "Come, let's get you out of the rain."

Though hesitant to follow, Lucia is drenched and shaking badly, so she lets herself be led away from the river, under the copse of trees. The leaves have barely begun to fall here, so the canopy of leaves and long, awning branches gives them an escape from the raging storm.

Lucia stares off into the far distance in worry, unsure of whether they will be able to make it back down the mountains in this weather. The sky is much darker than it had been before, and it is getting later by the minute. Soon, night will fall, and they won't be able to see a thing. Her overcoat now lies drenched where she left it on the ground. She will catch her death if she stays out here too long.

A glance over at the woman finds her already staring at Lucia, standing unnaturally still as if not affected by the cold and wetness at all. Lucia's eyes are searching as they meet with intense, dark eyes that she could have sworn were red before. Was it adrenaline that made them glow like embers?

Turning away from the woman's fierce gaze, Lucia peeks out from their little covering, trying not to feel like prey with her back turned, all alone with this stranger deep in the forest.

To herself, she mumbles, "Maybe if we hasten back down the mountain we could—"

An arm catches her, pulling her back as she steps out from the covering. Lucia stares at the paler arm in bewilderment.

"Where do you think you're going?" the woman asks, pulling Lucia back against her chest as she shuffles toward the trunk of the large tree. "Do you have a death wish?"

Lucia shakes her head, her sodden curls whipping around her face.

"If we don't leave now, we won't get back before dark," Lucia says, extracting herself from the woman's arms and peering back out into the rain. "If we get lost out here, we will surely die."

The woman sighs, her hand wrapping around Lucia's arm like a vice. Slowly, the woman pulls Lucia closer, and Lucia is beginning to feel irritated at the way the woman keeps handling her.

"There's no way you can go out there. You're freezing. With your constitution, you'll get sick."

Lucia tries not to take offense to that. With the woman's thick drawl, words like hot syrup, what she thinks is an insult sounds sweet.

Can this woman tell Lucia has no magisk or does she know who Lucia is already? It would be no surprise if she did. She must have been at the blooming and watched Lucia fail. Lucia knows everyone in her coven, but there are many visitors today.

"Well, I can't stay under these trees with you forever, either," Lucia snaps. "How did you get caught up in this storm, anyway?"

Everyone should be at the feast right now. Only Lucia was dense enough to run off like that, but she knows these woods like the back of her hand.

The woman's dress—a dark, velvet cloak with silver spiders along the trim—and manner of speaking aren't familiar to Naprait.

Lucia peers up and sees the shimmer in the distance. The barrier is still erect, so there shouldn't be an issue with the magisk holding it together. The woman can't be human for two reasons—she wouldn't be able to get through the Ife ring, and she wouldn't have been able to catch Lucia from such a great height.

"Those in rainstorms shouldn't cast stones," the woman quips.

Lucia is sure that's not how the saying goes, but she says, "It wasn't raining when I got out here."

Lucia's gaze falls back down to the woman.

"How did you catch me?" she asks, the adrenaline cooling and common sense breaking through. Most people would have died catching Lucia at the height and speed she fell. The only logical explanation is the woman is an Augure and was able to enhance her body to take the hit, but even so, that answer seems too convenient, and it is nagging at Lucia's mind.

"Are you going to keep asking unnecessary questions, Princess, or are we going to get out of here?"

Lucia tries not to bristle at the *princess* comment, but her shoulders relax as it proves that the woman does know who she is. That means she couldn't be...

Lightening cracks overhead as thunder shakes the ground. Lucia trips, hanging onto the woman to steady herself. The weather is getting worse. This woman may have the ability to manipulate her body, but Lucia does not. She feels the cold like nettles in her skin.

"I don't think I can—"

"We aren't going to your little town tonight; it is too far for you to travel in this weather. We're headed to the city."

"The city... *The human city*?"

Lucia's eyes almost bug out of her head. Her mother will kill her if she leaves Golden Griffin territory without permission. It is dangerous to leave the barrier.

"What? Scared of a couple of humans, Princess?"

"What, I'm not—Stop calling me Princess!" Lucia bristles.

The woman chuckles, moving closer to her once more. Lucia's next words are stuck in her throat.

"Here, take this."

The woman unties the cord around her neck, pulling her cloak off smoothly. She places the thick, warm fabric around Lucia's shoulders; the inside is warm and dry, which is a great surprise. It must be a cantus, but the woman doesn't look much older than her, so how could her magisk be so advanced? A gift perhaps—she looks like she comes from money, but her speech is crude.

The thick fabric is cozy and smells like roses. Lucia tries not to sniff it as her face heats in embarrassment.

"What are you—"

"Shhh," the woman whispers, tying the cord snug around Lucia's throat, her breath blowing across Lucia's cheek. "You ask too many questions."

"You're going to be cold now," Lucia stutters, her voice small and confused.

"If you haven't noticed, I'm *hot*, Princess. I mean, *I run hot.*"

The woman winks.

Lucia doesn't even comprehend the teasing as she stares up at the woman, in awe at the generous act. The woman is so odd. She is only a stranger, and yet she is being kind to Lucia.

"It's no big deal, Princess. Can't have you dying on the way to the city. The humans might give me some funny looks."

Lucia nods airily, but her attention is no longer on the woman's words. With her cloak off, she can finally get a good look at the stranger, bending back to study her face.

The woman's hair is damp, darkening the pale hair to amber. A bob shapes golden skin and a charming, chiseled face. Dark, smooth, angular eyes cut like diamonds observe Lucia, and she just can't look away from them.

"We should go." The woman pulls back, turning to peer out into the rain. It hasn't slowed any since they took cover, and the sky has only darkened, the moon rising quickly beneath the sheath of clouds.

Lucia nods, snapping out of her daze. "Yes, of course."

She follows the woman closely, quickly peeling off her only remaining shoe to steady her gait, and when she approaches the barrier nestled beneath the woman's warm cloak, she becomes wary. Lucia has never been outside of Golden Griffin territory before.

The stranger stops, turning back to look at her.

Lucia leans forward, running her fingertips over the warm, glowing barrier that had shocked her out of the sky. When her hand goes right through, she gasps, cocooned in warmth as she stumbles onto the other side. It's an odd feeling like being wrapped in heated sheets warmed by the sun or falling asleep laid out by the hearth.

On the other side, there is no rain, and the sky is indigo, bright without clouds to block the setting sun.

The woman entangles their arms, tucking Lucia into her side, and Lucia spares only a parting glance at the shimmering barrier before looking up to watch the stranger as they trudge down into the valley headed toward the human city—a forbidden pit in the countryside the sheltered witch has always longed to explore.

"I never got your name," Lucia says.

The other woman towers over her, sylphlike and leggy with a graceful gait. She directs a sly, humored smile down at Lucia.

"The name's Adelaide, darling."

"Adelaide," Lucia whispers. It's a beautiful name, but it doesn't quite capture the woman's alluring beauty. "My name is Lucia," she says, wanting to return the branch of intimacy. There is no harm in her name as the woman must already know of her.

Adelaide stops and closes her eyes as if committing Lucia's name to memory. The smile that stretches soft, bowed lips holds no air of the humor it's had since Lucia first fell from that tree.

"Lucia. Lucia, *Lucia*," Adelaide repeats, rolling the name over her tongue.

When she turns to Lucia, that smirk is back in place, discharging the crackle of heat gathering in the air between them and sliding over her skin.

"I prefer Princess, but Lucia is lovely as well."

Lucia is in awe as they descend upon the city. Wooden buildings with large lit-up signs and cobbled streets. A car drives by and she shouts as Adelaide pulls her off to the sidewalk. She has never seen one in person, but Gabrielle has told her all about them, self-driven, engine-powered carriages that are fast and loud.

Her sister has visited human cities before, with her friend Mia in Etryae.

"Hello, beauty," a rough, nasally voice calls. "Nice dress."

The older man with ink along his neck and a scruffy, grimy face winks at Lucia as they walk quickly past.

She pushes farther into Adelaide's side, her eyes wide and fearful. The arm over her shoulder is her only comfort as foreign people mill about the market, whistling at women who pass and are buying goods.

The street is loud and crowded, and Lucia feels so overwhelmed; her temples are beginning to throb from the sharp, clashing smells and neon lights flashing in her face.

"No need to be frightened," Adelaide whispers, her voice tickling Lucia's ear. "I'll protect you from the humans. You're safe with me."

The woman's tone is teasing, but it makes Lucia feel better anyway. With her strength, she could hold off many humans so long as they don't have those frightening weapons Lucia has heard about.

They pass quickly through the glowing market onto the darkened streets where the moon doesn't reach. Adelaide pulls her off the main road, heading toward a building shrouded in shadows, and Lucia can hear raucous voices coming from within.

Adelaide bursts in through the back, the swinging doors flapping behind them as she pulls Lucia along.

Lucia is assaulted with the sight of wild debauchery. The place is filled with shouting and boisterous laughter. A small band plays in the corner drowning out most other sounds, like the monotonous slide of drinks across a long counter and coins slapping the bar.

There are women in short skirts dancing or flirting with men at the bar, and the men tussle, tankards of ale sloshing and spilling onto the sticky wooden floor.

One man loudly boasts of his travels to anyone who will listen, some curious locals latching onto every word.

Lucia tries to take it all in. It is a shock to her system.

"Come, Princess, the tavern after dark isn't a place someone like you would want to be."

Adelaide steers Lucia over to the stairs, nodding to a barmaid as they pass. Lucia wants to argue about her ability to take care of herself because she doesn't like the thought that this woman thinks she's some weak damsel, but Adelaide looks so much more comfortable, navigating through the chaos as if she belongs within it, that Lucia keeps her mouth closed.

The room Adelaide pulls Lucia into is messy. The small bed against the wall is unmade, thin blankets in disarray, and clothes strewn about, hanging out of a trunk thrown on the floor. Smudged glass on a broken wooden frame is open to let an icy breeze in and air out the stuffy, dusty room.

Lucia's stomach rumbles, breaking the silence as Adelaide riffles through her bag.

"Are you hungry?" she asks, turning startled eyes on Lucia, who hides her face behind her hands in embarrassment.

Lucia nods. She hasn't eaten in two days aside from the small loaf of bread Haru gave her last night.

"I'm going to have dinner brought up to the room," Adelaide states like some grand declaration rather than something as normal as getting food.

"Stay here."

She moves back out of the room, squeaking as the rainwater rappels down the leather of her tight, black bodysuit. Lucia is also still wet, her damp dress sticking uncomfortably as she stands barefoot, dripping water onto the dusty, wooden floors.

Shivering and alone, Lucia lets her eyes wander. There isn't much. The room is barren aside from the trunk and satchel, clothes spilling out similar to the odd ones the woman is wearing now. A lot of leather and high-heeled boots, and very revealing, tight, sheer dresses.

Lucia hadn't seen any humans dressed like that when they passed through the town, so the woman isn't native to Domeg though she has a room booked here. Neither do any of these humans have bright hair, so it must be unnatural as Lucia had thought.

When Adelaide returns, Lucia is still standing beside the bed. There isn't much room to move around, and the small bed and stuffed chair in the corner take up most of the floor.

"You can get comfortable," Adelaide says, striding toward Lucia. She reaches for the knot of the tie around her neck, but Lucia jolts back like she's been shocked.

Adelaide stares at her confused, arms in the air like she means no harm.

"Sau-sau, I forgot touching is *djini*. But you're still wet, and you need to get warm if you have any chance of keeping from getting sick," she says in what Lucia thinks might be an apology. The language the woman speaks is foreign to her.

Lucia nods her face heating in embarrassment at her reflexive reaction. The woman has touched her quite a bit today already, but she came in so quickly Lucia got spooked.

With Adelaide's back turned, crouched to riffle through her trunk, Lucia takes a moment to catch her breath and removes the cloak with shaking hands.

In general, Golden Griffins aren't very physically affectionate, but hugs and cheek kisses are common amongst women. Lucia is very much like her mother in that regard. She doesn't like being touched. Not unless it's her sister who is incapable of keeping her hands to herself. Lucia got used to it.

Overall, today has been a very odd day and now that she has settled, everything is beginning to catch up to her.

"What did you mean by sau-sau?" Lucia asks as Adelaide turns back to her. She shakes out her hair, little droplets of water sprinkling the floor. The woman runs her fingers through it, pushing it back from her face and Lucia watches, mesmerized. The woman is unlike any Lucia has ever seen.

"You can set your clothes on the floor. I'll lay it over the balcony to dry," Adelaide says, and Lucia quickly picks up her dropped jaw.

R-right," she stutters, red-faced as she wets her dry lips.

Lucia folds the cloak, placing it on the ground, and then pauses at the top button of her dress. It has dried a bit, but it's still opaque and suctioned to her curves. She pulls it away from her skin, letting the damp fabric flair back out around her in a less revealing manner. She has no other clothes, but staying in this dress will make her sick.

Lucia's hands twitch with the need to cover herself as Adelaide's eyes rake up her body. The woman grabs Lucia's hand gently, the one that had been cut earlier. Lucia had forgotten all about that. Her face grows warm when Adelaide stands there too long, staring at her palm.

"It's not that bad," Lucia says, feeling the need to fill the silence. "It doesn't hurt at all."

Adelaide pulls her eyes away, searching for the truth in Lucia's face. Finally, she lets go and moves back to her trunk.

"Let me dress it. You wouldn't want to get an infection."

Adelaide grabs a shirt, tearing off two long strips of cloth. Moving toward the nightstand, she dips one of the pieces into the pitcher of water.

"Come."

Lucia hesitates, looking around as if someone might be watching before she steps forward slowly and raises her hand. Adelaide dabs at the cut with the wet cloth, Lucia's face twisting with discomfort. It didn't hurt before, but it stings as it is tugged and poked at.

Adelaide holds her hand tighter as if afraid Lucia might pull away. Then she wraps Lucia's palm with the dry cloth and steps back, admiring her work with a smile.

The wrap is a bit sloppy as if Adelaide has never dressed a wound before. She didn't even have bandages, ripping her clothing instead. But Lucia returns the smile and thanks her for the effort.

"I have something else for you to wear," Adelaide says, checking her out again. "Unless you would like to lie in damp clothes."

"I'll take the dry clothes, please."

Adelaide lays another cloak on the bed and turns around to give Lucia privacy. Lucia watches her for a moment, the curve of her hips, the dip of her back in the tight clothes. She wishes Adelaide would turn around again so she can stare at the bright red pigment on her bow lips and ink smudged under alluring eyes, black like a moonless midnight sky.

"Are you done?" Adelaide asks.

Lucia startles as if she has been caught, quick to grab the cloak off the bed.

"Ah, no. N-not yet."

Lucia fumbles around, trying to unbutton her dress and pull on the cloak at the same time. It takes some struggle, but eventually, Lucia is settled with the cloak around her and panting from exertion as she perches on the end of the bed.

The cloak is interesting, as it closes all the way around the body with buttons, and it's a cool, silken texture that feels like water against Lucia's skin. There's only a thin piece of fabric covering her nakedness, and it's hard to ignore.

Thankfully, a knock comes as Adelaide finishes changing too, and she strides to the door to answer it.

Lucia nearly gasps, her eyes bugging when she sees what the woman is wearing. Short pants that end just under the swell of her bottom that is more risqué than any of Lucia's undergarments back home, and a strappy top of a similar shiny fabric.

"Adelaide, your dinner."

The woman at the door is wearing a short dress cinched in the back with a tangle of strings, and high stockings under tall black boots. She drapes herself against the doorframe, the covered platter held out in one hand in a practiced move. She bats long, dark eyelashes up at Adelaide, a smile cutting madly into her face, which is painted with bright, messy colors.

"Thank you, Charlie."

Adelaide reaches for the platter, but it is pulled back.

"What, you're not gonna invite me in tonight?" Charlie arches a brow, tongue darting out to wet her lips. "You know you don't have to order food to get me to come up here. You never have before."

"I'm busy," Adelaide says flatly, looking in no mood for the woman's game.

Green eyes peek over Adelaide's shoulder to land on Lucia, who sits primly on the bed, her head turned away to make it seem as if she isn't listening.

Charlie's grin widens.

"You're busy with the stiff?"

Lucia's mouth drops open as her head snaps toward the server. Charlie is smirking at Lucia, her painted nails running up Adelaide's arm as if laying claim on the woman. Lucia splutters, her face burning like a furnace.

"She doesn't look like one of our girls."

"W-we're not— I'm not—"

Tongue-tied, Lucia turns away from the rude woman. There are too many implications in the words and the woman's eyes for Lucia to defend against and she's ashamed to even acknowledge half of them.

"We're done here," Adelaide growls, her voice deepening a few octaves, sending an involuntary shiver down Lucia's spine. She grabs the platter and closes the door on the tavern servant, whose offending huff is muffled through the wood.

Lucia kicks her feet up onto the bed, wrapping her arms around her bent legs, her eyes trained on the patterned comforter beneath her. She feels the bed dip, the platter set beside her hip.

Lucia just lets out a little huff. She is embarrassed and hungry and feels awfully foolish for letting some wanton servant fluster her. She tries not to wonder who the woman is to Adelaide. A friend, or...

Lucia shakes her head. It doesn't matter.

"Come on, you have to eat," Adelaide says as Lucia's stomach growls once more.

Adelaide reaches over and lifts the silver lid. Beneath is unfamiliar food, and it piques Lucia's interest. There is some sort of meat sandwiched between two pieces of bread and pale, crispy wedges. Lucia's eyes flicker first to Adelaide, who sits across from her on the bed, and then back to the platter. She pokes at the bun, which slides to the side to reveal vegetables—sliced tomato and lettuce.

"Is this a ber-burgu-burger?" she stumbles, searching for the right word, eyes wide as she studies it. Gabrielle used to go on about how she had one when she went to a human city with Mia. For a whole week, after she tasted it, she talked of it nonstop; Lucia could nearly taste it.

"Yes, do you like burgers?" Adelaide asks.

"I don't know," Lucia says. She grabs it in both hands, sauce dripping onto the platter as she stares down at its many folds. Gabrielle told her this is how you hold them, with both hands. Her neck craning to stay over the platter, Lucia takes a small bite out of the side. The seasoned meat and bread melt on her tongue. Her eyes close as she groans in delight.

"This is wonderful!"

Lucia's hunger catches up with her, oblivious to Adelaide watching her as she quickly eats the entire thing, licking the sauce from her fingers when she's done.

"It is quite messy," she notes.

Adelaide laughs, and Lucia finally looks up at her, noticing that she got no food for herself. "Are you laughing at me?" she asks, hurt, curling in on herself.

The woman is quick to get her laughter under control.

"No, no. I'm sorry. I'm not laughing at you. I'm... admiring your love for burgers. I never knew they were that good."

Adelaide hands Lucia a napkin.

"You don't like them?" Lucia asks, wiping her face. She wonders how anyone could not like them.

Adelaide shrugs. "I like watching you eat them more."

Lucia nearly chokes. She turns away from the woman as she has a coughing fit from swallowing wrong, then takes a moment to collect herself. She decides to ignore the comment and its possible implications.

"What are these?" Lucia asks, her voice high and nervous as she pokes at the pale-yellow things left on the platter.

"Those are fries. You've never had them, either?"

Lucia shakes her head.

"They're made of potatoes and fried in oil."

"Potatoes?" She likes potatoes. Lucia picks one up, nibbling on the end. They're salty and have a bit of spice to them. She eats those just as quickly as the burger. "Who knew human food was so good?"

"You keep saying that," Adelaide says, getting up to place the tray outside the door. "Have you never had human food before or been to human cities?"

Lucia shakes her head. "My mother didn't ever let me leave our town. She said it wasn't safe, being... Well, my mother is paranoid. And why would I leave when I have what I need already?"

Trade is good in Laesbury; they have crops and shelter, and they are safely tucked away in the mountains. Lucia was supposed to leave for meetings with other covens, but it never happened. Eventually, she stopped asking.

"Which coven are you from?" Lucia asks. "What is your family name?"

Lucia studies Adelaide closely. She isn't a human obviously, and she doesn't have any of the familiar features of the local wolves either. It's been a while since Lucia had seen them, but they had long dark hair and strong, handsome features. They dress nothing like Adelaide as well. And she couldn't be a... a... Lucia remembers the flash of red eyes and shivers. Well, there are none of them in Naprait. Her grandmother saw to that.

"I'm not from around here," Adelaide says dismissively. She comes around the side of the bed and begins pulling back the covers.

Lucia nods. She figured as much. If the woman is going to be ashamed of where it is she comes from, it must be a smaller, poor coven. Lucia wonders where she got all of the flashy clothes though. Maybe she's a scavenger, or maybe she's just a working woman. It is none of Lucia's business anyway. It's rude to pry.

"Where am I sleeping?" she asks.

Adelaide reaches over to flick off the light. "You can sleep beside me. I won't bite."

"I—I cannot sleep beside you," Lucia splutters. "It's against the rules."

"What rules, Princess?"

"The Holum Actus!" Lucia shouts, appalled.

The light flickers back on, and Lucia squints away from the sudden brightness. She gives Adelaide a curious look.

"If you're a witch of any standing, you should know of the holy acts obeyed in the worship of the Mother and great deities. Acts that ensure you pass on and join the ancestors..."

Adelaide stares at Lucia like she's grown a second head. Lucia takes a deep breath trying to calm her pounding heart. She's starting to sound like a *tradist*.

She isn't an extremist by any means, but she performs her holy duties and finds strength in her beliefs. Perhaps if she were a better Daughter and a more devout disciple, the Mother would have given her a gift. Perhaps the coven is right, and there is something wrong with her. If this woman who doesn't even obey their ancient traditions has gotten a gift from the Mother, then what does that say about *her*?

Lucia kneads her chest, her fingers digging into the flesh until her sternum feels bruised like she can reach within her chest and stop her wildly beating heart. It's like some wire is tripped; she feels breathless as yesterday's events come flooding in a frenzy.

This was Lucia's third failed blooming. She has truly been rejected by the holy deity and everyone knows it is all her fault. She must have done something the Mother found unforgivable. *Something dreadful.* The coven is right; she is bad. She is tainted.

Lucia takes deep, gasping breaths. *In, out... In, out...* Her heartbeat thunders in her ears as her vision goes dark and blurry like Adelaide turned off the lights again. She can't breathe, and her legs are shaking. She feels like she might faint.

"Lucia?"

Lucia closes her eyes. Her head is spinning. If she focuses on anything other than getting her shaking limbs to settle, she will lose the thin shred of control she has. She can already feel the threads unraveling, frustrated tears prickling at her closed eyelids.

She feels sick... dizzy... she is spinning round and round and can't get out no matter how hard she tries.

"*Lucia!*"

The voice is much closer now, sharp and panicked as a warm breath blows across the back of Lucia's neck and scalding hands grasp her arms.

"You're okay," Adelaide soothes, those hands moving over hers through the silk cloak. "You're okay, just breathe for me."

Lucia's eyes snap open, jerking away from the sudden heat. The light floods back in a surge, stinging her eyes again.

"What—" Lucia is a bit disoriented, her head pounding from all of the stimuli. It's always like that after one of her *"episodes,"* as her mother calls them. This isn't as bad as they usually are when she crashes hard. A mini episode.

"You need to sleep," Adelaide says, directing Lucia to the bed as she palms her aching forehead. "You've had a long day, darling."

Lucia can't look at Adelaide, afraid of what she might find in her expression. "I'm sorry. I—"

"It's fine. I will take the floor, just please, get some rest."

Lucia nods absently, climbing beneath the covers as Adelaide turns out the light. She has only the glow of the moon through the dirty window to see by as she blinks up at the spinning ceiling in confusion.

When Adelaide comes to the side of the bed to grab the bedding folded atop the stuffed chair, Lucia wants to tell the woman to join her on the bed. They can put pillows between them. It's no different from sharing a bed with her sister, isn't it? She was just overreacting...

But her tongue feels heavy in her mouth, and Lucia can't seem to make out the words.

There's shuffling in the dark as Adelaide settles in, putting together some cushioning from the extra bedsheets and pillows.

Lucia snuggles into the mattress, pulling the blanket up to her chin as her eyes drift closed. She tries her hardest to fall asleep.

Chapter Four

Eggs and Ambush

Sun comes streaming through dingy windows, sending light scattering across the room. Lucia is nearly blinded as she blinks awake. The world comes into a blurry focus, dust particles floating by her face shimmering like diamonds in the sun.

"Good morning, Princess."

Lucia startles at the voice, a high-pitched squeal leaving her mouth as she turns to the woman standing beside the door. Adelaide has re-dressed into day clothes, tight black leather with a zipper undone quite a bit at her chest. Lucia is beginning to think she doesn't know how to wear clothes properly.

The events of the previous night come flooding back; traipsing in the mountains, falling from that tree, Adelaide bringing her to the human city…

Lucia stands quickly, nearly stumbling over her own feet. The silk cloak isn't very warm, and the room isn't insulated well. She shivers, wrapping her arms around herself.

"I should probably be heading home," she says. "My mother will be worried sick if she finds me gone."

Lucia's mother won't be angry at her disappearance, so much as furious that Lucia disobeyed the rules. She doesn't even think her mother will notice she was gone, but Gabrielle certainly will. *Not that Adelaide needs to know this.*

Adelaide doesn't respond. The woman leans against the wall, staring hard at Lucia, who shifts uncomfortably under her gaze. She can't tell what the woman is thinking. She isn't easy to read. One moment Adelaide will be smirking, the next her face is dead blank. Lucia isn't sure if she thinks everything is a joke or if she just doesn't care at all.

Perhaps Adelaide doesn't want to take her back? It's light out, so Lucia should be able to make her way back to Laesbury on her own, but she would feel much more comfortable if she is escorted out of the human town first.

"I'm just going to—"

Feeling like she overstayed her welcome, Lucia makes her way toward the door. Adelaide steps right in her path, blocking the doorway.

Startled, Lucia steps back and stares at the woman. Adelaide's intense black eyes still have not left her, ruby red lips pursed. *A storm is brewing in those eyes.*

"Adelaide?" Lucia whispers, getting a bit worried now.

Adelaide was nothing but kind the day before, but as Lucia's mother always taught her, you can never be so sure of someone's intentions. Lucia has only dealt with two types of people in her life. Those who want to get close to her because of who her family is, and those who bullied her relentlessly in lower academy for being different. Lucia should have known Adelaide's kindness was too good to be true. Laying that cloak over her shoulders had some sort of ulterior motive.

Adelaide doesn't answer so Lucia tries to squeeze past her once again, but this time the woman's arm comes out, catching Lucia around the waist. Lucia gasps, that unnatural warmth the woman radiates shooting through her.

"Adelaide, what—"

"Why were you out in the forest last night?" Adelaide asks, her voice low and searching.

That is the last thing Lucia expected her to ask. Why now?

Adelaide's eyes bore into Lucia's, unfocused as if the events of yesterday are replaying inside her mind. "You nearly died, falling from that tree..." She looks right at Lucia, her eyes piercing. "You did fall, *didn't you?*"

Lucia's cheeks grow warm, her mouth falling open in shock.

"You think I tried to jump?" she asks. "Of course, I fell. I'm not kur ni nokami—*I'm not a nut.*" Lucia's face heats as she tries to defend herself, her mother's words playing in her head. "I was just... I was just trying to see the view!"

That isn't the full truth. Lucia hadn't just been up there for the view. She wanted to get away from everyone. Far from her coven and her mother's judging eyes. She thought that looking out at the humans going about their natural lives, unaffected by coven order or family expectations, would bring her peace.

She imagines what life would be like if she had been born human: eating burgers and staying up late in rowdy inns, traveling, and going on adventures.

"Lucia..."

Adelaide stares down at her, their faces only an inch from one another. The arm tightens around Lucia, every shift of the silk robe skimming her naked skin beneath. Lucia shivers under Adelaide's gaze, feeling bare in this small slip of weightless fabric. Her breath catches in her throat as she holds those passionate eyes with her own, unable to look away.

Adelaide breaks the moment too soon, closing her eyes as she turns her head. Lucia notices the woman doesn't take a breath. She hadn't realized before what seemed so... odd about the woman, but she is unnaturally still, like a statue under heated flesh. She doesn't seem to breathe or make unnecessary movements, and when she does move, it's as fluid as water. Even her face looks like it's carved in stone, so focused and pronounced. There isn't a hint of nuance in her expression. Maybe that is why she is so hard to read because Lucia isn't used to someone being so unguarded. The answers are right there if Lucia wasn't so afraid to look.

"I... I'll get you breakfast and then I'll walk you to the barrier," Adelaide says. She moves away from Lucia and the door.

Lucia's eyes linger on the woman. She can tell that isn't what Adelaide wanted to say, but she doesn't question it. There is no point. Lucia isn't sure she wants to know, and if she isn't sure then she should leave it unsaid.

Lucia follows Adelaide out of the room and down to the bar. It's very different than it was the night before, the rowdy nighttime crowd melded into subdued patrons eating breakfast, and quiet chatter.

They're silent as Lucia eats a classic human breakfast of eggs, bacon, and sweet toast that she leaves half-finished, and Adelaide watches her from across the table, pushing the salt back and forth. A chasm grows between them with all the words they want to say. Lucia humors the idea of saying a few of them, but suddenly the atmosphere shifts, going cold in an instant.

Without warning, Adelaide jumps up and grabs Lucia, whose fork is halfway to her mouth. The woman pulls her under the table only seconds before the swinging doors burst open with a *crack!* and three men come stomping in with heavy boots and hefty shimmering weapons in hand.

From the floor, across the wide room, Lucia watches the men and their large unfamiliar weapons with unbridled fear. Adelaide knows, tensing against Lucia's back where she's lying over her like a blazing shield.

Lucia tries not to wonder where Adelaide might have run into people like this. It's such bad luck that Lucia found them on her first journey out. She had heard of the advancements in human technology which fuel the Etryaen economy, but she had hoped to never encounter them herself.

Screams erupt around the room as patrons dive under their seats or try to flee. The three men pay their frenzy no mind, scanning the room as they walk slowly, cataloging everyone's faces. *They're looking for someone.*

Adelaide pulls Lucia away while the men are looking in the opposite direction, pushing her down behind the bar. She presses a lever that opens a small storage where the bartender is cowering. Adelaide shoves him over and hauls Lucia onto her lap.

The man looks like he's going to protest but Adelaide gives him a scathing look and he turns away, his jaw snapping shut.

Lucia holds her breath as the passage closes and the three bodies are squished in the small, dark space. Only small slivers of light come in through the cracks in the wood.

Heavy boots thud outside of their hiding space and Lucia's breath catches. She pushes further into Adelaide's embrace. She's frightened of small spaces.

"*Her* supposed to be here, eh?" one of the men says, his voice muffled through the wood. "The tip said her came to this here bar."

"Her might've left already, eh?" another voice responds in the same drawl, though his voice is high where the first was deep and gruff.

"She could be working with someone, you boneheads," the last one shouts, his speech clearer than the other two. "Someone tipped her off!"

The boots get quieter as they move away. The first guy says, "No, her was alone. Her doesn't have magisk, her can' 've take care of herself, eh?"

There's a ring like a shot, and Lucia jumps, squeezing her eyes shut tight. *Deep breath in, deep breath out, deep breath in...* She tries her hardest to picture she's anywhere but in this cramped, tight spot that is bringing nothing but awful memories to the surface. If she doesn't calm down, she might bring that classic breakfast back up.

"Why is she outside of the barrier? That's the only thing protecting her—" The man pauses. "*Where did you get the tip from, Big?*"

"Dunno, some nameless lass."

"Idiot! It makes no sense she would have left. The barrier was only down for a moment, the safest she would have been was surrounded by witches. Especially that mother of hers. Besides the girl, that family is skilled at magisk."

THE BALANCE OF FATES

Inside the bar, Lucia struggles to catch her breath. Adelaide's hand goes over her mouth to keep her from making any noise. She glares at the wide-eyed bartender across from them to make sure he knows to stay quiet too.

"Hey, you! What do you think you're doing with that? You're not who we have trouble with, so if you want to keep your life, I'd suggest you scurry right back out the way you came."

While the men are distracted by the newcomer, Adelaide whispers in Lucia's ear, "Stay quiet. I know you're upset but if you draw attention to us, we're both dead."

Lucia nods, blinking the tears back from her eyes as she tries to steady her racing heart. Adelaide's other hand rubs against her back in a calming motion and she matches her breathing to it.

Suddenly, there's an eruption of gunfire and Lucia can't hold back her scream behind Adelaide's hand as the bartender slumps back against the wood, a bullet through his head. Wood splinters as the bar is pierced by multiple strays.

Adelaide grabs hold of Lucia and twists to get a look out at the bar through the cracked wood. The men are engaged with another group, each firing at one another.

"Come on!" Adelaide whispers, grabbing hold of Lucia's hand as she busts down the door to the hidden space with incredible strength.

Keeping their heads down, Lucia is dragged toward the stairs off the back of the bar, using the distraction to escape.

They tramp up the stairs, pushing past a group of servers and waiting girls who are cowering in the hall, and make their way to Adelaide's room.

Adelaide's clothes are still strewn about. While she quickly flits around grabbing things, Lucia is frozen in the middle of the room, freaking out. Those men had mentioned the barrier, they said it had been *down for a moment*. What did that mean? Lucia is afraid her family might be hurt, and she wasn't there to help.

Lucia stands there frozen as Adelaide throws the cloak she wore yesterday over her and pulls the hood up. The cloak is freezing and a bit stiff from drying on the roof overnight.

Adelaide also covers herself and slips a knife into her boot. Lucia's eyes bulge out. *Does Adelaide plan to fight?*

"We have to leave right now," Adelaide says to a hysteric Lucia mumbling incoherently under her breath. She grabs Lucia's shoulders and shakes her. Recognition comes back into Lucia's eyes as she focuses on blond hair, light piercing through the fair strands.

Lucia realizes there are no more bangs of gunfire. She jumps as thundering footsteps come up the stairs and workers shout in the hall.

Adelaide wrenches the window open and jumps out onto the roof. She helps Lucia climb out of the small window and then slides down the wooden shingles, dropping down to the ground below.

Lucia stares wide-eyed as Adelaide disappears over the side of the building. They are three stories up; Lucia will break her legs trying to do that.

"Lucia, come on," Adelaide hisses.

"I can't," Lucia says, her voice shaking as she holds tighter to the ledge of the windowsill. The wood is weak and cracking beneath her sweaty palms. She closes her eyes, wondering how she keeps getting herself into these kinds of situations. She's good. She's a *good* girl. *So why does this keep happening to her?*

"Adelaide, I can't. I—I'm scared."

"You'll be fine, Lucia. I'll catch you."

"Adelaide..." Lucia whispers, squeaking when the wood cracks further and she drops lower down the roof.

"Don't you trust me?" Adelaide says. "I caught you before."

Lucia opens her eyes, looking up at the ceiling of the dingy room she slept in last night. She had spent a long time staring up at it before she could fall asleep, only her own breathing in her ears. Adelaide had been silent on the floor, with no sound of shuffling or labored breathing. It was like she wasn't there at all.

Lucia felt strength in Adelaide's peace; knowing the other woman wasn't scared or restless.

Taking a deep breath, Lucia lets go.

Lucia slides down the roof and pitches over the side. Her breath is punched out of her chest when she lands in Adelaide's awaiting arms, cradled against that strong, warm body just like last night when she fell from that tree.

Adelaide lets Lucia down and grabs her hand, pulling her down the street where they disappear into the morning rush. Behind them, three men stare out of the inn window, scanning the crowd.

Once the women are safely tucked into the woods, Adelaide lets Lucia fall apart, her eyes puffy and red-rimmed from crying. She saw a dead body and witnessed a gunfight all in one morning. That's what Adelaide told her they were. *Guns*. Her heart is racing madly in her chest and her hands are shaking. She still hasn't had time to process any of it.

"T-those men, were they *looking for me?*"

Lucia's mind is swirling with questions. *Why would anyone want her? Is this what her mother was talking about when she spoke of dangers outside of the barriers?*

"Who were those men? W-why—"

"I don't know," Adelaide says softly. "I don't have any answers for you."

Lucia begins to shrink, feeling exposed under Adelaide's gaze. Who is this woman and where did she come from? If she was at the blooming ceremony, why was she booked into an inn in Domeg, and how did she stay so calm when those men attacked? There is so much that Lucia doesn't understand...

Adelaide turns away, closing her eyes as if she's in pain.

"Are you hurt?" the woman asks.

Lucia looks down at herself. She pulls back the cloak. The silk robe beneath is splattered with blood, red soaking into the beautiful flowers.

"N-no, it isn't mine."

She had been sitting on Adelaide's lap, so the bartender's blood must have only gotten on her.

"I—I need to get home," Lucia says, dropping the cloak back over herself as her stomach churns. "My family—" She takes a deep breath of icy air. "My family might be in trouble."

Adelaide opens her mouth and then closes it again. She nods.

"Come on."

Adelaide moves away from Lucia, and Lucia hurries after her. This is the second time this morning that the woman didn't say what she had really wanted to, and once more, Lucia ignores it. No more words need to be said. *This is goodbye.*

The two women walk slowly to the barrier, back to the clearing where they met. Lucia drags her feet as they approach, spotting her overcoat and slipper still sitting out on the ground, sodden from the evening rain. It almost makes her laugh. Last night feels so far away.

"Thank you," Lucia says when they stand there staring at one another too long. "For catching me..." she says, motioning to the large oak she'd fallen from. "For saving me from freezing to death. For everything."

Lucia laughs, thinking about the city and burgers. It's nothing like she had expected.

"Humans are quite frightening."

Adelaide smiles, but it's a bit sad too. "You have no idea. This place is nothing like the inner cities. Not much different from your own town."

Lucia nods, humming. Adelaide would know much better than her. This was Lucia's first time in one. She doesn't really want to experience it again.

"It was fun, Princess," Adelaide says. She strides forward, her hand reaching out to cup the side of Lucia's face. Lucia goes still, staring wide-eyed at the woman as she leans down. Lips brush against Lucia's cheek and her eyes close as she melts into the touch.

When Adelaide starts to pull away, Lucia's eyes flicker open. Orange leaves flutter around their heads from the trees above. A breeze pulls at the bottom of her cloak making her skin pebble.

This is Lucia's second kiss in this place, and yet this one was nothing like the first. *It was...* Lucia can't even describe the heat blooming within her.

"Will I ever see you again?" Lucia asks. She doesn't mean to say it out loud, but the words come anyway.

Adelaide smiles, her eyes bleeding red.

"If the world is fair."

Scarlet eyes disappear from Lucia's sight as Adelaide melts into the forest. Lucia stands there for much too long, cold and confused, as the autumn sun is swallowed by a nest of clouds. She tries not to think about Adelaide or her red eyes as she makes her way back down the mountain, her feet bruising from rocks and sharp branches underfoot.

Tugging off the cloth still wrapped around her hand, Lucia stuffs it in her pocket, staring down at the thin, scabbed cut across her palm.

It will be weeks before it fades.

Chapter Five

Red Eyes Haunt

"Wʜᴀᴛ ᴛʜᴇ ʜᴇʟʟ ᴅᴏ you think you're doing?" a voice calls, pushing through the brush. A familiar face comes into view, full lips pursed in displeasure.

"F-Fabien," Lucia whispers, not believing her eyes. *"Huh?"*

Fabien's eyes darken. "What do you mean, *huh*? What the hell are you doing out here?"

He motions around at the trees and Lucia's eyes follow, still very confused about why he's here. Did her mother send him? She expected he'd be gone right after the ceremony.

"I was, uh..." Lucia scratches her head. "...exploring."

Fabien's eyes widen hysterically. "In a storm? Are you insane—did you hit your head, *Lady Lucia*? Your mother had people out all night looking for you and you've been out exploring the forest in an autumn thunderstorm overnight."

"D-did anything happen?" Lucia asks, afraid to know the answer. Why else would he be the one out here searching for her?

"The barrier flickered for a moment, but no hunters attacked. You should count yourself lucky, alone all the way out here."

Fabien marches over and grabs Lucia's arm. He does not look happy as he guides her back down the mountain, quickening his pace as rain begins to fall, the sky becoming darker overhead.

Lucia's thoughts go to Adelaide. *She wasn't alone.* She's glad everyone is okay though, her shoulders dropping in relief. She stares at Fabien's back as she stumbles along trying to keep up. He is the last person she would have expected to find in these woods, the first son of Linae Devroue, coven head of the Sea Serpents, and her mother's best friend.

Lucia thinks he's handsome, with smooth dark skin and coiled hair, but he is quite average by Swaydan standards. They are all unnaturally pretty. Like his kin, he has hardened features and a chiseled face. His curls are cropped short, and his plum cloak is thin, not suited for this weather. But more than his looks he is also exceptional in magisk.

Lucia envies that.

The first son of one of the four major covens, Fabien is a rare case. A mage—*a male witch who has abilities beyond coven magisk.* Due to his ability and his family standing, he was permitted to attend Swaydan's blooming ceremony the same year Lucia failed hers, and he presented as a Gaia.

"Why are you still in Laesbury?" Lucia asks. "Actually, I'm surprised you came to the blooming at all."

It's been a while since the Devroues have come to visit, even longer since Fabien joined his mother. Linae and Hatsia are good friends, but things have been tense in Swaydan over the years. *Because of the vampires,* a small voice reminds her.

Witches and vampires have never gotten along, but Swaydan is swarming with them. The vampires are meaner up in the swamps, and since the Silver Spider cult took up residence there, crime has gotten worse. Lucia has heard her mother talk to Linae over the sphaera about the trouble the Skullkins are causing, and the witches have been hard-pressed to do anything about it.

The Skullkins run the vampires and they're an old family. The oldest. They have money, connections, and whatever other advantages that make dealing with them difficult.

"I'm not sure why either," Fabien says, "but it's big news. My mother and Madam Hatsia want us all together before they will say anything."

Lucia shivers, following Fabien closely as she pulls Adelaide's cloak tighter around herself. *What could be so important that Lord Fabien and the Sea Serpent coven head had to travel all the way up to Naprait?*

❦

Lucia sits in the living room of the Dol'Auclair manor with her hands clasped between her thighs. She is between Gabrielle and Fabien on the sofa, with Linae across the tea table. Her sister is giving her odd looks, checking out her unfamiliar outfit, and Lucia shifts, paranoid her sister might spot the blood splatters on her robe peeking through the black cloak draped over her shoulders.

Hatsia stands above them, sipping from her cup of vanilla lavender milk, pacing back and forth.

"What is this about?" Gabrielle asks, one hand squeezing Lucia's thigh. She doesn't have the patience to wait for her mother to finish drinking her tea.

"Manners, young lady," Linae scolds, leaning forward with a pinched face. "Your mother will speak in her time."

Linae turns to her friend, smoothing out her sleek white dress. She wears a matching cape around her shoulders and a simple, fat green band with her family crest on it around her finger.

The Devroues are always elegant, but not overdone. They're one of the richest of the major covens, but they don't show it by way of dress like the Sacrenladre with their flashiness. There's an aura around them. One that means business. It must be the *Sway* in them. Swaydans are always so commanding and in control. She wonders what it is about the swamps that make them that way. Maybe it's the irritating heat that makes them grow tough skin or the dangerous vampires that overrun the place.

Hatsia sets down her cup and moves to sit beside the other coven head. She crosses her ankles and tips her nose up just a smidge, before addressing the three children.

"Last night, the Caput Trium sent out a sphaera to all of the coven heads." Hatsia pauses, sharing a look with Linae. "But it wasn't just the coven heads who were summoned."

Lucia swallows, anxiety climbing up her throat as she waits for her mother to drop the news. A call from the Caput Trium is big. The Caput Trium are the heads of the three Mystic families—the vampires, the witches, and the wolves. There is Nikolay Skullkin of the Silver Spider cult; Ayawa Anoki, interim chief of the Silver Fang clan; and Kaeda Dol'Auclair of the Golden Griffin coven. Each are powerful elders.

Lucia bets whatever is going on is the reason her grandmother missed the blooming ceremony.

"I'm going to play you three the message," Hatsia says, pulling her sphaera from beneath the high neck of her dress.

The black orb dangles between her fingers as she whispers, *"Jiji."* The glass shivers, and a sapphire glow lights from within. "Last call."

"A message from the Grand Elder," comes a shrill voice inside the orb. *"A summons to the Dome for a gathering of grand importance. All coven heads are to advance to Olympia at once! An assembly of the Mystic council commences at dawn in two days' time."*

The message repeats twice more before the sphaera dims back to black and the voice disappears.

Lucia sits in stunned silence.

A gathering of the Mystic council? Dread fills her all the way to her toes, her teeth worrying her bottom lip. The Mystic council hasn't gathered in Lucia's lifetime. Vampires, witches, and werewolves all gathered under one vaulted roof seem like nothing short of trouble. And the event that precipitated it must be important.

"What reason could they have for needing the entire council?" Fabien asks, sitting stiffly in his seat, stunned by the message. "Nothing good, I imagine, if the Caput Trium can't handle it."

Gabrielle squeezes Lucia's leg again, and when Lucia turns to her, a wide grin stretches her lips. Lucia stares at her incredulously. She is too excited about the news. Like how she looked back at lower academy when they would have battle simulations, she was always thrilled to fight.

Lucia hopes this is nothing like those traumatic days. She has seen what fighting does now, and it is *not pretty*.

"Serio?" Lucia mumbles, her fingers plucking nervously at the threads of her dress, unable to believe what she just heard.

The message said they were gathering at the Dome. The famed building at the outskirts of Zarun where the Caput Trium passes judgment on those who violate Paxum ex Cinis—*committing a crime against another Mystic or putting Mystics in danger from the humans.* Nothing good happens there.

Lucia flashes back to her own horrid memory of the place. A memory she thought she had forgotten. The first and only time she left the barriers of Laesbury with her mother. She had been twelve and so unaware of the way of the world. That day was a rude awakening...

A man knelt on the hard ground, his ashen skin bathed in moonlight. His face was waxen and gaunt, the skin stretched over sharp bones.

Lucia couldn't look away.

The Grand Elder cut an imposing figure standing over him, her face twisted up in a scowl. Lucia had seen her grandmother angry before, but a different type of fear hit her, watching her grandmother shake with rage. All of her magisk and authority as Grand Elder was felt throughout the room, the vastness and depth of brutality she could inflict with the wave of a wrist.

Lucia shivered, holding tight to her sister. Gabrielle was only ten, yet Lucia tried to hide behind her as the vampire's haunted red eyes turned to her. Caught in the stare, Lucia took a step back, struck by the hatred she saw there, and under that, his fear burned deep into her.

Flaming red eyes glistened like the rubies that hung around Lucia's neck. She felt weighted by them as she hunched in on herself, feeling exposed and raw. Like the vampire was seeing into her soul.

Gabrielle grabbed Lucia's clammy hand, pulling her back into line beside their mother. Lucia stood sandwiched between the Dol'Auclair women, the pulse at her neck jumping as hungry eyes flickered to it. The Grand Elder yanked on the chain around the vampire's neck, and spikes dug into his throat. A black liquid oozed down his pale chest where the silver pierced marble skin.

Lucia shifted away, watching the scene from the corner of her eye, her breath held tight in her throat. She shook, afraid to even breathe lest time play onward. She hadn't understood what was going on—what the man's crime was, or why he had to be subjected to such cruelty. Bolted to the floor and collared as rows of witches watched from above, the Dome was filled with spectators.

Lucia didn't understand why she was made to watch.

The Grand Elder spoke as the sun inched its way up the sky to replace the moon, lightening the Dome as a kaleidoscope of color rained down from the domed glass roof. Kaeda's voice boomed, echoing through the vibrant walls.

"Abhain of the White Dragon cult, you are here because you have broken Paxum ex Cinis. You were caught feeding on a witch, directly violating the treaty, which prohibits violence against another Mystic family. For that crime, you are sentenced to Ikun Una—*death by fire*. Do you wish to repent in your final moments, vampire?"

Lucia held her breath, her lungs burning as she watched her grandmother. There wasn't a drop of light or sympathy in her eyes. She looked down at the vampire as if he was a monster. He didn't look like a monster to Lucia. He looked... broken. He looked scared...

He looked no different from her.

"I couldn't help myself," the vampire cried. "I was so hungry."

Ink-black hair shone in the remnants of moonlight. When he turned his head, hands like claws came up in front of him, weighted by shackles. His eyes were like fresh blood, teeth sinking below his lip as he glared at the Grand Elder of the witches with a deep-seated hatred in his eyes.

Lucia caught her breath, her heart pounding like a drum as she stared at those teeth and claws.

So beautiful.

So deadly.

She had never seen a vampire before, only heard stories from her mother that gave her nightmares. The sinful, selfish creatures of the night. Even the reality was like something out of her imagination.

Kaeda strode forward, pulling a ring from the vampire's finger. The man was a daywalker—they wear rings to keep from burning up in the sun.

"That is your reason for killing one of mine, vampire?" Kaeda spat, her lip curled up to show her own blunt teeth. "A disciple of the Mother, Deipara. Your lack of self-control is so based, and your sins run so deep, as to drive you to your core nature. A murderer. A daemon."

Kaeda waved her hand and there was a creaking as someone started the mechanics to lift the domed roof, parting the stained glass to let in the first rays of sunlight. The vampire's skin began to blister, red blemishes disfiguring his smooth skin as light filtered from above.

It was horrifying.

"Repent to Deipara," Kaeda said, "and in your next life, may you be reborn a witch."

The vampire struggled against his shackles as he began to burn, and his skin peeled and cracked. He turned to Lucia once more, their gazes holding, looking into one another's eyes. As the man burst into flames, she lost contact, and a piercing wail cut through the night as a woman struggled in the arms of Olympian guards. The woman's own red eyes flashed brilliantly in her pain.

Lucia wasn't sure if she was family or a lover. But she remembers the eerie cry. She recoiled, a sob ripped from her throat as tears stung in her eyes. Her mother shot her a worried look and Gabrielle's hand held hers tighter trying to ground her in place. Lucia tried to hold on to her strength and to focus on the warmth of her sister's small hand, but she couldn't.

It was too much.

Lucia ripped away from Gabrielle's arms, running toward the door—an opening cut into the gray stone. The door echoed as it slammed behind her.

She ran out into the hall, her breath becoming harsh as it was torn from her throat. Lucia was burning up, sweaty, and uncomfortable in her restrictive dress. The high neck and jewels wove around, choking her. She couldn't stop the stream of tears, hot and endless down her face as the image of the burning vampire played on a loop behind her closed eyelids. She was suffocating, screams echoed in her ears as she bent over her knees, gulping in the crisp, biting air of the hall untinged with smoke like it was water.

Lucia was startled as a door slammed behind her and turned in time to see her mother's thunderous face before she was snatched by thin, biting hands. She stared big, wet eyes up at her mother as she was held by the front of her dress.

"How dare you?" Hatsia hissed, spittle flying at Lucia's face to join her tears. "Embarrassing your grandmother, our family, in front of the covens as she offers a sacrifice to the Mother avenging our fallen sister."

"I—I—"

Lucia's mouth gaped as she struggled to find words. She hadn't meant to run or disrespect the traditions and punishments of the coven, but she was so overwhelmed. Watching a man die.

It confused Lucia further, how she seemed to be the only one who was affected. Even Gabrielle hadn't batted an eye as the vampire was burnt before her. She'd never been as emotional as Lucia, crying over trampled flowers and dead birds. She was strong.

A stinging hand struck Lucia's face, the slap echoing through the winding hall as she fell to the ground. Dark green vines whipped out from thin air, created from Hatsia's mind, and wrapped around Lucia. They drug her flailing down the hall, climbing up the wall and wedging between the cracks of stone to open a door leading to a small, pitch-black storage.

"You disgrace our Mother deity and spit in the face of our Grand Elder's righteous judgment. You will stay here until you've dried your tears and thought about your shame. Feeling sympathy for a monstrous criminal? A heretic."

Hatsia tossed Lucia inside the dark room and slammed it shut. The vines retreated and Lucia's heart leaped to her throat, the familiar dark, crowded feeling closing in on her as she threw herself at the door.

A horrified "No!" squeaked past her lips as she hit the door, but it didn't budge.

Lucia continued scratching at the door, her nails chipped and bloody, and her chest constricted painfully against her ribs. She wheezed, her breath short and her head fuzzy like she might pass out. Her head hung between her shoulders as she whimpered to be let free.

"Mama!" she cried, though she knew the woman wasn't coming for her. She never had before.

Much time passed before Lucia heard a sound. Her head lifted weakly, her neck stiff and eyes crusted with dried tears as the sound of grating stone reached her ears. She flinched back as the door was slowly pushed open, and Gabrielle's head peeked in. Lucia tried to return her sister's small smile, relief at being found, but it didn't quite reach her eyes as the girl came to sit beside her, streaks of morning sunlight streaming into the small room.

Lucia shivered against the floor, the chill left her a shaky mess. Gabrielle pulled a cloak over Lucia's shoulders, and she leaned forward until their foreheads were touching, and Lucia's eyes fell closed as a fresh tear curved down her cheek.

"She hates me," Lucia whispered, angry at her own weakness. A weakness that even the terrifying punishment of being locked inside a confined room hadn't cured her of. No amount of punishment has. "Our mother hates me."

"She doesn't hate you."

Gabrielle pressed their cheeks together, the wetness of Lucia's tear imprinted on her face. "Our mother has always had high expectations of you, more so than of anyone else. Perhaps, that's because you are the Dol'Auclair heir, or because... because she doesn't see you as I do."

Gabrielle's voice was whispered and sharp. That of a child, and a wise one at that.

"Mother has her excuses for why she treats you as she does, reasons I know not. But know this Lucia—you don't have to change a thing about yourself to earn my love. You already have it, and you always will."

Chapter Six

It Speaks

LUCIA FACES THE FAMED building, the Dome, a pearly mound in the middle of Olympia's buzzing city square. Her pulse races, her heart beating staccato against her ribs.

Vampires, werewolves, and witches will be in attendance, squished together inside a stone cage. The last and only time Lucia had contact with a vampire is an unpleasant memory in her mind. She can still smell the burning flesh as if it is imprinted on these walls.

Lucia and Gabrielle are separated from their mother when they enter the Dome, escorted in by Olympian guards. As she enters, Lucia is enveloped by that same peculiar warmth she felt when she passed through the Ife Ring in the mountains, an uncomfortably sticky feeling rushing over her, like the invasive veil is caressing her skin beneath her clothes.

Lucia hasn't talked about her experience that day. Her mother had pulled her aside after she played the summons and scolded her for running off, but Lucia had told her the same as she had Fabien: she huddled in the forest overnight, exploring the mountains. Her mother thought it was a miracle she hadn't gotten sick, but she let it go. There were more pressing things to be concerned with.

The Olympian guards wear uniforms that mimic the Dome's exterior, and their armor is painted in repetitive geometric shapes with many shades of blue and yellow, which give it a vibrant and animated quality.

Lucia can hardly study the blurring colors and shapes decorating the walls as she's led in a dizzying spiral up the building. A door is opened into a room on the third floor, and then it's closed behind her. There is no handle for it to be opened from the inside. They're stuck in here until someone releases them. Lucia takes a deep breath to calm her racing heart, teeth worrying her bottom lip.

You're fine, Lucia. You're fine. It's not that small of a space. You're not alone.

Lucia is grateful when she feels Gabrielle's hand in hers, soothing the rising panic. It wouldn't do well to freak out right now, not with the many eyes of witches from major covens as well as royalty within the vampire and werewolf ranks. She has to be a good representative of the Golden Griffin coven and the Dol'Auclair family. Her grandmother's reputation is on her shoulders as the firstborn.

The room they've entered is more of a ledge, circular, with black marble benches that line the walls.

There are five rows, each opening up on a different floor, and at the center on the ground level is a round table that is currently empty of people. That's where the Caput Trium will sit.

Lucia shudders when she eyes the chains bolted to the floor, trying to push back that distant memory. The guards took Lucia and Gabrielle to the second row closer to the floor, but they are still fairly high up. Lucia is reminded of the last time she had been high up and tries to push away that thought as well. The thought of Adelaide. She will never see the woman again. The way the woman spoke when they parted made it seem that way.

If the world is fair.

Lucia never quite felt it was. If it had been, she would have been born with magisk and she would have bloomed in her eighteenth year.

But, being here, outside of her cage in Laesbury, thoughts of Adelaide come flooding in. She has been trying her hardest to ignore it, but it has wounded her to do so. Adelaide is a constant companion in her mind.

Lucia has to distract herself from errant thoughts, her gaze wandering the room looking for something to catch her attention. The room is much bigger and taller than it looks from the outside, and each row is far apart. When she looks up, Lucia wonders if the people up top can even see anything on the ground floor.

When someone enters their floor on Lucia's side, she leans into her sister without realizing it, their thighs and shoulders brushing.

"Are you okay?" Gabrielle asks, tearing her eyes from the flurry of activity around her. She's practically vibrating with excitement, scanning all of the new faces.

Lucia guesses she's cataloging who she's going to try and make friends with once the meeting ends. Gabrielle likes to make friends anywhere she goes, forcing herself into people's lives as she does.

Lucia would prefer that to the alternative—that her sister might be seeking out a vampire in the crowd. Gabrielle has been fixated on them since they were young when her grandmother told them horror stories about blood-sucking hedonists who prey on the weak and vulnerable.

What intrigued her about them, Lucia has no clue. Some things about her sister are a mystery. Gabrielle just... *is*. And she sweeps everyone along with her.

Lucia will have to keep an eye on her today. Knowing her sister, she will do something stupid. Or dangerous. For Gabrielle, with one comes the other.

Lucia smiles, waving her sister off. "I'm fine."

"*Hello.*"

Lucia's heart leaps to her throat as a face pushes up into her space. She holds her chest to still her beating heart as she leans back, looking up at the girl blinking big silver eyes at her.

"Hele," Lucia responds, swallowing the lump in her throat as she takes a deep breath.

The stranger looks to be about Gabrielle's age. She has long, auburn silken hair tied in braids and tawny skin that's practically glowing even in the low lights. *She's a wolf.* Or at least, Lucia thinks she is.

"I'm Blythe Kanoska—or you can call me Birdie. These are my brothers Boen and Beaur."

She moves back so Lucia can see the two boys who look eerily similar to her. One gives her a polite smile and the other doesn't even glance her way. Lucia misses the way Blythe's eyes rake her up and down as she stutters through a response.

"I'm Lucia."

Blythe hums. "Crimson Ash clan, the second oldest triplet of the Crimson wolves' chieftain."

Lucia's eyes widen as they flicker back to the two boys. *Triplets?*

"Uhh... first daughter of the Golden Griffin coven head."

Blythe gasps and even the stoic boy beside her looks Lucia's way.

"You're *that* Lucia!" she says, and Lucia's face heats at the attention being drawn to her. She's lucky the door on ground level chooses that moment to open and she's saved from answering.

What does 'that Lucia' even mean?

Lucia focuses on the figures filing in down below, pushing aside the comment as she watches with rapt attention.

The first to enter is a man with bronze skin. Inky black hair falls down his back, and a white-and-gold fur-lined cloak sits around his broad shoulders. He walks with a twisted staff Lucia doesn't think he actually needs, the dull *clack!* thudding against marble with every step.

Though she'd only met Ayawa Anoki briefly as a child, when he came along with his brother to visit the Golden Griffin coven, Lucia knows it is him. The interim chief of the wolves looks a lot like his nephew.

That brings Lucia to a thought that hadn't crossed her mind before now. *Hetan is here.*

He must be somewhere in this room.

Lucia whips around trying to spot him, but it's hard to tell in the dark room. There are so many people, and it has been ten years since Lucia last saw him. There are other wolves here, and he would have changed a lot.

Lucia's heart pounds wildly, and she grows nervous at the thought of seeing him after so long. She'd imagined it for years but never truly considered what she would do if it happened. Would everything be as it was before, or would time have warped them into strangers? The thought of the latter makes Lucia's heart sink in her chest, and she feels sick. Gabrielle asks if she's okay again, and she nods.

The second man to stride in is pale, white like the shining moon. He's tall and lean, with a smooth, gliding step. He wears all black, his shirt unbuttoned at the top to reveal satin skin like pearls. He turns and red eyes pierce Lucia. His presence makes the hair stand on the back of her neck, hands clammy against the thighs of her silk dress.

He reminds her of that man she saw here all those years ago. The man her grandmother sentenced to death.

Vampires are known as solitary creatures. They live in cults, but they act for their own pleasure. They don't have much structure or authority, but they *will* and *do* answer to one man. The head of the Swaydan Spiders—*Nikolay Skullkin.*

Lucia holds her breath until the man looks away, taking his seat at the round table, equilateral to Chief Anoki. The room is tense with the arrival of two such powerful people, but when the last arrives it's as if all the air is sucked from the room.

Kaeda Dol'Auclair strides in with her head held high. She's in a traditional gown that sweeps the floor with a matching headscarf of many patterns and colors that the older witches favor.

But beneath that power, something feels off. Gabrielle's breath catches beside her and that's when she sees it. Their grandmother looks... unwell. She's always been old, for as long as Lucia can remember, but she has never looked it. Now, under the vivid lights shining only on the ground floor, she looks haggard and hollow-eyed, her skin touched with gray.

Something painful twists Lucia's heart at the sight.

Lucia's eyes flick to her mother, who sits in the row below her, but she can only see the back of the woman's head. Her shoulders are stiff though, her back straight and tall.

When the room has gone silent, the crowd watches and waits with bated breath, as the chief rises from his seat, leaning forward on his staff to address the room.

Anoki's voice echoes up to the highest floor, deep and commanding as he says, "I am the chief of the wolves, third of three seats on the Caput Trium, and I welcome you all here today. Kiora Hai—*hello, friends.*"

Nikolay stands next, a chilling smirk gracing the corners of his marble lips. Lucia feels uneasy at the sight of him. She misses most of his words as he stands there, still as a statue, with no breath in his lungs or rises in his chest as he speaks. It's with a chilling realization that she thinks of another.

She pushes the thought away.

"Nikolay Skullkin, Master of the Silver Spiders, second of three on the Caput Trium. I'm honored you all came to gather on such short notice."

A fang descends as one side of his lips curves upward, the ivory bone pointed in a deadly tip.

Lucia shivers.

Kaeda seems to struggle to get up, shaking slightly before she stands firm, head raised up in a proud tilt. Lucia finds Gabrielle's eyes, sharing a concerned look with her sister in the dark. Lucia's becoming increasingly worried, her curiosity about the call for this meeting turning sour.

In her age-rough voice penetrated with decades of power and authority, she says, "Kaeda Dol'Auclair of the Golden Griffin coven and Grand Elder of the witches. The daughter descended from the hallowed deity, Deipara. Kaab ogbo owan ti—*Welcome, all who gather."*

The Grand Elder retakes her seat, and Anoki stands once more, circling the ground floor as he speaks to everyone. Lucia holds her breath, tugging nervously on the flame necklace Gabrielle gave her, the time arriving that they'll get answers for the sudden call of the Mystic council. She's been a wreck, nervous the whole journey as her mother's unsettled energy permeated the carriage, stuck for two days with no escape from the woman. She spent more uninterrupted time with her mother than she has in years.

The only thing grounding Lucia right now is Gabrielle's hand, which digs nearly painfully into her thigh, fingers carving crescent moons in the skin.

"As you all know, this world—our three great Mystic families—rely on the magisk we were born to. Some for survival, strong lethal bodies, immortal lives, power to raise crops and manipulate minds... The foundations of who we are and the legacy of our ancestors. But—" Anoki says, raising his voice, and slamming his staff against the floor as he meets eyes shadowed in the darkness, some glowing red or silver. "—there is something that even we fear. Something that has long threatened that very magisk, the core of our being. *The Orbis Libra*. A powerful, destructive celestial magisk that wishes to devour our own magisk and would bring chaos should it ever have the chance."

Lucia gulps, breath unsteady as Anoki meets her eyes in the dark. She knows of the Orbis Libra, of course. Her grandmother is its holder and has been since long before Lucia's birth. She took over from its previous wielder, Sonya Mitsu, the only witch to hold it that wasn't a Golden Griffin of the Dol'Auclair line.

A beauty and prodigy of the Black Basilisk coven with thick, ink-black hair that touched the back of her calves and deep black eyes like a boundless ocean.

During her reign as the Orbis Libra's holder, she brought her coven to riches, and the Sacrenladre still sits as the wealthiest family because of it.

Lucia sweats, dreading the chief's next words.

"I speak on behalf of the Grand Elder. The reason for this gathering is to inform you all that she is ill. So afflicted by this *sickness* the great and terrifying magisk she wields is waning and with it the power to hold the Orbis Libra."

The crowd around Lucia erupts into chaos. There are shouting and horrified gasps, people jumping to their feet. All Lucia can do is sit there frozen, eyes wide and trained on her grandmother, who sits trembling even as she tries to look strong—back straight and head held high like the regal woman she taught Lucia to be. That Lucia *failed* at being.

It can't be true. Her grandmother can't be sick. She's strong, she's a powerful mystic—the strongest in recent history. Lucia never imagined there would be a day that ended. That she would see her grandmother weak. It might not look like it to anyone else, but Lucia, who has looked up to the woman her entire life, sees it beneath the veneer, a vulnerability she tried to ignore...

"Settle. Settle!" Anoki slams his staff once more, bringing the room quickly under control. "I know this news is shocking, but there are pressing matters at hand. Firstly, is the selection of a new holder of the Orbis Libra."

Anoki motions to the marble table where a box sits. Lucia hadn't even noticed it before, she was so focused on the three powerful leaders. Anoki holds it up for all to see, and Lucia leans forward to get a better look. The small chest is made of an unfamiliar white wood, with intricate carvings on its side that she can't read from so far away. Red tendrils wind around it, bloodied vines strangling the wood beneath. *Like they're guarding the box.*

"When Kaeda fell ill a few nights ago, we were extremely lucky she had enough strength to return the Orbis Libra to rest inside of this ancient chest, a remnant of the Old World it descends from, *Ashad Escana*. But it cannot stay there for long. The ancient chest is old and many of its magisks fail. The Orbis Libra can only be in it for a short while before we need to give it a new host. If we don't, there will be certain chaos."

Anoki looks to Kaeda, who nods. She is ashen and drawn, like just sitting there keeping up appearances is taking a toll on her. Lucia can't keep the distress off her face, rocking nervously as she tries to keep her eyes from straying to the woman. She feels guilt crawl through her, that only days ago she'd been so happy her grandmother wasn't at her blooming ceremony, while she was suffering.

Selfish, horrid, wicked granddaughter, Lucia scolds herself.

Anoki motions to Nikolay, and the man stands fluidly as the chief takes his seat. Nikolay doesn't move about, rooted in place as he straightens his cuffs. He then turns red eyes up to the gathered audience, that smirk gracing his lips once more, but this time there's a tinge of satisfaction in it that makes Lucia's skin crawl.

"The Orbis Libra needs someone strong and young to take over. Someone who can handle the strain it demands on a person's body. In the past, that role has been filled by wise and powerful young witches such as Kaeda Dol'Auclair herself, *in her prime*. But this is a unique time in our history. One in which the major Mystic families are not at war, or spilling blood amongst each other. A time when we can pick a vessel from not only a witch but a vampire or a wolf, as well."

A hum of conversation follows those words, less chaotic than before as people begin mumbling and muttering amongst themselves. Gabrielle grips Lucia's arm, saying, "Isn't that awesome, Lucia? A vessel from any of the three families."

Lucia hums, giving Gabrielle a small smile. *No,* she doesn't think it's amazing. Anyone can become the vessel; anyone can become the holder of the greatest power in the New World. A power that aided her grandmother, an already powerful witch in her own right, in becoming the most powerful mystic in all of Hontaras. It's frightening. Everyone will want to get their hands on it. *And who knows what they'll do once they have it?*

Lucia turns down to the row below, only to find her mother already looking at her. The look in Hatsia's eyes tells Lucia what she already guessed. *She is expected to take her grandmother's place.* To bring the Orbis Libra back to the witches. Never mind the fact Lucia doesn't even have any magisk, and she failed her blooming just days ago. How can she be expected to fill her grandmother's role?

"We are going to choose from—"

Lucia's eyes flick to the Orbis Libra, which begins to glow brighter from within the chest, enveloping it in an indigo glow. Little tremors like electricity race through it, and she's unable to look away, leaning farther and farther forward in her seat, being drawn toward it—the living, *writhing* thing. Like it's in pain.

Lucia's heart begins to beat fast. The room feels too small, and the air is sucked from her lungs as she is transported, body and mind, like falling into a dream.

Lucia is floating in a sea of warmth, drifting out in a great big ocean that soothes her like a hot bath. Her face bobs above the surface, staring up at the sky; the stars and moon are big in the night above her, hovering right over her head like she can reach out and touch them. Slowly, she raises her hands to do just that. Everything is so warm... floaty... and nice. *If she could just reach—*

Gabrielle?

Distantly, Lucia can feel her sister; she hears Gabrielle calling her name like a faraway whisper carried on a breeze.

There's a stinging in her side, a prick—*are there jellyfish in this ocean?* There's another on her arm. Lucia cries out, arms flailing. Suddenly, she begins sinking, going under the water deeper and deeper like she's being sucked up by a whirlpool, or falling through the sky, and then...

"*Ouch*. Kein u kila, Gabrielle?"—*What are you doing?* Lucia snaps.

Lucia blinks a few times like she's coming out of a trance, her hand rubbing her stinging leg. Lucia's eyes fall on Gabrielle, a small needle clutched between her fingers—a pin from her hair.

Lucia's eyes widen as she whispers, "Did you stab me with that?"

Gabrielle only gapes at her, a sort of relief passing over her eyes. "Uh... Gabrielle? What in tofet's name was *that*?"

"S-sorry," Gabrielle says, pinning her braid back up into place. "You were... like... glowing. Your eyes were blue, and it was kind of freaky. I tried speaking to you, but your eyes were fixed on that—the Orbis Libra."

Lucia follows her gaze to the table, where the Orbis Libra sits, no longer glowing or surrounded by the electricity Lucia saw only a moment ago.

Lucia blinks a few times, but it still looks normal. *It must have been a trick of the light.*

Lucia nods, fingers bunching in her dress to dry her nervous hands as she tunes back into Nikolay's speech about choosing the Orbis Libra's holder. She ignores her sister's worried eyes watching her.

"We are going to choose from—" he says, and Lucia could have sworn he said that already. Before she has time to question it, the room is shaking. Lucia jolts forward and is nearly knocked off the platform, but the wolven woman from before, Blythe, grabs her arm, hauling her back into her seat.

"T-takke." Lucia stutters her gratitude, looking around the room where many others are righting themselves. Even the Caput Trium look stunned, staring at the Orbis Libra on the table, which is glowing even brighter than Lucia had seen before. The chest is shaking, expanding, and contracting like it's taking a breath. Then, it speaks:

"*Lucia Dol'Auclair, Mia Sacrenladre, Cassius Draik, Azeume Skullkin, Boen Kanoska, Hetan Anoki.*"

The chest takes one last monstrous breath and then it goes dim, falling back to the table with a dull clatter. The room is silent.

Lucia is holding her breath as she stares at the dormant chest, and when she looks up, there are eyes on her. Gabrielle, her mother, her grandmother, and the other witches in attendance are all staring right at her.

Blythe, beside her, is staring at her brother whose name had also been called by the Orbis Libra.

Lucia's heart races, unable to breathe as her throat is thick with fear. *Why did it call her name? What is happening?* By the looks on the Caput Trium's faces, this wasn't meant to happen. They're just as shocked as she is.

Lucia's fingers tug at Gabrielle's dress, clenching the fabric between shaking hands as she pushes closer to her sister to shield herself from the many stares. *Is she supposed to get up—or* do *something? She wasn't prepared for this.*

Boen a few seats over seems to be just as confused, frozen in his seat as his sister and brother try to pry information from him. There is chatter across the room as the others whose names were called are hassled. They're all saved from answering by Chief Anoki, who stands, bringing the room back to attention.

"We seem to have an... unexpected development," he says, fingers red as he grips his staff tightly. His eyes are meeting someone across the room, and Lucia remembers another name the Orbis Libra called off—*Hetan Anoki.*

Lucia's chest constricts as she follows the chief's eyes to a figure on the other side of the room. It's hard to make out the details, but she can see the shadow of broad shoulders and silver eyes shining like beacons. *Hetan? Is that really him?*

"The plan has changed." Anoki goes on. "The Orbis Libra seems to have chosen... *it's contestants.* Lucia Dol'Auclair, Mia Sacrenladre, Cassius Draik, Azeume Skullkin, Boen Kanoska, and Hetan Anoki. Our six warriors will compete in the Triune for the honor of becoming the next vessel for the Orbis Libra!"

A slow clap builds up until the room is shaking with applause. Lucia's face burns from the attention, her mother's proud gaze on her. She doesn't deserve it. She has no magisk, *how will she compete against these other contestants?*

Lucia meets the woman's eyes. She's never seen her mother look at her like that. Hatsia is a severe woman, and she has always been hard on Lucia, but for once she actually looks pleased. Almost happy. Or, as close to it as she can get. It fills Lucia with a strange warmth, though she did nothing to gain that affection.

"There will be a gala," Nikolay drawls, his voice rising over the commotion. "In one week, we will hold a celebration at the Hallow Tower in the heart of Olympia, a joining of the three major families to commence a three-month, three-event tournament to seek our next Eidan—*the holder of the magisk core.*"

Chapter Seven

Only a Skull Remains

Stepping out into the city square is like emerging from the deep recesses of an underground cave, the light burning Lucia's eyes as she steps outside. Olympia is a busy place, always moving; the people are in a hurry with important things to do. Sentinels patrol the area, keeping an eye out for thieves or anyone who might try to enter the Dome without permission.

Olympia is a rich city, full of color, art, and invention. It's the epicenter of Hontaras, positioned dangerously among human cities, and as such, there is much value. Things someone might want to get their hands on. Gabrielle had warned Lucia to watch her pockets when they first arrived.

Baron and the handmaidens stay with the Dol'Auclairs as they stand around waiting for the other two guards, Falex and Gisela, to go fetch their carriage.

"My daughter." The Grand Elder approaches the group surrounded by Olympian guards. They stand back as Kaeda takes her daughter's hand.

Bowing, their eyes to the ground, Lucia and Gabrielle show respect to their grandmother.

"Are you coming home to Laesbury?" Hatsia asks, surprised her mother followed them out.

"I will not. I have some things to settle here in town, but I will be heading to Laesbury at the week's end. I haven't visited for a long while, and we have much to speak of."

"Yes, of course. I will prepare for your arrival."

Kaeda's eyes stray to Lucia, her pupils narrowing as they settle on her. Lucia gulps, unable to meet the woman's stare. Her fingertips dig into the meat of her palms as she swallows the shame that falls over her.

Her grandmother must know about her failed blooming; Lucia knows she does. She wonders if her mother sent it in a letter or thought it urgent enough to send with the projice cantus through the sphaera around her neck. Perhaps she didn't have to tell her at all; perhaps the news reached her with the quickness of a forest fire. The title would read something like this—*The Dol'Auclair heir is a failure; she wounds the Dol'Auclair name once again.*

When the woman raises her hand Lucia closes her eyes, preparing for the strike. She's proud she only flinches slightly. Except, her grandmother's hand moves past her. It lands on Gabrielle's shoulder, the other coming up to present a velvet box. Lucia's eyes fly back open as she leans in to watch Gabrielle open it, gasping at a set of turquoise hairpins that glow beautifully in the morning light.

The pins are of the family crest, the Golden Griffin, and are heirlooms that have been passed through generations of Dol'Auclair.

"I had Eshana Sacrenladre see that it was restored. I was going to bring it to your blooming ceremony, but the situation with the Orbis Libra and my health held me. I am proud of you, *my light.*"

Gabrielle thanks her grandmother, in awe over the beautiful gift, and Lucia turns away from her family, grateful for once that no one is paying her any mind as tears well in her eyes. They burn as they track down her cheeks, blurring her vision, and she quickly wipes them away with the sleeve of her dress.

Lucia shouldn't be surprised. Still, she remembers a time when her grandmother had promised her those hand-carved pins. When she used to call Lucia *my moon*.

Lucia hides her shaky hands in the folds of her dress. It was silly of her to think that being chosen by the Orbis Libra would change anything. Nothing short of winning the place of Eidan could restore her grandmother's respect.

As she's blinking tears from her eyes—her family advancing toward the carriage pulling forward without a glance back toward her—she spots a pair of red eyes. Faltering in her step, she turns and watches as they disappear into the crowd. Her heart squeezes in her chest, her breath coming faster.

Red eyes.

She's reminded of that moment in the forest when she had first looked up into vermillion eyes. At the time she had thought it was a trick of the light but... *could it be?*

Lucia feels something well up inside her. Anger? Excitement? She isn't sure. But she wants the truth. She has to know for sure.

Lucia doesn't spare a thought of warning before she's racing after red eyes, swallowed into the crowd.

"Wait. *Wait!*" Lucia wheezes, running down the street, cutting through alleyways as her mind spins eerily out of control. Her head is filled with images of Adelaide. It's like she can feel the woman's hands all over her body, setting fire to every place that she'd touched.

Lucia has ached since they parted. She's done everything to forget the woman, but she can't. The woman had said if they met again, it would be because the world was fair. Lucia isn't sure where she stands on the subject of fate, but as she pushes through the throng, she hopes it is true.

Lucia stands alone in a passage between two buildings. Her eyes dart around, turning at every sound.

"*Adelaide?*" she whispers, the hair on the back of her neck rising. Lucia doesn't know what she plans to do if she finds the woman. All she knows is that she has to see her.

"Well, well, well. If it isn't Hatsia's *bairn*, herself," a voice behind her trills. "Lucia Dol'Auclair."

"Who are you?" Lucia asks, whipping around, her heart beating quicker.

The figure is tall; a broad presence in the narrow pathway. His face is shrouded by a black cowl. The man steps forward, and Lucia takes one back. Her eyes drop down to the dagger in his scarred hand, the silver glinting at his side. There are shining red rubies in the eyes of a skull. Lucia's blood runs cold. *It wasn't Adelaide.*

Lucia turns to run, but the man is fast. He charges toward her, his knife held high, and when she tries to dodge him her high heel catches on a raised bit of cobblestone, sending her airborne. Lucia hits the ground with a smack, an arm coming out to catch herself. She can feel the bruise forming under her skin.

Lucia turns over, and the man's blade comes down hard on the stone beside her head. It chinks away a bit of rock as the man groans at the reverberation shooting up his arm. Lucia pushes her arms out, trying to launch up from the ground, but her foot is grabbed, slamming her back down. Her teeth rattle in her head as her chin bounces off the ground, knocking her dizzy. Her vision swims as she tries to bat the man away. He's much stronger, climbing atop her, one hand grabbing her hair and pulling her up by her curls.

The headpiece Lucia wears pinned across her forehead for Dai Gemus in honor of the great deities is ripped free. The crystals scatter across the ground as she grabs for her attacker's hands, her fingers digging futilely at his thick skin. Her eyes clench closed as she tries to gather all her strength to push against him.

"*Agh!*" Lucia cries out as the dagger slides across her skin, carving into her thigh. For a moment she thinks that's her own voice, but the weight disappears, blood from the short blade dripping down onto her as the man falls away.

Lucia turns to see an arrow in the man's arm. He jumps up, trying to flee at the arrival of his attacker—Gabrielle stands at the mouth of the alley, a bow-and-arrow in her hands.

Lucia's mouth drops open in awe. She wonders if the bow is a summoning and how her sister was able to conjure something so big. *Her blooming was only days ago.*

Gabrielle's eyes widen as she takes in the scene, Lucia's dress bloody. Her hands shake as she notches another bow. The hooded man is headed right for her, his weapon stained red with Lucia's blood.

"Gabrielle, stay back!" Lucia shouts, pushing to her feet. The man charges at her sister, who stands in his way of escape.

Lucia tries limping forward to stop the man, but she's too slow. Her injury holds her back. Her arms stretch toward him as if she could grab him from this distance and send him away from her beloved sister. The earth that separates her and Gabrielle feels like the space that separates the sun and the moon, and as her sister's eyes widen, arms coming up to protect herself, Lucia's heart seizes in her chest as if caught by an invisible hand.

"Stay away from my sister!" Lucia screams, her hand curling into a fist. As if by force, the man stops right in his tracks, leg raised and arm poised midair. He freezes.

"Get away!"

Lucia can't think clearly. All she sees is the man headed toward Gabrielle with evil intent, an image of Gabrielle bloodied on the ground driving her to madness. With one final push, her hand flicking to the side, the man jolts to the right like he's been shoved and then—*disappears.*

With a *pop* crackling in the air, he's gone. The dagger clatters to the cobbled stone with a sickening ring.

Lucia drops to the ground in fatigue, her face gone ashen as all her strength flees her. She stares bewildered at the place the man had just been standing, the sound of thundering footsteps approaching alongside the clatter of her sister's heels.

Falex's voice washes over her. "Lady Lucia, are you all right? Speak to me."

"Lucia, *oh my goodness.*"

Lucia groans as Gabrielle's cool hands grab at her face, pushing back her nest of hair, which the stranger had tugged sore. Lucia distantly registers that there are tears in her sister's eyes. She's never seen Gabrielle cry before... It's an odd and unpleasant feeling, knowing that she was the cause. "Are you okay? We have to get you to a healer right away."

"I'm okay," Lucia says, breathily. "Just a cut." She looks down at her ravaged dress, the fabric dyed red. It looks a lot worse than it is. She just wishes for a slumber and then a hot bath. *Maybe she's delirious from adrenaline?*

"Get back, Gabrielle," Hatsia says, moving swiftly down the alley, her dress kicking up with her steps. Gabrielle jumps aside as her mother comes to stand before Lucia, lifting her dress just enough to see the wound. Lucia winces at the hand against her leg, and her mother catalogs the reaction.

"Where's the attacker?" Gisela asks sharply, as she comes to join them. The head guard is on high alert. Her eyes cut to the people standing around—the other two guards, Baron and Falex, and then to Gabrielle.

There is nothing left of the attacker but a dagger with a skull carved into the hilt that lies on the ground.

"I—I don't know," Gabrielle whispers. "He just disappeared." Her eyes cut to Lucia, who lies in Falex's arms, eyes fighting to stay open.

Gisela doesn't look pleased by the answer, but she nods, her head on a swivel, always looking out for danger. "Let us move quickly before the madam loses too much blood. We can dress her wound at the carriage."

The group moves quickly out of the alley, the three guards surrounding them. Some eyes are drawn to them, curious and horrified as they spot Lucia being carried, her body bloodied. When she's maneuvered to lie across the carriage floor, the Olympian guardsmen block the outsiders' view.

Maile scurries to the trunk sitting at the back end of the carriage to retrieve the medical aid. She pushes everyone aside as she drops down to clean and bandage Lucia's leg.

Lucia lies there, barely coherent, and she's reminded of Adelaide dressing the cut on her hand with a scrap of her T-shirt. She grits her teeth as pain sears her leg, wondering how she got here. She hadn't even been thinking when she'd gone after that stranger, putting herself and then Gabrielle in danger. *Adelaide couldn't have been here.* She was so foolish.

"Prepare yourself, Lady Lucia, this is going to hurt," Maile says, pulling out a vial of orange liquid.

As Lucia watches her sister explain what happened in the alley to the Olympian guards in greater detail, she sees her mouth moving but is unable to make out any of the words. A severe pain shoots through her, and her vision fades away.

Lucia spends the next few days in bed, off her feet. Her sister sits up in her room to read with her, and the tutor comes to teach her for an hour. She relies heavily on the handmaidens, though she wishes she didn't need to. She likes to do things for herself.

She asks Mila to help her to the window so she can look out at the mountains above, staring out in the direction she had fallen from the tree only a week earlier. Since that night, so much has happened.

Gabrielle tries to pry from her the reason for her disappearances—after the blooming ceremony and then in Olympia—but Lucia has no words for her sister. She doesn't even understand her own reckless actions.

How does she tell her sister that she met a stranger in the woods and hasn't been able to stop thinking of them? Her dreams are filled with flashes of scarlet eyes.

On the third day since the attack, Lucia is let out of her room. Falex stays nearby in case her legs give out on her. Lucia thinks they're being dramatic—it was only a cut—but she's allowed to walk around the house and come down for breakfast, so she doesn't complain.

Hatsia is absent until dinner, and even then, she is distracted and distant. She only hums when Gabrielle asks her a question, then rushes away to her study as soon as she's finished with her meal. She's holed up in there with Lucia's grandmother and coven elders who come in and out of the house.

On day five, Lucia is allowed outside, breathing in the crisp, fresh air. She joins her arm with her sister's as they stroll down the street, smiling as she turns her face up to the feeble warmth of the sun, dimmed by a pale and foggy sky. Falex and Baron trail behind at a distance, keeping an eye on them. The sisters don't usually need their guards in Laesbury unless there are outside visitors, but they've been keeping a closer eye on the two women since the incident.

"Gisela has been asking around about the dagger," Gabrielle says as Lucia hands a vendor some coins and accepts a large, spiny wood fig. "Mother asked her to find out what she can about the man who attacked you."

"Has she found anything?" Lucia asks, nervous to hear the answer. She's not sure if she'd just prefer to forget about it and move on or to look the man in the eye once he's been caught. She's still unclear on what happened to him, and the thought has kept her up. Gabrielle said he just disappeared, which sounds crazy. Lucia barely remembers. It's all a distant, foggy memory. It was like she blacked out as soon as she saw the man charge toward her sister.

It worries her that his sudden disappearance might mean he's a mage. *Why would another witch want to hurt her?*

"From what I hear, no. She sent Eldrich out to the west following some woman who said she'd seen it before, but I think it's a dead end. The woman was a *hound* and hung around some bar overrun by thugs. She probably doesn't even know the season, let alone whether she's seen a dagger with a skull hilt."

Lucia hums, trying not to seem too interested in the information. If Gisela's information is leading her to Whoynia, whoever sent the hooded man to her might not hesitate to send another.

"Do you really not remember anything?" Gabrielle asks. "You didn't see his face?"

Lucia shakes her head.

It's all a fog. She knows the man hadn't been familiar, nothing about him rang any bells in her head. A perfect stranger. He was pale maybe, with light hair, but his hood was drawn over his head and Lucia had been too distracted to notice anything further.

The two women travel to a nearby meadow, sitting out in the grass. Lucia tucks her dress underneath her legs, wincing at the pull of her wound as she does so. She doesn't want to think about thugs and assassins. The day is nice, and she's just happy to be back outside, though the cold stings her nose when a breeze blows through.

Digging her nails into the spiked green skin of the wood fig, she cracks the fruit into two uneven halves, revealing a bright yellow center. She hands the smaller one to Gabrielle, and they bicker over it for a minute until Gabrielle relents. They eat for a while, peeling off wedges of the tart, juicy fruit. They point out shapes in the clouds, and Lucia listens to Gabrielle talk on and on about some boy she has a crush on.

"He's *a shy boy*," she says. "A hand-aid for the Priestess."

Lucia teases her about it, as all good sisters should. It takes her mind off everything else. Adelaide, the Triune, and the attack. That is, until Gabrielle asks, "What about you, Lucia? Do you have any secret crushes?"

Gabrielle tips back her half of the fruit to drink the sweet nectar hidden beneath the sour fruit while Lucia's thoughts drift. Her pleasant smile wanes a bit, her finger absently tracing the faint scar across her palm.

"Me?" she asks softly, her thoughts floating to Adelaide. She shakes her head, trying to clear them away. "When would I have time for such silly things?"

"Relationships aren't silly, *Luc,*" Gabrielle says, putting aside the husk of her fruit and lying beside her. They face each other, their breath warming the air between their faces. "Come on, you never talk about boys. There has to have been someone."

Lucia smiles. Of course, her boy-crazed sister would think she couldn't live without fancying someone.

She shrugs. "I don't know, Gab. Perhaps there was someone."

"*Ooh*, do tell!"

Lucia rolls her eyes. "If I do, you have to never badger me about this again."

"I promise," Gabrielle says, holding up her sticky hand. Lucia smiles, rolling her eyes at how serious Gabrielle is making this, but she puts hers up too, threading her fingers through her sister's. *"There, now it's sealed."*

Lucia tucks her hand back under her head, taking in a deep breath of yellow and red heleniums and fighting back the urge to sneeze. She ignores Gabrielle, who's watching her intently as she lets her thoughts go to Adelaide. A stranger in the night.

"I don't know if I'd call it a crush," she says. "Just a kind stranger who made me feel something. I didn't have to be anyone or play some part. S—*They* didn't seem to care about any of that. I... I think they liked me. I'm not sure. It was hard to tell beneath all of the teasing."

She plucks a flower from the ground, twirling the stem between her fingers and watching the colors spin and blur. Her voice goes soft.

"I'm not sure it was anything more than a budding flower torn from the ground before it could bloom. But *when our skin met,* it was like every nerve ending fired at once. I could feel them in places they didn't even touch me."

Lucia's heart is heavy as the colors of the flower blur before her. She drops it to the ground mournfully.

"*Wow,*" Gabrielle whispers when she goes quiet. "You're right," she says, "I don't think you can call that a crush."

Lucia hums, her eyes closing and the feeble sun heating her face. She drifts off in the haze.

The rest of the week goes by in a blur. Lucia's fretted over by the tailor as he prepares her and Gabrielle for the gala, and she walks on eggshells staying out of her grandmother's way, afraid to be stuck alone with the woman.

Lucia tries her best to make herself scarce, but it isn't necessary. Her grandmother doesn't seek her out, not even to scold her for failing to bloom. She is pale and withdrawn and often needs help from the handmaidens to get around. An uneasiness sits between them that Lucia doesn't know how to bridge, and when she leaves, Hatsia lectures her on the pressure she carries being in the running for Eidan.

The duties once placed on Lucia's grandmother are slowly shifting to her.

Lucia only has one goal. Win the place of Eidan in her grandmother's honor to secure the power of the witches. She can't let her family down, or her coven. It just isn't an option.

Chapter Eight
From Memory to Man

It's finally here, the gala. Lucia's nerves ratchet higher and higher as they take the magisk lift to the top floor of the Hallow Tower, soaring over the city below. She steps out of the metal box and is hit with so much noise and madness. It's nothing like the parties back home in the covens, they are much quieter affairs. This... *is overwhelming.*

Lucia's heart pounds quickly, her pulse jumping in her throat as a storm of color twirls past her. Figures dance as the music plays softly over a shower of conversation. The periodic crash of lightning that illuminates the windows makes her jump.

Lucia takes a step forward toward the crowd, pulled away from the machine that drops back down to the first floor to pick up more guests as her eyes flit back and forth, taking in all of the sights and sounds. The smell of sweets clouds the air making Lucia feel almost sick, and she waves away a man who tries to offer her a drink atop a silver platter. Her hands are shaking too badly to hold a glass right now.

It's a shock to Lucia, the sight of vampires and witches and wolves all around. So many new sights and smells she is unused to. At the Dome, everyone had been gathered, but there was still some order to it. Here, everyone is mingling, brushing elbows and even stopping to chat. It's a sight Lucia had never imagined, surrounded by only witches all her life.

"Tama hei," a deep voice calls behind Lucia, and she freezes, turned to stone in her place. A chill races up her spine as the endearment plays over and over in her mind—*Hey, kid.*

The voice, familiar if not for the deep bass that accompanies it, cuts through her heart worse than being struck by lightning.

I-it can't be, she thinks, dizzy as the breath is knocked from her. That nickname... stirs something in her. A memory.

Tama hei—tama hei—tama hei.

Greetings flash through the years. Five years old, seven years old, ten years old. Parting under the glow of the setting sun. The last time they had seen one another...

"*Hetan,*" Lucia breathes, wide-eyed with disbelief. They had left so quickly from Olympia that Lucia hadn't been able to find him. Her mind had been so preoccupied and then *the attack.*

"I always wished if I were to see you again, it would go something like this." Hetan's eyes rake Lucia. She wears a siren dress in a deep blue that trails the polished black marble beneath her, gold-and-russet detailing around her hips, and parting the middle of the dress to her feet. Gold jewelry hangs around her wrists, and a matching fan headdress sits in her big, free curls like a crown.

Lucia's face warms at the attention, her own eyes scanning Hetan. She's not sure she would have recognized him in the crowd, so different from the young boy she once knew. His dark chestnut hair is tied back showing off a well-defined jaw that was once soft and round, and straight white teeth no longer missing a gap.

Before, his hair was cropped short, and he was much, much smaller. Lucia used to tease him for being shorter than her, but now she is the one who stopped growing whereas he towers as tall as the rest of the wolves.

Hetan wears a red tunic under a black fur-lined cape with golden detailing and buttons, much more dapper than the wild, dirty kid who hated wearing the tight, fancy clothes his parents dressed him in for visits to Laesbury. He looks like a man.

As Lucia stands in the middle of the floor, struck dumb, Gabrielle jumps at the wolf, her arms wrapping around his neck. She laughs as he spins her before setting her back on the ground.

"Looking lovely, Gabrielle," he says, kissing her hand. Lucia had forgotten Gabrielle was even beside her. She is at a loss for words.

"I do, don't I?" Gabrielle says, spinning; her dress, one she had a heavy hand in creating, is a deep purple with rainbow, cape-like butterfly wings down the back, twirling around her.

"*Hetan,*" Lucia repeats, still breathless.

Hetan pulls Lucia into a hug. He smells lovely, like pine and smoke, and Lucia closes her eyes for a moment to breathe in the comforting scent of childhood and pleasant memories. She had forgotten how touchy the wolf was.

"It's been so long," Lucia says. "How you've grown."

"Is that all you notice, little witch, *how I've grown?*" Hetan teases.

Lucia laughs. "Well, you were shorter than me the last time I saw you." They stare at one another, unblinking, that easy banter coming back to them.

Gabrielle giggles, stepping between them.

"Don't take it so personally, Hetan. Lucia never notices any men. You look very handsome."

Lucia flushes, mouth dropping open. "Not true! I just don't..." Lucia trails off. She just doesn't think about those kinds of things. Not like Gabrielle, who fancies every man she meets. She thinks her sister could spend a little less time thinking about men.

"There are more important things to do than ogle guys, though my sister wouldn't think so," Lucia says, staring pointedly at Gabrielle. Gabrielle winks, her eyes flickering between the two. Lucia knows that look. She shakes her head, hoping whatever thought is racing through Gabrielle's head will leave immediately.

Lucia shuffles over as people edge around their small group in the middle of the floor. Hetan looks around, noticing how crowded it is.

"Come with me. I'll show you somewhere I found where we can get a little privacy. To catch up."

Hetan holds out his hand, and Lucia's eyes trail up to his expectant face. A familiar look, like the one she'd seen many times as kids whenever he wanted her to do something daring, like jumping over a stream or running from their parents.

Lucia gulps, eyes darting around before she takes a deep breath and grabs his hand. It feels so different, his hand large and firm, the palm warm to touch. She can't help but think—*Not as hot as Adelaide's*. His smile grows as he squeezes his fingers around hers, and Lucia's grows to match.

Hetan turns and begins pulling her through the crowd, Gabrielle's voice behind them.

"Don't just leave me!" she calls.

"I'll be back. I'll see you later, Gabrielle," Lucia shouts, giggling as she weaves through the party. She feels exhilarated as she runs behind Hetan, her heart pounding fast in her chest.

The pair bump people as they pass, others jumping out of the way. A feeling Lucia hasn't had in a long time rises within her.

Hetan takes her to one of the grand staircases and pulls her under the deep purple drapes that hang down over the side. It's dark, except for patches of light filtering in through the steps. Lucia and Hetan laugh, holding their stomachs as they fall to the floor in the small space.

"Did you see that woman I bumped into?" Hetan gasps between breaths.

"You nearly knocked her drink from her hand! The look she gave you was *scathing*." Lucia struggles to catch her breath as Hetan leans forward, wiping a tear of laughter from her eye. She stares at Hetan, his hand burning her face where it still sits, her chest aching as she nearly stops breathing.

Beautiful.

Lucia pulls back, startled, her cheeks burning. "What?" she stutters. Her eyes dart down to his lips, and for a moment she wonders whether they'd feel different than they had all those years ago.

"What?" Hetan echoes, his confusion mirroring her own.

Did he mean to say that? she wonders.

"Never mind," Lucia says, not wanting to embarrass him further. It must have been a mistake. "So uh, what did you want to talk about?" she asks, getting comfortable as she leans against the back of the stairs, her dress fanned out around her legs.

Hetan leans back as well, turning to his side to face her. They're so close, leaning in toward the ray of light, whispering under their breaths though they probably wouldn't be heard in the loud room under the chatter and music. They're in their own little world.

"There's so much," Hetan says, eyes gaining a faraway look. "I don't even know where to start. From the beginning perhaps? I swear I remember that night like it was yesterday." He looks back down at Lucia, and she wonders if he's thinking of the kiss too.

Something odd squirms in her stomach when she remembers it now. Something different from before. Even from just a week ago when she had sat in the place where it happened. She doesn't know what it is that has changed, but it has.

"Yeah," she whispers. "That day plays on a loop in my mind. What I might have done differently had I known it was our last."

Hetan heaves a breath. "I don't think I'd change a thing. That day was perfect. It was... what got me through the years."

Lucia swallows. The look on Hetan's face is heartbreaking. He looks so sad. One of the things that got her through the years was the hope that wherever he was, he was doing better than her.

"I never... No one ever told me what happened. Why did you leave? I tried many, many times to get my mother to send a letter to you, and she just kept saying you didn't respond."

Hetan's face twists into a scowl, lips pursed. "I never got a letter," he says. "I don't know if..." He takes a deep breath. "It was a long time before I could think of you. I'm not sure if a letter would have helped. That night, all of my thoughts were focused on one thing. One life-changing thing." He laughs bitterly, staring down at the floor between them.

"I had come back down from the mountains that night, after being with you, so happy. So, so, happy. But it wasn't my parents who greeted me in Domeg on the other side of your boundary line. It was my uncle, eyes rimmed red and looking broken. He said—he—"

Lucia lays her hand on Hetan's arm, squeezing. "It's okay, Hetan, it's okay."

Hetan shakes his head. "My parents were attacked in Domeg. T-they *died*."

Lucia gasps, her eyes widening in shock. *His parents died that night?* She sits back against the staircase, remembering her night in Domeg. Those people with the weapons... She never told her mother about that. She was too afraid of getting in trouble for leaving and worse for having nearly died. When she arrived and everyone was fine, she just... tried to push the memory away.

Lucia had known the chief and her mate died. Her younger brother—Hetan's uncle, Ayawa—took over as interim chief, because Hetan was too young to do so.

She remembers thinking, selfishly, that she and Hetan were the same. With so much responsibility on their shoulders. And she had felt sorrow for him. But Lucia didn't know they died that night. No one ever told her. It wasn't for a few more years she learned of their deaths. *Why? Why keep that from her?*

"Hetan, I—I don't know what to say." Lucia lays her head on Hetan's shoulder, melting into his side. It feels so natural, to be close to him. Comforting him. Like this closeness might burn away years of longing.

Hetan lays his head atop hers. "You don't have to say anything." He sighs. "This is good. Just being here. I had wanted to see you after the meeting in Olympia but..."

The pair stays like that for a long time. The world spins on, laughter and footsteps coming and going outside of their small cocoon, people dancing and celebrating, bartering and arguing, and everything in between as the witches, wolves, and vampires try to coexist under one roof together. Pretending to get along for the sake of the occasion, while under the stairs a wolf and witch sit in comfortable silence, eyes closed and breath mingling in the air.

"I missed this," Hetan murmurs. Lucia peaks an eye open, trying to look up at his face from where they sit.

"Me too."

Hetan pulls back, laughing as he smooths out Lucia's curls where his head made a dent in them. Lucia smiles, fixing her lopsided headpiece.

"What about your blooming?" Hetan says. "You should have had it already, right? Well, what did you get?"

Lucia looks down at her hands, fiddling with them as her face heats in embarrassment.

"It was two years ago. My uh—well, my first ceremony."

Hetan's face scrunches, probably trying to remember what he knows about witches. "Your first?"

"I—*I didn't get a magisk nature because I didn't bloom,*" Lucia says in a rush.

"What?" Hetan repeats.

Lucia takes a deep breath, looking back up at Hetan. His face looks so open and curious. Not a hint of the ridicule or unkindness she is so used to within her coven. *Right*, Lucia thinks. *Hetan isn't a witch. He doesn't care about these things. And even if he were, he wouldn't care. He's... he's my friend.* Even after all the years apart, that hasn't changed, the intimacy Lucia feels with Hetan.

"The Mother didn't give me a gift," Lucia says sadly. Tears well in her eyes, her lip wobbling as all of the shame and disappointment hits her again, now that she's able to sit and think about it. With the Triune and her grandmother's sickness, Lucia's failure is more poignant. She'll have to take her mother's place as coven head soon. If her grandmother...

Lucia shakes her head. She doesn't want to think about her grandmother dying. She can't. The Golden Griffins are counting on Lucia. She can't rest on the fact that Lady Mia of the Black Basilisks is competing too; she's also Lucia's competition. The Golden Griffin lost the Orbis Libra to a Sacrenladre once before. Sonya Mitsu. They wouldn't forgive her for letting it happen again.

"Even the great deity, a Dol'Auclair legacy, didn't think I was good enough."

This time Hetan is the one who lays a hand on Lucia's arm.

"Hey, I'm sure that's not true. There must be another reason. I couldn't see why anyone, deity or not, would think you were unworthy."

Lucia laughs, a tear trailing down her cheek. She roughly wipes it away with her sleeve as she takes a deep breath, then sighs.

"It's been a long time since you saw me last," she says.

Hetan shrugs. "Not that much could have changed."

Lucia smiles, feeling better than she has since the blooming ceremony. Hetan just has a way of saying exactly what she needs to hear.

"Thank you," she says. It's not lost on her that she is going to be competing in the Triune against him, but she tries not to think about it.

Lucia doesn't know what the tests will be, but looking at the contestants, she knows she has no chance. The wolves and vampires have physical strength over her, and Lucia remembers when coven head Eshana Sacrenladre had visited after Mia bloomed to tell her mother she presented as a Gaia. Mia is Gabrielle's age and will be attending Eirini Academy of Mystics this year. It's another thing Lucia envies.

Even if Lucia had bloomed, as the first daughter she couldn't apply to Eirini. She will receive private lessons at home in Laesbury. Gabrielle will get to live in Olympia for the academic year, in dorms, surrounded by other witches from all over Hontaras. She convinced their grandmother to let her go since her friends were too. Both Lady Mia and Lady Caitlyn, two women in major covens, are going this autumn. Gabrielle promised she would stay within the witches' circles, which Lucia doesn't believe for a moment.

Their mother was worried about Gabrielle attending, as to her it's controversial that anyone can enroll at Eirini so long as they're Mystic. It's a famous school for Mystics, the first to allow witches, vampires, and wolves to cohabitate, though they have separate dorms.

It's also one of the best magisk schools in Hontaras, which is why her mother eventually agreed.

Lucia is jealous. She has always dreamed of going to Eirini. She wants to leave Laesbury and experience life outside of the coven. Mystic relations has always interested her, and she thought it would be a good course to take as a future coven head of the Golden Griffins, and possibly Grand Elder—if she'd ever been able to bloom. Her mother doesn't think it's important, but *why not?* Lucia thinks it's fundamental that the Caput Trium's first of three have intimate knowledge and skills in dealing cross-culturally.

How could she lead people without understanding them? Maybe it's the harsh truth that her mother doesn't actually believe she will lead one day.

"Finally, I found you."

Lucia turns to see Gabrielle, light flooding under the staircase as she holds the drapes open.

"I was worried," Gabrielle says, "when I didn't see you and Hetan anywhere. Have you guys been here all this time?"

Lucia shares a sheepish look with Hetan.

"We lost track of time," Hetan says, standing. He helps Lucia up, and they file out from under the stairs. Hetan stretches, groaning from being cramped for so long. Lucia realizes she had been in a small space for nearly an hour and didn't panic. The realization throws her.

"Taste this," Gabrielle says, handing both Lucia and Hetan a glass. "It's s-so good."

Lucia squints up at Gabrielle, her eyes adjusting to the bright lights.

"Are you drunk?" she asks, incredulously. She looks at the fizzing purple liquid in her cup, then back to Gabrielle, whose braids are falling from her updo. She looks flushed, from dancing probably. "How many of these have you had?"

Gabrielle shakes her head. "Too many to count!" She raises her glass, nearly spilling the liquid. Hetan takes the glass from her.

"I think you're good on these for now," he says.

"You guys totally should have been there. I was dancing—dancing, with *so many people*. A-and I met this guy." She looks around for anyone nearby and then leans in with a whisper. "He is *so hot*. He's a vampire and my future husband."

"Husband!" Lucia's eyebrows shoot up in alarm. *What has Gabrielle been up to in the last hour? Surely, she couldn't have gotten into* that *much trouble.*

"Well, he doesn't know it yet," she says, a finger over her lips. "But you should have seen him, Luc, even you probably would have thought he was charming."

Lucia's eyebrows furrow. *What is that supposed to mean, even you?*

"Hetan. Lovely to see you catching up with an old friend," a deep voice drawls.

Lucia turns to see Chief Ayawa Anoki approach, leaning on that same warped cane of redwood and feathers. Lucia bows.

"Chief Anoki."

The man gives her a twisted smile. "As sweet as I remember, Lady Lucia. Gabrielle, you're much bigger than when I last saw you." He tips his head to both women.

"Yes, I've grown a fair bit, if I do say so myself," Gabrielle says, giggling. "And you've... gotten *older.*"

"Gabrielle!" Lucia gasps, eyes widening as her sister stumbles around a bit.

"It's okay." Anoki chuckles. "Fair observation."

Hetan grabs Lucia's arm and begins dragging her off. His uncle lifts his staff to block their path.

"Whoa, whoa, off so quickly? I wanted to speak with you, Hetan."

Hetan hesitates, looking torn between her and his uncle.

"It's okay," she says. "You can go speak with your uncle. I'm sure we'll find time to catch up more later."

Hetan nods slowly. "Yeah, of course."

Before Lucia can walk away with Gabrielle leaning heavily against her side, Anoki stops her again.

"Odd, isn't it?" he says. His nearly black eyes sparkle with mirth. "You'll be competing for the place of your grandmother. Following in her footsteps."

"Uh, yeah," Lucia says. "It's a bit weird. I never really considered she would ever *not* be the Eidan."

Anoki hums. "Mhm, yes. The witches have held that power for a long time. *Some* would even say too long. Who knows, maybe it's time for a change. Maybe my nephew here will even win the spot of Eidan, eh?" He taps Hetan with his staff, and Hetan grimaces.

"Come on, Uncle, you said you wanted to talk?"

"Coming—coming." He turns and then glances back at Lucia once more. "Have a good night, Lady Lucia."

Lucia stands there for a moment, confused by the interaction. It was a bit odd, but she doesn't quite know what to make of it.

"Come on," Gabrielle says, tugging on Lucia's arm to get her moving. "You have been flirting with Hetan all night, can we go dance now?"

"Nuh-uh," Lucia says, defensively. "I was not flirting."

Gabrielle smirks, watching Lucia bite her lip nervously.

"Sure."

Lucia lets herself be dragged toward the dance floor, a song starting up as they approach. On the way, Fabien intercepts them, stepping into their path.

His dark skin is glowing under the bright white lights and his hair is cropped shorter than the last time she'd seen him, an intricate design braided up one side.

"Lady Lucia, would you care to dance the Malovei with me?" he asks, approaching Lucia with a hand out in offering, the other behind his back. He's smirking at her, eyes alight as if in a challenge. His long black cloak has a sea serpent going up the side.

"Of course, Lord Fabien."

Lucia takes his hand. Even if she wanted to, it would be impolite to turn him down, but she has no reason to. He's a family friend, though she doesn't know him very well due to their long distance.

Lucia lets Fabien bring her close, but not too close to be touching more than the hands. The Malovei is about the feet. A swaying, stomping rhythm. Except, the goal is to be light on your feet and not make a sound.

Lucia and Fabien glide across the floor, the bottom of Lucia's dress sweeping the marble as she swishes and turns, moving like a whisper. They don't speak at first, Lucia concentrating on the steps of the dance. It has been a while since she's done it. She used to perform it during ceremonies as a child, a solo performance for the Mother on Dai Gemus—*the day of the spirit.*

"I'm glad you're in the running for Eidan," Fabien says as if he read her mind.

"I don't know about that," Lucia says, breathless as he spins her.

"You're having doubts?" he questions as if the thought is absurd.

"Well, I—I don't have a magisk nature, now do I? I can't even do *cuma*," she says, the words painful coming out though he and every other witch already know it. There's no point in trying to hide, especially not now. Once Lucia is in front of all of the Mystics, weak and magisk-less, she will be an embarrassment in the eyes of vampires and wolves, as well as witches.

"You are a Dol'Auclair," Fabien says firmly. "Have some respect for that title. You are not just any witch, Lucia; you are in the succession for Grand Elder. If you don't have pride in who you are, how can you expect anyone else to?"

Lucia bows her head in shame at Fabien's words. *He's right.* She hadn't thought of that before. That she was leading her own condemnation. She should look at the Triune as an opportunity for victory, rather than a guarantee of failure.

That's easier said than done though. Fabien himself has done the impossible, a man with a gift from the Mother.

"Besides," Fabien says, "having one of our own take control of the Orbis Libra is paramount. A witch. Especially a Golden Griffin. That power can't fall into anyone else's hands, not even those of another coven. The Black Basilisks are kin, but they aren't family. And I don't trust those Sacrenladre. Their ancestor Sonya Mitsu used her position to set them up with gross wealth. Wealth that can be used to take power from the Golden Griffin."

Lucia's brows furrow, mouth pinched. "Why would they want to do that?" she asks, bewildered. *What could the Black Basilisks have to gain by taking down another coven?*

Fabien clicks his tongue. "Power. Control. They want what your coven has. What the Great Mother Deipara built for you. Who wouldn't?"

"Do you?" Fabien might be forgetting but he isn't a Golden Griffin either.

Fabien is silent for a moment.

"I'd have nothing to gain by becoming your enemy. I could never be the Grand Elder, and I am my mother's only child. Besides, our mothers have been friends for a long time. The Sea Serpents are your ally and your spear. All I am saying is you cannot be so naive. You see your lack of magisk as a failure, and I won't lie, it is. But it is not the end. The Orbis Libra chose you for a reason. Do not lose faith."

Lucia nearly trips during a complicated maneuver, her mind spinning with every word Fabien says. She figures he must be exaggerating. Being paranoid. Because why else would he say such mad things?

Lucia is silent as they continue the routine, focusing on the dance rather than Fabien's disturbing thoughts until she hears the bitter musings:

So ignorant. To have such grand ideas of harmony. Witches can't simply co-exist with vampires and wolves. The covens are meant to rule Hontaras as we once ruled the great nation of Ashad Escana.

Lucia stops dead in her tracks, mouth agape as she stares incredulously at Fabien. He nearly knocks her over, stumbling as she brings him to a halt.

"What?" he says, face twisted in confusion.

"How could you say that?" she asks, appalled by what she's hearing, and so freely in a room of people no less. Some with extraordinary hearing. Hopefully, the loud music confuses sensitive ears.

"What? It's true, you'd have to be naive not to know. Ask your mother. The other covens—"

"Not about the other covens. The other thing."

"Lucia, what are you—"

"May I cut in?" a deep, melodic voice drawls. The stranger doesn't wait as she scoops Lucia's hands into hers. It's customary during the Malovei, to steal partners, but it's not something people usually do. In polite society, you wait for agreement by the chosen or their partner.

"What are you—" Lucia hears Fabien start, but she isn't listening. Her breath catches as she looks at the woman who grabbed her.

"Dais holum,"—*Holy days*, Lucia whispers in awe. Her eyes travel up a forest-green leather body suit that clings to every curve of the woman's lean figure, darker cut-outs framing her stomach and breasts.

Chains hang across the shoulders and chest—mimicking a ribcage—and fall from the stranger's hips. The hands that grip Lucia's are traced with bleached clay along the knuckles like a glowing skeleton and are decorated by many thick rings.

Lucia bites her lip, heart beating a staccato rhythm, hands sweating where they're held by the stranger as she finally reaches the face. Red lips slanted up in a devilish smirk. Familiar, mocking lips...

Lucia hears Fabien's words just as she meets the woman's fierce, burning red eyes.

"*—vampire.*"

Chapter Nine

If the World is Fair

Lucia is in shock, staring into the eyes of a vampire, the woman's long, unusually warm hands holding hers tight.

"Don't worry, I'll bring her back in one piece," the vampire says, winking at Fabien as she whisks Lucia away. The pair get swept up into the crowd of dancers.

Lucia's face is burning, hands sweating as the vampire stares down at her. Lucia can't even meet her eyes, staring at the clay down the woman's neck disappearing below her body suit.

"My eyes are up here, *Princess*."

She shivers, that nickname washing over her as memory takes her through every single moment she spent with the woman.

Lucia gapes, her head snapping up to meet the smug woman's gaze. The woman has shocking pale hair like dried wheat, warm, tawny skin, and brilliant vermillion eyes.

Did she just— "My name is *Lucia*," she huffs. "Lucia Dol'Auclair."

The woman's voice pitches low in whispered mockery. "Well, okay, Lucia—*Lucia Dol'Auclair*. I already know that."

The woman pulls Lucia close, moving her hands from Lucia's hands to around her waist, pulling her in until their bodies are flush. Lucia gasps, arms flailing awkwardly as the vampire moves them around the dance floor in an intimate embrace.

"Name's Azueme. Nice for you to meet me."

Lucia scoffs. *The woman is arrogant.* Not that she didn't already know that when they first met.

"So your name was a lie too," she says, looking up at red eyes that had been black when they met before.

Lucia hadn't wanted to believe the flash of red was more than her imagination. That would have meant being honest with herself. The woman is a vampire, that is undeniable.

"What do you mean lie? I never told you I was a witch, you assumed."

Lucia rolls her eyes. *This woman is unbelievable.* Was everything she told Lucia a lie?

"And Azueme is my given name, Princess, but you can call me Adelaide. It's like a nickname."

"Princess is *not* my nickname." Lucia tries to pull away, growing frustrated with this interaction. She doesn't know what to think or feel. "You're not doing it right. This is not how you dance the Malovei, we're not meant to touch."

Adelaide raises a brow. "Well, I'm not doing the Malovei. For vampires, dancing isn't about the movements or the music. Dancing has no rules. It's just about you—" She pulls Lucia back to her, nothing but fabric between them. She whispers in Lucia's ear, "—and your partner."

Lucia splutters. Her palms are sweaty where they sit on Adelaide's shoulders, digging into the leather. Butterflies jump in her stomach, tickling her ribs as the vampire leans in close.

Lucia thinks there might be something wrong with the woman. *Why would she ask Lucia to dance just to get under her skin?* Or maybe that's *why* she asked her to dance, she seems to love doing just that.

"You're insufferable. Let me go. If you're not going to do the dance properly then—"

"You don't want to dance with me?" Lucia yelps as Adelaide spins her, then brings her down in a dip. "You only dance with dickheads, *shi?*"

Lucia's mouth falls open. "He— Fabien is not— You can't say things like that!" Lucia argues, shocked by the colorful language. She squeezes her eyes shut as the vampire lifts the corner of her mouth, and a descended fang pops out. A shiver races down her spine.

"Isn't this meant to be about the celebration?" Adelaide sighs like she's annoyed Lucia isn't playing along with her game. "That old *dog-man* at the Dome said we were supposed to be getting along. Inter-Mystic mingling and all that. You're not being very hospitable, Princess."

Lucia takes a deep breath, and blood rushes back out of her head as she's righted once more, gripping the vampire's arms tight to keep from being dropped to the ground.

"I—" Lucia groans. *Adelaide—Azueme—whoever she is, is right.* She is meant to be getting to know the guests. Wolf, vampire... Lucia feels a bit silly about how she's acting. It's just a vampire. Just a... sharp-fanged, blood-sucking, cocky, no-boundary-having vampire woman. Lucia isn't obtuse. She's old enough to sort through the *"scary stories"* her mother and grandmother told her about vampires growing up. Like, if she misbehaved one would sneak through her window and snatch her up.

She also knows Adelaide, sort of. The woman saved her life twice.

Lucia lets out a deep breath, straightening her spine as she meets Adelaide's eye with much more confidence than she feels. She's grateful for the drink Gabrielle gave her, which made her loose enough to even get on the dance floor in front of all these people. She takes a look around. The party is in full swing, everyone focused, deep in conversation, no one paying any mind to one witch and a vampire. They too have probably had many drinks.

Adelaide perks up, possibly noticing the shift in Lucia, and her grin grows wider. "Do you think you can keep up, Lucia?" the vampire purrs. Lucia smirks. One thing she's confident she's good at is dancing.

"Give it your best shot, *Adelaide*."

Dancing with Adelaide is completely different from dancing with Fabien. The vampire is fast, and her movement is like water, so graceful and delicate. She swings Lucia around the floor like they're floating. Lucia struggles to keep up the pace at first, sweating and breathing hard.

Adelaide holds her so close Lucia can hear her heartbeat, and she would be embarrassed at the obscenity if she wasn't so fully focused on Adelaide's movements, the way their bodies fit and move together.

"The way vampires dance," Adelaide whispers, "it's a push and pull. Like that of a beating heart. You don't stop until you're fit to burst."

At this point, Lucia's feet are barely touching the ground. She holds tight, her hands gripping Adelaide's shoulders and the vampire's are wrapped around her hips. She lets Adelaide lead her and trusts that the woman won't let her fall. She gets lost in the beating of their hearts and the pounding of the music.

Adelaide dips Lucia down as the room goes silent; Lucia stares up at the vampire, red eyes shining with passion and a smirk gracing cherry lips. Her eyes flicker to the bow lips, trained on their movement as her heart beats in her ears, drowning out all sound. She's breathing heavily, her chest rising and falling like the pull of the tide. Adelaide's face is so close. *So, so close.*

"I'm impressed, Princess, even wolves have a hard time keeping up."

Lucia blushes further at the compliment, her heart in her throat as she's held suspended in Adelaide's arms. She never wants to move from this position. She wishes she could stay right here in this moment. She feels outside of her body, floating. And it's just her and Adelaide there.

Looking into her eyes Lucia remembers their parting and the aching longing she has felt since she last saw the vampire.

In the quiet of this moment, Lucia says, *"We met again."*

She holds Adelaide's stare, and a softness comes over the woman's eyes like she too is remembering those words whispered in the forest.

"Ahem."

Lucia jolts in Adelaide's arms, the moment lost as she turns to see Fabien standing above her. Adelaide quickly rights her, and the blood flows back down to reawaken Lucia's liquified bones.

"Good, you're done," Fabien says, hands behind his back and voice tight. He holds his head high as he speaks to Adelaide and then turns to Lucia. "Come?" he says, holding out his arm to her. "Your mother wants your company."

Lucia nods, taking Fabien's arm as the shame under his stare begins to fill her. She danced—*like that*—suggestive and completely immodest. With a vampire, no less.

Lucia looks to Adelaide, who watches her with undivided attention, her gaze like knives. Lucia gives a small bow, still holding on to Fabien.

"Thank you for the dance, *Ad*—Azueme." With Fabien in earshot, she doesn't say the name used just between the two of them.

"It was my pleasure," the vampire responds, red lips almost taunting as her gaze flickers over to Fabien. Lucia watches Adelaide leave, her hips swaying in a tantalizing beat as an intricate web of silver chains sways around her sultry figure.

Lucia is led away by Fabien, but her mind is on Adelaide.

"Disgusting," Fabien spits. "I'm sorry you were subject to that, Lady Lucia. If it wasn't impolite, I would have rescued you sooner."

Lucia looks up at Fabien, the displeased curl of his lips. She tries to forget what she heard earlier, about vampires and wolves needing to be controlled by witches. Surely it was a slip of the tongue. An exaggeration. *It must be.*

"It's fine," Lucia says. "The dance was... different from what I'm used to, but I think it gave me a bit of insight on the vampires. Their culture seems fascinating."

Fabien scoffs. "Nothing is fascinating about undead killers. Those thugs. Especially not the Skullkins. They cause my mother endless trouble up in Swaydan, piles of bodies, poisonous medicines, weapons dealings..."

"Well, surely Azueme isn't one of those vampires. She seemed no different from you or me."

Fabien nearly stops in his tracks, jolting Lucia as his step falters. He turns to Lucia, revulsion burning in his eyes. "Do not compare yourself to them, Lady Lucia. Especially not that one. She's the worst of them all. Azueme Skullkin, daughter of *Nikolay Skullkin*—the Father of Vampires."

When he tries to move, Lucia is the one who stops this time, her eyes wide with realization. Azueme. *Azueme Skullkin.* She remembers now, the woman's name had been called at the meeting with the Caput Trium. Lucia had been so distracted she didn't pay much attention to the other names called by the Orbis Libra.

Is that why she hid her name in the forest? Because Lucia would recognize her name. While Lucia had been an idiot, giving hers away, the vampire had been thinking ahead. Except, what was Adelaide doing in the forest beyond the border in the first place? She must have gotten in when the barrier dropped because vampires cannot get through. When Lucia was falling, the barrier had lifted. *As if it was fate.*

"*She* was Azueme Skullkin?" Lucia asks, turning to try and find the vampire in the crowd. "It can't be," she whispers. She's heard wild rumors of Azueme—of the entire Skullkin family. Among her family's stories of vampires, they were at the forefront. The worst of them all. Azueme is known for her ruthlessness. Her ability to get what she wants. She has no regard for life or *love*.

Not that Lucia cares. But she feels cheated and lied to. Betrayed. And she doesn't know why.

The Skullkins have a reputation. They commit many crimes but manage to get out of punishment and blame every time. The Silver Spiders cult to which they belong is the biggest in Hontaras. They're old money, filthy rich. And they're *trouble*. Lucia bites at her lip, letting Fabien pull her along.

What has she gotten herself into?

Chapter Ten
With Mouths Closed

"**M**ama."

Lucia joins Hatsia's side as the woman stands before a white-and-gold stage, surrounded by grand pillars and gauzy drapes hanging from the ceiling. Lucia eyes the thing on stage, like an oddly shaped pole.

Hatsia is speaking with Madam Devroue and another woman. She's in a flat yellow dress with faded coloring that looks like it's seen better days. Her gloves are fraying, and she rubs them together anxiously as she whispers to Lucia's mother. The woman looks familiar, but Lucia can't place her face.

"Hatsia please, *the money—*"

"We'll speak about it later, Amelia," Hatsia says through gritted teeth smiling as she waves the woman off. *Amelia*! Now Lucia remembers, Madam Coflar, the Starlight coven head in Whoynia. Gabrielle is friends with her daughter Caitlyn. She looks different here. Her hair is pulled back and she's more dressed up than Lucia has seen her before.

"Lucia, darling, you look stunning."

Madam Devroue moves from Hatsia's side to press a hand to Lucia's cheek.

Lucia bows, respectfully.

"Madam Devroue, it's good to see you."

"My son has been treating you well, I hope?" the woman asks, glancing at Fabien. "He's been making sure you don't get snatched up by any of these beasts?" The woman throws her head back and laughs at her own joke, the drink in her hand sloshing as she raises it.

Lucia's eyes flit from Fabien to his mother. "He has been very respectful, madam."

"Good, good."

Hatsia brings out a hand for Lucia's. She pulls her daughter to her side. "Join us," she says. "They're going to be announcing the rules for the Triune soon."

Lucia listens with only half an ear as the women gossip, humming appropriately as Fabien speaks of cantus and expanding the magisk tongue while they wait for the speech to begin. All that is on her mind is Adelaide—*Azueme*—She can't get the names straight in her head. *Which should she call her?* Lucia shouldn't be thinking of her at all—a Skullkin of the Spider cult, and her competition for the Orbis Libra—but in such a short time the woman has captured her thoughts completely.

Even her nerves about the Triune have dampened in the tide of her musings. Lucia's skin still burns in all of the places she and Adelaide touched, re-imprinting on the places from before.

Lucia is freed from her thoughts when shoes clack across the stage. She looks up to see many people filing on, starting with a peculiar man, strikingly short with long, twisted ears and snakish skin. Behind him trail the three members of the Caput Trium. They step back as the man comes to stand at the front of the stage.

Lucia winces at a soft, ringing voice in her head. There's a bit of an uproar as people react unkindly to it. The man's lips aren't moving and yet his voice echoes in everyone's minds.

"Sorry," the creature says. "People are usually thrown off guard by that."

"Who is he?" Lucia leans into Fabien to whisper.

"Ekrul—the *Orun-kun* of Eirini Academy. He's a bogy."

Lucia's eyebrows furrow as she studies the man once more. *The principal of Eirini is a bogy?* She didn't know a mystic creature could be in such a high position. It's fascinating.

"That's a class of chimera?" Lucia says, trying to remember her studies.

Fabien nods.

"Welcome, esteemed guests," Ekrul says. "I am Ekrul-Kizingll, and it is a glorious sight to have vampire, wolf, and witch under one roof for this celebration. I still remember the dark times of the War of Mystics, when a meeting such as this would have ended in bloodshed. Though I was a hatchling then, and times have changed."

The War of Mystics? Lucia thinks. That would make Ekrul centuries old.

"I am proud to have you here in the Hallow Tower. This building is the tallest in Hontaras, built at the end of the aforementioned war as a sign of peace. That makes it all the more significant to host this gala in honor of the chosen six who will be competing in the Triune, in this place. If those six would join me now, I will call out their names."

Lucia's heart races as Ekrul calls up the competitors of the Triune, first Cassius, a vampire Lucia hasn't met. He's introduced as a part of the White Dragon cult in Etryae, up in the mountains of Kudo—*the city of caves.* The White Dragons are another old cult known for getting themselves into trouble. The difference, is they're not as good as the Spiders about not getting caught.

Cassius swaggers up onto the stage, red eyes narrowed as he sneers down at the bogy, sharp teeth on display in a devious smile. The man makes Lucia feel uneasy, a shudder racing through her at the thought of having to meet him in some sort of battle. In a battle of strength, she has no chance. Against anyone. Though, she's trying to keep a positive outlook.

Next, a wolf Lucia just barely recognizes. The quiet kid who sat near her at the Dome. One of the triplets, Boen, his sister Blythe had called him. He is royalty of the Crimson Ash clan, the second born of the triplets, and from one of the wealthier clans. He takes measured steps across the stage, his face an unreadable mask as he stares blankly forward, giving Ekrul a small bow of his head. He takes his place next to Cassius, ignoring as the vampire jeers at him.

Mia of the Black Basilisks is called up. She is in an extraordinary red dress displaying her flamboyant wealth. Hetan is next, his stride confident and powerful. Lucia's eyes stray from him to Adelaide as she walks past, her signature smirk in place.

"—Lastly is Lucia Dol'Auclair of the Golden Griffin coven."

Lucia's hands shake as her name is called, her breath wavering as she takes quivering steps onto the stage. The lights seem too bright, and she's aware of every pair of eyes on her as she ascends, pleading not to trip and embarrass herself as her train drags behind her. All of the confidence she displayed while dancing with Adelaide—the poise and grace—has fled her.

Lucia joins the end of the line beside Adelaide, heart pounding and hands slick with sweat. She resolutely ignores Adelaide's gaze, keeping her eyes forward so as not to lose her nerve. Lucia has to plaster on a mask of confidence so that no one can see just how terrified she is. She meets her mother's gaze, the woman nodding to her with a small smile. Lucia clenches her eyes shut.

Bad idea, bad idea. She should not *look at her Mother.*

Lucia bites her lip, focusing on that stinging sensation as Ekrul's voice is in her head once more.

"On behalf of the Caput Trium," he says motioning to the three leaders, "and all of the Mystics of Hontaras, we thank the six of you for your participation in this esteemed competition. The first of its kind, all three Mystic families will take part in the trials. For your sake, and that of everyone here, I am going to tell you the rules of the Triune and what will be expected of each of you. First, it is non-negotiable that the six of you will attend Eirini Academy of Mystic this autumn, where I am orun-kun."

Lucia's eyes widen at that proclamation. *We are to attend Eirini Academy?* She can't believe her ears. She has wanted to attend Eirini for years, burning with bitterness that her mother wouldn't let her, both due to her status as Hatsia's firstborn and as Koyan—*without magisk.*

"We demand enrollment at Eirini for many reasons—safety, scrutiny, and we think it of utmost importance that any young Mystic that commands such great magisk should be well rounded and educated. Eirini is the best school for that. As well, the trials you undergo will take place on campus."

Lucia is buzzing with excitement now, tugging the sleeves of her dress in enthusiasm rather than nerves. She tries to tamp down the huge smile wanting to stretch across her face as she meets Gabrielle's eyes, her sister now standing beside their mother in front of the stage. Gabrielle is to start at Eirini this year, and now Lucia will get to join her! A swell of joy fills her chest at the thought.

"The Triune will span three months, concluding on the Winter Solstice, and there will be three trials, which you will gain further instruction on in the future. Strength, speed, intellect, empathy... the things you'll need to make a great Eidan."

The bogy looks excited, blue scales shimmering a deep purple across his cheeks, but Lucia's heart plummets. *Strength and speed* are not her strong suits. She tries to fix her face, which must be reflecting her misery. She thought she would at least have a chance. At least make it somewhat far, but a test of physical aptitude against bodily-enhanced opponents is impossible. Lucia is in no way a skilled fighter and her genetics work against her.

Lucia walks off the stage feeling dejected. How does she stand any chance of winning? She walks back over to her family, ashamed to meet her mother's eyes. She peeks up at her to see if the woman can see through her false bravado, but Hatsia isn't looking at her. Curious, Lucia turns to follow her eyes. Hetan is coming down the steps off the stage, a big smile on his face as he chats with—*or to*—Boen, who is silent beside him.

Lucia is startled by a voice.

It's a shame. And the poor boy is so handsome too, just like his father.

Lucia's brows furrow, looking from Hetan to her mother, who is still watching him with a regretful expression.

Is she talking about Hetan? Lucia goes to ask when her mother speaks again.

It's a shame they had to die. Ukaih. Talulah. My old friends.

Lucia's eyes widen, her mouth dropping open as the words begin to come together.

"No. No, no, no, no, no," she chants, her legs moving on their own, taking her away from her mother. Her mother turns to her, looking worried by the outburst.

"Lucia, are you all right?" she asks as if Lucia's entire life hasn't just turned over.

Lucia shakes her head, mouth moving but no words coming out. Her heart races, slamming against her ribs as tears pool in her eyes, stinging as they waver there on the cusp.

"*Mama.* Why would you—" Lucia clasps her hand over her mouth. Is this some sort of sick joke? Because it isn't funny.

Why would she say that? Why would her mother...

The night replays in Lucia's mind as lightning claps outside of the big windows of the Hallow Tower. They're so high up it's like they're in the clouds, right there in the eye of the storm. As lightning illuminates the room, Lucia understands what is happening. *Something terrifying.* Something like out of a dream.

Twice this night, Lucia heard things she wasn't meant to. Things she played off as her imagination. Like Ekrul, when these words were spoken, no lips had moved. Except, they aren't bogy. *First*, Hetan calls her beautiful. He had been so confused when she questioned him on it. And then Fabien, his unfiltered thoughts about the place of wolves and vampires, things he hadn't wished for her to hear. Things he hadn't said aloud.

Even now, as Lucia's mother revealed the most horrifying truth, her lips didn't move. The thoughts—no, the memory—of killing Hetan's parents hadn't been said aloud, because Lucia wasn't meant to know. No one was.

"Lucia? Lucia!"

Hatsia shakes her daughter, her lips moving, but Lucia can't hear the words over the thunder, her heart like a stampede in her chest. Lucia turns and runs, racing through the crowd not caring as she pushes through strangers, knocking them out of her path. She needs to get away. She needs to go right now. To still her heart that just might leap out of her chest, and her labored breathing that has her faint and dizzy, the white room spinning and blurring in her vision as those tears now fall like raindrops against her cheeks.

Lucia nearly trips over the end of her dress as she slips and slides, turning the curve around the grand staircase and ripping back the thick curtain to hide inside. She falls to her knees, collapsing against the floor as she presses her hot cheeks to the cool marble, her face wetting the floor as she curls up and cries, thankful for the music that starts back up as the party continues, drowning out her sobs. She feels numb, her heart carved from her chest as she's torn between her mother and her childhood friend.

Her mother is *a murderer. An evil person.* But she is Lucia's mother. And she's the coven head of the Golden Griffins.

Why? Why would she do it? What motive did she have to kill the chief and her mate? Lucia almost wishes she heard more. She *needs* to know, but she can't just *ask* her mother why she killed someone. Hetan's parents...

Lucia can't even sort it in her mind, trying to search for another explanation. There has to be some sort of misunderstanding. This gift is new to Lucia, *maybe she heard wrong?*

Lucia breaks down on the dusty floor, biting into her wrist to keep from crying out too loud as she heaves and sobs, having a panic attack right there in the middle of the gala with no one the wiser. She cries until her eyes are red and raw, her chest hollow and aching from the contractions.

She lies there, her mind blank. She doesn't want to think. She doesn't want to feel. She doesn't know what to do.

Lucia feels so cold, tears dried and sticky down her face and neck. She stares blankly at the wavering light flickering through the slats coming in and out of the space under the stairs as people walk past. She clutches Gabrielle's golden necklace in shaky hands.

When a familiar voice, loud and playful, filters in and caresses her ears, she stirs just slightly, raising her head to listen. *It's Adelaide.*

A touch of warmth thaws Lucia's heart at the sound of the vampire. She's speaking with a man whose voice is the soft tumbling of smooth pebbles.

Lucia pulls herself closer to peek out of the slats of the staircase. Adelaide has her back to the stairs, and the man she's speaking with is turned sideways to face her. From what little Lucia can see of his face, he has delicate features with skin like silver diamonds and night-black hair down his back, swaying as he moves. He wears silken red robes with a delicate print.

Adelaide seems annoyed and upset as Lucia strains to listen. After the things she's overheard tonight, listening in on this is probably the last thing she should do, but she does it anyway. *That voice.* Her heart beats a little faster.

"She cornered me, what did you want me to do?" the robed man says.

"Siphon—" Adelaide takes a deep breath, grinding her face into her palm. "You should've never been alone with her. Do *you* know who she is?"

"She's a Dol'Auclair. The younger sister, Gabrielle. I'm not a child, Adelaide, I'm much older than you. Of course, I know who she is, who doesn't?"

Lucia perks up at the mention of her sister. *Why are they speaking of Gabrielle?* Lucia thinks. And then, *what did Gabrielle do this time?*

"Since you know who her mother is I shouldn't have to remind you that being found alone with her is not a good look. You shouldn't have even spoken to her."

"As opposed to dancing with her?" Siphon bites back. Adelaide seems to freeze for a moment, the response dead on her lips. "Do *you* know who *she* is?" Siphon continues. "Because I'm sure Lucia Dol'Auclair is a lot further up the forbidden witch list. She's your opponent in the Triune, might I remind you? I know you like sleeping with witches, but that one's off-limits."

Adelaide swallows, silence stretching between her and Siphon before she turns from the dancing to glare up at him. That familiar smirk slips back on her lips, sending a chill up Lucia's spine as she purrs, *"But the forbidden ones are the most fun to play with."*

Lucia falls back from the stairs, plunging into darkness as that small flame in her heart shrivels up. She takes a deep, shaky breath as she presses herself back against the smooth patch of wall, going numb once more.

Chapter Eleven
If All You Do is Fail

It's a long week of avoidance, Lucia dodging through the halls and feigning sick to get out of meetings with her mother.

Lucia used to ache to have her mother call her to her office, to speak with her, or look at her with that sense of pride, and now all she wants to do is run and hide. She can't face her mother after what she learned. And worse, she can't even tell her mother she has a gift. A gift Lucia has been agonizing over all week. *She's a Sage.*

Lucia had gone to the library but there isn't much information on them. Sages are extremely rare, Lucia herself has never met one. And, their abilities are still greatly unknown.

Lucia had read Fabien and Hetan and her mother's thoughts at the gala, but she can't share this information with anyone. Not with what she knows. Becoming a contestant in the Triune and going to Eirini was supposed to make her feel more connected, but now Lucia just feels... alone. She finally has a gift but she is too afraid to reveal it.

How would people feel if they knew she could read their minds? She can see the secrets they hide.

The ability is still unpredictable, she hasn't heard another thought since the gala, but she is on edge, dreading the next one.

It's odd, that Lucia got a gift outside of the blooming ceremony. She didn't even feel when the power hit her, like it was already there, simmering under the surface. Lucia thought it would be more noticeable, like being hit by a giant wave.

Now she has no one to turn to for advice or to celebrate with. It is her secret.

At least, now, as the carriage rolls up to the academy, she won't have to hide her feelings or magisk from her mother day after day. The only one she'll have to lie to is... *Hetan*. She still hasn't let herself think deeply about what she heard that night.

Lucia looks at the wolf out of the small window of the carriage. He stands at the entrance with the students in lower level one and the other contestants who have arrived. Lucia's heart squeezes painfully as she looks at her old friend, knowing she'll have to keep this secret from him. *For now.* Just until she can think of what to do.

Eirini Academy of Mystics casts a long shadow over Lucia, a portrait against an orange-and-red sky. With rolling hills to the front and a dark forest behind, Eirini is hidden away up in the mountains of Olympia.

Lucia's breath catches as she takes it all in, a sight she has dreamed of for years. Attending Eirini is one of the dreams Lucia had let die, but now here she is.

Five colossal buildings are positioned in a curve to make a U-shape, curling inwards toward the entrance, each with varying sizes and styles, from grim to golden.

"Okay, everyone, gather around," a whistle voice calls. "I'm Naris, a professor at Eirini, and I have the pleasure of being your guide for the day."

Naris, a small fairy who flutters in the air before the group, has translucent light green wings and skin a shocking pink. She's around the size of a large bird that could perch comfortably on Lucia's shoulder.

Lucia is awed. First Ekrul and now Naris. Eirini is truly the inclusive academy she had heard of. She's never even met a magisk creature before; part of her didn't think they were actually real, let alone a professor and orun-kun of the most prestigious mystic academy.

The sun is setting, casting a warm glow over the group. It gives the academy a romantic feel, and Lucia's hope for a pleasant experience here only grows.

"There are five buildings," Naris says, "one for each Mystic. Though this is a blended school, the dorms are still separated. It was built decades ago when even this—"she waves her hand over the mixed group"—was considered *progressive*."

Naris starts left, pointing out each building, starting with the vampire dorms at the end, then the wolf dorms. The academy building is in the middle, and it curves around to a training center called the Noxidome and the witches' dorms are on the far right. As Naris explains each of them, giving a bit of history, Lucia tunes out her voice.

The vampire dorms are dark and gloomy, a moat surrounding them with water too dark to see below. The building is made of dark wood faded from the sun, and large spires extend from the top with stone statues wrapped around the peak.

Lucia shudders at the sight of the gawking figures with bulging stone eyes. A snake coils around one tower with four tails diverging at the ends. A monstrous creature with long wings and pointed claws looks right at Lucia like it can see into her mind—to the twisted, dark secret she is hiding—and next to it is a one-eyed beast with a curved nose like a beak and four arms and legs.

As Lucia stares up at it, Adelaide moves beside her. She startles when she notices the woman's presence, recoiling back from the vampire.

Adelaide smirks, raising a perfect eyebrow at the reaction.

"You okay, Princess?"

Lucia presses a hand to her chest trying to push down the pattering of her heart, ignoring the way her stomach swoops at the nickname. She turns away, hurrying to Gabrielle's side as the vampire watches her. The last thing Lucia needs right now is to let the vampire get under her skin. She allowed it once only to be made a fool.

Of course, Adelaide was trying to rile her up before the competition. They're rivals. Why she would bother with the witch who is obviously going to lose, Lucia isn't sure. To mess with the granddaughter of Kaeda Dol'Auclair possibly?

Whatever the intent, Lucia wants no part of it. She has too many things to be worried about. She isn't some jester to be mocked.

"Why is there a bridge connecting the dorms?" Hetan asks, glaring up at the large stone bridge that links each building.

Naris pauses to think for a moment before saying, "I am not sure, it has been like that since it was built. I believe it was a personal choice of the builder. These metal slats over the windows were another of his creative liberties." She motions to the wolf dorms, made of red brick. The building is rounded with a flat roof. It's also the smallest of the three dorms. It makes Lucia wonder whether the wolves have a smaller population at Eirini.

The academy building is huge, and Lucia thinks it looks like an ancient castle, all gold with domed roofs. There are too many windows to count.

"This place is beautiful, isn't it?" Gabrielle says arms splayed wide. She spins, giggling like a child. "Mother isn't here, and we don't have to worry about the elders breathing down our necks."

"Yes," Lucia says, staring up at the witches' dorms, white stone with bronze spires and stained-glass windows that shower a rainbow of colors onto the lawn. Lucia's heart twists. "But I'm not here to relax or for fun. Once the first term is over, I'll have to return home." Lucia had nearly forgotten she is only here due to the rules of the Triune. Once it's over—whether she loses or not—her time at Eirini is over. Her mother would never allow her to stay.

Gabrielle's face falls. "I know that, of course. But that doesn't mean we can't enjoy it for now. Students come here from all over Hontaras, witches, wolves, and vampires from dozens of cults and clans. Imagine what they've seen and done. The *stories* they could tell."

Lucia is becoming giddy just from watching Gabrielle's excitement build. She sighs, letting herself smile at her sister. "Of course, Gab. It'll be fun."

Lucia knows she has to be focused on winning the Triune. She'll have to study and train if she wants to be at the level of any of her opponents. She's never been a great student, not when it comes to magisk, so she'll need to put in twice as much work. But she can stand to have a little fun. At least until everything—the secret, and her magisk ability, all come crashing down on her.

※ ※

Professor Olivio stands in front of the class, his brown hair falling around his ears.

The Mastery of Cuma professor is young, and he looks it, but his cuma and knowledge of coven magisk is vast. If he had a gift, he would probably be more powerful than the Magisk Nature professor, who had demonstrated her abilities in class the other day.

Olivio gestures to the class.

"Who can tell me how many classes of magisk there are?" he asks.

A girl raises her hand, nearly jumping out of her seat. Her red hair spills over her shoulders. Lucia's eyes widen at the young girl, Mairan, who just shared a blooming ceremony with Lucia. Lucia is surprised she didn't notice her, with how much she stands out.

"Yes, Mairan."

"There are six, Professor. There are also five levels of magisk difficulty, or grades, and four magisk natures."

Olivio smiles. "Thank you, Mairan, for the extra information." The classroom breaks out into laughter. "But there are six magisk grades, counting Asa-o—zero grade. There is Asa-o, Neno grade, Odua grade, Tri grade, Attan grade, and Quen grade. Quen is the highest level of difficulty you can achieve, and realistically most of you will never reach it. That is the level of the likes of our Grand Elder, where a coven head would probably sit around Tri or Attan grade. Most students don't go higher than Tri grade, which is the highest you will be learning in depth at this school."

Lucia thinks of her own grandmother and the fearsome power she wields. People shake at the sound of her name, even Lucia herself. Her grandmother's magisk, even before she became the Eidan, was on a different level.

"As an L One—or lower one—teacher, we will focus on Neno grade, specifically coven magisk. In lower two you will learn a bit more about singular cuma, which as you should know is never as strong as the cult, but with practice can be very useful to know. I'm going to put your lower academy knowledge to the test. Harif, can you tell me the two types of magisk?"

"Uh... koy and cuma?" Harif stutters, his cheeks turning pink. He pulls away from Mairan beside him, who he had been trying to chat with. "Koy is your magisk nature, which you can only get from the Mother, and cuma is the innate power within every—" he glances at Lucia "—almost every witch. Also known as coven magisk, and as its name implies it is made stronger when used with others."

Lucia's blood boils and she tries not to feel shame at the eyes on her. Though she knows that she has a magisk nature bestowed by the Mother, no one else does. It's a secret that is driving her mad. She should be over the moon that she has a gift. She should be able to celebrate it like everyone else, but she cannot.

Lucia can't help but wonder why the Mother gave her this gift.

"Great," the professor says, reaching into his pocket and pulling out a small marble. The colorful orb glows in the sunlight streaming in through the large skylights as he holds it up. "In this class, we'll focus on cuma, as koy is your Magisk Nature professor's job." He places the marble on the center of his desk. "We got a bit off-topic, but as I had been saying before, there are six classes of magisk: Ariraan—divination, Ifyai—enchantment, Irujui—illusion, Oporaa—permutation, L'Paeru—conjuring, and Itoju—abjuration."

Olivio points to the marble on his desk. "If I were to have this marble come to me by way of cuma, which class of magisk would that be?"

"That would be considered a L'Paeru cantus. Since you are having the marble move from a place it was before."

"Correct. And if the marble were already moving toward me and I commanded it to stop?"

Mairan raises her hand again. "That would be considered under the class Itoju."

"Yes, good job, Mairan." Olivio waves his hand, and many more marbles appear in his hand of different colors and sizes. "Even though I do not need to protect myself against a rolling marble, it would still be under the class Itoju, because of the nature of a stopping or *halting* cantus. Now, I want you to get into groups and take one of these—"

Lucia's magisk skill classes are getting the best of her. Even though she has developed her magisk nature, it seems she still can't access her cuma. Olivio paired the class off into teams, and every single time she was the one throwing the cantus off.

Lucia strides down the hall, fingers gripping her tote tightly as she replays her blunder in class. The professor had asked her to activate a simple charm, a marble he wanted Lucia to stop. It was a simple abjuration, with the cantus yogun—a blocking cantus in the class Itoju. But when Lucia repeated the word, her tongue was heavy. Her pronunciation was way off, and the marble kept going until it rolled right off the table. Lucia was humiliated, her classmates trying to stifle their laughter as the professor gave her the marble and told her to "keep practicing."

That marble burns a hole in Lucia's tote as she chokes back the lump in her throat. Technically, her classes at Eirini aren't important. Most people who come to the expensive academy don't care about grades anyway, they're here to hone their skills and make important political alliances. And Lucia won't even be graduating, but she wants to try and make the most of her time here and learn all that she can in these three months she was afforded by the Triune.

"Lucia—"

"Oof."

Lucia groans, rubbing her head as she pulls back from the figure she bumped into. When she sees the red eyes, she freezes up. Adelaide is looking down at her with a toothy smile. *No, no. Not right now.*

Lucia has been trying hard all week to ignore Adelaide, but the woman is persistent. Isn't it obvious she doesn't want to talk? Adelaide might not be aware Lucia overheard her at the gala, and all the better. Lucia would rather the vampire think Lucia is just too wise for her games. A witch she couldn't toy with. It's better than the latter—*Lucia had been fooled*, if only for a moment. That maybe this vampire could want... what? Friendship? Lucia doesn't know what she was thinking, but she won't be played again.

"Hold up, Princess," Adelaide says, grabbing Lucia's arm when she tries to bolt off. Lucia pulls her arm, but the woman is too strong. She huffs irritably.

"I'm busy," Lucia says, ignoring the heat that races across her skin as she glares up at the vampire. "So if you'd let me go, that would be nice."

"Busy with what, with this thing?" Adelaide holds Lucia's marble between three fingers, the light shining through it.

"Hey!" Lucia shouts, eyes wide as she tries to snatch the marble back. "How did you even get that? Did you go through my bag?"

Is Adelaide so fast that Lucia wouldn't notice that?

"*No*," Adelaide says like it was obvious. "It fell from this pocket when you bumped into me, and I caught it."

Lucia looks at the small front pocket of her satchel hanging open and then back to the marble. She plucks it from the vampire's fingers, feeling a jolt of electricity where their skin touches. Lucia's face heats as she shoves the marble into the bigger compartment.

"Thanks, now are we done here?" Lucia snaps.

Adelaide tilts her head at Lucia, a look of confusion on her face. "Did I do something to piss you off, little witch, because you're being extra snippy? And, dare I add, you've been avoiding me." Adelaide pushes closer, blocking Lucia against the wall. Lucia's heart beats quickly, her pulse bobbing in her throat as she swallows. She tries not to let her eyes travel downward to all the skin the vampire has on display. A skirt that sweeps the floor, gauzy and nearly see-through, with large slits displaying long legs and toned thighs.

"Y-you wish I was avoiding you," Lucia stutters, fingers sweaty as they grasp her tote straps.

"We made a connection at the gala," Adelaide says, "and now you're acting like that didn't happen." She brings her voice nearly to a whisper. "Is it because of the Triune? You can't be friends with the competition?"

Lucia snorts, fully distracted by how close Adelaide's face is to hers. The vampire smells like iron and something sweet and earthy, like old leather. Her dress is black with a high neck, a purple flower wrapped around her neck like a choker, and her hips enveloped in chains. It's pretty—*if* Lucia was into that sort of thing.

Lucia's voice is a whisper as she answers, "Of course not. I danced with a lot of people at the gala. I just didn't think you'd take it so *personally.*"

A flash of hurt melts red eyes, but Adelaide's smirk doesn't falter. "Ouch, Princess," she chokes. "That was almost mean, shi."

Lucia shrugs, unable to meet Adelaide's eyes. The vampire takes a step back, giving Lucia room to breathe where she's trapped between her and the wall. Lucia's grip tightens on her bag as she inches sideways along the wall, motioning somewhere behind her.

"As I said, I uh... gotta go."

Lucia turns in front of the vampire, heels clicking and stiff hoop dress swishing across wooden floors as she scurries quickly in the other direction. She was headed to her dorm to practice with the marble, which is the opposite direction, but she can't afford to turn and see Adelaide again.

"Lucia!"

Lucia jumps, thinking it's Adelaide caught up with her before she registers her sister's voice. She turns a forced smile on her lips, as Gabrielle races toward her. That smile falters as she sees what her sister is wearing.

"What are you—"

"Like it?" Gabrielle asks, spinning. She's wearing tight black jeans and a purple-and-black corset, her arms and chest bare. Lucia's eyes are wide as they rake over mahogany skin. She is speechless. Their mother would have a fit if she saw Gabrielle like this. In *human fashion*, and wearing pants.

"Where did you even get this?" Lucia asks, still stunned.

Gabrielle looks smug as she says, "From Blythe. They're a wolf in one of my classes, and they are friends *sort of* with Cait. They said the wolves go into human cities all the time. They don't even have to ask! Isn't that awesome? They lent me some clothes."

Lucia takes note of the way Gabrielle is speaking, saying they instead of she. If Lucia remembers correctly, the wolves have a third gender, neither male nor female. Is this how she is meant to refer to Blythe? Lucia remembers the nice, pushy wolf she met at the Dome. They are exactly the kind of person Gabrielle would befriend.

"Well, I'm glad you're making a friend, Gab," Lucia says, not wanting to be the downer who tells her she can't wear what she wants. She isn't their mother. Though, if it gets back to her, Lucia will be the one in trouble.

"Just be careful who you surround yourself with, okay? We're away from home, but you are still a Dol'Auclair."

"Of course. Anyway," Gabrielle says, pushing the reminder of her status away, "you should join us for lunch."

"With who? And isn't it early for lunch?"

Gabrielle scoffs. "Do you ever just go along with things, Lucia?' She grabs Lucia, tugging her in the direction of the canteen. Lucia sighs, letting herself be dragged.

"I do let myself go," she grumbles. "That's how I always get into trouble." Growing up, every bad decision she made was her going along with one of Gabrielle's wild ideas. She's not sure if she ever really decides anything on her own, always doing things for other people. Like the Triune. And keeping her mother's secret...

The canteen is as busy as it always is. Lucia doesn't think there's a time of day that there are not at least a few dozen people here. It's open at all hours. You could wake in the night and come down to get a snack if you wanted to. Nothing at Eirini is closed besides the academy building, which is locked up after sunset and opened at sunrise. The dorms have no curfew, and the training center is always in use.

The canteen is kind of like a small market, with many booths selling different foods and sweets. Lucia heard it is modeled after something the humans have. Everything Lucia learns about humans seems exciting. If not a bit dangerous. *Definitely dangerous,* if her outing to Domeg is to be remembered, but it still kind of excited her.

There's a hot food side that has home-cooked meals that rival what Lucia's cooks make back home, and honestly, it's the best part of Eirini. Lucia loves to eat, so the canteen is her dream come true. The kitchen back home is not open at all hours.

Lucia goes through the line looking for something to eat. She wants to try something new every day to make the most out of the experience while she can. Eyeing some sort of twirly noodles with a green sauce, Lucia decides she just has to have it. She chooses that and some strange fruit before Gabrielle takes her arm again.

"Let's eat outside," she says. "The girls are waiting."

They make their way out to the garden where Gabrielle's friends, Lady Mia and Lady Caitlyn, sit under an acylwood. The beautiful flushed pink petals look like they're woven across one another. They release a light, almost sweet fragrance. You can suck on the petals, and they taste like raw sugar. Lucia isn't a fan of sweets, but they're a nice autumn snack, especially on sleepless nights.

Lucia recognizes Gabrielle's friend Caitlyn Coflar, the youngest daughter of the Starlight coven head. Then there's Mia Sacrenladre of the Black Basilisks, one of Lucia's opponents for the Triune. She's meant to be a talented witch. When her mother visits Laesbury she goes on and on to Lucia's mother about what a prodigy Mia is.

Mia has bronze skin and long hair like a shadow, which is currently covered by a scarf. Caitlyn has short dark brown hair cropped around her chin with bangs that fall over her eyes that burn like violet ice. And her heart-shaped lips are unnaturally red like a dark wine.

Both girls are close to Gabrielle's age at eighteen and nineteen, so Lucia never got very close to them. She never really got close to anyone. Gabrielle, on the other hand, could make friends with a teapot.

Though the sun is out, there's a bit of a chill in the air. Lucia wraps her cloak tighter around her shoulders, wondering how her sister isn't freezing. Gabrielle moans over her cornbread slathered in butter as Lucia removes her silk, fur-lined gloves, rolling her eyes at her sister's dramatics.

"You're making a mess, Gab."

Gabrielle looks down to see a slab of butter has fallen on her corset top.

"My goodness, let me." Mia dabs her handkerchief in her water glass and reaches over to dab at Gabrielle's top. Gabrielle just sits there, continuing to eat her bread as her friend dabs away.

Lucia raises a forkful of what she learned is called *pasta*, marveling at it as it bends and wiggles funnily. Lucia takes a hesitant bite and immediately descends into the same noises as her sister. She loves the food of her home, but the flavors and creativity of these foreign dishes are unmatched. Maybe it's because it's something new, but whatever the case it's wonderful.

"This is divine!" Lucia moans, and the other girls chuckle at her reaction. The other covens aren't as strict as the Golden Griffins are with human things, not even the other major four. The only one who probably rivals them in that aspect is the Sea Serpents. They're terribly traditional.

"Ooh, look at Lord Hakim," Mia says, giggling behind her hand. "He looks so handsome today. Well, every day."

Caitlyn rolls her eyes. "You're gross, Mia."

"No, I agree. He's very cute," Gabrielle says. "You're just jealous, Cait, because Mia is engaged to him, and you can't seem to find your own beloved."

"It was an arranged marriage," Caitlyn says indignantly, swaying away from Gabrielle's playful swat.

"Arranged or not, he's mine." Mia puffs up her chest, her cheeks reddening. She leans into the table, whispering low. "And we've already kissed."

"You kissed!" Gabrielle shouts.

Mia shushes her. "Well, don't go yelling it to the entire room. I'd be dead if it got back to my mother. The entire coven would shame me."

"It's just a kiss," Gabrielle scoffs, acting cool. Lucia knows it's an act. She hasn't kissed anyone either. Her sister would tell her.

"You don't understand since you aren't the firstborn," Mia says to Gabrielle. "You and Caitlyn are allowed more... *freedom* than I or your sister. I bet your mother would have a heart attack if Lady Lucia was seen kissing a boy."

"I'm going to say it again, Mia," Caitlyn says seriously, "and as my best friend, you won't think too poorly of me for it—*Yuck*. Also, I may not have the pressures of being firstborn but that doesn't mean life with my mother is roses. Her goals for me may be harsher than yours."

Mia just rolls her eyes. "Anyway, Lucia, what do you think of Hakim?" she asks, excited.

"Or better question, what is your type, Lady Lucia?" Caitlyn asks, looking Lucia up and down. "I think you like nice, *tradist* boys. The ones who only wear their traditional clothes and go to the temple on Trin Dai to Holum."

Lucia ponders it as she chews her pasta. The two girls lean in to hear her answer.

Trin Dai to Holum is the three holy days of the witches. Dai Sanctum is a day of rest and inner reflection. It's also known as the day of the divine eye. Then there's Dai Dimi Dei and Dai Gemus, the day of accordance or selflessness, and the day of celebration also known as the day of spirits. People claim to find their soulmates on Dai Gemus, or they become *enlightened* and find their higher purpose.

Lucia has always gone to the temple on Trin Dai to Holum. Her grandmother has always expected it, and she never questioned it or missed a service except for illness. Does she care if her partner is a traditionalist? She's never thought of it. She doesn't think about relationships much. As Gabrielle often laments, Lucia is boring.

While Lucia's thinking, Gabrielle cuts in, "Lucia doesn't need a tradist. She needs to have fun. I think she's too stuck in the elder life and should enjoy being young while she can. I mean, who's to say you should stop at just one partner?"

Mia squeals. "Gabrielle, you minx! You can't just say such things."

"Gabrielle," Lucia scolds, her face heating up. More than one partner? Preposterous. Her sister does say such wild things. Lucia thinks she only does it for the shock.

Caitlyn buries her face in her hands as if embarrassed by her friend. "Well, what about the first son of the Sea Serpent coven? The Devroue boy. Madam Linae's bairn?"

"Fabien?" Gabrielle scoffs. "He's an imbecile."

Gabrielle has never been too fond of Fabien. She thinks he's stuck up and haughty. Lucia can't disagree, but he's a nice, proper boy and their parents are close. Her mother sent him to Eirini to keep an eye out for her and help during the Triune, which nearly sent Gabrielle over the edge.

"Well, I just assumed you'd get together," Caitlyn says, cutting up a red desert squash. "You're both of high-born families, and he's the first son. Not to mention, the Devroues are very rich. Almost as rich as Mia's family."

"Yeah," Mia says. "It kind of makes sense. He has the money, and you're a Dol'Auclair. Plus, he has a powerful magisk. Your children would be unstoppable."

The table goes a bit silent at the thought of magisk, all thinking the same thing—that Lucia herself doesn't have magisk, and he helps keep her children from the same fate. Except, Lucia *does have magisk*. She just can't tell anyone.

"Ladies," a voice croons.

Lucia startles, her head whipping back at the voice. Fabien appears as if summoned by their mention of him.

"Fabien," Lucia breathes, almost glad for the distraction. Caitlyn scoots across the bench so Fabien can sit beside her.

"Thank you," he says. "Lady Lucia, looking beautiful as ever. How are you?"

The two girls giggle into their hands, while Gabrielle glares at him.

"Thank you, I'm good." Lucia dressed up for Dai Gemus in a pink-and-green floral corset over a white blouse and a magenta skirt. She even has butterfly charms in her hair. She wears the most color on this day, to please the great deities.

Especially now that the Mother has answered her prayer, she is especially grateful. She might not be able to reveal her gift yet but soon. She has to talk to her mother and settle whatever it is she heard at the gala. It must have been a misunderstanding. It couldn't be anything else. Lucia doesn't know what she would do otherwise.

"Will you join me for temple tonight, Lady Lucia?" Fabien asks.

Lucia's heart stutters. *Join him for the temple?* She plays with the hem of her sleeves, unable to meet his eyes. What a forward request. And in front of

Gabrielle and her friends, no less. She can't exactly say no. Not that she wants to exactly, but the talk of dating makes her feel a bit odd.

Lucia nods. "Of course, it would be my pleasure." She ignores her sister's eye roll from across the table. She knows she'll get an earful from her later, but she is the one always complaining Lucia never speaks to boys.

Chapter Twelve

Things You Find in the Forest

Lucia stares down at the scroll with apprehension. She had been studying in her room when Theia, the messenger fairy for the witches' dorms, who brings the students' packages and letters, dropped it off along with a basket of treats.

The small scroll is made of black parchment on a roller of redwood. A white seal is holding the parchment closed—the seal of the Caput Trium.

It must be about the Triune. Lucia has been dreading this day.

"Well, what are you waiting for? Open it," Gabrielle says, hovering over Lucia's shoulder. She had come to study with Lucia but she hadn't been doing any work. Only distracting Lucia as she blabbered and riffled through Lucia's drawers. Now, she has a bar of chocolate hanging out of her mouth and a blue-and-yellow flower crown on her head. Lucia stares at her wide-eyed, her mouth open.

"Is that my stuff?" Lucia gasps, looking at the unwrapped basket on the bed. Gabrielle looks guilty as she meets her gaze.

"Maybe... but you don't like sweets. And I'm only borrowing the crown."

Lucia snorts, shaking her head. She turns back to the scroll, her hands still shaking.

"Do you want me to do it?" Gabrielle asks.

Lucia shakes her head again, taking a deep breath. "It'll be fine. I can open a scroll, at least." Gabrielle nestles up to Lucia's side, laying a head on her shoulder as she watches. Lucia snaps the white wax, slowly unrolling the scroll to reveal white ink against the dark parchment.

In calligraphy at the top of the page, it reads: *For Lucia of the Golden Griffin coven, by your humble Caput Trium.*

Each of their names is signed below it. Lucia closes her eyes, her heart beating quickly. She can't bring herself to read further, she's too nervous. The letter, she assumes, contains the rules for her first trial. The contestants were told they would be receiving them at some point. Lucia can't bear to look and resigns herself to the inevitability of her failure.

"Gabrielle, can you read it?" Lucia says.

"Are you sure?" Gabrielle's voice is close to her ear, Lucia's eyes still clenched shut. She can feel her sister's warm breath and smell the minty chocolate.

"Yes, please. I'm too much of a coward."

Gabrielle shifts beside Lucia to get a better look, and then she begins to read:

"Champion of the Triune here is your first task. A game of pairs to test your ability to work with others. A test of power to decide your strength. You will complete a timed obstacle course with your partner, a race you both must finish to come to an end. When two have won, the last group has failed. Both members of the losing team will be eliminated from the Triune."

Gabrielle pauses for a moment, looking up at Lucia, who has opened her eyes, head tilted up to the ceiling.

"Lucia, your partner is... *Hetan Anoki of the Silver Fang.*"

Lucia lets out a long breath, deflating as she leans her head against Gabrielle's.

"Isn't that a good thing?" Gabrielle asks, confused. "You'll be working with someone you know."

Lucia's grip on the scroll is tight, crinkling the parchment. *That's what makes it so awful,* Lucia thinks. *She's going to hold their team back and her friend will lose because of her.*

"I—Yeah, it's great."

Gabrielle doesn't look too convinced, but she nods. "Oh, and look," she says, reading the last part of the letter. "In your gift baskets is the uniform you are meant to wear for the Triune." Gabrielle knocks over the basket, spilling sweets and fruit, and other trinkets. Folded in black wrapping at the bottom is Lucia's uniform. Gabrielle rips it open and out falls a robe. Blue and gold, Lucia's cloak is ankle length with two slits up the sides. She wonders if the other contestants have similar ones.

"Why would the Caput Trium pair me with Hetan?" Lucia asks, folding the uniform in her lap. "Wouldn't it make sense to pair me with Mia?"

Gabrielle hums. "Well, it would be easier to work with Mia, since you're both witches. Maybe they also want to test how well you work with someone from another Mystic family. Or maybe it's to even the playing field magisk-wise. Witches, wolves, and vampires have very different skill levels. For example, a vampire paired with a witch. The vampire has speed and strength, but they don't have the magisk skill of a witch—things like my conjuring, or nature manipulation. There will probably be something to test everyone."

Lucia nods. *Maybe.*

"Lucia... can I keep these?" Lucia looks over to see Gabrielle in her basket again, this time pulling out a pair of boots. They're yellow to match her uniform, tall, sturdy-looking shoes with a lot of buckles. Lucia has never worn anything like them before, preferring to stick to her silk slippers and heels.

"Okka, Gabrielle."—*No way.* She rolls her eyes.

Lucia changes into training clothes—a thin, lightweight dress over a long-sleeved body suit with a high neck—then makes her way to the Noxidome where Hetan waits for her.

Gabrielle is with Hetan when Lucia enters. They don't notice her at first as they banter. Lucia is glad the two are getting along. Gabrielle was young when Hetan first came around, and they didn't bring her along when they would play. It's nice to see her two favorite people together.

"Tama hei, come race me," Hetan says, lighting up when he sees Lucia. They don't know what the obstacles for the first event will be, but they figure any practice will help.

"Coming."

Hetan throws his arm around her shoulders. "You and I have an advantage because we work well together. The other teams will be too busy trying to rip each other's heads off to win."

Lucia can only hope.

She positions herself beside Hetan on the obstacle course. The top floor of the Noxidome is tall, and it's set up with different terrains and dangerous practice equipment. It's perfect for practicing. Most of the stuff was sent over from Etryae, which is far more advanced than the other three regions.

"Just try your best," Hetan says. "I just want to see where we are in terms of skill and what we need to improve on."

Hetan nods to Gabrielle, who presses a buzzer starting the match. Lucia takes off, running toward the ladder right in front of her. She doesn't know what she's doing. She isn't athletic and has no fighting skills whatsoever.

When Lucia is near the ladder, a *Niveus* pops up, blocking her path. She nearly trips, so caught off guard by the thing. The creatures are pale, sickly blobs in humanoid shapes, creations of Etryae and their sophisticated technology. One appears right before her as she's reaching for the first rung. It swings at her, and she quickly dodges, nearly falling over as she does so. She sweeps out with her leg, dropping it on its back. It disappears.

Ah, so these are lower levels. They shouldn't be too hard to fight.

Lucia rushes up the ladder to a platform a few meters in the air. She jumps when a beam comes out, trying to knock her back down.

Her foot catches, dropping her to her knees, but Lucia catches herself right before the edge of the cliff. As the bar comes back around, she scrambles back to her feet, breathing hard as she jumps out to grab a rope and swings to another platform.

Another Niveus appears, and she dodges the first hit but not the second. A painful punch lands on her stomach, then another to the side of her rib.

Lucia dodges and tries to side-sweep it again, but it learned. It grabs her leg, pulling her. She lands on her back with a painful thud that knocks the wind out of her.

Lucia's head is at the edge of the short platform. She rolls over when the Niveus tries to hit her on the ground, kicking out wildly until her foot connects. The Niveus goes flying over the side of the platform and disappears.

Lucia groans, holding her stomach. She can feel painful bruises forming. *Is this how hard the first trial is going to be?* If so, she has no chance.

The Niveus is going easy on Lucia, and still, she's struggling. She wonders briefly how Hetan is doing, but she doesn't have time to look. She's sure he's far ahead by now.

Struggling back to her feet, Lucia climbs the lattice rope ladder, arms burning as she does so. Her eyes widen when an object comes hurtling toward her. She lets go, rolling back down the rope, her foot tangling in one of the rungs before she can fall off.

Using what little upper body strength she has, hands burning, Lucia pulls herself up so she can free her leg. She's panting, sweating all over, but she rights herself and begins climbing again.

This time Lucia watches, dodging the flying objects that come at her.

A close call has her hanging by one hand, her fingers twisting in pain at the strain to hold on. She quickly gets her other hand on the rung before she dislocates them.

"*Oww,*" Lucia hisses. One of the objects comes barreling at her, colliding with her left shoulder. A blunt but fast arrow. She thinks it might have broken the skin a little bit.

Eyes stinging with tears, Lucia pulls herself up onto the next platform, now even higher above the ground. She's too afraid to even look. She collapses, rolling over onto her back as a tear trails down into her hairline, fingers prodding at the place she was hit. She winces at the pain.

There's still a lot of obstacle course left; Lucia just hopes no more Niveus will show up. Aching, muscles protesting the movement, she stands on shaky feet. Hetan is nowhere to be found, and she wonders if he has passed already. She can't give up, even if he did. They will both have to pass the finish line, and that's all she can focus on. Being a good partner for him. She can't let him down.

Gritting her teeth, Lucia jumps into the frigid water before her. Immediately, sharp waves come crashing down on her.

Lucia hasn't done much swimming, only in the small rivers and ponds with Hetan as a kid. Taking a deep breath, she dives under, figuring she'll have a better chance that way, and since the water is too dark to see much of anything, she closes her eyes and paddles her arms as hard and fast as she can. She comes up twice, gasping for air, before diving back down below.

The worst part is the cold, like needles across her body, and the fear of not being able to tell where she is. When she hits a solid platform, she pops up, sighing in relief as she hauls herself up onto dry land. *Thank goodness,* she thinks with relief. Her lungs are burning as she blinks water from her eyelashes to clear her vision. She can feel the pins in her hair have come undone, and her curls are a mess around her face. She pushes them back and goes on though her limbs feel heavy, and walking feels like wading through the sand.

This is only practice. If she's struggling now, she will have no chance at the trial.

When another Niveus pops up, Lucia's reactions are much slower than before, and she takes many hits. She drops to her knees, surprising the Niveus, and throws her shoulder at its stomach. It disappears before hitting the ground.

Lucia falls many times, trying to get back to her feet. Her legs are shaking badly from the cold and exhaustion.

"Come on, Lucia. *Come on!*" she mutters to herself. She gets to her feet, trembling as she tries to take a step toward the next obstacle: three floating islands she's meant to jump onto to get to the other side. Backing up to get a running start, Lucia charges forward, but when she goes to jump, her legs buckle. She barely gets off the ground, arms stretching out to grab the first island but only hits the air.

Oh no.

Lucia sees Hetan and Gabrielle far below her on the ground, which comes rushing toward her. Screaming, she closes her eyes as she falls.

"*Oof.*" Lucia hits something soft before bouncing, turning over and over before coming to a stop. Peeking open her eyes, she sees what she was caught by. *A net.* Lucia lets out a long breath as she's slowly lowered to the ground, then crawls out of the net to stand before Hetan and Gabrielle, who come to meet her.

Gabrielle looks worried, taking in Lucia's chattering lips and soaked hair. Her cotton dress clings to her curves and soft belly, her underclothes like a second skin.

"I promise, it's not as bad as it looks," Lucia jokes tiredly, her words slurred. She wants to curl up and take a long nap.

Hetan wraps a towel around Lucia, and she whispers, "Thank you," embarrassed that not only did he finish much sooner than her, barely even breaking a sweat, but that he had to watch her fail so miserably.

He's probably thinking how unlucky he is to have her as a partner.

Lucia clasps the soft, warm towel around her head, freezing when she meets a pair of red eyes across the large room.

Adelaide stands beside two boys who are sparring, the smaller one a wild hellion as he jumps and claws at who Lucia recognizes as Cassius. Cassius has thick curls, two long, braided strands swinging wildly as he expertly dodges and blocks, putting the dual-haired vampire on his back.

Adelaide's arms are crossed over her chest, eyes burning as they lock on her. Lucia feels heat rise to her cheeks, chasing away the chill like a raging inferno. She has to tear her eyes away as she moves to sit, sliding down the wall. She's exhausted, and it takes everything in her to not collapse in a heap on the floor.

"So I guess that means you won," Lucia says. *That's an understatement.* Lucia didn't even finish. Hetan puts his towel over a bench, stretching his limbs.

"Something like that, *tama*," he teases.

Lucia scowls up at him. She never did like that nickname and he knows it.

"Hetan, go with me," Gabrielle says.

"Way ahead of you, *pup.*"

Lucia's mouth drops open at the nickname, one she knows Gabrielle definitely won't tolerate. Gabrielle's face turns stormy. Her arm snaps out beside her, so fast that Lucia barely registers what's happening as a large, hooked club appears in Gabrielle's hand. She whips it around, catching Hetan's leg. His face turns from amused to shocked as he goes down, landing flat on his back. Gabrielle's atop him quickly, legs caging his chest and a hand at his throat.

"Call me pup again, *wolf*," she growls in his ear. "Stop treating me like a child."

Both Lucia and Hetan are shocked; Lucia at the skill with which her sister called upon her *Apparo*, and Hetan at being caught off guard. He was so surprised by Gabrielle's speed and skill he hadn't had time to block her.

"Cheat," he groans, getting to his feet once she climbs off him.

"Not a cheat. You shouldn't have let your guard down. That's what you get for underestimating me."

Hetan smiles, shaking his head. "Yeah? Prove it on the course."

"I will."

All of Lucia's practices follow a similar route. Lucia is far behind Hetan in skill and doesn't seem to offer much in the way of teamwork. She feels more and more defeated as the days drag on.

"Where are we going, Hetan?"

Lucia follows Hetan out into the forest "*to practice*" he had said.

"Come on, tama, just trust me. You've been down during our practices. I can tell something is off. So, I figured we should change things up for today. Instead of practicing your physical ability, we should be focusing on your magisk. That's where you excel."

"But I can't—" Lucia pauses. She can't tell anyone she got her magisk nature yet, too uncertain about the response to *reading minds*. Being a Sage is one of the rarer natures, but that in itself isn't weird. If Lucia had telekinesis or the ability to read emotions, that would be perfectly fine. But reading someone's thoughts is an entirely different thing. She doesn't feel comfortable sharing that information, especially not with what she already knows. It might put her in an unnecessarily dangerous position.

But that doesn't mean she can't try to learn cantus. If she has a magisk nature, that means she has magisk. She just has to try harder. "Okay, but I don't know how you're going to be able to teach me. You're a wolf."

"Was that meant to be an insult?" Hetan teases.

"No, I just—"

Hetan laughs, removing his tan cloak and setting it on a boulder. "I'm playing with you, Lucia."

They're deep in the forest. There's a light breeze whistling through the tall trees, the branches high above swaying rhythmically. Hetan's warm skin glows with a thin sheen of sweat from their trek, muscled arms displayed in a sleeveless tunic.

"What do the other witches do when they're trying to make magisk?" Hetan asks.

"Cantus. It's not *making magisk*," Lucia corrects.

"Okay, well, cantus. Is there anything they do before or during these cantus that stands out to you?"

Lucia tries to think back through the years of watching and failing at being a witch. She shakes her head, letting out a frustrated breath. It's different for everyone. Everyone has their way of being a witch that's unique to them. Like Gabrielle, she doesn't even seem to have to try. It comes effortlessly, and she looks beautiful while doing it.

The other day Lucia failed miserably and hasn't been able to complete the obstacle course at the Noxidome since, while Gabrielle completed it on her first try. It's getting harder and harder to believe her sister shouldn't be in her place. Why couldn't she have been the firstborn?

"I don't know how this is going to help me," Lucia cries. "I've done it all. My mother even got me a private tutor, because she thought it would help. Nothing *worked*. I'm broken, Hetan."

Hetan's chuckle snaps Lucia's angry eyes up at him. "What is so funny?" Lucia asks, annoyed, hands fisted on her hips. "This is serious, Hetan. I'm a witch who isn't good at using their magisk. That's, like, the entire reason for being a witch. A witch without magisk is... Well, they're nothing."

Hetan shakes his head, mouth forming a straight line. "But that isn't true, is it? Aren't you in one of the most revered covens? Also, from what I know of witches, it's hardly unusual. Especially amongst the men. Are they any less a witch?"

Lucia hesitates as she thinks over Hetan's words. It's true, there are many without magisk, even more without magisk natures, but not in one of the big four. Not a Dol'Auclair. Sure, Lucia can read minds now, but that means nothing if she can't control it. And this situation with her mother, and the Triune, are just making everything worse. Lucia feels like she might explode.

Lucia looks up at Hetan, who is staring down at her, waiting for her answer. Her eyes roam over his skin, up to his kind face with the setting sun behind him. His hair is in a bun, the flyaway strands blowing in the wind. He's so beautiful. And so kind. She doesn't know what she would do without him here helping her.

Looking at Hetan is painful. As is training with him, being so near him when she knows she's keeping such a big secret from him. One that would change everything between them. But... not just them. What her mother did breaks the Paxum ex Cinis. That'll not only send her mother to death by the wolves' hands but given who her mother is, it could start a war between the witches and wolves.

She pictures the vampire Abhain chained down to the floor of the Dome, burning alive. She flinches in horror.

"Come on, Lucia, focus."

Lucia's eyes snap back up to Hetan.

"Sorry—I, uh, no. No, it doesn't make them any less a witch."

"Okay, now stop feeling sorry for yourself, and let's practice."

Lucia nods, taking a deep breath of fresh air. "Cantus. A lot of witches say that an important part of it is feeling the words. If you're trying to start a fire, you have to picture the warmth against your skin and see the colors—orange, red, yellow—flickering in front of your eyes. The smell of smoke. You have to ignite your senses."

"Good," Hetan says. "That's similar to shifting: feeling the wolf, imagining it in your mind's eye. Let's start there."

They've been at this for an hour.

Lucia is dripping sweat, her cotton dress clinging to her curves. She feels like she's going to overheat and pass out.

"Don't give up, Lucia."

"I'm trying!" she shouts, hands raised in front of her, curved like she's cupping something. She faces one of the smallest trees she could find, trying to convert the tree into water. It isn't too difficult a technique, and she knows the steps, but somehow, she can't do it.

"Oporaa—Igi I omi," she chants, trying to focus her energy on the tree. "Oporaa—Igi I omi... *Igi I omi!*"

Lucia groans, her hands dropping when Hetan's lands comfortingly on her shoulders.

"You know what, I think that's enough for the day. You're exhausted, and you're distracted by something."

Lucia shivers when a cool breeze rushes through the trees, cooling the sticky sweat on her body and suctioning her clothes to her skin. Her hair is currently pinned up under a headwrap, which matches her training outfit.

"It's just... hard," Lucia says. "There's so much pressure I think I might burst."

Lucia knows she shouldn't be so hard on herself, but she can't stop. Because everyone else will be—her mother, her grandmother, the covens. With her grandmother getting sicker, Lucia only has so much time to prove to her that she can do this. That she isn't a disappointment. She's held to a higher standard than most. She always has been. She isn't just a disappointment to her family and her ancestors, but to all witches.

"How do you do it? How do you channel your... What is it? Your spirit changes."

Lucia has never actually seen a werewolf shift before. She just knows what she's learned. Wolves undergo a shift in puberty where they gain the ability to harness the spirit of the wolf. Their body can shift from human form to that of a beast.

Hetan kicks a stone in his path. "It's different for us. The shift a werewolf undergoes isn't anything like the magisk that comes from your words or your hands. I was an early bloomer. Most homolupus get their first shift around age thirteen, sometimes as late as fifteen. Mine was right before my eleventh year. When my parents died, I became the rightful chief of the wolves."

"But you're not in charge now, are you?" Lucia asks. If he had so much responsibility, how could he be here right now, at Eirini? His people would need him back home.

"No. I have many duties—to the Silver Fangs and all of the clans—but I was so young when I became heir it was decided my uncle would act as interim chief and sit as three of three on the Caput Trium until I was ready. He handles all of the higher duties and manages relations between clans. I'm still learning. I was meant to have more time to shadow him, but now, with the Triune, things are moving so quickly. If I win, I might have to take over the reins. Honestly, I'm still not sure if I'm ready. There is so much going on, so much stress and responsibility. Real-life issues that *terrify* me."

Lucia leans against a large oak. She looks up at the overreaching branches that shade them, and then back to Hetan. He's changed a lot since they were kids. He's tall with bronze skin and wide shoulders. There is power in his body, his muscled legs, and arms like those of an animal. His long hair is a silky dark brown that looks reddish when it catches the light. Lucia has never been more aware of how much he's grown. They both have. They used to talk about climbing trees and racing with each other along the river. Now they're becoming leaders.

"Can you show me?" Lucia asks, her voice soft. She doesn't want to push and make him nervous, but she's curious.

Hetan turns, his eyes burning into hers. They glow silver for just a second, and her breath catches. "I'm sorry if that's a personal question. I don't know if it's something you can—"

Lucia blushes, turning quickly as Hetan begins to pull his clothes over his head. Her face is hot as she stares out at the trees, the sound of rustling clothes accompanying the swaying of leaves blowing in the wind. She can hear Hetan's muscles move and shift, the sound of cracking making her wince. When she turns, the forest gone quiet and a brush of fur against her side, she is breathless at Hetan's beauty.

Standing beside her is a large wolf. His head reaches her hip, and his fur is blinding, the pearlescent white of freshly fallen snow.

"*Dais Holum,*" she whispers in awe—*Holy days.*

Captivated by the beauty, Lucia reaches out to touch. She slowly brings her hand to his head, feeling the soft fur between her fingers. His wolf is a gorgeous creature, but also so powerful with rippling muscles and strapping hindlegs.

"Wow, Hetan. If only you could see yourself."

Lucia watches Hetan for a bit as he moves around. He begins loping through the woods, dodging between trees, and jumping over a small stream. Laughing, Lucia chases after him, trying to keep up. It's different from when they were kids and Lucia was right on his heels. An obvious gap has risen between their abilities.

Hetan is going slow for Lucia's benefit. He even chortles when she slips, her foot dipping into the river and soaking the bottom of her dress. She's glad to see he's kept his playful spirit.

Lucia thought she lost this side of herself. The carefree part. But when she's with Hetan it all rushes back.

Hetan nudges her with his big snout, preventing her from falling any farther into the water as he helps her back onto the shore.

"Thank you," she says, collapsing breathlessly onto the grass.

Hetan shifts back to a man and she hands him the clothes that she carried over. He sits beside her with a large smile on his face.

"It's more incredible than I imagined," Lucia says. Werewolves are truly far better than she'd been told. Even Hetan himself had never talked too much about being a wolf when they were kids. True, he hadn't had his shift yet, but to be surrounded by such beauty, she would have shouted it from the rooftops.

"Does it hurt?" she asks, remembering the sound of the cracking of bones.

Hetan shakes his head. "No. It feels a bit odd at first. Uncomfortable. But you get used to it. It can even be quite an enjoyable sensation, like stretching or sneezing."

Lucia laughs, bunching grass between her fingers. She pictures a bunch of sneezing wolves doing the downward dog. Gabrielle showed her that pose once when she came back from the city.

"I don't know why magisk is so hard for me. Trying to make something out of nothing or forming something in my mind. *Something new.* Gabrielle makes it seem so easy. She's good at cantus. She can even do some without saying a word. She just pictures it in her mind."

Hetan hums. "When I shift, I don't imagine becoming something different. I'm not a man and then a wolf, I'm both of them at the same time. It's like emotions. People aren't happy or sad, they are not angry and then calm. They're all at once. Certain experiences can bring one to the forefront, but they're all inside of us. The wolf is always inside of me. When I change, I just call the wolf to the forefront."

Lucia and Hetan watch the sun, nearly sunken below the horizon, bits of orange sunlight shining between the cluster of trees as the forest darkens. Hetan stands, holding his hand out to Lucia to help her up.

"Takke'," she whispers, brushing off her dress.

"Maybe," Hetan says as they head back toward the academy, "you shouldn't think of your magisk as a thing separate from you. Think of it as a part of you."

Lucia ponders what Hetan said for a long time, distracted as she follows him through the forest. When she looks up at Hetan, he seems to be lost in thought as well. She asks, "You're not upset with me, are you?"

Hetan looks down at her, his eyebrows furrowed. "Why would you think that?"

Lucia looks down at her feet as she walks, arms wrapping around her torso. "It's just... you've been helping me so much with my magisk. But we're competing too. Technically. I mean, I know we're partners now and you're helping me so you don't fail too, but—"

"Lucia," Hetan says, stopping her. "I'm not upset with you. And I'm not just helping you because we're partners. Yes, we're both competing for the vessel of the Orbis Libra, but that doesn't mean we can't still be friends. If you win, I would be happy for you. You would make a great leader."

"I know but—"

"Stop worrying. You don't have to feel bad about wanting something. I know you have just as much pressure on you as I do. We have to do things, and sacrifice things, for our people all the time. But my friendship with you won't be one of them."

Lucia smiles up at Hetan, letting out a breath. Things are so easy with him as if there was no time separating them. Her smile sours a bit as Hetan turns around. Staring at his back she wonders if he would be so kind and forgiving if he knew what she was keeping from him.

"Aah—"

Lucia jumps, hands gripping her skirt as she draws up short. Her heart thumps hard and fast in her chest, her mouth going dry as she tries to convince herself this isn't real. She's just imagining it.

"Is that a—a—"

Lucia turns to Hetan, gripping his arm tightly. His face is ashen, but his shoulders are back and he's standing tall as he finds her hand. Lucia is rooted in place, eyes trained on the prone body facing down in the dirt, trying not to lose the contents of her stomach.

"Let's go, tama," Hetan says gently, tugging her. Her feet move slowly; her eyes still on the body as she follows him. "Come, look at me."

Through tears gathering in Lucia's eyes, she moves her gaze up to his. With her eyes glued on him, to the strong set of his jaw and confidence, they walk slowly until the body is far behind. Lucia takes a deep breath once it's out of sight, picking up speed. She's like a puppet following the wolf blindly, but inside she panics.

A dead body. *They just found a dead body.*

Lucia's head whips around, her heart battering her ribs and her hand sweating in Hetan's. She wonders if the person was murdered because if so, the culprit could still be in the woods.

"Gabrielle!" Lucia shouts as they break through the trees.

She spots her sister instantly; Gabrielle is walking through the field, a textbook cradled in her arms. She turns to Lucia with a confused look on her face but moves quickly toward them.

"Lucia?" she says sounding worried. "Hetan..."

Hetan thrusts Lucia's hand toward Gabrielle. "Take her, please. Get her to the nurse if you must. Just stay out of the woods."

Hetan turns in the opposite direction, looking so brave and assured. Lucia thought she had seen how much he grew up, but she hadn't truly. When they were kids, he was the more sensitive one. The smallest things would make him weep.

"The nurse? Lucia, what's going on, are you hurt?" Gabrielle's eyes are wide and nervous as she takes in Lucia's blank stare. Lucia drowns out Gabrielle's voice, replaying the sight of the lifeless body in her mind.

Lucia can't sleep. For the last few nights, she has tossed and turned in bed worrying over the dead body she and Hetan found in the woods. They said the young man's name was Orion, a wolf in lower two. There's no news of how he died, whether it was foul play, though they're trying to figure it out.

Ekrul updated the rules about coming and going from campus, and now students need permission from the teachers to go into town. Lucia's mind goes to the hunters she ran into when she went to Domeg with Adelaide. She hasn't thought of that for a while, almost like it was another lifetime, but she can still remember the large weapons they carried. They were hunting for Mystics. She worries whoever killed Orion might be the same people that had been looking for her. They might have already entered Eirini. *Somehow.*

Her grandmother is getting sicker, and the barriers are weakening. If they don't replace the Eidan soon, Mystics will have no protection from humans and the outside world.

Lucia feels guilty. There is nothing she can do about it. Adelaide told her she knew nothing of the men who attacked the bar, and Lucia can't tell anyone in her coven without revealing she snuck out of the Ife ring. She's alone with this, once more hoarding secrets she can tell no one.

And now the first trial is tomorrow, but Lucia is restless. Her mother is going to be there. She's going to watch Lucia fail. Fail at the first trial.

Lucia groans, burrowing her head in her arms. It's midnight, and she's in the canteen, tucked away in a private booth. The lights are low and there are only a few other students here, most people are either sleeping or off partying. Lucia never realized how much of that went on at Eirini.

"You can't sleep either?"

Lucia stiffens at that voice. *Adelaide.*

"Don't—leave," Adelaide says, sliding into the booth. Lucia slowly sits back down, swallowing as she watches the vampire sitting across from her. The lights are dim, the one above them flickering.

"What do you want?" Lucia asks, eyeing the plate the woman sets on the table. Some sort of orange pudding with a thin crust.

"Is this a sweet?" Lucia asks, eyes lighting. She tries to tamp down her excitement, but eagerness squirms in her belly. She doesn't love desserts, but she does love sweet potatoes. It *smells* like a sweet potato.

"Yes. Do you like sweets?" Adelaide questions, folding her hands atop the table.

"Not really," Lucia says. But she grabs the plate with both hands to bring it closer. She takes the spoon Adelaide holds out to her and digs in. Her eyes close as she groans in delight. It's a dessert but very light and savory. Salty-sweet.

"This is wonderful!"

Lucia's hunger catches up with her, oblivious to Adelaide watching her curiously as she quickly eats the entire thing, just like she had in that room in Domeg. Lucia is getting flashbacks to that meeting, the warmth she had felt with the woman, just the two of them alone in an unfamiliar place. Before Lucia knew who she was and what she was after. She had known who Lucia was all along; it was all an act. This probably is too.

"It truly is fascinating to watch you eat, Princess. Like you're starving. You're deprived up there in the mountains, aren't you?"

Lucia snorts. Is that a come-on?

"I'm not deprived of anything. I have everything I need." She pushes away her plate, which she scraped clean. She waves her hand over it. "This is good, but I don't need it. It's a distraction."

"Mhm. But is that any way to live? Just because you don't need to do something, doesn't mean it wouldn't be fun. Haven't you ever taken a risk, Princess?"

Lucia scoffs. "Why do people keep saying that? Of course, I have. Just being here is a risk." Lucia looks the vampire up and down. She's leaned back with her arm over the booth, a lazy, smug smile on her face and eyes knowing. Adelaide wears a red body suit today, like the color of her eyes, which glow in the low light. A chill passes over Lucia as the vampire watches her. Like she can feel the touch of that gaze.

"Why are you here?" Lucia asks. "To taunt me—to shake me before the competition?"

Adelaide bites her lip and Lucia's gaze strays to it unconsciously. "To wish you luck."

"Luck? But we're competition."

Adelaide hums again. "Maybe."

"Maybe? I'm not stupid, *Azueme Skullkin*. And I'm not something for you to toy with. So if you're going to just run back around saying how naive and stupid I am, good luck. I'm not falling for it."

"Falling for what?"

Lucia groans, wanting to wipe that satisfied look off the vampire's face. "T-that face. Like you're trying to seduce me or—"

"Or *what?*" Adelaide says, sliding out of her seat to move next to Lucia. "Are you aroused by me, Lucia?"

"I—I— What?!" Lucia splutters, backing up against the wall of the booth as the vampire leans in toward her. Lucia puts her arm out to keep space between them, her hand pressing against the vampire's chest. Her heart is beating fast, her face burning up in embarrassment as she gets flustered. "Y-you wish, vampire," Lucia says breathlessly. It's not her fault if the vampire is confusing her. *She's a vampire.*

Lucia grew up hearing the stories. This is what vampires do best. They're sex demons, wanton and sinful. They have no shame in the pleasure of food or who they bed. It's all to get the kill. They were designed for it—wickedness and immorality. The witches have worked hard since the time of the War of Mystics to keep them in line.

Adelaide gets closer and closer, her face only a breath away. Lucia stops breathing, staring up into glittering vermillion eyes.

"It's okay," Adelaide whispers. "I'll keep your secret. No one has to know what you are. What you *really* want."

Adelaide pulls back, slithering smoothly out of the booth. She displays a toothy grin as she looks down at Lucia, whose eyes are wide, her shaky hand pressed against her chest over her quick beating heart.

"Good luck tomorrow, Princess. I'll be first, but I'll still be rooting for you."

Adelaide winks and then she's gone, leaving Lucia feverish and disoriented.

Chapter Thirteen
Two Things are True

Lucia thinks she's going to be sick. There are so many people here for the first trial, and her mother is in the audience somewhere. Lucia hasn't dared try and look for her, but she can hear Gabrielle's whooping and cheering from the sidelines.

The six contestants stand at the starting line of the obstacle course, the end nowhere in sight. They are at the edge of the akokora dei—the *little forest*—that sits in the center of campus between the dorms, with the Siren Lake behind them.

The other contestants are in the uniforms they were given, similar to Lucia's but not the same. They all wear cloaks in different colors and styles, and their boots match their clothes. It's hard for Lucia to rip her eyes from Adelaide down the line, whose cloak is to mid-thigh, fair skin on full display in the expanse between her boots and hem.

Lucia tries to tune out the noise of the crowd and her exploration of Adelaide's distracting outfit as she focuses on Ekrul who is explaining the rules of the first trial. His scaly skin glows under the morning sun, an almost reddish tint to the usual blue, and a black robe over his small shoulders.

"You will all go into the forest," Ekrul says, his voice echoing in her ear, "where a path has been marked out for you. And you will make sure to stay within the path that the lovely witches on staff have cast a charm on to alert them if anyone strays too far. Going off path will result in an automatic disqualification for both teammates."

Ekrul motions to the line of professors standing in the audience, and Lucia's heart skips a beat when she sees her mother standing in the throng. Her mother's eyes gleam with a stern look that says *you better win,* and Lucia's stomach drops. She turns back to the orun-kun, palms pressing into her thighs.

"To win the obstacle, both partners must pass the finish line, and whether you work together or go off on your own is your own choice, but again *you will not be marked as complete until both have finished.* There will be many obstacles—magisk creatures and enchantments—in your way, some dangerous and some meant to test your might, so be warned this will not be easy no matter how strong or fast you may think you are."

Lucia peeks up at Hetan beside her, whose face is a mask of calm determination. The complete opposite of how she's feeling right now, her stomach twisting in knots. Looking down the line, she thinks she might be the only one worried.

Adelaide looks bored, ready to start the trial. Cassius is smiling like a loon, and his partner wears his usual blank expression. Lucia can't see Mia, but she's sure the prodigy witch with the Mallei magisk nature is doing fine. Even if Lucia knew how to use her Sage magisk, an ability of the mind wouldn't be much help here. Not unless they were fighting humans.

"You'll have an hour to complete this trial, and there will be a horn blown at every twenty-minute interval, three blown in your final ten. Only two teams will pass, and both members of the third will be disqualified from competing to be the Orbis Libra's vessel. I'm going to give you the count of dece—*ten*—and then you will start. Ready? Nen, odu, trium, atta—"

Lucia's heart pounds, turning to Hetan, who meets her gaze. He gives her a small nod, mouthing, "*On dece run to the trees' edge and wait for me.*" Lucia is confused, but she trusts her partner. If she wants a chance of winning, she'll have to follow Hetan's lead.

"—octin, novo, dece!"

And with that, the contestants take off. Lucia nearly slips right at the start, still unused to the large, clunky boots, but races to the trees as Hetan said. The wolf is there waiting for her right inside the forest.

"We need to make a plan real quick," Hetan says, his wolf's eyes shining through. He must be using them to see ahead for any traps. "We stay together, and we cross the finish line together. If any obstacles come our way, we'll work through them as a team. I think that's our best course of action, understand?"

Lucia nods.

"Okay, let's go. Stay close."

There are no traps for a while as the pair weave through the trees. It's when Lucia's thighs start burning that she sees the first obstacle, some sort of vine maze with an opening large enough for a person to crawl through.

"Does it look like we can go around?" Hetan asks, scanning along the wall of vines. Lucia takes a step back, trying to see out into the dense forest. From what she can see, there is no other way, but it's hard to tell.

"Maybe we could head left and try to find another way, but I don't think there will be one. No Gaia would take the time to build something this intricate to leave a weak point." Lucia's mother is a Gaia and a powerful one at that. She's seen what they can do. If the professors at Eirini are as good as Lucia thinks, this trap will be airtight, and dangerous.

"Okay, we'll go through."

"Be careful, Gaia can manipulate nature. There could be additional traps beyond a tricky maze."

Hetan nods, peering into the tunnel. It seems to move and writhe like a living, breathing beast. He unsheathes his claws, testing them against the vines. As he tries to hack away at them, there is no damage to the durable plant. Lucia hadn't thought of it, but that rules out the option of having Hetan hack through them rather than playing the maze.

"I think we can both fit side by side, so let's go in together."

Lucia and Hetan climb in on their hands and knees. It's too low to walk normally, so that will be a hindrance for the other teams too. They won't be able to speed through it as quickly. Lucia also has the advantage of knowing a Gaia.

For the other teams, the unknown works against them, since they don't how far the maze goes. Lucia knows some of the limitations of the ability, so she estimates it can't be much more than four hundred meters long. With that, Lucia feels a bit more confident. There are things that she can do after all.

Lucia and Hetan crawl in silence until they come to a fork in the path, five different directions splitting off.

"Do you think they all lead to the end at different places, or could some be dead ends?" Hetan asks, turning to Lucia. She hesitates, looking down each dark path that curves off into another direction.

"I'm... not sure. There are probably dead ends. It would make more sense than having to keep up multiple tunnels. It's also possible there is only one right path. That would allow the wielder to make the tunnel longer..." Lucia groans. She hadn't considered that. The tunnel might be longer than she originally calculated.

"Let's just play it safe," Hetan says, "and keep going straight. Whichever way we go, the choice is only conjecture."

"Right, if it's all guesswork we can't go wrong with either."

The pair heads down the straight path, the tunnel curving left and right, and eventually up, climbing at an incline. Lucia's knees feel bruised from the pressure against the thick vines, her back hurting from being in a hunched position for so long. The deeper they go, the narrower the tunnel gets, and the more Lucia's breathing begins to pick up.

Lucia has never liked confined spaces—too many memories of being locked into closets or going into her wardrobe to hide during panic attacks.

"Is the air getting thinner?" Lucia rasps, feeling lightheaded as she squeezes her wide hips through an even smaller space with Hetan in front of her. There's no longer room for them to go together.

"Lucia, are you okay?" Hetan calls, hearing her harsh panting.

The memory of her mother throwing her into a storage closet at the Dome after she witnessed that vampire burn up plays in Lucia's mind—her echoing cries gone unanswered, fingernails bleeding as she scratched at the stone. She can't even hear Hetan's worried voice as her nails dig into the vines below her, pulling herself along as if in a daze.

"You're all right, you're all right. You're all right," she whispers over and over to herself, closing her eyes and continuing to move forward. She tries not to lock herself in the darkness where her panic will overtake her, focusing on her breathing and the task at hand. It's only the first of who knows how many obstacles. She can't let Hetan down or disappoint her coven. Not so soon. Not without trying.

Lucia keeps her eyes closed and hums her favorite tune from a love song she heard once from an Enchanter during the Summer Solstice celebration the year of her first failed blooming. Though Lucia has never experienced romantic love, nor has she sought it, those words the man sang had struck deep within Lucia since that day. It has been her go-to tune for relaxing.

Finally, the maze opens to a larger room. Lucia nearly falls as the floor drops out beneath her, but she's caught by Hetan and set on her feet. Lucia opens her eyes, letting out a long breath as she gets her shaky nerves under control.

"Are you okay?" Hetan asks. Lucia nods, not wanting to worry him. He shouldn't be focusing on her. It's so unfair. He should be able to compete without being weighed down by her.

"Should we stop for a minute to catch our breath?" Hetan lays a hand on Lucia's arm, his warmth a great comfort as the heat sinks into her skin. She shakes her head.

"I'm good, we should keep going," she says. They're probably already behind the other competition, having stopped at the start of the race and with Lucia holding back the pace. She doesn't have supernatural stamina or speed, nor is she skilled enough to use an Oporaa cantus to help.

The pair keeps going, Hetan taking the place behind Lucia instead so he can see if anything goes wrong. The two of them move quicker, Lucia's arms aching and legs burning as she pushes onward, not even thinking as they turn down random paths and hope for the best. There's no logical decision they can think of, so it's best not to think at all. That motto seems to be working for a while as Lucia finally sees a bright spot of sunlight and trees ahead, crying out to let Hetan know. She starts to move even faster, but she's caught by a vine wrapping around her leg.

Lucia cries out, the maze shifting and expanding as it lifts her by her leg. She doesn't have time to think of modesty as her bodysuit under her competition robe is revealed by the position, and she looks to find that Hetan is in the same state as her, swinging upside down.

"Lucia!" Hetan shouts. He's facing away from her, fighting with the vines. As he releases himself new ones come and grab him up again.

"Hetan, I'm here!"

Lucia is lightheaded, trying to struggle with the sentient plants as they begin dragging her back away from the exit. *No. No.* They're almost out. Lucia can't do that again. She can't get stuck in here.

Lucia tries thinking of a cantus as she kicks her feet and writhes her body hoping the movement will frustrate the vines, though it seems not to be even a minor annoyance. Nothing comes to her mind; blood rushes to her head making her unable to think.

Useless, Lucia. Useless, she bashes herself, tears of frustration stinging her eyes as she's powerless to overcome the vine's grip. Even with what she knows about Gaia, there's nothing she can do to help herself.

"Lucia, don't give up!"

Hetan is close now. She can hear his labored breathing and the sound of flesh against a solid vine. She struggles to bend her head so she can look, and Hetan is slicing his way toward her, cutting and knocking away the vines. This time they split easily. Whoever designed the maze made the vines weaker to enable them to attack. They must have run out of energy after creating the rest of the maze.

Lucia brightens at the realization, wiggling harder as Hetan begins hacking at the vines attached to her as they try to keep their grip and keep her away from Hetan. When he gets the one around her leg, Lucia twists as much as she can, squirming right out of the vines' grasp.

Lucia puts out her arms as she falls headfirst to the tunnel floor, not missing a beat as she begins rushing toward the exit, the space tall enough now for her to crouch. Hetan is the stronger of the two. She just needs to get herself out so he doesn't have to worry about saving her.

The weight on Lucia's chest is lifted as she crosses out into the open forest, the bright sunlight stinging her eyes. Hetan comes crashing out behind her, nearly running into her back as he exits the maze. The vines immediately go still as soon as they are both out, not bothering to chase them.

Lucia nearly collapses in relief, her legs shaking from crawling for so long. As they catch their breath, a horn sounds in the distance.

Twenty minutes are down in the first obstacle.

Lucia and Hetan run, cutting through the forest. They can't waste any more time. They already spent so much time on the first task with an undetermined number of obstacles ahead of them.

"Three!" Hetan shouts out of nowhere, startling Lucia, who almost trips over a log. "There must be three obstacles," he says, "because we've already been running for so long, and there was a lot of distance to the maze. That, plus there are three twenty-minute intervals, probably to give that much time for each t ask."

Lucia thinks over Hetan's words, and she has to agree it makes sense. If it's true and there are only three obstacles, that means they only have two to go. Without knowing which place their team is in, it's hard to determine their likelihood of passing, but if they are indeed in last place, fewer obstacles mean fewer chances to catch up. They'll just have to keep going as hard and fast as they can and hope another team made a mistake.

Lucia was a huge hindrance in the first challenge, so she has to step it up. Even though her lungs burn, she can't stop. She has to drive harder than she had during practice training in the Noxidome.

"Do you hear that?" Hetan whispers, coming to a stop to listen. Lucia stops beside him, trying to strain her ears but she hears nothing.

"No, what is— *Hetan!*" Lucia shouts as Hetan is snatched before she can finish her sentence and pulled off into the sky. She doesn't have time to go after him, mouth still wide in shock and horror, as a second creature comes slithering toward her.

She jumps out of the way of the large beast, its body long and agile with huge webbed wings tucked into its side along scaly red skin.

Lucia hits the ground hard, kicking up dirt and grass. She can feel the bruise forming along her ribs from the impact but can't think too hard about that as the Ere'akahi, or as her mother calls it, Ejof—*the flying serpent*. It twists around and heads straight back for her.

Lucia can't get taken away like Hetan, as she has the least likely chance of getting free. Not only for the competition but for her life, getting caught by the Ejof isn't a good idea. It will take her back to its mountain cave to be dinner.

Lucia dips between the trees, jumping and dodging out of the way as the serpent strikes. She's dripping with sweat, her cloak ripped farther up the sides from throwing herself against the ground and snagging on tree branches.

THE BALANCE OF FATES

Lucia fears she's going to die, her blood boiling under her skin as she tries to outrun and outwit the Ejof. There is only so long she can hold her luck until the creature gets her. It's stronger and faster, a predator made for the hunt.

Lucia almost laughs at the thought that this might be the way she goes out. If she had any breath in her lungs, she might. She had resigned herself somewhat unhappily to the knowledge of her life. It would be long and hard and spent following someone else's rules—her coven, her family, even her mother. Lucia is meant to do so as her ancestors before her, yet here she is running for her life, about to be killed before she can prove herself worthy.

Lucia slips as she rounds a large tree, and the Ejof snatches her in its tail as it unfurls its great wings and takes up into the air. Lucia tries uselessly to dig her fingers into its tough skin, but her nails crack against the armor and she goes limp with resignation in its grasp as she's taken up, up...

She is sobered by the realization that she has done nothing to bring honor to her family, yet she finds peace in the knowledge that she will die fighting for her coven. For her grandmother's place as Eidan.

It's a more noble death than she thinks she deserves.

Lucia closes her eyes, arms spread as she flies up through the tree branches like the great Idkiniu—the deity Griffin of Lucia's beloved coven.

Zruuuuphf-crrrrr—this is the sound Lucia hears before a great piercing cry, and she's pitched sideways toward the trees. Her eyes fly wide and see an unbelievable sight.

Adelaide jumps through the tree to catch the Ejof and flings herself at the great beast, using her razor-sharp claws to tear a gash in its delicate wing. She then races down the Ejof's back toward Lucia and grabs hold of her as the creature loosens its hold.

Adelaide is angry, teeth bared and eyes hard as stone.

Lucia wraps her arms around Adelaide, her heart beating like a drum as the vampire jumps from the flailing tail, dodging the appendage as it nearly whacks them out of the sky, and latches onto the trunk of the nearest tree. She holds

Lucia with one hand, nails digging into the tree with another, and Lucia bites her lip to muffle her cry as they slowly come to a stop.

Lucia slowly opens her eyes, looking up at the vampire. She's shaking from the waves of anger she feels radiating from the usually playful woman, who begins descending the tree, using both hands now as Lucia holds on, arms wrapped around her neck.

When they are on the ground, Lucia checks for the creature, which seems to have slithered off, and takes a huge breath of relief as she collapses against the tree.

"Thank you," Lucia wheezes, wiping sweat from her brow. The vampire is standing still, head bowed and hands clenched at her sides. After a few moments of silence Lucia pushes herself upright, walking toward the vampire on shaky legs. She lays a hand on Adelaide's arm, a small electric shock jolting her where they touch. "Seriously, thank you. I would have died if you hadn't—" Lucia swallows. *"Takke."*

Lucia feels guilty. She may have judged Adelaide too quickly, overhearing her conversation at the gala. They're competing and yet the vampire saved her life when she could have let her die. Lucia mentally kicks herself. This is the exact reason reading minds is a curse, and why she can't jump to a decision about her mother until she knows more.

When Adelaide lifts her head, her loose smile is back in place as if it never left.

"Anytime, Princess. I can't resist a damsel in distress." She looks over the broken tree the Ejof crashed into and leans at an angle, the branches and bushes flattened. Adelaide whistles. "That feishe caused quite the mess."

Lucia nods, still, a bit rattled from that traumatic near-death experience, heart in her throat. She doesn't care why Adelaide saved her, though the thought that she would have saved anyone stings a bit. Lucia won't fool herself into thinking she's special.

"I need to find Hetan," Lucia says, her voice sounding distant to her own ears.

She doesn't even realize she said it aloud until Adelaide says, "So I'm not the only one who's run off from my partner."

Lucia's head snaps to the vampire, the fog clearing from her mind. "You *left* your partner?" she says incredulously. "Why?"

The vampire shrugs. "She was slowing me down. Whining. Honestly, she wasn't much fun."

Adelaide says this like it's all perfectly reasonable, and Lucia's eyes nearly pop out of her head as she stares at the woman crazily.

"My partner would never leave me, first off," Lucia corrects. "And second, do you take this competition seriously at all? You do realize you both need to cross the finish line to win, right?"

Adelaide strides up to Lucia, flicking one of the curls that have fallen loose from her pins. Lucia leans back a bit as the woman invades her space.

"I am aware, but we don't have to cross together. I'm sure the witch is fine; she was holding her own. Give your people some credit, *kuai-yuel*. You're just as capable as the rest of us."

Lucia blushes at the inflection of the word *kuai-yuel,* though she isn't sure what it means. Something in Chiskae, just like that word she used for the flying serpent—*feishe*. In its mother tongue that beast is called the Ere'akahi, and for the witches familiar with their native language of Azes—of which Lucia knows little—it's called Ejof.

A horn blows once again, closer this time. *She's getting close to the finish line.* Lucia looks up at Adelaide. If the vampire is in the same place as her, then it's safe to assume the other contestants might not be too far ahead. She still has a chance!

"I have to go," Lucia says, stumbling away from the vampire. She needs to find Hetan and makes sure he's okay. Her heart aches at the thought he might have been killed by the Ejof, but she has to push that away. Hetan is strong. He's strong, and he got away. They still have a chance of making it to the next trial.

Stay safe, Princess.

Lucia's heart thunders in her chest as she takes off through the woods in the direction Hetan was carried off. Adelaide's unfiltered thoughts play through her head as she runs. *Stay safe.*

"Hetan, where are you? Hetan!"

Lucia runs through the forest shouting Hetan's name. She has been running a long time and has found no sign of him, and she's beginning to worry he might not have gotten away from the creature. A painful pit grows in her stomach at the thought. Hetan has to be okay. *He has to.*

Lucia fears she will never get the chance to tell him the truth about his parents. Would she be punished by the great deities? For being a bad friend—for keeping the truth from him?

Would Hetan gain peace if he died without the truth behind his parents' deaths?

"Lucia, stop it. You're being ridiculous," she mutters. "You'll find Hetan. He probably went on without you. He probably thought you kept going."

Comforted by that thought, Lucia goes on, hoping she'll bump into Hetan soon. She runs along the barrier, a shimmering wall similar to the Merin Korua that borders the major covens. She was pushed towards it during her search for Hetan.

Lucia enters a clearing as the horn blows at the ten-minute mark. Her heart begins racing. *The competition is nearly over.* She wonders how many people have passed and whether she would be informed if it was over yet. As long as there isn't a sign, she will keep going.

The clearing Lucia happens on is not like the rest of the forest. The ground becomes cracked and rocky, making some sort of staggered staircase she has to cross over.

The last obstacle. Lucia is giddy that the end is near. She just has to get past this last test and the finish line should be nearby. The horn didn't sound very far away. Hopefully, Hetan will be on the other side.

Lucia climbs up onto the first platform, the shortest one. Then she jumps to the next. *Not so bad so far.* She wonders whether it was made by the same witch who did the maze. If so, they must be extremely powerful.

Lucia is slow and steady as she jumps across the unstable ground, some higher, some lower, and some with a greater rift between them. She can't be in last place, but she won't risk slipping. She's fairly far off the ground now. If she lands wrong, she could be badly injured and then there's no way she'd be able to finish. Besides, she's exhausted. She doesn't know how she keeps going, but she does.

Lucia is about halfway across when she hears a noise behind her. She turns to see Boen and the vampire Cassius come leaping across the platforms. They're fast, not even looking down as they slowly gain ground on her.

No. If Adelaide's team has passed already, Lucia and Hetan will lose if they pass her. She can't go back to her coven if she loses now.

Lucia quickly jumps to the next platform, her heart thundering as Boen passes her. She's jumping down to one below her when suddenly, they begin shifting, the one she jumped to shooting up higher. Lucia's breath is knocked from her lungs as the rock slams into her stomach, and she scrambles to get herself fully onto the platform before she's knocked off.

All of the platforms are moving up and down, some faster than others. Lucia groans, hoping that Hetan has somehow passed this already because it has suddenly gotten a lot harder. She watches the platform a bit off to the side of her, one that's bigger and moving a bit slower than the others. She'll have to play it a lot safer now.

Lucia lets out a proud huff when she lands on her hands and knees, and she's moving to stand when something bowls her over. Lucia is knocked to the ground, rolling over to the edge of the platform. She lies flat on her back, chest aching from the hit. When she blinks her eyes open, Cassius stands above her, eyes shining brightly and teeth dangerous. The man is grinning wildly down at her.

"There, there, little Griffin, I'll put you out of your misery quick."

Lucia scrambles away from the ledge and away from the crazy vampire. She jumps over to another larger platform, but she hits her head against the rock as her foot is grabbed mid-air.

Oof.

Lucia's head is ringing, and she thinks she might be bleeding. Her vision is blurry as she blinks her eyes rapidly, groping around the ground under her to help her stand to her feet. The vampire lunges at her again, but another figure crashes into him and the two go flying to the next platform.

Lucia is dizzy and terrified as she stumbles on shaky legs toward the edge as the two men fight. It was Boen who jumped, knocking his partner away from her, trying to tug him across the obstacle. Cassius struggles in his grasp, desperate to get back to Lucia. She watches the next platform for a moment, the ground warping in her delirious mind. That hit knocked the sense out of her.

When Lucia looks back, she sees Cassius coming at her again. Boen is heading across the platforms quickly, seeming to have given up on getting his partner under control. Lucia jumps, nearly missing the fast-moving platform, her legs hanging over the side. She scrambles to get atop it and leaps for the next one without thinking. She can't let Cassius catch her. The vampire is crazy, and he seems to be trying to make her fall to her death.

Lucia does this a few more times, hopping platforms and narrowly missing close calls before Cassius is on her again. He knocks her onto her back as the platform shakes and moves.

"What are you doing?" Lucia shouts, trying to push him away. It doesn't seem like he is trying to beat her but *kill* her. "I lose okay; I'll give up. You can go and cross the finish line, just leave me alone!"

"I don't think so, *witch*," Cassius growls through his fangs. He drags Lucia toward the edge of the cliff, her scalp burning as his fingers dig into her hair. Tears burn at Lucia's eyes, her chest heaving with exertion as she tries to dig her boots into the rock to stop his movement. "You're not so strong, are you? What a joke, being born to the Golden Griffin coven and being so weak. I'm sure you've made your family proud."

Adelaide's voice echoes in Lucia's mind as she's hung over the side of the platform—*stay safe.*

Tears drip down her cheeks as she curses her uselessness. This is the second time today she's been at the edge of death and has been unable to do anything but wait for it to come. She is broken. All her life Lucia has been unable to do anything her peers could do. She isn't a good witch, and she's no match for the vampires and wolves. Her body just won't listen to her.

When I shift, I don't imagine becoming something different. I'm not a man and then a wolf, I'm both of them at the same time... Certain experiences can bring one to the forefront, but they're all inside of us...

As Lucia dangles in the vampire's grasp, fingers digging into his tough arms, Hetan's words play back in her mind. What he'd said to her as they trained in the forest.

Is that what she's been doing? Thinking of her magisk as some foreign entity—a stranger within her body that she's trying to tame.

"Goodbye, Hatsia's bairn," Cassius sneers. He lets go of her and she begins to fall. Those words trigger another memory in her. *Well, well, well. If it isn't Hatsia's bairn, herself...* The words of that man outside of the Dome. The man with the skull blade had disappeared without a trace.

Lucia's heart stutters.

Disappeared. Lucia had been so terrified for her sister that she had screamed for him to get away... she had wished that he would just disappear, and he did. Lucia had magisk, even then. She used it to get rid of the man. *She has used magisk before.*

"Itoju—yogun!" Lucia shouts, palms facing toward her feet. When a glittery apparition wavers in her sight and she lands, crumpling down onto an invisible platform, she nearly wails with relief.

"I—I did it," she says in awe. She used her magisk successfully.

"What the hell?" Cassius stares down at Lucia from his moving platform above, angry that Lucia didn't topple to her death. Cassius rides the platform down and tries leaping at her again to knock her off—a fall that he would probably survive—but she's filled with the confidence of accomplishing her first cantus, and her determination not to die like this, not after enduring three near-death experiences in the past month. Her hands come flying up in a cross in front of her and she shouts, "Itoju—uugun!"

Cassius's eyes widen as he's stopped mid-air, the yogun-extension incantation of magisk class—Itoju—creates a barrier around him. Cassius punches and kicks, throwing himself at the shimmering barrier, but it holds strong.

Lucia laughs, a pained sound of joy mixed with disbelief. *She did it. She really did it...*

"Lucia?"

Lucia's heart nearly stops at her name, before she registers the voice. *Hetan?* Lucia turns around, tears of relief springing to her eyes as her eyes meet the wolf's. "*H-Hetan*," she gasps, her heart released from the painful constriction she has felt since he disappeared with the Ejof. A part of her feared he was truly gone. "You're okay."

Hetan collapses against Lucia, wrapping his arms around her in a tight embrace. She winces as her straining muscles and bruises are tugged, but she's too happy to make him pull away. When he finally does, it's with a twinge of sadness that she lets him go.

"We have to go," Hetan says, eyeing a furious Cassius shouting profanities muffled from within Lucia's Itoju. "If we make it back before the horn, we win, Lucia. Cassius won't be able to move."

Lucia's eyes widen moving from Cassius to her partner as his words sink in. Cassius is stuck here. He can't cross the finish line...

"We can win."

Lucia and Hetan leap across the last obstacle, crashing through the forest toward the finish line. Nearly the whole campus is there waiting on the other side of the forest. Lucia's mother and Gabrielle stand there, her sister with a smile and Hatsia with an unreadable look on her face. But Lucia thinks she sees a twinkle of something in her eye. Perhaps she's *proud* of Lucia.

The other contestants—Adelaide, Mia, and Boen are there. Boen's eyes widen in surprise as he doesn't see Cassius with them. Many people look to be in shock that it's Lucia's team coming up.

Lucia grips Hetan's hand tighter, her chest feeling like it might burst as they pass the orun-kun waving a white flag, collapsing in a heap at the feet of the crowd. A hysteric laugh explodes from Lucia's lips as she lies in the grass, the cool breeze blowing her ripped and dirty cloak.

She passed the first trial.

Chapter Fourteen
What Not to Do at Parties

LUCIA ACHES ALL OVER, and her head is full of cotton. Despite the soreness, she feels quite happy and giggly.

"That's the tonic," a high, young voice says.

Lucia blinks her eyes open to blue hair, deep like the Valbien Sea. It glitters in the dim light as the moon shines outside the large windows.

"You're in the medical wing of the Academy building, you were badly bruised from the first trial. I gave you some herbs to help with the worst of it."

The girl comes to stand beside Lucia. She gently pulls back the collar of her dress and replaces the herbs over her shoulder on a bruise that is particularly bad from Cassius's hits, the skin a deep purple, splitting where the impact busted the skin.

"Himari—" Lucia breathes. She hasn't seen the young healer in more than a year. The girl had grown up at the Golden Griffin estate but was sought after for her gifts. She left to study at Eirini a year ago. Lucia has been so distracted with the Triune, she forgot.

Himari gives Lucia a small, shy smile as she pulls back. "You've been sleeping the entire day, Lady Lucia. You were quite exhausted. But you'll make a full recovery, just make sure you don't get into any more fights with vampires."

Lucia snorts, warmth spreading through her chest at the familiar face. "I promise I'll try," she says.

Back in her room, Lucia is snuggling down into her warm, comfortable bed when the door bursts open. She jumps, eyes flying wide as she stares at her sister in the doorway.

"Gabrielle!" she cries as her sister skips over and plops on the end of the bed, dropping the bags in her hands. When Lucia tries to reach for them, she snatches them away.

"What are you doing in here?" Lucia asks. "It's late, I'm going to bed."

Gabrielle's eyes widen in horror like Lucia saying that is a crime. "It isn't even midnight! Besides, you can't sleep, we're going to a party. *Your* party."

Lucia looks at Gabrielle like she's crazy. *A party? What is she even talking about?*

"My party? How am I having a party, Gabrielle? I just got out of the medical wing."

"Well... it isn't your party necessarily, but it's for all the finalists of the first trial. The vampires are throwing it in their dorm."

"No way."

"*Yes,* way," Gabrielle whines. She pulls a dress out of the bag she is holding, a thin, lacy white dress. It doesn't look like it would reach past Lucia's knees. Her mother would lay her on a pyre and set her aflame if Lucia was caught out in it.

"I am not wearing that, Gabrielle, what are you thinking? Are you trying to set me an early death?"

Gabrielle looks at it like she's trying to figure out what the issue is, before clutching it to her chest. "Fine, I'll wear it then. But if you say you're not wearing this then that means you are going right? Just please don't wear one of your stuffy old lady dresses that cover every inch of skin."

"Gabrielle!"

No matter how many times Lucia says her name her sister is not listening. What part of *she's trying to sleep, she feels like she got run over by a carriage* is not registering in Gabrielle's mind?

Gabrielle takes Lucia's hands up in hers, squeezing them. Her voice is soft when she says, "I knew you could do it, Lucia. I knew you would win. Don't you deserve a night to have fun? To celebrate. Mother isn't here, or Grandmother, or any of those old bats on the elder council. Live a little, Luc. You won, you did a good thing—showed those elders that you have what it takes to follow grandmother's footsteps."

Lucia bites her lip, her heart beating fast from her sister's praise. She's right. *Lucia did it.* Lucia wishes she could see their faces right now, everyone who gave her *that look,* that hated look, and said the Mother was angry with her.

Lucia used magisk, and she passed the first trial of the Triune. She wouldn't have been able to do it without Hetan, or Adelaide who had to save her from the Ejof, but it's still something.

"Now come on, let's get you dressed," Gabrielle says, seeing the acceptance in Lucia's eyes. "I've never even seen you show a slip of skin. I don't think I know what your elbows look like. *Your elbows!"*

Lucia pushes her shoulder. "You've seen my elbows, Gab; you used to help the handmaidens dress me."

"Okay, well, that's not the point, is it? I'm not the one who needs to see you naked."

Lucia raises an eyebrow. "And who is it that needs to see me naked?"

"Anyone! Or, not anyone, obviously. I'd murder anyone who tried to peep on you. I just mean you need to get out there and seduce some lucky bastard. You're hot, and you're young. You need to stop thinking of what Mother would think and live a little."

Lucia's face blooms in embarrassment. She does not need to live, not like that at least. Boys are not on her mind right now.

"No one needs to see that, not until I'm married. It's against the Holum Actus," Lucia says.

"Fine, you're a tough cookie. But I'm still helping you pick out the dress."

• • •

Lucia is undeniably nervous. She's never been to a party before. Not one that wasn't crawling with elders and her mother around the corner. The baby blue silk piece around her waist feels suffocating, and she has to rub the flaming moon hanging around her neck for strength.

"You'll be fine, Lucia, this isn't like back home. You're wonderful, and anyone would be an idiot not to see it."

Lucia nods, taking a deep breath as she looks up at the vampire dorm. It's much taller than the other buildings, the spires at night standing stark against the dark sky like they're piercing the moon.

Gargoyles stare down at Lucia, watching her every move, judging her for daring to enter. The dark water of the moat glistens under the moon, and she thinks she sees something moving within its murky shadows.

When Lucia is safely inside the building, it feels as if her mother's eyes are on her, even within the vampire's walls. She tries not to think what the coven would think of her, knowing she willingly entered the vampires' den.

Lucia shakes her head. *What is she thinking?* The vampires are no different from the witches, and neither are their living quarters. A little darker, maybe, but not odd. Not *too* odd. The floors are all wood, with vaulted ceilings and murals covering the walls. She's mesmerized by the work. She never would have pictured from the outside that it would be this beautiful within.

Across the cracked walls are paintings of what Lucia assumes to be the War of Clans. There are vampires and witches on either side. The paintings are almost abstract, the blood—splatters of red and pink—the soldier's deformed figures with claws and pointed teeth. Flashes of color like bombs depict the witches' magisk. But the couple, her eyes are drawn to them. They're the most realistic thing there.

Lucia runs her fingers over the lovers amidst the battle. The woman and man cling to one another, their eyes desperate as they hold each other close, molded to each other's bodies. Blood pools on the ground around their feet. Lucia traces the teardrop trailing the woman's dirtied face, and it takes effort to tear her eyes away.

When she does, she notices Gabrielle is gone.

"Giuseppe H. Skullkin," a voice says near Lucia's ear. Lucia nearly jumps in surprise she was so distracted. She turns to find Adelaide beside her. The color around her eyes is a dark red, with red and silver streaked beneath them like falling tears, and she wears an intricate headpiece made of metal and chain and shining crystals that highlight the Skullkin's immense wealth. Blood money, many would say.

They're in the dorm's common room on the first floor, the sound of chatter and music loud from out in the hall. The two of them are alone. Lucia's face burns hot as she turns back to the wall.

"The piece," Adelaide continues, "was made by my great-uncle when this dorm was first built. He was an amazing painter and has pieces all over Hontaras. He mastered almost every style, but this... was his most underrated. No one would allow him to paint it anywhere else, so he put it here at Eirini. Back then, it wasn't even an academy yet. No one wanted to come here. The idea of vampires and witches studying together sounded mad. It was meant to be sacred land, a place where Mystics could come together, but not everyone liked that idea, and horrible atrocities were committed here before it was turned into an academy. If only he could see it now."

Lucia tilts her head to get a better look. Her face gets hotter the more she looks at it, the piece's intricacies revealed to her. It's quite an erotic piece, very vulnerable and open. She can almost read exactly what Giuseppe felt when he created it. She feels creeping jealousy for whoever inspired it.

Sweating, Lucia extracts herself from between Adelaide and the wall, stuttering, "I-It's beautiful. Very beautiful."

The pair circle each other for a minute, eyeing one another as they pretend they're looking at the art. Eventually, Adelaide says, "Join me. I'll show you around."

Lucia hesitates, looking out at the common room, crowded even despite how big it is. She should go and look for Gabrielle. She worries about not keeping an eye on her here. Then she remembers Gabrielle's quite good at taking care of herself. If she wanted Lucia hanging on her all night, she wouldn't have run off at the first opportunity. And Lucia does owe the vampire for saving her. The least she can do is stick around for a few minutes.

"Okay," Lucia says, following Adelaide into the busy room. She's mesmerized by the light that hits the crystals dangling on the vampire's headpiece.

The room is almost too dark, a hypnotic red haze over everything. Lucia coughs from the smoke, which seems to stick in the back of her throat. She tries not to look too hard into the dark corners of the room, following closely to the vampire so she doesn't get lost in the crowd.

"Kai," Adelaide says, approaching a boy with two-toned hair, blond and brown. He's small with short little fangs that peek out from his gums as he smiles wide at Adelaide. "Two drinks, make the witch's light."

Kai looks from Adelaide to Lucia, eyeing the witch up and down. "Got it," he says, turning to the bar—which, Lucia notes, the witches do not have in their dorm—and begins mixing a few different glowing bottles. It looks nothing like the lavender wine Lucia has at coven gatherings.

Adelaide nods, taking the drinks, and turns to hand one to Lucia. Lucia is hesitant as she watches the vampire throw her drink back. She smells it first and gets a fragrant, floral smell, which is nice.

"It's stronger than you're used to, Princess, but it won't kill you."

Lucia narrows her eyes, the cup halfway to her lips. "How would you know what I'm used to?"

Adelaide smirks, leaning back against the bar. She raises her voice over the pounding music— Lucia has no idea where it's coming from as she doesn't see any Enchanters around.

"I *know*," Adelaide says smugly, eyebrow raised as she looks Lucia up and down. Lucia should take offense to that, but she knows it's true. She just scoffs and quickly throws back her drink, wincing as it goes down.

Lucia smacks her lips, surprised that she doesn't hate it. It does make her lips a bit numb though.

"Witches tend to like that one," Adelaide says with a wink, and Lucia shouldn't feel a sinking feeling in her stomach at the thought of these *"other witches"*.

Lucia turns away from Adelaide's intense gaze under the red lights, gripping her drink tighter. Her heart is beating too fast. Though she's only had one drink, she feels intoxicated. The music changes, beating to the pace of Lucia's pulse, and Adelaide holds out a hand decorated with rings.

"Dance with me."

"Oh no. Not again." Lucia tries to resist when Adelaide pulls her up.

"Yes, come on, Princess."

Lucia tries to turn away, not wanting her head to get mixed up with the feelings from the last time they shared a *too-intimate* dance, but Adelaide spins her and then dips, staring long into her eyes.

Though her words are a whisper, Lucia can hear every one.

"You're so alive, Lucia. Let me be alive with you."

Lucia has no idea what the vampire means, but she doesn't fight as Adelaide slowly pulls her to the dance floor. Her eyes don't leave the vampire's bright red gaze, even when someone bumps into her. She listens to the music distantly, watching the way Adelaide rolls and sways her hips. She remembers what Adelaide told her when they danced at the gala, which already seems so long ago. That there were no rules. That it was about feeling your partner's energy.

THE BALANCE OF FATES

Lucia's movements are stilted at first, getting used to the way Adelaide dances again, but Adelaide guides her, hands hovering over her hips until they're moving in sync.

Lucia raises her arms over her head, something heavy and stuck lifting from her chest. Music in a language Lucia doesn't understand blares from the rattling speakers, the haunting melody wrapping around the dancers. The vampires are moving so quickly they're blurring right in front of Lucia's eyes. The pulse of the music is fast, and Lucia is swept up in the adrenaline, sweating, her heart beating fast as she follows Adelaide's steps.

When Lucia closes her eyes, it almost feels like she's floating, drifting in the current of the bass and writhing bodies. Adelaide is fluid like the tide, going in and out, moving Lucia's body as she sees fit. Lucia doesn't have to worry about her mother or other witches watching like at the gala. She's free to give herself up to the madness and lets herself be swept offshore into the greater unknown.

"That was—" Lucia rushes to catch her breath as the third... fourth... she has no idea how many songs they danced, ends. Lucia and Adelaide stand in the middle of the floor among dancing bodies, but Lucia's stamina is not as great as the vampire's and she's already exhausted. The courage from her drink has begun to fade, burned up as she moved and sweat.

Lucia wipes the damp beads from her forehead and fans her hot face.

"Let's let you rest for a bit," Adelaide says, guiding Lucia away from the dancing. "I forget sometimes, you witches have more needs than the undead."

Lucia's eyebrows furrow in displeasure at Adelaide's wording.

"Why do you keep saying that? That you're *dead*," Lucia questions. Adelaide pulls her down to the couch, and Lucia is aware of the vampire's heat and the way their legs almost touch. Adelaide turns, bending her knee so she's facing Lucia.

"I *am* dead. In the ways that matter."

Lucia's eyes roam over Adelaide's face, her smooth, tan skin. She wears a long, sleeveless black dress with golden chains around her shoulders that drape down to connect at the center of her chest where a spider amulet sits between her breasts. Lucia blushes trying not to stare too hard, but Adelaide's chest rises and falls. Her heart beats.

"You aren't dead," Lucia whispers. "If you were you wouldn't be here talking to me. You wouldn't have wants and needs, or—" Lucia is hesitant as she lifts her hand. Her heart is in her throat as she stares at it, afraid to meet Adelaide's questioning gaze. She touches Adelaide, her hand soft on the vampire's bare skin as she places a hand on her chest. "I wouldn't be able to touch you."

The room is quiet as Lucia watches the rise and fall of Adelaide's chest under her hand. She almost startles and pulls back when the vampire catches her hand, pushing it harder against her scorching skin. Lucia nearly stops breathing herself, looking up to meet the vampire's gaze.

"Do you feel that? Nothing. My chest rises not because it has to, but so I won't stand out. I don't want anything," Adelaide says. "I care for nothing."

Lucia shakes her head, caught by that stare and her hand in Adelaide's.

"That's not true. You're in the Triune and you cared enough to win. You cared enough to... to save me."

Adelaide's face scrunches in like she is trying to understand Lucia's words. As if wanting or caring about anything is a foreign concept to her. They sit like that for a while, just looking at one another, before a body drops beside them, startling the pair.

Lucia pulls back, her heart thundering from the intimate moment. It takes her a moment to realize a body is draping itself over Adelaide's lap.

"I figured you could use another drink." That same boy from before hands Lucia another glass as he plops on Lucia's empty side. "Both of you," he says with a wink, nodding to the woman crawling all over Adelaide. Lucia is confused by what he means at first, but when the understanding hits, she gasps.

"*Master Adelaide*," the woman practically moans, baring her neck to the vampire. The scantily clad witch looks up at Adelaide with seductive eyes, a familiarity in the way she moves against her. When Adelaide sinks her menacing fangs into the pulse, Lucia clenches her eyes shut, turning away from the sight. It was easy to forget Adelaide was a vampire as they spoke and danced—to forget what it *meant to be a vampire.*

She doesn't know if she is more sickened that a witch would willingly bare her neck as if she were a feast or that Adelaide would take her up on the offer. From the looks of it, not for the first time.

"Adelaide," a deep voice calls, drawing Lucia's attention and that of the feeding vampire. Cassius stands with a hip cocked, shuffling some sort of flashing cards in his hands. He wears a sheer top, and his two braids hang down the sides of his face as he leans in, pushing aside the woman Adelaide's feeding on.

"It's your brother," Cassius says. "You have to go to him right away."

Adelaide is quick to jump to her feet, a worried look passing over her eyes. She turns to Lucia, who is still stunned on the couch. "I'll be back," she says in a rush, before hurrying after the man. Kai hops up and follows.

Lucia is wide-eyed, still clutching her drink and wondering what just happened. She turns to the witch who is lying against the arm of the couch looking loopy and dizzy with pleasure.

Lucia downs the second drink and stands, needing to get out and get some air. She's a bit light on her feet from the haze and the strong spirits, pushing through the crowd trying to find the exit. Her head is swimming, and everything is red. She keeps imagining Adelaide's teeth in that woman's throat, sucking her blood, until the image blurs together and it's her lips on *Lucia's* neck. Lucia doesn't notice someone is in front of her until she bumps into them, stumbling back from the collision.

"Sorry—Gabrielle?"

Lucia clutches her sister's arms. Gabrielle looks drunk. And upset. Lucia is immediately worried. "Gabrielle, what—" A memory plays in front of Lucia's eyes. One that doesn't belong to her:

He's beautiful, Gabrielle thinks, watching as a tall, black-haired vampire heads out alone to the balcony. The music and the noise from the gala play behind her, but all she sees is him—Siphon Skullkin. The mysterious older Skullkin sibling.

Checking to make sure no one is watching, Gabrielle slinks over to the double doors and quickly slips out after him. The balcony is long, with large plants scaling the sides, and vines wrapped around the railing. The angered sky has settled now—though it still smells like rain, heavy and woodsy—clear as the moon stretches out on the horizon, illuminating Siphon. He stares out over the city, and his coal-black hair looks like it's bleeding out into a halo of stars, blending with the sky.

Gabrielle hesitates at the door for a minute, afraid to break the calm, pleasing sight, but she comes to stand beside the vampire.

"Hele," comes Siphon's voice, low and flat. It's pleasant but weary, and for an instant, Gabrielle questions whether she should have followed him out here or left him to be alone. He turns to look at her and his eyes are the darkest of greens like the leaves of a Twilight fir, staring so intensely that she can't meet them for long.

He makes her nervous. Huh. Gabrielle didn't know that was possible.

The silence grows long and uncomfortable between them, Gabrielle's palms sweating as she grips the railing tightly. She tries to make her voice work, to say something rather than stand there like a coward. She looks out at the city stretched before them; the city of Olympia doesn't sleep, even after the sun goes down. People move about the streets like ants, illuminated in the neon glow of tavern signs and night markets.

"It's beautiful," Gabrielle finally says. "I've always loved the city. I prefer it to the countryside, where everything is slow and ancient. The city is full of humans and all of their odd inventions."

Siphon only grunts in response, but that doesn't stop Gabrielle. When she starts, it's hard to get her to stop. Her arms flail as she speaks about all of the things she wants to see and how she longs to get out of Laesbury. Going to Eirini

Academy is going to be the breath of freedom she has been waiting for, away from judging witches and her mother's moaning over what Gabrielle does and wears, and her fascination with different. Her coven has never understood that.

And, though she feels shame for thinking it, Gabrielle will be able to get away from Lucia. Her big sister, the firstborn, to whom she is always compared. *Gabrielle, you have to apply yourself... Gabrielle your magisk is better than your sister's so you can't throw away your talents. Gabrielle... Gabrielle...*

Gabrielle doesn't want to be a backup in case her sister fails. She wants adventure. She wants love. She won't settle for anything less than absolute worship.

Maybe Siphon, a strikingly beautiful vampire, can give her that.

Gabrielle peers up at Siphon from under her lashes, trying to look seductive. He hasn't said a word since she began speaking, standing there silent as the night after a storm.

"I must go back inside," Siphon says curtly, turning to leave. Gabrielle lifts her head from where it rested atop her arms on the railing, her eyes widening in distress.

"Wait!" she says, desperate to make the vampire stay. She can't just let him slip through her fingers. This is the first time she's finally getting to meet one and there's so much she has to say.

Growing up, Gabrielle's grandmother used to tell her horror stories about vampires, stories that gave Lucia nightmares but only left Gabrielle curious for more. As she grew older, so did her interest, intrigued by the dangerous, lustful, powerful demons of the night. Demons that did what they wanted and were free. Free to explore their every desire. Gabrielle has so many questions. Things she planned to say are now stuck in her throat.

What is bloodlust like?

How does blood taste—is it sweet?

Do they need it to survive, or can they eat normal food too?

What does it feel like to hurt someone, to kill? To crush someone's bones just because it'd be easy... An uncontrollable impulse.

Siphon is frozen in the light over the door, and Gabrielle notices for the first time that he almost looks sad. His mind isn't here, his eyes looking far past her.

"Siphon—"

A noise rips from the vampire's throat, low and long, a pained mixture between a growl and a groan. Siphon doubles over, grabbing his head as if in pain. Like something is splitting his head in two.

Gabrielle tries to run to him, terrified by what is happening. The look on his face is frightening, and she's scared for him.

Siphon holds out a hand to stop her. "Don't get any closer."

Gabrielle hovers her arms out to let him know she won't hurt him. "Should I get you help?" She moves to grab the handle leading back into the ballroom.

"No! I can't go in there," Siphon pants. "Leave. You shouldn't even be here. Haven't you ever heard it isn't safe to be alone with a vampire?" He backs into the corner of the balcony to let her get to the door.

Gabrielle shakes her head. "I don't care. I'm not some weak witch. I'm not afraid of you." She strides forward, forgetting about her nerves. She's Gabrielle Dol'Auclair, the youngest child and badass. When has she ever been hesitant about anything? "I've heard all about vampires. My grandmother used to rant about them endlessly. It doesn't matter to me."

"It should," Siphon growls, his eyes flashing bloody red at her. The lovely green is gone, swallowed by scarlet, but Gabrielle thinks they're just as stunning. His teeth are different, too, fangs elongated and sharp as daggers. Gabrielle shakes her head, tossing aside the warning.

"Where does it hurt? Just your head?"

Siphon growls, the sound cutting through her like rumbling thunder. "Serious?" he asks. "Do you have a death wish? One wrong move and I lose control; you'd be dead in seconds."

Gabrielle doesn't respond. She has no answer. Sometimes, she doesn't even understand the things she does. She just feels something, and she acts on it. There's no prize or praise for sitting back and waiting for things to come to you.

There is no prize for second place, and you don't get to cash in regrets. She lives her life for now, and her head is telling her to go to Siphon.

Gabrielle grabs Siphon's face in her hands, tilting it down to her. The vampire looks stunned, his mouth wide in shock. Gabrielle tends to do that to people.

Gabrielle has to stand on her toes, even in heels. Leaning in so close, she can feel the unusual heat emanating from Siphon's skin. She blows gently across the bridge of his nose and forehead and Siphon's eyes flutter shut. He blinks in confusion, the red bleeding from his eyes as the green makes another appearance.

Im-It Sinaxiam—*Breath of calm.*

It's a cantus Gabrielle perfected years ago to help Lucia when she had panic attacks. It pained her to see her sister so vulnerable and in pain all the time and she wanted to do something about it.

Gabrielle pulls back, but she doesn't let go. She stares into Siphon's eyes, which now have their full attention on her. "If you were truly a danger to me, you wouldn't be so worried about hurting me," she whispers.

Gabrielle has heard a lot of things about vampires over the years, some true and some wildly unbelievable. Mostly things to try and scare little frightened witches. Siphon doesn't seem like any of them, but even he doesn't seem to think so.

"Does that happen a lot?" she asks. She's not even sure what that is. *Is he sick? Can vampires even get sick?*

Siphon doesn't answer. He slowly leans down, and she holds her breath as he lays a kiss on her cheek, breath like fire on the side of her face.

"Go back inside, little witch," he whispers, a smirk crossing his lips. "It's cold, and there are dangers all around."

With a smile on her lips, Gabrielle leaves the way she came, slipping quietly out of the doors. She thinks she's free when she runs right into someone, a squeak drowning under the music as the figure goes flying back. Gabrielle thinks quickly, summoning her hooked club to her hand, the amethyst glinting under white lights as it hooks around the woman, keeping her on her feet.

"Caitlyn?" Gabrielle's eyes go to the closed balcony doors at the same time as her friend's. She smiles. *Don't be suspicious...*

The room comes flooding back to Lucia. She drops hard to the floor of the vampires' common room, disoriented as the room rights itself. She stares up at Gabrielle, who looks concerned.

"Are you okay, Lucia? Have you had too much to drink?" Gabrielle laughs at her own question, wobbling in her heels—because she actually *has* had too much to drink. And Lucia is standing slowly, still so confused and disoriented. She was *inside* Gabrielle's head. Not just hearing her thoughts or seeing flashes of events through her eyes, but she was reliving that moment with Siphon at the gala as if she was Gabrielle.

What is happening?

Lucia stumbles away mumbling to Gabrielle that she's going to get some air. Now she *really* needs it. She can't quite make sense of the things she saw in Gabrielle's head, her sister's thoughts about her and the coven and this *Siphon*. He's the same man Lucia saw from under the stairs. The vampire Adelaide had been speaking to when she said that nasty thing about her.

Wait—*Siphon*. That name clicks again, the name that Cassius whispered to Adelaide right before she disappeared. He had said that Siphon was "acting odd."

Lucia stumbles out onto the front lawn trying to piece together everything that has happened tonight. It's quiet, with no noise coming from inside the dorm, even though it was just deafening inside.

Lucia takes a deep breath, the air cooling her heated flesh, refreshing after all of the smoke and fog.

Lucia turns, heading to the stone bench along the building, but stops in her tracks at the sight of beaming red. The night is dark, with clouds covering the sky, so she can't make out much of a face, only a silhouette.

Lucia goes to call out, Siphon's face still in her mind as she strains to see the man's face. When the clouds part for a moment, the breath is knocked from her as all she sees are the eyes of a predator. Cassius. The vampire is Cassius Draik.

The last time Lucia was alone with him was bad. She'd like to think it was only the competition, but the look in his eyes is saying otherwise.

"W-Where's Adelaide?" Lucia calls, looking around to see if the woman is nearby. They had gone off together.

Cassius doesn't answer, his eyes trained on her. Lucia swallows, backing away slowly. With predators there are two big rules of thumb: either move slowly and look non-threatening, or run. As soon as the vampire starts following her, saliva dripping down its chin like a rabid dog, Lucia knows which one she's dealing with... *Run.*

Chapter Fifteen

Vampires Can Play Doctor

Lucia turns, sprinting away from Cassius. Her muscles ache as she runs across the massive lawn. She can't turn and make it to the vampire's dorm because he stands between her and the door and she can't be sure they would protect her even if she made it there. Her body is still suffering from the first trial, but she knows she can't stop running. She saw it in the vampire's eyes—he wants blood. He looked like the horror stories Lucia grew up hearing. She needs to get to the witches' dorms.

"Y-yogun," Lucia tries to call, her voice shaky. The vampire's too fast. Lucia can't concentrate while running full out, fear shaking her. *It's too far, she'll never make it.*

Lucia curses the large campus. She screams as she falls to the ground, slipping over soft grass as the vampire swipes at her side. She throws her arms out to push him and give the vampire something other than her soft underbelly to swipe at. Her hands knock away the wild arms for a moment as her eyes lock with his.

"Uugun!" Lucia shouts, hoping to replicate earlier that morning, how she trapped him in an Itoju cantus, but nothing happens. Claws rake out, slicing the skin of Lucia's cheek as she turns her head at the last moment. His movements are jerky and feral, so Lucia is able to catch him off guard, shoving him as his fingers raze the ground, sending grass and dirt flying.

Lucia turns, scrambling to her feet as the vampire is flung to his back. But she doesn't get far before the vampire is on her again. Cassius knocks her face-first into the dirt, a sharp branch digging painfully into her forearm. Lucia cries out as the thin skin of her wrist is torn.

Cassius has got his claws around her neck, keen points nicking her skin, and just when Lucia thinks it's all over, the weight is suddenly lifted from her back. She turns in time to see the vampire sprawled on his back in the grass. Adelaide is crouched in front of her, between her and Cassius, hissing like a furious viper ready to strike.

Tears of joy spring to Lucia's eyes at the sight of her vampire. *She came back.*

"Cassius," Adelaide growls, eyes widening with shock and anger. Cassius leaps back onto his feet, facing off against Adelaide as she yells, *"Touch her, I dare you!"*

Lucia watches in horror as they both strike, leaping toward one another in sync. Lucia holds her bleeding arm, shaking as she tries to stand. She feels dizzy, and the movements of the fight are too fast to keep up with. She might be sick.

Lucia is stumbling toward the dorm to try and find help when Cassius sends Adelaide flying and turns back to her. Lucia is frozen in place out of fear, lightheaded from the blood loss and aching prior injuries. Not a single cantus is coming quickly enough to her mind.

"No!" Adelaide shouts, sprinting to get to Cassius before he gets to Lucia, his arms out, ready to deal her a deadly blow.

Wham!

Another figure appears in the night, coming from the side and tackling the crazed vampire.

It's Siphon. Lucia recognizes him. He looks exactly as he had in Gabrielle's memory. Long-limbed, his pale skin glowing silver in the moonlight. Lucia can see why her sister thought he was beautiful. Siphon's hair is onyx, whipping around his face as he fights.

Lucia is in awe of the way he moves, so quickly and his movements are fluid like water. A ripple across the moonlit lawn. He subdues Cassius quickly, pinning him to the ground.

The feral vampire stops struggling, going limp under Siphon's grasp. He is no match for the eldest Skullkin, who takes him down him with quick, graceful moves, his dark cloak billowing behind him.

"I'm sorry," Cassius croaks. "I don't know what came over me." His voice is rough, like two boulders clashing against one another. The vampire looks horrified. He looks over to Adelaide from where his head is pushed into the grass, eyes less clouded and confused than they were when he was chasing Lucia. But Adelaide's gaze is harsh and unforgiving, her teeth bared at him in a warning.

"I've got him," Siphon says, his voice heavy with strain. "Go help the witch."

Lucia looks up as she hears a pained shout. A small figure rushes across the grass like a shadow. Kai throws himself down beside Cassius, pulling the man's face into his hands.

"What happened?" Kai shouts, looking up at Siphon who is pinning him. "Why are you hurting Cassius?"

Adelaide stares at her brother for a long moment, some sort of understanding passing between them. "Make sure this never happens again, or I will," Adelaide growls.

Siphon nods.

Lucia doesn't hear the rest of the small vampire's protests. She recognizes him as Kai, the man she had met earlier as Adelaide takes her arm, leading her back to the vampires' dorms.

"Come," she says when Lucia tries to resist.

"Shouldn't we go to the healer? And wouldn't it be a bad idea to go in there when..." Lucia raises her bloody arm. She has been attacked by one feral vampire tonight, she doesn't want to double it.

"Too far," Adelaide barks, her eyes hard and angry. "Besides, we're not animals, we can control ourselves."

Lucia doesn't mention the event that just happened where a vampire didn't control himself. Her head is foggy as she leans on Adelaide. Besides, the look in the vampire's eyes right now is already scary enough.

Lucia's first party, mauled by a vampire.

Lucia is led upstairs to a room she assumes is Adelaide's. The vampire's room is much bigger than Lucia's, the walls a deep red, and the carpet soft under her feet. Lucia wants to sink into it. She's so exhausted as the adrenaline settles, her eyes drooping as she lets Adelaide guide her to a large, stuffed settee in front of a huge vanity mirror.

"I'll be back, don't move."

Lucia nods absently, not really listening to what she said. She doesn't think she could move if she wanted.

Adelaide returns a minute later with a bucket of warm water and some rags. "Sau-sau—er *sorry*—I don't own medicine for obvious reasons, but I was able to find some salve for the cuts." Adelaide motions for Lucia to lift her arms. The witch does so reluctantly, wincing as it tugs on the old and new cuts.

When Adelaide begins pulling off her dress, Lucia quickly puts her arms back down and stands, wobbling from the quick movement and loss of blood.

"What are you doing?" Lucia gasps. Adelaide pushes her back down before she can topple over.

"You're in no condition to be modest, Princess. I can't clean your cuts while you're in that torn-up dress, and if I remember correctly, you people do die from stupid shit like that. Now stop being stubborn."

Lucia bares her teeth at the nickname and the insult but sits still to let Adelaide do what she has to. Lucia feels a dizzy spell and groans, holding her head. She is still a bit muddled by the spirits and the blood loss.

Lucia doesn't resist when the strings of her corset are loosened, and her top garments are removed. Her face is a furnace by the time she's left in her white chemise and ripped stockings. Lucia appreciates that Adelaide only rips the bloodied right sleeve of her chemise to get to the cut without leaving her bare.

The vampire sits beside Lucia on the cushion and begins cleaning the dirt and grass from her wound. By the time she's wrapping it, Lucia is half asleep and swaying in her seat. Adelaide pats her cheek to rouse her.

"Not yet, Princess."

Lucia groans. She can hardly keep her eyes open.

The vampire finishes wrapping and grabs a large T-shirt for her to put on. Lucia stares at it blankly. "A *T-shirt?*"

It's human clothing, a long black shirt with a large pair of red lips stretched across it. She has never worn something so common, not even to bed.

"It's comfortable," Adelaide says. "And there's no way you're getting in my bed in that bloody monstrosity."

Getting in her bed? "I am not sleeping here," Lucia says. "I have to get back to my room."

"You're not going anywhere in this state, *shi?*" Adelaide says, clearly frustrated.

Lucia starts to the door. "I'll be fine." She wobbles after a few steps and would have collapsed if not for Adelaide catching her. A knock on the door has them both stiffening for a moment before Adelaide sets Lucia back on the settee and makes her way to the door. Lucia covers herself with her arms as the boy from earlier, Kai, stands in the doorway. He averts his eyes when he sees her.

"I—uh, I got some things," he says, handing a covered dish to Adelaide. "It will help the witch regain strength from the blood loss."

His eyes are red-rimmed and he's shaking a bit. He looks like he's going to open his mouth to say something, and then he closes it. Then he opens it again.

"Cassius will be... he will be fine. Nothing like this will happen again."

Adelaide stares at Kai for a long moment. The vampire's eyes are on the floor.

"Look at me, fledgling," Adelaide snarls. His eyes snap up to hers. "Cassius is a... He's..." She sighs, clear annoyance on her face. "We'll deal with it tomorrow, in the box."

Kai nods, his shoulders relaxing.

"Xiex," Adelaide whispers gratefully, motioning to the tray. The smaller vampire passes over a pitcher of orange liquid before disappearing. Adelaide closes the door and makes her way back to Lucia, setting the things on the vanity. She uncovers the dish to a plate of steaming fish and beans.

"It's squeezed fruit," Adelaide says when she sees Lucia eyeing the pitcher.

Lucia rolls her eyes. She knows what juice is, she has just never had any that was orange before.

"I can't eat right now," she whines. "I need to sleep."

"Eat first," Adelaide says, a vein throbbing in her temple at Lucia's stubbornness. "Kai studied medicine, and he says you should eat this, so do it."

Adelaide removes her twisted headpiece and lays it on her vanity. Lucia watches as the vampire stares at her reflection in the mirror, an almost sad expression on her face. Lucia can't quite place the look.

"Why don't you just take me to the healer?" Lucia says. "I think they can take better care of me."

"I can take care of you just fine!" Adelaide growls. Lucia stares at her wide-eyed at the outburst. "I—I'm sorry," Adelaide says. "Xiex—xiex. I didn't mean to shout. Just, please eat. I can't take you to the healer because... Well, they'll ask questions about the attack."

Adelaide looks vulnerable right now, biting her fist as she turns away. Lucia feels a pang of sorrow. She's never seen Adelaide look so worried. She has a feeling that whatever the vampire is thinking, there's more to it than Lucia knows.

"I'll take care of Cassius, okay?" Adelaide says quietly. "He is a respected figure in the cults. A friend to my brother and a warrior. What he did he—he'll pay for it. But we can't let this get out, especially not with that unresolved murder on campus. It wouldn't be good."

Lucia bites her lip, staring down at the plate of food. The smell wafts up to her nose and her stomach growls. *When was the last time she ate?*

"Okay," Lucia says. Adelaide's right, a vampire attacking a witch doesn't look good. Not just for Cassius, but for all vampires. Lucia doesn't know why he attacked her, or what was going on with him, but until she knows more, it would be bad for the vampires and the treaty to say anything crazy... Just like with her mother. She can understand Adelaide's struggle. If she can keep that secret about the witches, she can keep one more for the vampires. Besides, Adelaide has helped her many times.

Lucia quickly eats as much of the food as she can, and it's delicious. Kai must have gotten it from the canteen. When she's done, Lucia eyes the shirt. It looks big enough to cover her most intimate bits, at least.

Lucia gets her first good look at Adelaide since following her up to her room. The vampire is watching her carefully as if afraid she might fall over at any moment. Lucia motions the vampire to turn around, and it hits her just now as her stomach begins to feel all fuzzy, that she's in the woman's *private chambers.*

Lucia groans as she takes off the formless shift, now stained with blood, aching as she pulls on the black shirt, which lands mid-thigh on her short form, but is quite snug around her hips, which are bigger than Adelaide's. She's surprised she has enough blood to heat her face as she realizes she's going to be nearly naked beside the vampire. She doesn't dare take off her tights, though ripped and grass-stained. At least there isn't any blood on them.

"You have to stay on the far side of the bed," Lucia says seriously as Adelaide turns, eyes lingering as she looks her over. That cocky smirk is back on the vampire's lips and it's unsettling. Lucia squirms at the attention, clearing her throat. "Why aren't you affected by my blood?" she asks, trying to draw the woman's eyes from her legs. "Aren't you—Don't you want to—"

She can't even say it. She's a coward.

"Despite what you may think, I'm not a monster. Your blood doesn't call me to feast. Not in any way that would bring harm to you at least. Besides, I'm not *fully* undead."

Undead? There's that word again. "But at the party..." Lucia watched the woman drink from that human. It was like ecstasy. Lucia has never seen someone experience that much pleasure. It was indecent... It was almost terrifying.

Adelaide clicks off the light. "I drank from that witch because she wanted it, Lucia. And because it's fun. I drink because I can, not because I have to."

Lucia's head is spinning, and not from the blood loss. Everything Adelaide says is more confusing than the last. *Do vampires not have to drink blood to survive?* More and more, Lucia realizes there is so much about vampires that she doesn't know. So many things she's been told are beginning to feel like lies. Adelaide is nothing like she imagined the woman would be. Nor is her brother from Gabrielle's memory. The *"terrifying Skullkins"* don't seem much different from her own family.

Lucia slides under the thick red covers, watching Adelaide as she gets in on the other side. The vampire is... beautiful. Her skin glows in the moonlight streaming through the large windows. Lucia puts some of the pillows between them to make sure the vampire doesn't cross, and her breath hitches as Adelaide's blood-red lips turn up in laughter. *They look so soft... Adelaide's bow lips would probably feel nice pressed to hers...*

Lucia shakes herself, turning away from the vampire. *What is she thinking? It's fine, it's no different from lying beside Gabrielle.*

Lucia closes her eyes, pressing the covers tighter around her body as she finally lets herself succumb to sleep.

Lucia wakes with a shout, her heart pounding like crazy as moisture stings her eyes. As she struggles to get her breathing under control, she's startled by a pair of arms that wrap around her torso.

She relaxes minutely, letting out a breath. The larger, paler hand moves Lucia's, which rests over her beating heart, and instead rubs at the spot on her chest. There's no physical bruise there, but the motion is comforting. Lucia leans back against the scorching presence, the heat sinking into her back and loosening her muscles.

Adelaide's hand presses down quite hard, almost like she's trying to faze her hand into Lucia's chest. It doesn't hurt. It's more like a rough massage. The slight soreness works to ground Lucia, whose mind is still fractured between dream and reality, keeping her from being drawn back into the nightmare.

Once she's limp against Adelaide, the vampire traps Lucia's hands across her chest, just holding her. Adelaide whispers in her ear to follow her breathing and when Lucia's breathing is stable, she whispers back.

"Thank you."

No one except Gabrielle has been able to help Lucia through her panic attacks, stopping them before they can get too bad. It's enough that Lucia doesn't feel awkward as she lies pressed against the vampire.

The pair lie in silence for a while, Lucia exhausted but unable to go back to sleep. Her arm throbs beneath the tight wrapping Adelaide applied earlier in the night. She glances at the windows; the sky is still dark. She must not have been asleep for long.

Adelaide shifts behind Lucia, getting up and moving across the room. She sits on the settee, flicking on the vanity lamp.

"Do you always get nightmares like that?" Adelaide asks gently as she stares at Lucia across the room. Lucia feels colder now, with Adelaide so far away. She wraps her arms around herself as she stares at the red comforter. She shrugs.

Lucia has dealt with nightmares most of her life. It's weird talking about it, though. It's always been something that she pretends doesn't happen. The few times Gabrielle witnessed it, they didn't speak of it afterward. Gabrielle is a great comfort, but she doesn't understand. She has never truly gotten what Lucia has gone through.

When Adelaide does nothing but stare at her, she follows with, "It depends. Sometimes, when there's a lot on my mind or things get too much for my brain to handle, it affects my sleep. Sleep panic, I c-call it."

"Is there no *witch-y* cure for that?"

Lucia scoffs. "For anxiety? Who knows? My mother would never let me try anyway. It's not worth the trouble. The witches think something's wrong with me. That I'm weak. I suppose they're right. When Cassius attacked me, I was powerless."

Even the word—anxiety—is something Lucia knows from Gabrielle. Something her sister learned about in the human cities.

"You're not weak."

Lucia scoffs. *Sure.* Adelaide herself has had to save Lucia several times. And Hetan. During the first trial alone, she would not have made it if not for the two of them. Not to mention how often she leans on her younger sister for support.

"What?" Adelaide asks her voice like gravel. "Why is that so unbelievable?"

"It's just odd, is all, that a vampire is the one telling me this. You can't even be affected by these things. *Mental illness* or whatever. You can't get sick, your injuries heal in minutes..." Lucia clutches her arm, wrapped sloppily but securely in gauze and bandages. "You don't understand what it's like to not fit in."

"Who's to say I don't? Who's to say you know anything at all."

Lucia looks up, trying to read the guarded expression on Adelaide's face.

"I didn't mean it like that. I just meant it would be nice to be as confident as you are. You thrive as a vampire. You belong to that world. It was easy to see at the party, the way you were so comfortable with your friends and... I've never had that. As a kid, when I'd have a panic attack, my parents would just lock me in the closet until it passed. My mother said it would make me strong, but look how well that turned out."

Adelaide is quiet for a moment, jaw clenching under the illumination of the lamp.

"I don't think you know how strong you are, Lucia. How lucky you are to be born as you are. I guess it's hard to see from your vantage point."

"You say that like you know me."

"I don't know you, but I know those like you, *kuai-yuel*. But you're different, I could tell from the moment I met you. Now I can see why."

"Why do you keep calling me that—*kuai-yuel*? What does it mean?"

Adelaide chuckles. "Ah, so there are things you don't know." Lucia rolls her eyes. "If you're so curious, you should learn Chiskae. You would think the witches would, as they should understand the language of those they rule over."

"We don't—we don't *rule over* the vampires. My grandmother isn't the only one on the Caput Trium," Lucia defends.

Adelaide hums as the lights flicker on and off with the storm of Lucia's thoughts. The window that wraps around the bed is battered by rain, a rhythmic pitter-patter against the pane as a swirl of leaves and flower petals create a miniature tornado outside the glass.

"Family is a funny thing," Adelaide says as she fingers the strap on a journal sitting on her vanity. "Your pain seems to stem from yours."

Adelaide pulls the journal off the desk and faces Lucia propped on the bed. She opens the book to the middle.

"This was my uncle's," she says, looking down at the page. "He was talented. A great painter and writer. He lived in this dorm and studied here at the old temple before these grounds became an academy. He practically grew up here; fell in love here. *Died here.*"

Lucia shudders. "Was he not..." She can't finish it. There's so much she's ignorant of. She doesn't even know what questions to ask because there's so much she has wrong.

"He was a vampire yes. But there is an emptiness more final than death. That's what he thought, at least. *He was dead long before he was gone.*"

She motions to the book. "Giuseppe was a romantic. If it wasn't for the words inside these pages, I wouldn't believe there to be love as strong as he claims."

"What happened?"

Adelaide shrugs. "Too much."

Lucia shrugs off the blankets, waving Adelaide away when she tries to get up and help. Lucia climbs from the bed, wobbling and aching as she comes to sit beside the vampire.

"Read it to me."

Adelaide doesn't respond at first, staring down at the pages. Lucia looks up at her, studying the side of the vampire's face—smooth, warm skin and prominent cheekbones. Their eyes meet in the soft orange glow of lamplight.

"Fine, but only a little, then you must sleep."

Lucia nods. Maybe it's the soft warmth of the dead night or Lucia is still intoxicated from the strong spirits, or the elixir Himari gave her, but she lays her head on Adelaide's shoulder, which stiffens for a moment before the vampire flips the book open to the beginning.

Lucia leans over to look at the doodles and sketches of a beautiful woman. Full lips, dark curls, and wide, curious eyes. *Kind eyes.* Lucia closes hers as Adelaide begins to speak, her voice enchanting:

"From the time of Eve, things forbidden have been most beautiful. I was tempted the moment I saw Corseia, but it wasn't her beauty that captivated me most. It was how vibrant she was, like the sun. Like she was Mother Nature itself. I'd never felt as alive as when I was with her, not even from my birth. I craved that feeling more than air in my lungs..."

Lucia falls asleep like that, slumped over. Her head is on Adelaide's shoulder as the woman speaks softly, that idea—*of forbidden things*—on her mind. The light flickers, the throbbing in Lucia's arm only a dull ache.

Chapter Sixteen

As My Eyesight Began to Fade

A knock on the door makes Lucia jump. *Is it Gabrielle?* Lucia looks at the time. It's still early. She's making her way to the door when she hears a voice.

"Lucia. Lucia, dear, wake up."

Lucia freezes. *Mother?* Eyes wide, Lucia rushes to the wardrobe throwing off the T-shirt she borrowed from Adelaide and slipping a nightgown over her head. The thick fabric falls at her feet.

"Coming! Just a second," she calls, out of breath and anxious as she pulls up her hair and moves quickly toward the door. She throws it open to reveal her mother, Hatsia, the woman in formal dress for so early in the morning.

"Mama, I—I wasn't expecting you," Lucia says as the door closes behind her mother. The woman raises a single brow, taking measured steps inside the room, scanning Lucia's space. She hopes her mother doesn't notice the untouched sheets or the spot of black fabric peeking out from under the bed.

"I didn't get a chance to congratulate you on your win at the first trial." A warmth spreads across Lucia's face. Her mother has never praised her before. It's a foreign feeling that tightens her chest and chokes her up.

"Of course, it was a close win," Hatsia continues, perching on Lucia's chaise. Lucia moves to the end of the bed, folding her legs under herself. Hatsia's eyes finally land on Lucia, giving her a critical examination. Lucia tries not to squirm.

"You didn't tell me your magisk bloomed."

Oh no. "I didn't— I didn't know," Lucia stutters, searching for a plausible lie. "It just happened during the last obstacle when one of the contestants attacked me. I remembered my magisk application classes and it just burst out of me."

Lucia sweats, head bowed. She can't meet her mother's eyes, afraid the woman can see the lie.

"Well, that's wonderful. I can't wait to give the coven the good news. They will be thrilled."

"It isn't a magisk nature or anything, but it's something."

"Yes, it is." Hatsia stands abruptly, fingering the orb around her neck. "I want you to spend more time with Fabien. He can teach you and help your magisk grow. Your grandmother is getting sicker, and I need to be able to rely on you. I need your magisk to be as strong as possible, do you understand?"

"Yes, Mama."

"I also want you to keep a close eye on your opponents. Keep them close."

"What do you mean?"

Hatsia smirks, and it sends a chill down Lucia's spine. She lays a hand on her daughter's shoulder.

"Be nice and friendly, and sweet as you are... But keep in mind that at the end of the day, they want your downfall. They're betting on you to lose, and they'll use your sweet nature to do so. It would be helpful if we were aware of their weaknesses as well. Living in such proximity is good for one thing after all. Learning secrets."

Lucia's heart beats fast, and she tries not to meet her mother's eyes. Last night is running through her head. Getting attacked by Cassius. That is the sort of thing her mother would want to know. Except, she hasn't asked yet.

"Of course," Lucia says, her throat tight.

Hatsia smiles. "Good girl. *I will be watching.*"

Hatsia stands there for a moment and the thoughts of what Lucia had overheard at the gala plays in Lucia's mind. She squirms, anxious to blurt out what has been on her mind for weeks, to beg her mother for answers to clear up the confusion. To tell her that what she saw was *wrong* and that she had to have been mistaken. Her mother couldn't have possibly had Hetan's parents killed, could she?

Lucia feels like she might burst, and right when she thinks the words might slip out, Hatsia says, "It has been decided you are going to have your spirit walk soon, and the more magisk you have the stronger the elder you will meet. The wisdom the ancestors can give you is great, but whether you get that will be up to you." She strides to the door. "I will see you at the second trial."

When Hatsia is gone Lucia collapses back against the bed, muscles unclenching as she lets out a long groan. If she had been any later coming back from Adelaide's room, that would have gone a lot worse.

Gabrielle shadows Lucia as she makes her way to the canteen, sticking by her side, staring at her as she gets her food.

"You didn't go to bed last night," Gabrielle finally says.

"Yes, I did."

"Correction. You didn't go to bed in *your bed* last night."

Gabrielle's eyes squint at Lucia as they sit below the acylwood in the corner. Mia and Caitlyn are in deep conversation when they arrive. Something about Caitlyn being too busy to hang out lately and Mia feeling slighted by her friend.

Lucia feels guilty because she has also been quite busy. She hopes Gabrielle doesn't feel ignored too. But she wants to put space between herself and her sister. After seeing into her sister's mind, and the thoughts Gabrielle had about coming to Eirini and being her own person, Lucia felt bad about leaning on her so much. And she knows Gabrielle loves her too much to say anything, so she had to be the one to do it.

"I was..."

As Lucia searches for a suitable lie, Gabrielle says, "Were you drunk last night? I remember you acting weird. Did something happen?"

Lucia nods slowly, taking this as the perfect out. "Ah, yes. I got drunk and hurt myself. Ended up back at the healers."

Gabrielle gives Lucia a look of pity. She prefers that over the scandalized look she'd give if she learns Lucia shared a bed with a vampire.

It's not *bad*. Lucia did nothing wrong. Adelaide may not be kin, but they had pillows between them. So, why is there a twist of guilt in Lucia's gut?

"That's what happens when you're a lightweight," Caitlyn says, leaning her elbow across the table in an ill-mannered gesture as she tunes into the conversation. Mia still seems to be staring at her, like she wasn't done with whatever they were whispering about, but obviously, Caitlyn is.

Gabrielle launches off into conversation with her friends, and Lucia can sit back and breathe as she slowly picks at her breakfast. Her night with Adelaide and the unexpected visit from her mother still play in her mind.

"I'm not surprised you're one of those people who come early to class."

Lucia looks up from her notebook. She was studying cantus in her last class. Her face heats when she looks up to see Adelaide sauntering toward her. The vampire has always shown up late to class, so it's odd to see her here so early.

Lucia tucks her notebook against her chest, curling into herself. She tries not to think about last night. How Adelaide saved her from that crazed vampire or how they fell asleep beside each other. Lucia had run out as soon as she woke, without even saying goodbye. She wanted to get across campus before anyone woke so she wouldn't be seen in the vampire's clothes.

Lucia sits stuck between her chair and the desk with Adelaide looming over her. The vampire is smirking, hands in the pockets of her leather jacket. Lucia takes a breath, schooling her features before looking up at Adelaide with a blank face. She can see the tick in the vampire's jaw when she does this and refrains from grinning. She knows her disinterest will only make the woman angry.

"Yes?" Lucia says. "Is there anything you needed..." She pretends like she's searching for the woman's name in her memory. There's no need, she couldn't forget it. Alluring eyes squint at her in annoyance, and Lucia gulps. She feels like she's being dissected. Like those eyes are seeing too much of her.

"*Funny*. You know you don't fool me, Princess. With that cutesy facade. You're a feisty little—" Adelaide's words are cut off when the door opens. Students start pouring in. Lucia just looks up at Adelaide, a faux look of confusion on her face. She's a bit disappointed they were interrupted so soon. It's fun riling up the vampire.

Adelaide's fists clench, and she huffs her annoyance at the interruption. After a few moments of standing there, she marches over to her own seat at the back of the class. Lucia turns to the front, smiling to herself. She never understood her grandmother when she spoke of the rivalry that exists between witches and vampires like it was some innate thing. But now she gets it. The sight of the vampire's face triggers something inside of her. Some sort of unexplainable heat in her belly.

"Now, class, we're going to look at a poem on page one hundred twenty-three of your textbooks. This is a rare document, discovered over a decade ago in the aftermath of the Battle of Shante'sha during the War of Mystics, and has been the topic of much discussion in the literary community. We're going to read it, and then talk about it briefly."

Professor Webber, their Mystic Literature professor, looks across at his students. He's a vampire, the only one at Eirini. His employment is the topic of many whispered conversations. It makes Lucia a bit sad. His class is her favorite. She enjoys learning about Mystic history and she enjoys poetry more. Any type of art. Her mother never really let her explore it, always pushing her to study cantus, so Lucia had to smuggle books up to her room, hidden in a cubby under her bed.

Professor Webber calls to Faith, who sits beside Lucia. "Read the first paragraph. The poem is, 'As My Eyesight Began to Fade'. The author is unknown."

Lucia's eyes widen and she tries to tamp down her excitement. She knows the poem; it's one of her favorites. The original diary sits in a museum in Olympia city square which Lucia has always longed to visit. The poem reads:

My dreams became more vibrant as my eyesight began to fade. It was like my mind knew what my body didn't. Every night was a new adventure, and last night was the most thrilling.

As a babe, the thought of children had only been a fantasy of the future, but this dream painted my life like a map behind unconscious eyes.

To meet my daughter is to know she is beautiful. She belongs to the woods, but she is still mine.

With hazelnut eyes and sparse blonde hair, the bundle of joy was wrapped in cloth and abandoned in the wilderness.

I took my precious offspring from the hardened earth. She affected the trees and darkening sky with her smile. The wilted flowers and browning leaves swayed as we passed, bowing to their mother.

The giggling, squealing girl, wiggled in my arms as I passed the threshold of my home, and my family looked up as I entered, as we'd intruded on their dinner.

Walking farther into the room, my sister gasped, and my mother scowled, each demanding to know who the babe was.

She's mine, I defended, and all eyes turned on me as if I too was an intruder from the wood.

My girl began to cry as foreign eyes betrayed her, and hating her distress, I turned and fled.

At that moment my childhood was left behind and the cloak on my back was all we had.

As we were chased by the fear of those who'd never understand our bond, the wind embraced us, whipping around our heads and ankles in a frenzy.

The sharp barbs from the branches of trees leaped out of our way as we ran into the heart of the forest.

I didn't belong in this place, but it was all my daughter had known.

I fell into the darkened woods, collapsing to my knees, arms wrapped around my daughter's peaceful form.

For the pair of us, a bed was made within the leaves, and as the stars materialized above our heads, we descended into a peaceful slumber.

I slept with the knowledge I had just become a mother.

The class is silent for a moment as they digest what they have just read. Professor Webber stands at the front of the class, eyes closed and hands on either hip. After a minute, he opens his eyes, taking a deep breath. He looks out at each of them.

"That was powerful," he says. "Who would like to take the first shot? What do you gather from the poem about the meaning of the text or the woman who wrote it?"

Someone raises their hand. "Yes, you. Liam."

"Uhm, the woman seems to be an outsider in her own home. She doesn't have a good relationship with her family."

"Yes, and what gives you that impression?"

Liam, a wolf, adjusts his glasses, looking down at the page. "There are a few different lines. First, *My family looked up as I entered, as we'd intruded on their dinner.* And *All eyes turned on me as if I too was an intruder from the wood.* She uses the word *intruder* multiple times. Her family doesn't seem to understand her or like her. It makes me think that this child, which she just kind of acquires, is a replacement for a family she never fit into."

Lucia thinks of her relationship with her own family. Maybe that's why from the first time she read it, she loved it so much. She too feels like an intruder from the woods.

"Aha!" Professor Webber says, tapping his temple. "I love that. Good eye. What can we infer about what the woman may have been going through, to write something like this? What does it tell you about her and the world she lived in?"

He looks around. "Miss Dol'Auclair," he says, smiling down at Lucia. "You're a bright young woman. I'm curious what you think of the piece."

Lucia's face heats, looking up at the professor and then the students around her. The piece is so personal to her, she's not sure if she can dissect it critically. But with all eyes on her, she has to be confident in her answer. Everything she does here, even just answering a poem in class, reflects on her family.

"From what I know of this poem, it was written near the end of the War of Mystics. Or so it is believed. With that knowledge, I can only assume that this woman's woodland baby is metaphorical. In that, she was not actually found in the woods, but the woman gave birth to her there. Possibly without her family's knowledge or at least knowledge of who the father was. I would assume the young woman was a vampire and had a child with a witch. I say so," Lucia rambles, getting nervous now as she plays with her fingers under the desk, "because of the line about belonging to the wood, but again, looking at the time, women would often give birth outside, in the forest. If the birth was out of wedlock, sometimes the mother and babe would be abandoned there by their families and disowned. The family didn't accept the baby, and by extension, the mother, because she was *other*."

The class is silent, staring at Lucia. She shrinks in her seat as Professor Webber stares at her with a look Lucia can't read. Interest, maybe. "That is such a beautiful analysis, Miss Dol'Auclair. Except, vampires cannot have babies. With witches or otherwise."

Lucia nods, trying to keep the embarrassment from showing on her face as a heavy weight settles on her chest. She knew the theory was crazy, but Lucia has read the poem a million ways and that's the analysis she lands on every time.

"Ah, Miss Skullkin, you have yet to speak in my class. I'm thrilled."

Every eye turns to Adelaide and Lucia is relieved to have the attention away from herself. She turns in her seat to look at Adelaide, who's slumped lazily in her seat, wearing skin-tight leather that is unzipped at the front to show off her cleavage. Lucia struggles to keep her eyes locked on the other girl's, red eyes staring straight at her.

"I think that was a well-thought analysis by the missus, er, *Auclair*, but I disagree."

Lucia's face burns at the insult, a response to Lucia pretending not to know her name earlier.

"I'm quite a poetry fanatic. Art and its many interpretations are beautiful, but I do not believe that all ideas are good. That being said, this poem is an enigma to many, so it's of no fault to the witch that she is mistaken about the intent of the writer. One thing many scholars often overlook is the first paragraph, and that's a great shame. I'll read it for you. It says, *My dreams became more vibrant as my eyesight began to fade*, and again, *This dream painted my life like a map behind unconscious eyes*. She mentions dreams twice. Isn't that odd? Too odd to be overlooked. I don't think this was based on a woman giving birth, at least, not as the focus."

Adelaide's gaze never leaves Lucia as she speaks. *"As my eyesight began to fade, it was like my mind knew what my body didn't.* This is someone who was losing not her literal eyesight, but a lie she has been told. A veneer lifted. As the lie was unraveling, the truth of the world was becoming clear to her. An awakening. At the core of magisk, what is most powerful? Women and children. Especially to witches who worship *the Mother*. So yes, it's probably a witch who wrote it. And the woman never said the child was born in the woods, she specifically said that the baby was abandoned in the woods and that the woods accepted her. Treated her like a God, almost. Once she acknowledged that babe, she was cast out by family, or maybe society in itself. She is cast from society and all she knows, but embraced by magisk, beauty, and the wood. She's reclaiming her power. And sometimes, you have to lose people to do that."

Adelaide sits back in her seat, feet up on the desk, and has a smug smile on her face. The professor, and even a few students, begin applauding. Lucia's hands clench below the desk as the woman winks at her. *That infuriating vampire.*

Lucia turns away, eyes glued to the professor and face blooming in embarrassment. Lucia is embarrassed, not only that Adelaide said she was wrong, but that Lucia herself hadn't thought of the points Adelaide brought up. For some reason, Lucia never once considered the Mother may be involved in the meaning of the poem. That changes everything.

"Great discussion," Professor Webber says, nodding. "I can tell this is a passionate and intelligent class, so I'm excited to see what you all come up with. Your project for this semester will not be easy. I want a well-thought-out report and analysis dissecting a text of your choosing. It must be nonfiction and have a section about the time it was written and how that translates to today. I would prefer you use pieces within your family histories, as most of them are vast, but if you wish I have alternate works you could choose from. Also, you will be working in pairs."

The class groans and he quickly quiets them. "This is important because given your different backgrounds I expect there to be much debate about the meanings within the work, which will make for a more thrilling assignment. I expect you and your partner to come to some sort of agreement by the end. Now, partners—"

Professor Webber begins assigning the pairs and Lucia waits anxiously for her name. She doesn't like group pairings for many reasons, as evidenced in her partnership with Hetan for the first trial. But this being her favorite topic, it'll be more infuriating having to decide on an answer with her partner.

"Miss Dol'Auclair and Miss Skullkin."

Lucia's eyes widen at the sound of her name right next to Adelaide's. She turns to the woman, her heart beating fast. *No way.* Adelaide doesn't even meet Lucia's gaze this time, but a dimple forms in the corner of her mouth giving away the woman's amusement. *Aggravating. Infuriating. Conceited.* The list of names goes on.

Professor Webber motions to three of the classroom walls. All but the one behind him with the large window and his desk against it are floor-to-ceiling bookshelves covered in old books. It makes the room smell like vanilla and smoke.

"Get with your partner. Find a piece of text from family libraries or heirlooms that means something to you. Find a way to connect with it in the present. The past, in many ways, can leave an echo in the present. Scars, if left unhealed, will haunt you in the future."

"Hetan, where are we going?" Lucia complains, huffing as she tries to keep up with the wolf. They climb up the mountainside deep in the forest surrounding Eirini, the full moon high in the sky above. Lucia can barely see and continues stumbling over the branches and brush beneath her feet. Hetan grabs ahold of her arm to keep her upright.

"Are you all right, Lucia? You always struggle to keep up with me, but you're especially clumsy today."

Lucia hits the smug wolf's arm. "I've been practicing with Lord Fabien all week. I'm sore," she groans.

"Practicing what?"

"My magisk. My mother thinks he'll be able to help me get ahold of my cantus faster, but it's useless. I haven't gotten a single one right since the first trial."

"Well, good thing you're with me tonight. It'll distract your mind from having to put up with that asshole all the time."

Lucia rolls her eyes. "He isn't that bad."

"To you."

Lucia ignores that, following her friend out into a small clearing. "Are you going to tell me what happened to your face?" she asks. His nose is a bit crooked and there is purple bruising under his eyes like he got punched, but he won't tell her what happened. The thought of Hetan getting into a brawl is almost laughable to Lucia. "You know, if I didn't know any better, I'd say you were the academy killer and were luring me out here as your next victim," Lucia jokes.

"Hetan, a killer?" Someone cackles, their voice echoing in the night. A bonfire sets the trees aglow, and a group is gathered around it. Lucia pushes closer to Hetan, nerves alight at the sight of strangers. "Honestly," the feminine voice goes on, "I'd have a better time believing Hetan was set to flame and what we are seeing is his apparition haunting us."

Lucia gets closer and sees the voice belongs to Blythe. Their brothers sit beside them around the fire. The sight of a familiar face makes Lucia relax slightly.

"Hetan is scary enough for it to be true," Lucia jokes, gaining a betrayed look from her friend that makes her burst into laughter.

Hetan pulls her down to sit beside Blythe and introduces her to the group. When he gets to Blythe, the wolf says, "She knows. I saved the witch from face-planting at the council meeting." Lucia's face flames at the memory. "If I'd known she was *your witch,*" Blythe goes on, "I might have let her fall."

Hetan splutters as he takes a drag of the medicinal cane someone hands him on his other side. He turns his head up, letting the smoke out slowly as the herb smolders.

"Lucia is not *my witch,*" he says, cheeks growing pink. "She's my friend."

Hetan offers the cane to Lucia who shakes her head. He leans over her to pass it to Blythe.

"Oh, come on, witch," Beaur, who Lucia hasn't heard speak before, says, his voice a deep rumble. "You're not going to have a little fun with us? It's ritual if you're going to be hanging with wolves."

Lucia waves her hands. "I can't. My mother would kill me."

"Your mother isn't here, is she?" Blythe laughs as Beaur looks around the trees, the firelight flickering against the shadows. "I don't see her. Maybe she's behind that boulder."

"Very funny, Beaur," Hetan says dryly. "If she says she doesn't want to then that's the end of it."

"Oh, come on, you don't have to speak for her. Living with that nightmare of a mother, she's got to have tough skin. Isn't that right? Your mother is one scary witch."

Lucia swallows, her heart thumping quickly at the ribbing. She never realized anyone outside of the covens sees how terrifying her mother is. She peeks over at Hetan who is glowering at the other wolf. Does he agree with him? Does Hetan think her mother is scary? It makes her wonder what he knows about his parents' death. She never asked and now she's regretting that. But thoughts of her mother are the last thing she wants right now.

"Fine," Lucia says, putting out her hand for the cane. It looks like a slender shoot of purple sugar cane, hollowed out in the center.

"Are you sure?" Hetan asks as Lucia fumbles with the thing, putting her lips against the side that isn't glowing. She squints her eyes at him.

"What? Don't think I can keep up, Hetan? Or are you afraid I'm going to leave you behind?"

Hetan shakes his head, a dimple popping on his cheek when he smiles. "*Hiahi na,* tama—you'll eat those words, Lucia."

"Don't scare her, Hetan," Blythe says. "A little *ronga* never hurt anyone."

The medicine burns to fill Lucia's lungs, her eyes watering as she drags the smoke into her mouth. Her head feels like cotton as she lets it out, hitting her harder than the spirits from the party a week ago.

"*Whoa,*" she breathes, head spinning as warm hands take the cane from her. "Yeah, that'll go to your head, witch," Blythe says.

"Are you okay?" Hetan asks, his voice closer to Lucia's. It sounds like he's whispering in her ear. She nods, her vision spinning a bit. The fire is an orange swirl and the faces of the wolves around her blur at the edges. She feels *very good.*

"Let's get some music going!" Blythe says, standing. "I want to dance."

"*No,*" Beaur groans, slapping his forehead as Blythe grabs a string instrument lying in the grass and hands it to Boen. Lucia blinks at the wolf who sits nestled by his brother's side. He's so quiet, she had forgotten he was even there. "Boen, I swear—"

Boen starts strumming a song, and Blythe sings the lyrics, their voice carrying atop the mountain. Others join in singing the song, wolves getting up to join them in dancing.

Lucia is fascinated, wide-eyed, and dizzy as they romp around the fire. Their dancing is different from the witches or even the vampires, moving their whole bodies and making lots of noise. Every inch of Blythe's skirt clinks and rattles, body and clothes an instrument. Lucia almost wants to join them except she thinks she might fall over if she tries to stand now.

It's beautiful though, watching the wolves dance. They wear a mishmash of bright colors and furs, loud, clanging beads wavering in the moonlight.

She sits beside Hetan, the fire warming her face and his arm heating her side as they press close. There's nowhere that Lucia doesn't feel like she's burning. It's a different burn than when she's with Adelaide, a warmth rather than an inferno. It's safe. She doesn't think she'll be consumed by it.

Blythe grabs multiple wolves, man and woman, to dance with.

"Don't mind them," Beaur says as his sister tries to get Lucia up to join them. "They're a bit of a nymph."

Lucia can't help the laugh that punches out of her at that. She gets a bunch of stares for it. It's an odd thing to learn as she spends more time with vampires and wolves, that talk of *sexual relations* is a casual conversation.

Blythe plops back down beside Lucia, nearly sitting on their brother, who jumps out of the way with a startled shout.

"Watch it, *Birdie*," he growls.

"Oops." Blythe giggles. They throw an arm around Lucia's neck, pulling her in until their heads bump. Lucia closes her eyes feeling a bit lightheaded. "You know, *witch*," Blythe says in a way Lucia has come to realize is an affectionate title as much as it is teasing, "your sister was a lot less squeamish than you."

"You know my sister?" Lucia says before she remembers Gabrielle mentioned Blythe once. She said she borrowed clothes from the wolf.

"Yeah, cool witch. That Caitlyn girl introduced us."

"You're friends with Caitlyn?"

Blythe shrugs. "Not really. Her family came up to Swaydan to visit and stopped by the Crimson Ash clan."

"When?"

Blythe gives Lucia an odd look.

"Sorry, I was just curious." Lucia doesn't know why she cares; it just strikes her a bit odd that the Starlights went up to visit Swaydan.

"It was a few weeks before school started," Blythe says, then laughs. "You know, you're almost as weird as your sister. She kept asking all sorts of odd questions." The wolf is still swaying to their brother's strumming, eyes closed. "She's a lot of fun though. You could learn a thing from her. Loosen up a bit. I bet you'd be really cool if you did."

"Blythe..." Hetan warns.

Blythe waves absently at Hetan, scoffing. "Chill, I didn't mean it like that. I like your witch."

Lucia's pulse thrums in her neck from being pressed close to Blythe for so long and the comment about being more like Gabrielle. Lucia's been told that her whole life and she gets it—her little sister is *amazing*. Lucia knows it and so does everyone else. But Lucia thought she was opening up. She has done a lot of things since coming to Eirini that she never would have thought she could.

"Can you get your grubby little hands off her?" Hetan says, pulling Lucia back to his side. "You Crimson Ash wolves, I swear..."

When Hetan stands Lucia nearly tips over from lack of support on her side. She watches as the wolf stretches and cracks his neck. "Come on, pups, who's up for a run?" He looks up at the full moon which sits big and bright in the sky above them. The other wolves whoop and holler as they jump up in excitement.

Lucia forgets that Hetan is a chieftain now. A leader for his people after the death of his parents. His uncle may be the interim chief, but Hetan is the rightful heir of the wolves.

Lucia stands, a bit wobbly from the one puff of ronga. Hetan grabs her arm when she stumbles.

"Do you want to come?" Hetan asks, leaning down to whisper in Lucia's ear. His breath is warm against her skin, and she shivers as she looks up at him in question. Her eyes meet his, which sparkle like liquid silver in the moonlight.

"How?" she asks, uncertain of what he means. She isn't a wolf; she can't keep up with them.

"Get on my back," he says. "You can ride me when I'm a wolf."

Lucia's pulse thrums at the thought of riding down the mountain with the wolves, and her hand tightens around Hetan's arm. She nods. "*Yes,*" Lucia breathes. And maybe it's foolish, especially while she's still reeling, but she trusts Hetan.

Howls echo atop the mountain, the wolves throwing their heads back and shouting up into the sky. Hetan nudges her and Lucia laughs, joining with a much fainter call that merges with the voices. Lucia's face blooms with heat as men and women unashamedly begin pulling off their clothes, stripping down so they can shift.

One after another the sound of cracking bones fills the clearing until Hetan is the last. He squeezes Lucia's hand before removing his final article of clothing, tossing it into the bag along with everyone else's, shoulders popping as he hunches over, back morphing to that of a four-legged beast. Lucia is just as awed as the first time she saw it, a white wolf surrounded by wolves of all sizes and coloring, from ebony black to dusky orange.

Lucia shoulders the bag with everyone's clothes and pours the pail of water on the fire until it hisses, a plume of smoke rising into the air. The wolves are restless, snuffling and pawing at the ground, while three tawny, flaming-amber wolves wrestle across the grass, nipping and jumping at each other.

Lucia approaches Hetan slowly, swallowing down her nerves as he lowers his head to the ground. She climbs onto the giant wolf, grabbing fistfuls of fur to keep herself atop his large back, her heart racing at the thrill of it.

Hetan's wolf is like a beacon, an argent pearl leading the way through the forest, the rest of the wolves falling in line behind him as they tear through the trees. Lucia bites back her shout as her legs clamp tighter around the wolf's rumbling torso, leaning forward until the long fur tickles her chin. The sharp wind whips her curls around her face, stinging the clarity back into her mind.

The sight is magnificent—the trees blurring around her as Hetan's powerful body leaps down the mountainside, kicking up dirt and rocks. She can't imagine a sight more beautiful—such calm and chaos—Lucia is almost envious that she can't experience this view all the time. She never wants it to end.

Lucia lays her head atop Hetan's silken fur as he begins to slow, taking in the campus framed by moonlight as the trees part. They approach from the back of the buildings. Lights flicker inside the vampires' dorm, and Lucia looks up at the upper level and wonders whether Adelaide is still awake.

She's exhausted as she slips off Hetan's back, stretching her cramped legs as the wolves slowly shift back to human form. She drops the bag so they can find their clothes, turning away from the sight of so many tanned naked bodies with long, sleek hair swinging down their backs.

Lucia can feel Hetan behind her, and she turns slowly, ripping her eyes from their search for Adelaide's window.

"*Hele.*"

"*Hei—hei*," Hetan whispers back, his dark hair falling loose around his shoulders like a curtain. His face is shadowed as he blocks the light, and Lucia swallows, heart racing in her chest. *Is he leaning in?* She panics, unsure of what to do. Her hands are sweating against her thighs.

"I have to be up early to practice with Lord Fabien," she says quickly, trying to ease the air of tension between them. Hetan leans back, a look of disappointment crossing his face. Lucia tamps down the knot of guilt in her belly as she lets out a breath.

She had thought about it many times before, kissing Hetan again. Growing up she would think of that first kiss they shared. But now, the thought makes her feel guilty.

"You should come back to practicing with me," he says, that prideful swagger returning as he puffs his chest.

Lucia laughs. "If I could. My mother made this request. The Dol'Auclairs and Devroues are longtime friends."

When Hetan opens his mouth to respond, a growl sounds behind him. Beaur's chest rumbles, both his and Blythe's faces angry. Lucia is taken aback by the hostility from the obnoxious, slightly rude, but fun-loving pair.

"That asshole," Blythe snarls. "He and all of the Devroues can *waokit ai mat*."

Hetan's eyes widen. "Blythe!"

The wolf turns away, arms crossed over their chest. Lucia looks on confusedly, unsure of what is happening.

"The Crimson Ash clan isn't far from those Sea Serpents," Beaur spits, lip curled up to reveal his canines. "Between them and their damned rivalry with the Silver Spiders, Swaydan is hell. Food is scarcer than ever, and more and more wolves go missing—"

"Beaur, enough. Both of you," Hetan says, eyes flitting between the pair. The wolves bow in submission, as authority drips from his words.

"Whatever," Beaur finally scoffs. "Don't tell your little witch that her vampire friend is the one who beat you." He kicks up dirt, stomping off toward the dorms with his brother on his heels.

Blythe calls, "Tell your sweet sister to come to see me again soon!" and rushes off after them.

Lucia's eyes widen in shock, turning to get a better look at Hetan's face in the dark. It's hard to see because she doesn't have magisk sight.

"Adelaide did this?" she asks. "Why—Why were you fighting?"

"We weren't fighting," he snaps. "She's just crazy."

Lucia shrinks back at that word. She hates that word. Hetan must notice because he sighs, shaking his head.

"It's nothing. We got in a bit of a disagreement, and you know those vamps, they love to solve things with their fists."

"That's not okay. She shouldn't have—"

"Again, it's fine, Lucia. I can handle myself."

Lucia takes a deep breath as the tension dissipates, her heart thumping as she looks up at Hetan. She'll have to talk with Adelaide. It's not okay that she hit him.

Hetan seems to have masked his face back into something pleasant, but she can still see the lines of stress that she hadn't noticed before. A pit of worry grows in her stomach.

"They're fine," he says, leading her away from the wolves and toward the witches' dorm. "Things are a little... tense in the clans right now. Especially with Orion's death. He was of the Crimson Ash clan, just a pup, so the wolves are grieving his loss as well as searching for the killer. No one else seems to be doing anything about it."

Lucia shudders, the sight of the lifeless body she and Hetan had found what feels like so long ago coming back to her mind.

"I'm so sorry," Lucia whispers, feeling guilty that she had forgotten about the young man, and that she stirred that pain back up for the triplets. Hetan shakes his head, grimacing as he looks away from her.

"It's not your fault, Lucia. You didn't kill him nor are you responsible for the clans' problems. I am."

"But—" Lucia tries to find comforting words for her friend, but he cuts her off.

"Goodnight, Lucia," Hetan says dismissively, laying a hand on her shoulder. "Good luck with your training."

Lucia is left alone outside of her dorm as Hetan rushes back across the lawn, once again helpless when her friend needs solace.

Chapter Seventeen

If You Have to Hate Me

Gabrielle bursts into Lucia's room, sweaty and out of breath. She holds Lucia's gift basket and a scroll in her hands.

"Aren't they supposed to hand those directly to the recipients?" Lucia questions, looking up from her coursework. She sees the impish look on her sister's face. "Never mind, I don't want to know. Just—tell Theia I'm sorry for whatever you did."

Gabrielle bounces onto the bed, Lucia's paperwork slinging up into the air and scattering. Lucia has to take a deep breath and bite back her first response as Gabrielle sets down the basket.

"Sorry."

"It's okay," Lucia grits through her teeth. "Let's just look at the rules for this next trial. Hopefully, it's not teamed again."

This time Lucia unwraps and reads the scroll herself, Gabrielle once again stuck to her side.

"For Lucia of the Golden Griffin coven, by your humble Caput Trium," she reads slowly. Impatient with her pace, Gabrielle reads it with her to speed her along:

"A will of the mind to test your mental strength. Reach into the deep recess of your mind to see what it is you fear. The things that keep you up at night and thoughts you hold most dear. This test will weed out those without the mental fortitude to push through when it gets tough, a weak mind that will bend under the dark magisk touch. The last to make it out of the Sage's test is cut."

Gabrielle is silent beside Lucia. It is no secret that this will be a difficult test for Lucia. Gabrielle used to help Lucia when she would have panic attacks. But another worry Lucia has that she can't voice aloud is how her ability as a Sage will affect the second trial.

Lucia puts a hand up to push back Adelaide's face as she leans close. The vampire keeps doing that, and it's distracting her from their project. The woman was across from Lucia in the small booth, but she moved a few minutes ago claiming it was hard to hear Lucia over the table. Lucia wasn't buying it, but Adelaide squeezed in next to her anyway, squishing Lucia against the wall.

The pair is in the canteen, back in the booth they had sat at together the day before the first trial. It's late, but Lucia has no other time to meet up between practicing her cantus with Fabien, and Gabrielle helping her prepare for the second trial.

Lucia is more nervous about this than she was for the first trial, even though it isn't meant to be physical. Her mother has berated her throughout her entire life for how mentally weak she is, so she has no idea how she will be able to do this.

Lucia yawns, leaning her head against her palm as she blinks watery eyes down at the journal.

"This is all just—*lovey-dovey* stuff." Lucia groans.

Adelaide scoffs, sliding the journal from under Lucia's hand. "You're the one who chose it for our project," Adelaide reminds her, flipping past the next couple of pages. It's a thick journal, two hundred pages, and bursts when it's tied with the thick leather cord. Giuseppe stuck notes and drawings, and all sorts of things into it.

Lucia thumbs the raised *A* etched in silver on a coin she found stuffed inside.

"You know, I'm surprised," Adelaide says, laying her arm across the seat behind Lucia as she leans in. "I would've taken you for a romantic."

Lucia blushes, turning her head away so the vampire doesn't see her burning cheeks. Lucia isn't a romantic, but something about Giuseppe and Corseia draws her in. Lucia hasn't had much time to think about love or marriage or any of those silly things most girls, like Gabrielle, dream about, thinking only of making her family proud and taking over the Golden Griffin coven someday.

As she reads through the transparent, heart-bleeding manifestation of Giuseppe's love for the beautiful witch, Lucia can't help but long for that too. A desperate, unmistakable declaration of love.

Whatever that might be.

Lucia doesn't think she has ever felt love. The closest she can get is Gabrielle, and even then, she knows that's not the same. It doesn't come even close to what Lucia has read on these pages.

Lucia pushes Adelaide away again, shaking her head. "I don't have time for that," Lucia says. "All that's important is the Triune. Besides, whether I like romance or not isn't the point. The point is I don't want to do my magisk history project about two lovers. We need to find something intellectual in this journal."

"You don't think love can be intellectual?" Adelaide teases.

Lucia rolls her eyes. She sees what the vampire is doing. She's behaving as she has during all of their meetings so far: pushing Lucia's buttons and riling her up. Testing her wits.

"No, I don't think so," Lucia says, rising to the bait as she snatches the journal back from Adelaide. "From what I know of love, it is the complete opposite of intelligent or reasonable. It's beyond comprehension. Love is... Well, the love Giuseppe illustrates in these pages is passion and lust. It's instinct and, quite frankly, frightening."

"You're afraid of love?" Adelaide murmurs, staring down at Lucia through red, heavy-lidded eyes. For a moment Lucia gets lost in that stare, her heart thundering against her rib cage and words heavy in her throat. When Lucia speaks, it's through that lump.

"Not love. I'm afraid of the piece in between. The parts before and after falling. The unknown and then... stuck. I don't think—once you've fallen in love—you can ever be free. As you said before, Giuseppe believed there to be worse things than death. He died when he lost Corseia, and I don't think that's a fate anyone deserves."

The air is tense between them. Lucia's eyes stray to Adelaide's lips as they have many times since the night of that party. As usual, they're bright and red like her eyes, glossy and hard to look away from.

A dull thud snaps Lucia out of it. The journal slips from her fingers onto the floor. Embarrassed, Lucia quickly scoops up the spilled contents, stuffing them haphazardly back into the journal and then bolting to her feet. Adelaide stands too.

"I have to go," Lucia says breathlessly, squeezing past the vampire. She backs away nervously, sloppily tying the journal back up. "We'll meet again tomorrow, same time, okay? Okay."

Lucia doesn't wait for an answer from the stunned vampire before she races out of the canteen, sweaty and breathing fast.

She is embarrassed to admit she races back to her room and collapses against her bedroom door. With her hand under her skirt, she touches herself for the first time, so overcome by the memory of Adelaide's eyes under the dim, amber lights and the woman's lips, which she ached to press to hers.

She doesn't understand what is happening to her. She has never been wound so tightly before. The vampire is making her feel things she never thought she would.

※ ※ ※

Fabien is angry and purple in the face as he stands over Lucia. She's on the floor, panting, dripping with sweat. Her dress is sticky and clings uncomfortably to her body.

"Do you not take this seriously, Lady Lucia? Is learning how to control your magisk just a joke to you?" he yells.

They have a small room in the middle level of the Noxidome all to themselves. He requested it for her training.

"I'm trying, Lord Fabien—"

"We've been at this a week, and you have yet to do any of the cantus I've asked of you. Again and again, you fail, and I have half a mind to believe you have no magisk at all. That you lied and that filthy White Dragon vampire hallucinated the whole thing."

Lucia's breath is ragged as she tries to calm her racing heart. *She can't focus while Fabien yells at her.*

"Are you even listening to me?"

"Yes—yes!" Lucia stutters, wincing as she pulls herself up off the floor. "I wasn't lying, I just..." Lucia doesn't know. She has no idea why her magisk worked then and not now. It never seems to come when she calls it. It's almost random in its use. Lucia is frustrated, more so than Fabien is, worried that she won't ever be able to master it.

"I'm here to help you, not the other way around. I cannot be coven head because I am a man, but you who are *gifted everything*, the firstborn of the Golden Griffins, ought to have a bit more pride and a better work ethic. It's like you're not even trying."

Lucia has nothing to say, staring down at the geometric patterns on the gray floor. No matter what she says, it won't please Fabien, so all she can do is stay silent as he berates her.

"This is important to me, and I promise I will try harder. I will follow your every instruction," she says quietly.

Fabien turns away, taking a deep breath as he runs his hands through his thick curls. "Good. I shouldn't have snapped at you, Lady Lucia. But this is exactly why your mother sent me to be your guardian."

His hands hover beside Lucia's shoulders like he's going to touch her, and she leans back almost on instinct. He drops his hands.

"You can come to me for anything. I'm here to help you—to guide you. To be your partner. I know you're prone to *fits*, your mother made me aware of this defect. If that's the issue, or you feel one coming on, you can tell me, and we'll work through it. You can come to me for anything."

Lucia swallows hard, eyes stinging as she takes a small step back. She doesn't know what exactly her mother told Fabien about her, but the thought makes her stomach drop.

"Of course," she croaks, blinking away the moisture. "I trust you."

That couldn't be further from the truth.

Fabien smiles at this, stepping back. He lays his hand on top of a large box sitting against the wall, which is the height of his hip. Lucia had been wondering what that was. It wasn't usually there when they practiced.

"I'm glad that we could work this out," Fabien says. "With your full cooperation, I think I'll be able to help you." When he lifts the lid, a Niveus pops out of the box. Lucia nearly jumps back at the sight of the twisted thing.

"Do you know what a Niveus is, Lucia?" Fabien asks eyes squinted in question.

"They're creations of Etryae?" Lucia says unsure. She doesn't know much.

Fabien shakes his head and his face lights with the opportunity to tell her. "They're Jaedou—shadow creatures. A rare magisk creature genetically modified by Etryae to be used in situations like this, training exercises to test our magisk."

Lucia's eyes widen in horror, the creatures becoming more terrifying with the knowledge. Lucia struggles to look at it, the pale indents where a mouth and eyes should be, and the nose that's just two slits in the center of its face.

"I want you to use magisk to get the creature to come toward you. That's all you have to do, a simple Ifyai cantus in neno-grade. Do you understand?"

Lucia nods though it sounds anything but simple. A *first-grade enchantment* might be easy for other witches, but the Jadeou is a living creature the size of a human, and Lucia can't even get small inanimate objects to obey her cantus.

Fabien moves back, jumping up to sit on top of the empty box as Lucia turns to the Niveus.

"Awa Nib."—*Come here*, Lucia says weakly. She's still exhausted from the training Fabien's had her do all week, and between that and everything else, all she wants is to lie down and sleep. She hasn't done much of that since coming to Eirini, spending many late, sleepless nights sucking on acylwood petals and nursing a cup of lavender milk in the canteen as she tries to get through her class lessons and practice neno-grade cantus'.

"I jiji I, Lucia!" Fabien shouts, clapping his hands—*Wake up!* "Say it with a little more confidence. Your words have intention. To guide them, you have to communicate your convictions. If you don't believe what you're saying, then it *won't work.*"

Fabien's words are loud and condescending, but he's right. Lucia knows he is, so it frustrates her more. This is all basic magisk skill.

Lucia stares at the white blob, eyes trained on the concave eye sockets.

"Igob—siw igbes. Siw nib." *Step—step forward. Come forward.* Lucia stares at the Niveus for a long time, getting lost in her mind.

She wonders if this is how the Niveus looks before it has been tampered with and whether it has thoughts and feelings—a family, like her, that it wants to make proud. Does the creature feel pain?

Lucia shakes her head questioning if she can go through with this training. *Is it worth helping her coven if she has to do something so inhumane?*

"It's a— I can't. Could we get a witch who can consent to be tested?" Lucia asks.

"We can't use a real person, Lucia. You could lose control of your magisk and hurt them."

Lucia looks back at the Niveus. *Is it not a real person?* She can't mess with a living creature's mind like her own personal puppet. It has a humanoid shape and consciousness. *Is that not enough to be considered deserving of basic rights?*

This was easier when Lucia thought it was just an imitation—something created in Etryaen labs.

"Stop overthinking it. They don't think as we do. They don't care or feel pain. This Niveus has been programmed to obey us."

"Fabien—"

"Are you saying no, Lucia?" He hops down from the box, getting close to her. He stares down at her intensely, dark eyes flashing. "The Mother granted you with magisk. I would think you'd be a little more grateful; she could take it away."

Lucia shivers at the thought. *Could she... would she?*

"I'm sorry," Lucia apologizes, voice strained and panicked. "I'm trying my best, I promise. It's *hard*."

"Yeah? Are you going to give up every time something gets hard, Lady Lucia? Because if you are, you will never be coven head and you will never lead the Caput Trium as your grandmother does. You will disgrace the Dol'Auclair name—disgrace your dying grandmother."

Lucia feels those gritted words like a slap across the face. Using her grandmother's name was a low blow.

Fabien backs up, his face hard and resolute.

"If you can't find the strength to do it yourself, I'm going to have to help you." He turns to the Niveus, lips pursed, eyes narrowed in passionate, barely restrained anger. "O Kulo!" Fabien commands. "O kula uugun i okan." *Attack! Attack her and don't stop.*

Lucia's eyes widen, her heart beating fast. The Niveus snaps to focus as it turns to her, its new target.

"W-what are you doing?" she stutters as fear strikes her. This isn't the easy training dummies used upstairs and it won't just disappear with a light tap.

"I've told it to attack you," Fabien says, voice hard and unwavering. "And it won't stop until you make it."

Lucia cries out, falling to the ground as the Niveus strikes her across the face. Pain blooms over her cheek as she cradles the wound. She can feel a bruise forming where the skin split.

The Niveus comes again, so Lucia jumps quickly to her feet, despite the exhaustion, backing up until she hits the wall.

The creature aims for her head, so she spins, the wood splintering as its white fist hits where she had been standing only moments before.

"Fabien, stop this!" Lucia shouts, her face throbbing in pain. "I can't do it. I don't know how I used the cantus before, but I can't call it on command."

"That's why we're doing these lessons," he says, not meeting her eyes. "Fear activated it last time; let's see if it does again." He looks cold and calculating as he sits atop the white box, his arms splayed wide.

Lucia cries out, her arms struck with bruising force when she puts them up to block. Her right arm drops loose at her side, a punch landing square in her stomach. Lucia lurches forward, coughing up spit and a few drops of blood.

What is Fabien trying to do?

Lucia wheezes, trying to catch her breath. She thinks she might suffocate like this, unable to get any air into her lungs.

"Come on, Lucia! Do you think you're going to win the Triune, let alone be able to control the power of the Orbis Libra if you can't do a simple cantus? Easy magisk a baab could do in their sleep! *Kein u Kila*; Do you want to be a disgrace to your family legacy? The legendary Dol'Auclair's—*the Mother* herself who bore magisk into Hontaras!" Fabien screams.

Lucia puts an arm out to push the Niveus away, but it doesn't budge, the skin hard and unyielding beneath her fingers. It sweeps its leg out in a graceful move, and Lucia's feet come out from under her as she lands on her back with a painful thud, head bouncing off the ground as the breath punches from her once again.

Lucia flails, face red and eyes bulging as she chokes, vision blurry as she stares up at the Niveus above her. Its foot comes up, aimed right at her stomach. As the foot comes down hard, with a force that could crush her, Lucia throws her arms out in an act of desperation—using no words—as her breath has yet to return.

Stop!

Lucia commands the Niveus in her mind. Her eyes clench shut as she anticipates the impact that never comes.

Peeking an eye open, Lucia sees the creature above her, foot poised an inch from her face. Slowly, it lowers its foot and steps back as if waiting for another order.

It listened to her. Not the cantus, but her Sage magisk.

Lucia lets out a painful breath, falling limp against the floor. She hears footsteps, and then Fabien is above her, his eyes wide in shock and awe.

"See, Lucia," he breathes. "You did wordless cantus. I'm going to make a witch out of you yet. I will do anything for the covens, even *hurt you*. If you care about your family's legacy, you'll understand. One day, you'll even thank me. Also, be careful who you hang out with and the message it sends."

Lucia lifts her head up, body sore and weary as she looks into Fabien's eyes. *Is he talking about Adelaide, has he seen them studying together? Or is he speaking of Hetan?* Fabien has always hated him.

"Mother told me to keep an eye on the competition to learn their weaknesses."

"Oh, yeah? And?" Fabien stares hard, searching her for answers.

"I—I don't really have anything yet. All I know is that Adelaide's brother Siphon gets bad headaches," she says quietly, guilt eating her up.

Fabien hums. "Madam Hatsia needs you to find the vampire and that wolf's weakness, but that doesn't mean you have to be so familiar with them. Make sure to keep your mind on the goal, or else I might need to send a message to your mother myself."

Tears track down Lucia's face, ribs stinging as Fabien's footsteps retreat.

She did it. Lucia used her gift to stop the Niveus. So, why doesn't she feel happy about it?

It's late when Lucia finally drags herself from the practice room, a group of young wolves coming in to use it. Limping out into the hall is one of the hardest things she has had to do, as the heavy weight of her emotions accompanies the pain.

Each inhale is like trying to breathe beneath a rushing current, taking in lungsful of water with every breath. Lucia ducks into the next hall as she hears laughter coming from the large gym. Gabrielle and Hetan walk out, disappearing toward the stairs. Lucia hadn't known they were training together.

"Imagine finding you here," an annoyed, mocking voice says. "You couldn't even tell me you were ditching our meet-up."

Adelaide is close, so close Lucia can feel the heat against her back. Her eyes close as she tries to gather her patience, trying not to think about Fabien's harsh words. He made it very clear that he doesn't like the friendship blooming between her and Adelaide. He's trying to control who she spends her time with by threatening to tell her mother she's misbehaving.

Adelaide sniffs the air. "You smell like that witch. The asshole. Is that who you ditched me for, Lucia?"

Lucia snaps her head around, turning so quickly that she loses her balance. The vampire is quick, her arms wrapping around Lucia to catch her, squeezing her wounded ribs.

"Whoa, I've got you," Adelaide says, her tone completely changing from snappish and playful to concerned. Adelaide's eyes rake over her, taking in her pained gasp and the bruise forming on her cheek. Her eyes darken so quickly, the red deepening to near black. "What happened?" she hisses. "Who hurt you?"

Adelaide's head whips around like the assailant might still be standing around, before locking back on her. The gaze hits her harder than any of her physical injuries.

"I'm fine," Lucia gasps, pushing away from the other woman. Adelaide doesn't touch her again, but she moves with her as if blocking her from going farther. Lucia is not in the mood for this. For the vampire's sass and meanness. She doesn't need more people trying to tell her what to do.

"You're not fine. Just tell me who did it and—"

"So you can hurt them like you hurt Hetan?" Adelaide is silent, her mouth wide in shock. Lucia pushes on. "Why do you care?" she snaps, continuing her slow limp down the hall, shaking as Adelaide hovers beside her, hand in the air like she wants to touch her. Lucia almost wants her to. Almost. But she's too angry. Too *hurt*. And she wants to hurt Adelaide at this moment.

"What is that supposed to mean? Why wouldn't I care that you've been attacked? You stand me up for our meeting with no warning, and then I find you here covered in bruises. Tell me what happened. Tell me who did it before I have to question everyone on this campus to find out who it was."

"You have no right to demand anything of me," Lucia snaps, glaring up at the vampire with all the anger she feels at this moment. Anger Adelaide doesn't deserve. "You're just like the rest of them. You all only care about yourselves. You're selfish."

"Where is this coming from? I thought we were—"

"What? Two lousy dances at some lame party and you think you can tell me what to do? Follow me around everywhere. If I had known you'd be this clingy, I wouldn't have—"

"Don't say it."

Adelaide has Lucia caged in against the wall, jaw clenched tight as she stares deep into Lucia's eyes. "Don't finish whatever cruel thing you were going to say." Adelaide looks down at her, and she looks angry. But Lucia thinks she also looks miserable. Almost as miserable as Lucia feels, inside and out.

Lucia keeps her mouth closed, looking away from that imploring gaze. She doesn't finish her thought. She can barely even remember the lie she was going to wield like a stinging whip at Adelaide.

"Lady Lucia?"

Caitlyn comes down the hall toward them, and though painful, Lucia puts distance between herself and the vampire. Adelaide draws back, uncaging her from the wall. She meets Caitlyn halfway, not sparing a single look at Adelaide over her shoulder. She can't. It would hurt too much. It's best for both of them that they don't speak. This way her mother can't get information from her about the vampire.

Caitlyn eyes the vampire warily and then turns back to her.

"What happened, Lucia? Do you need to see the healer?"

Lucia lets out a breathy chuckle. "Yes, if you could help me, please. I went a little too hard in training. Those Niveus don't pull their punches." Lucia isn't technically lying; all of her injuries were caused by the creature in one way or another.

Caitlyn drapes Lucia's arm over her shoulder to help her walk, sparing one last suspicious glance toward Adelaide, whose eyes bore into Lucia's back.

Chapter Eighteen

A Siren's Love Prophecy

LUCIA WAKES ONCE AGAIN on a cot in the medical wing. After Caitlyn dropped her off, Himari gave her a scolding for practicing so hard and a heavy elixir that put her to sleep due to the rapid healing.

Lucia looks around the quiet room, empty cots beside her and the sky still dark outside the windows. She turns over to face the window, looking out at the beautiful night sky. The moon and the stars look prettier in Olympia than they did back in Laesbury.

"I do my best thinking at night."

Lucia turns, startled to find Himari standing beside her bed. She hadn't heard the girl approach. Himari joins her looking out over the campus. Her hair shines like the deep sea in the dark room, inky and calm.

"I haven't slept much since I left Laesbury. There's too much to keep me awake. I love to look out at the sky and imagine what all is out there."

A small smile turns up the weary corners of the girl's lips. It warms Lucia a little, though her heart is still heavy.

"Mhm. Is that what all your books are about? Traveling—adventure." Lucia remembers Himari used to spend all day when she wasn't training with Madam Anais in the library.

Himari nods. "It's a wonder there are so many things to do and see and *be* in this world. I find myself getting caught up in it sometimes. It can be hard to pull myself out."

The young healer grabs a fresh jar of salve from the table and motions for Lucia to lift her chemise. Lucia winces at the movement, letting out a pained hiss as cool fingers run across a deep purple bruise.

"Then why don't you go out and see it? You could," Lucia says, her voice tight. She knows how gifted Himari's healing is. She was well sought after in Laesbury. For years people tried buying her services, to take her away from the Dol'Auclair estate, but she turned them down each time. It was always the same answer: *I'm happy here.*

Lucia could never understand how someone could be happy and stuck in the same place forever. She used to think that if she was as free as Himari, she'd go everywhere.

She never thought of it before, but she wonders why the girl changed her mind. Why she chose to leave.

Lucia notices Himari is too quiet behind her where she went to fetch the binding patch.

"I was seven when I came to Madam Anais," Himari says softly. "And when I came to stay at the Dol'Auclair estate. It was the first time I ever felt like I belonged somewhere, the first time in all my years that I had a home I didn't feel would be ripped away from me. No one expected anything from me, and Anais never scolded me when I made a mistake. And you and Lady Gabrielle had always been so nice to me. Kind of like having big sisters, if I'm not overstepping saying such a thing."

Lucia shakes her head, turning to look at the girl. "Of course not."

Lucia had never thought much about the circumstances that brought Himari to them. She'd been twelve at the time, and her mother said Anais was taking on an apprentice. In all her years, Anais had never done such a thing, so Lucia was curious about what was so special about the girl. When a young Himari had stepped out of the carriage on a bright spring day, with riveting blue hair and such desperate eyes, Lucia had wanted fiercely to protect her. A feeling she had only felt before with Gabrielle.

Lucia groans as she sits up. She pats the empty space beside her, and Himari hesitantly perches on the cot. Talking to the young healer must have been exactly what Lucia needed because she doesn't feel any of the hostility she had earlier, or any of the guilt for her reaction to Adelaide's jest.

"You have a lot of people who care about you," Himari says, fingers playing with the green patch in her hands. "They were in and out of here checking up on you. And Lady Gabrielle is still as passionate as I remember."

Lucia chuckles. She can only imagine the annoyance Gabrielle was for the young healer. For someone who doesn't take much seriously, Gabrielle worries and protects relentlessly.

Himari peeks up at Lucia as if she's nervous about what she's going to say next. "And um—that vampire, the one with the pale golden hair. She came to see if you were okay. It was hard to get rid of her."

Lucia goes rigid, her heart beating faster as heat rises up the side of her neck. *Adelaide checked on her... even after what she said?*

"Is she, ah... a friend of yours?"

Himari says it lightly like she couldn't care either way, but Lucia detects the curious sparkle in her eyes. Lucia smiles, melting back against the wall as she stares out the windows at the vampires' dorms across the big lawn, the statues atop the building imprinting monstrous shapes against the sky. In this room with the little healer beside her, under the dark blanket of night, Lucia feels laid b are.

"Kind of. I'm not sure anymore," she whispers too honestly. "It's funny how quickly matters of the heart shift. Almost without realizing..."

And that's what it is, matters of the heart. *Adelaide makes Lucia's heart hurt. In a good way... In a bad way. She doesn't know what it all means. It's terrifying.*

Himari scoots back, shifting to fold her legs underneath herself. "I wouldn't know. I'm only fifteen."

Lucia chuckles. "Of course." Lucia forgets she's so young, because of how talented and wise she is. "Weird question, but do you ever treat any vampires?" It's a question that has been floating around her mind since she saw Gabrielle's memory. "Like, can vampires get sick?"

Himari hums, thinking about it. "Yes, I've treated some vampires before, but not often. Vampires can't get sick in the way a human or a witch would, but if they go too long without blood, they begin to mimic some of the signs. It won't kill them obviously, but yeah, they can get sick. And if they're particularly emaciated their healing slows."

Lucia's eyebrows scrunch in worry. "Slows? If a very hungry vampire, one who hasn't eaten in a long time, were to get critically injured, could they die?"

Himari shrugs. "I don't know. Again, I don't work with vampires often. They're very secretive creatures and I'm sure there's a lot I don't know. But it's possible, I would say."

Lucia is quiet for a long time, sitting in silence with Himari as she thinks about the girl's words. After a while, Himari breaks the silence and for a moment Lucia is confused about who she's talking about.

"She's pretty," Himari says, almost like a secret. "But scary. And I like seeing you happy."

Lucia stares at the girl beside her, lost in thought. *Does she look happy?* She reaches up to touch her face, fingers brushing her cheeks and lips as if her joy might be imprinted there.

"If my books have taught me anything," Himari says, leaning back against the wall, "it's that the best things always seem much harder than they are. Fate will catch up no matter how hard you try to avoid it."

***

Lucia slumps down in her seat in her Magisk Creatures class, trying not to draw attention to herself. She's still tired from the elixir's healing and aching as it hadn't been able to mend all of her wounds.

Professor Gael, whom Lucia learned was the Gaia who constructed the vine maze and rock platforms at the first trial, sits back on a rock formation she created as a stool.

"I'm curious, who knows about creatures of love?" she asks. Her excitable nature is usually endearing, but today it's making Lucia agitated. She ignored Adelaide in the hall this morning on her way to class. She didn't know what she could possibly say to her—*Sorry?* No, that wouldn't be nearly enough. And to make it worse, Adelaide didn't seem to care.

Lucia groans, laying her head against the desk. *Why does she even care? It's not like they were... anything.* It's actually best she doesn't speak with Adelaide anymore. This way she won't be able to gather information for her mother.

The girl behind Lucia raises her hand, nearly bursting out of her seat. Everyone in this class is jumpy today.

"The early wolves who are indigenous to Hontaras believe magisk creatures of love to be the children of the love Goddess Aroha."

"Good. Yes, in a time before Mystics came to Hontaras, and magisk creatures were still greatly thought to be a folk tale, those who lived here depicted the unknown as children of various Gods. For creatures such as the Sirens"—Gael points to the projection on the screen—"that Goddess was Aroha. Sirens, in particular, are the children of Aroha and Wai—God of the Sea. The origin of Sirens is still unknown, as is their method of reproduction since no male of the species has been discovered, but some believe they do so asexually. The earliest records we have are drawings discovered in an oceanic cave on the coastline of Amesia. They're said to come at the call of this tune—" The professor whistles a sharp, shrill note that makes Lucia grimace, her head feeling like it'll split in two.

Professor Gael claps excitedly, hopping down from her rock. "Now follow me!" She ushers everyone out of their seats, who seem to have as bad a day as Lucia grumbling as they make their way out of the building and down to Siren Lake at the edge of the little forest. Lucia has passed it a few times, but she never saw any Siren in there, though they're told to sometimes be found splashing around in the deep waters.

The morning is cold, and the air is crisp. The professor motions for Beaur to do the call. The boy whistles the enchanting tune, and the class waits a long while, growing restless by the time a head bobs up from the edge of the water. That grabs Lucia's attention, and she's wide-eyed as she leans in to get a good look.

The creature that appears watches them curiously. Lucia is stunned by its eerie beauty: a human-like face and torso, but its eyes are a depthless black. It has fins for ears and gills along its neck, the body covered in large scales the size of a fist, which glow iridescently. Startled, Lucia nearly falls into the lake as its long tail thwacks the surface of the water.

The oddest part about the Siren is that where there should be arms, the Siren instead has wing-like fins with scales attached to webbed human-like hands.

Professor Gael cheers, a large, goofy smile overtaking her face. "What a beauty," she breathes. She hands another student some snacks and urges them forward. "Go on, feed her."

The boy approaches shakily, hand outstretched with the food in his palm. The Siren snatches the food so fast it's a blur and then begins eating happily, with long, sharp, terrifying teeth.

"You see her hair and the markings on her face? These are a bit different from the ones depicted in the underwater caves in Amesia, though aside from the fables and ancient drawings, we've never had any verified sightings there. It's unknown if they have evolved or are a subspecies of their ancestors, but we believe the two have some distant relation to one another. Some magisk evolutionary biologists think they're just in different stages of life, but who knows, we still have so much to learn. The study of magisk creatures is still a young profession. Many of our creatures aren't native to Hontaras and no one knows how they arrived here."

The professor walks around the edge of the lake, pointing to a dark mass deep below the dark blue surface of the water. "It's hard to tell, but here you can see a slightly darker part of the water. There's an underground cave in this lake that goes through layers of the earth and out into the deep sea. That's how the Sirens travel to this lake and many other lakes and caves around Hontaras."

Lucia sits back and watches the students play around, splashing water at each other, and the snacking Siren in awe. Her eyes stray to a lone figure standing at the edge of the group, looking out of sorts, her short, dark hair covering her downturned face.

"Caitlyn?" Lucia says, approaching her sister's friend. The girl is so quiet Lucia had never even noticed she was in the class. Without Mia around, Caitlyn always seems to look so different from her upbeat, playful self. Like a shell. "Uh, are you okay?" Lucia asks. She doesn't really know how to do this. Comforting people. But since the woman helped her get to the infirmary yesterday, she feels like she should try.

The young witch turns, and Lucia sees her face, teeth gritted and eyes hard as she stares at the gaggle of vampires laughing by the water.

"They make me sick," she says. "They're like wild animals, running around here with everyone like they aren't itching to rip someone's throat out."

"Excuse me?" Lucia says, shocked by Caitlyn's words. The girl is normally so sweet.

She's wearing a thin smock today, her arms clutched around her middle. She looks like she's freezing. Lucia knows her coven, despite being one of the big four, isn't very rich. How she affords to go to Eirini, Lucia isn't sure.

"Would you like to borrow my cloak? I'm not very cold and you look like you're freezing."

It isn't true; Lucia is very cold, but her thick, long-sleeved dress will keep her warmer than Caitlyn right now. The witch looks taken aback for a moment, looking down at the gooseflesh on her pale arms and then Lucia's thick clothing. When she hesitates, Lucia pulls it off and pushes it toward her.

"Go on."

Caitlyn takes the cloak with a small smile, her shoulders hunching in relief as she wraps the fabric warmed by Lucia's body over her small frame.

"Thank you," Caitlyn says, shaking her head. "Mia offered me her cloak this morning, I shouldn't have been so stubborn to take it. And sorry about that. I... I was just feeling a bit out of it. Maybe I shouldn't be telling you this, it's not my business, but I'm worried. Gabrielle—your sister is meeting with someone. A *vampire*. I don't trust him."

Lucia's brows furrow. "You're worried about Gabrielle, why?" She doesn't see why seeing a vampire would be cause for alarm given Lucia herself hangs out with a particular blonde one. Also, she knows her sister can handle herself.

"Well, he's Siphon Skullkin of the Silver Spiders. There are some nasty rumors about him. One I've heard recently just doesn't sit right. And I mean, just look at the guy and you can tell something is off. He's so pale and his eyes—they're unnerving. He just looks... sick."

"What was the rumor?" Lucia asks, turning in toward the witch curiously. She shouldn't listen to gossip, but if Caitlyn is truly worried then Lucia should know.

"It—" She looks around like someone might hear. "Apparently, this isn't Siphon's first time at Eirini. He came here a few years ago and met a girl. A wolf. So I've heard, they fell in love, like, crazy fast, and he even proposed."

Caitlyn shudders like the thought of a vampire and wolf marrying repulses her. "Anyway, they were engaged, and then suddenly she just disappeared. No one had any clue what happened to her, and shortly after, Siphon left the academy."

Lucia is in shock. She hadn't been expecting that story at all. "It can't be true," she says. "I mean, he couldn't have hurt her or anything, or he would've been taken to the Caput Trium. It would break the treaty."

Caitlyn growls, eyes hardening again. "Yeah, except he's the son of Nikolay Skullkin. *Adopted son*. Those Spiders never get caught for anything despite there being heavy evidence they deal weapons and drugs to human gangs in Zarun."

Lucia soaks this information in as Caitlyn wanders away. She knows she shouldn't believe it; she saw Gabrielle's memory, and the vampire seemed perfectly nice aside from—

Lucia grows cold at the memory. He acted a bit weird at the end of their conversation, but he never hurt Gabrielle. And he's Adelaide's brother. *He can't be all bad.*

"Sirens are known for their love prophecies," Professor Gael says, making her way over. Straight to Lucia. She places a hand on her shoulder, steering her back toward the water.

"No, no, no," Lucia says, trying to back away. She does not want to be a part of any sort of demonstration.

"Come on, don't be shy, Miss Dol'Auclair." She has Lucia kneel at the edge of the water. "Lean in close."

Lucia hesitates but gives in, holding her breath as she leans out over the water. The creature stares into her eyes, a scaled hand coming out to touch, cold and slimy against her forehead. Water drips down the center of Lucia's face as the black eyes glow an eerie gold, and the Siren speaks. Her voice sounds like a mimicry of human speech. The prophecy reads like a poem and Lucia can almost see it in her mind:

Three loves but only one that is true.
Your great love will bring loss,

So be warned of the path you choose.
If you choose wrong, your death might await.
Or life in a cage, walking the trail of fate.
But if you choose the last,
Another will grow to hate.

Lucia pulls back from the Siren, her pulse throbbing as her heart batters her chest. She laughs, wiping the cool water from her face as she turns to her stunned classmates, her professor's mouth wide and eyes bulging in shock.

"That was less a love fortune and more a cryptic omen," Lucia jokes, trying to make light of the eerie encounter. *This is all a joke.* Lucia laughs to herself. Rumors of the Siren's powers are greatly exaggerated, and for some reason, it has chosen to play along. Maybe for the snacks.

Three loves? Lucia doesn't even have one. *There is no epic love in my future, nor life in a cage. That's just ridiculous.*

The Siren reads a few more love prophecies while Lucia stews, cold and annoyed. She almost misses it when her class begins leaving, she is so caught up in her thoughts. She turns to join them and bumps into Kelsy, whose eyes are wide and frightened, mouth open without a sound.

"Are you okay?" Lucia asks, creeped out by the woman's face. She turns back toward the water where Kelsey is staring—as if she has seen a ghost. She finds something floating toward them in the water. Lucia is confused at first, still distracted by the love prophecy, but when the large, dark object hits the shore, bobbing against the short grass, Lucia realizes what she's seeing.

The Siren dives away quickly, her tail sending up a great big splash that sends water over Lucia and Kelsy, who stands frozen in shock. Lucia's face grows cold with fear.

After a moment, Kelsy stumbles forward, falling to her knees. Her scream pierces the morning silence as a young girl floats face down, her bloated body battering the shore.

Dead.

THE BALANCE OF FATES

***

Lucia can't even celebrate being at her mother's side for a meeting of the council, as the event that brought her here is less than cheerful. The girl found dead in the lake was Mairan Barlow. The sweet, red-haired, cherub-faced girl who had her blooming ceremony only months ago with Lucia. Now she's gone.

Lucia's mother called for the meeting, as Mairan was a Golden Griffin, and the Caput Trium wouldn't take on the case since there was no clear sign of who killed her, and they only take on cases that break the treaty between the witches, wolves, and vampires.

Hatsia has witches on the job, using their magisk in whatever way they can to try to find the secrets of Mairan's death.

Lucia bites her lip, fingers digging into her thighs as she stares around the silent table, some sort of battle of wills going on.

Hatsia stares down at the other members of the council, the ones who showed up. There are six in total out of twenty council members. Kamlan Hoover, the head of the Committee of Magisk Creatures, is a young man with big, round glasses and mousy brown hair. Linae Devroue, Siphon Skullkin, Cassius Draik, Hetan Anoki, and Ayawa Anoki—on the council not as third of three on the Caput Trium but as the chief of the Silver Fang clan.

They sit at the round table in the Dome, the spectator seats dark and empty.

"I am Hatsia Dol'Auclair, coven head of the Golden Griffin coven. I called this meeting on behalf of the murders at Eirini Academy of Mystics, murders which have no perpetrator to enact justice upon. The latest was my own, a young witch. It's hard to tell since she was waterlogged, but it looked as if she was drained of blood before she was dumped into the lake."

Hatsia's eyes flit to the two vampires. Siphon's face is drawn and blank, not acknowledging the implication of the witch's words.

Hatsia's expression is pained, a look Lucia has never seen toward her or her suffering, only for the love her mother has for her people—the coven. Lucia tries not to feel hurt by this discovery, as she watches Cassius's face grow dark with anger. The man looks better than the last time Lucia saw him, the memory of the attack still imprinted in her mind. He wears flashy clothes and has silver beads in his braids.

"One of your own," Cassius says, teeth gritted and eyes narrowed dangerously. "Interesting, because I was under the impression we were all one people. If anyone is to point fingers, what about the Sirens? It was found in their lake after all."

"*She*," Hatsia snaps, "was a young woman. Mairan Barlow."

"Yes, Hatsia, so sad," Anoki says, slow and measured. His hands are folded atop the table, white fur across his broad shoulders. "Many wolves have been killed. Wolves die daily due to famine and the group of human hunters that border the great forests of Whoynia. Where was everyone's concern then, from the vampires or witches? It took only one of yours to get you here, Hatsia Dol'Auclair. Where was that urgency from the start?"

Hatsia is seething, eyes barely concealing her rage from under her mourning veil.

Kamlan raises a hand. "I concur," he says. His tie is askew, and his glasses sit precariously at the brink of his nose. He looks like a child sitting at the adults' table. "Magisk creatures are killed at an alarming rate. I have come time and again to the Caput Trium on their behalf, yet no one listens. It isn't important unless it's one of the *major four*. The curriculum on magisk creatures is lacking and so is empathy. You, vampires, blame the Sirens for this, yet Sirens are gentle creatures. Though they may look scary to some, they are creatures of *love*. Yet your hate would have them tried for a murder they didn't—*couldn't*—commit. And they would have no way to defend themselves."

Lucia's heart beats quickly, hands sweating as she watches the elders argue. She doesn't like this. She doesn't understand why they can't work together to find the culprit.

She looks to Hetan, whose head is bowed, and Siphon, who still hasn't said a word. Lucia has no input; all she can do is listen. Listen and learn. If she becomes Eidan, she will be at this table again, and she'll be expected to talk. She doesn't like it, but it is her duty. That is why her mother brought her here. She's finally giving Lucia a chance.

"Might I note none of theirs"—Hatsia points to Siphon—"are dead. It's no wonder Nikolay wouldn't see to the issue when the vampires aren't dying. But when his vampires needed rings to walk in the day, we provided them."

Siphon says, "Are you implying this is our doing, just because your people are weak?"

Hatsia's eyes narrow, fingers drumming against the tabletop. "I'm just stating the events. I'm not implying any conclusion you can't draw on your own."

Cassius smirks. "Might I remind you, we vampires are simply superior to you? In strength, speed, and healing ability. It would be hard for this killer to catch one of us off guard. I wouldn't put it past the witches to kill their own for war, especially if it meant incriminating my vampires. What's a little blood sacrifice, to get what you want? The witches have done it before," he says smugly.

Lucia fears her mother might fly right out of her seat, that anger she reserves for behind closed doors close to bursting, but the woman takes a deep breath and when she opens her eyes again, she laughs.

Linae speaks up, not holding back her wicked tongue. "You aberrant beasts have the strengths you do because you feast on the blood of others—rely on them to live like retched scavengers. Vile, immoral, stains upon the human form. And, it seems, you could never get over the past and the fact that you lost the War."

Cassius's chair flips as he jumps to his feet, moving like a blur as he tries to cross the table. Siphon is behind him, arms wrapped around his torso as he pulls him back.

"Enough... enough," he repeats to the raging vampire, setting him back in his seat. Lucia's heart is racing, and images of him attacking her come to mind. Adelaide said they were handling him, yet here he is. She doesn't know what to make of that. It's obvious to her that he is someone high in the vampires' ranks, but she still can't forget the way he attacked her. Like he wasn't in control. Like he was *rabid*.

Hatsia looks smug leaning back in her seat. "Like Linae said, bloodsucking beasts who can't control themselves."

The meeting ends with Cassius storming off. Siphon is quick on his heels. Lucia lets out a breath, clammy and stunned from the events she witnessed. It's nothing like the calm, civil conversation among adults and leaders that she had expected. The meeting was a disaster with no resolution.

Without proof, there's only so far that accusations will take this. Not unless someone wants to risk shaking the tentative peace that exists between the Mystic families. And despite the murders, Eirini Academy can't be closed. It's still the safest place to hold the Triune and with her grandmother's magisk waning the Caput Trium can't wait much longer to replace her.

Is this chaos what Lucia has to look forward to?

Lucia slows as she follows her mother outside, watching Hetan and his uncle. Hetan looks angry, turning from his uncle who tries to speak with him. The man's face is red, staff striking the ground. His lips move harshly as Hetan flees back inside, and Lucia wishes to go to him, but her mother's hand on her back guides her into their carriage.

"I need to speak to—" The look on Hatsia's face has Lucia closing her mouth, climbing inside without a word.

"You have to be careful," Hatsia says, leaning in toward Lucia, who stares out of the carriage window, troubled as she watches the other carriages depart and head off in different directions. "Those wolves and vampires are dangerous. They aren't like us—they're wild, animalistic. They aren't your friends, Lucia, or your allies. They're your competition. I said to get close, but you have to keep your head on. Close *but separate.*"

The atmosphere is quiet and tense, Hatsia's displeasure known in every inch of her body. Lucia presses her head atop the window ledge, the cool breeze and her mother's words lulling her into a restless sleep.

Chapter Nineteen

Topsy-Turvy Past

LUCIA IS EXTREMELY NERVOUS as she stands beside her fellow competitors on the first level of the Noxidome.

There wasn't anything she could do to prepare for this trial, as the hint at what they were doing was so vague. Something to do with memories and mental challenges. That should have been reassuring because it means she is on a level playing field with the other three competitors, who look just as confused as her, but it isn't. Lucia worries about everything. And she hates surprises.

"We are gathered here today for the second trial." Ekrul's voice echoes as he motions a scaled hand to the crowd.

The competitors stand in the middle of the room beside a man Lucia doesn't recognize, but she's sure he is a mage and a strong one. She can feel his power.

Ekrul motions to the man, bald with dark skin and golden rings around his neck. He must be Etryaen, from his style of dress.

"This is Aamad, a witch—a mage—and an old friend who was kind enough to help with the second trial. He is extremely skilled in Sage magisk."

Lucia's eyes widened at those words.

THE BALANCE OF FATES

This man is the Sage?

She looks him over. He looks fine. He looks unhindered by his ability. She hadn't thought of it before, as there aren't many Sages, but maybe she needs a Sage to help her with understanding her own ability.

Lucia grows nervous at the thought, wondering if he would be willing to help her, as she wipes her sweaty hands on her dress.

"This trial is very simple. Aamad will devise a test for each competitor, a mind maze using the thoughts, feelings, and emotions that most hinder them." He turns to the four contestants. "You will have to overcome those challenges to escape the trial, and when you do you will wake. The first three to wake will move on to the third and final trial to become the vessel of the Orbis Libra."

Simple? That sounds downright frightening to Lucia, who returns her mother's nod, giving the woman reassurance she doesn't feel. Lucia doesn't see Gabrielle though. Scanning the crowd, her sister is nowhere to be found. Gabrielle is always Lucia's comfort in times like these, so Lucia wonders where she could possibly be right now.

A hand on Lucia's back sears heat through her. She glances up with a flick of her eyes so as not to draw her mother's attention. Adelaide. The vampire isn't looking at her, but there's a quirk of her lips where the side of her mouth rises in an affectionate smile. Lucia shivers when the heat draws away, and Aamad approaches with his cupped palms raised toward them, golden jewelry clanging around his wrists.

Lucia feels an odd tugging at her navel. She feels like she's being dropped, a grand big ocean and the starry sky above her even though it's morning right now. It's the same place she visited before, at the Dome. Lucia begins to wonder if it's a real place.

This time she isn't in the water, and when she looks over, Hetan, Mia, and Adelaide are there too, all looking up at the giant moon that takes up most of the sky.

Lucia takes a step toward Hetan beside her, opening her mouth to speak, but then she's falling again:

Lucia blinks awake, sunlight streaming into her bedroom window and warming the side of her face. She sits up, stretching her arms over her head as she lets out a large yawn. She's exhausted and, for some reason, sore. She runs her hand over her stomach, but there's nothing there. Weird.

"Lucia! Lucia, Lucia!"

Lucia smiles as Gabrielle bursts into the room, her braids bouncing wildly, and she's smiling wide. Her younger sister is always so full of energy.

Gabrielle jumps onto the bed beside her.

"Today's the day. It's the day you get your gift from the Mother!"

Lucia's eyes widen.

"Is it?"

Gabrielle gives her a funny look. "Of course it is!" She reaches forward to feel Lucia's face. "Hmm, you don't have a fever. Are you okay? You've been dreaming of this day for years."

Lucia nods. "Right." For some reason, she thought that happened already... How could she have forgotten?

Lucia smiles as the importance of today hits her, and she scrambles out of bed, rushing to get dressed. She'll finally get her gift, and everyone will start respecting her. She can put those years of teasing behind her.

"What gift do you think you'll get? Gaia, like our mother?" Gabrielle asks from the bed.

Lucia shrugs. She doesn't care which she gets; any would be cool. She flexes the nonexistent muscles on her arms.

"Maybe Augere?"

"Ooh, you could pick up really heavy things," Gabrielle teases. Lucia throws a dress at her, which falls over her face.

"And run fast," Lucia adds as Gabrielle struggles to untangle herself from the clothes.

The day passes in a hectic blur as Lucia prepares for the blooming ceremony, but something lingers in the back of her mind, some odd feeling that tugs at her gut. She pushes it away. She's probably just hungry. The cook is preparing a huge feast for the celebration breakfast and Lucia's stomach growls. She tries sneaking a roll from the kitchen, but the cook shoos her away.

Whatever, Lucia thinks as she slinks away rejected. She has a lot to do today. It's time for the honorary maturing ritual. Most witches do it on their eighteenth birthday, but Lucia was saving it for the blooming ceremony because today, her life truly changes. It's a tradition for witches, one they have to complete alone.

Lucia gathers up a few of her old things—the first picture she ever drew, a baby tooth, and one of her favorite stuffed bears. She heads out to the forest alone and sits underneath a willow tree. She likes to come here to think. It reminds her of her old friend Hetan. Except, when she comes here today, an odd feeling of guilt settles in her stomach.

Guilt for what?

Lucia shakes off that feeling again and places each item inside a metal basin. Since she can't use any cantus, she makes a small fire by hand, then places a burning stick atop the bear, the cotton catching fire and igniting all of the items. Burning these items from her childhood symbolizes letting go of the past to make room to grow into the future, an adult version of herself. She should feel lighter when she trudges out of the woods, yet something heavy and bleak sits atop her shoulders.

"What is wrong with you, Lucia?" she mutters as she walks up the path to the manor house. "Today is a good day. Don't worry."

Lucia sees her grandmother's carriage come into view and her eyes light up as she races to the house. She had sent a message on the sphaera to her grandmother a week ago and never got a response. She wasn't sure if the woman would show. She doesn't see her grandmother much because she's very busy, and her work is outside of Laesbury. But this is an important event, and Lucia wants all of her family there. Her grandmother will see her bloom and finally be proud of her!

The sun has gone down, and Lucia changes in the back room with the other girls while they wait to be called out by the Priestess. She ignores the taunting from the other girls. They won't be laughing when Lucia presents with the best gift.

The Priestess calls Lucia up first, holding out a hand to her. She goes quickly, cutting across the stage, bathed in moonlight and shaking with excitement. Her chest swells with pride and she holds her head high.

"In the far northern mountains of Naprait, on the eve of an autumn new, the Golden Griffin coven ushers in the next generation of budding witches. Each woman will display the gifts the Mother bestowed upon her."

Lucia closes her eyes. She thinks hard, trying to relax and leave herself open for the Mother to place a gift in her. She waits... and waits...

And waits...

Lucia's eyes open in confusion. She opens her eyes, mouth moving to speak with the Priestess, but she isn't there. When her eyes flutter open, she looks up into her mother's face.

A cold chill sweeps over Lucia's skin, a weight sinking in her gut.

"What is going on?"

Lucia looks around the temple. The place is quiet as a whisper. All of the witches who have gathered are in dark robes that hide their faces and sit stiffly like the dead. The room is dark, the moon above covered by dark, eerie clouds, and candlelight flickers over her mother's face. The statue of the Mother Deipara behind her is like a looming shadow.

"W-what is happening?" Lucia stutters, stumbling back from her mother as the ground begins to shake.

Hatsia smiles, the sinister grin spreading slowly across her lips.

"You have not bloomed, Lucia. The Mother has not granted you a gift."

"No. N-no." Lucia shakes her head in denial. *It can't be. She's supposed to bloom today. She's supposed to get her gift so she can finally live up to her mother's and grandmother's standards, the legacy of the Dol'Auclair. It just doesn't make sense...*

All of a sudden that deep ball in her gut that has plagued Lucia all day starts to make sense.

"But I've done nothing wrong. Mama, believe me. I have listened and done everything that's asked of me! I've followed the Holum Actus—" Lucia tries grabbing onto her mother's robes but the woman steps back from her, prying her fingers from the golden fabric.

"You have not. You have disappointed the Mother—you have disappointed us all." Lucia turns back to the pews, rows, and rows of witches staring at her with judging, angry eyes. Lucia turns again to her mother, desperation in her eyes. Desperation and fear. "You don't deserve to be my daughter. You are broken. You. Are. Unworthy."

Lucia stumbles, her eyes flying open as the ground beneath her becomes unsteady. Suddenly, a great big crack splits down the room with a sound like striking lightning, separating Lucia from the pews where the witches still sit, unfazed by the commotion, and her mother who stands beneath the shadow of the Mother. Her sister and grandmother are standing beside Hatsia now, and they are all looking at Lucia with disgust.

Lucia is floating all alone, on a small marble island. Her heart races as she stares at the growing gap between her and her family. She reaches out toward Gabrielle, her lovely sister. She is wearing white, and she looks so beautiful in the candlelight.

"Gabrielle—" She gasps. "Gabrielle, help me."

The crack is growing larger and larger, and Lucia needs to get on the other side before she gets stuck all alone. When she goes to jump, a cold hand grabs her, pulling her back. She turns and meets warm brown eyes.

Lucia studies the man who looks so familiar. Long, dark hair braided with feathers, and a fur robe around his shoulders. But it's the eyes... the eyes remind her of...

Lucia's breath catches in her throat.

"Hetan, what are you doing?" Lucia looks the man up and down. The man. Hetan is a man now. When did he grow so big?

"You are not going to the other side."

"Hetan, there is an earthquake," Lucia says, trying to pull herself from his tight grasp. "We have to get over."

"You have failed, Lucia, you are not worthy. I will not allow you to take anyone else down with you."

"No, you don't understand. I didn't get to finish the test. I haven't failed, just give me a chance!"

Hetan shakes his head, beads clacking together over the rumbling. "No more chances."

Lucia is horrified by the anger she sees in Hetan's eyes. *What did I ever do to you? Why are you so angry with me?*

"I'm sorry, Hetan. I'm sorry I left you. I'm sorry that I didn't try hard enough. But... I can't die here."

Lucia wrenches her arm from Hetan, stumbling away and nearly tumbling right off the platform into the dark abyss below. She rears back and then leaps across the chasm to where her family is. Her mother grabs her hand as she pitches backward toward the hole.

"Mama!"

Hatsia holds Lucia from falling, staring down into her daughter's eyes. For a moment Lucia sees a tenderness there she has never seen before, and her heart begins to soften. But her mother's face grows dark.

"You are the daughter I wish I never had. Gabrielle should have been my firstborn." Hatsia lets go of her daughter's hand and Lucia goes falling back.

THE BALANCE OF FATES

Her dress and hair whip around her as she falls, down, down, her eyes squeezing closed as her heart plummets along with her.

"Lucia—Lucia!"

Lucia slowly opens her eyes. She is lying on the hard marble floor, her sister's face above her, braids dangling down into her face. What—she's not falling anymore?

"It is so tragic my older sister has passed. May she always be remembered," Gabrielle says, wiping a tear. A sinister smile that looks so odd on her sweet sister's face spreads rouge lips. "Now I will be the inheritor of the Dol'Auclair legacy. As I deserve."

Lucia looks down, and she is no longer on the floor but inside a coffin, her body surrounded by beautiful wildflowers. A veil covers her face. A wave of bubbling anger builds up inside of Lucia as she pulls the lace from her eyes and climbs out of the wooden box, pushing past her sister.

She is not dead.

"Mother!" Lucia calls up to the statue of their great deity, "I have done everything you've asked of me. Everything! So what is this? Why are you doing this to me?"

The massive stone head of the Mother begins to shift and move, gray eyes opening as Deipara's head turns to look down at Lucia like a bug beneath her.

"You're a mistake I must rectify."

"No!" Lucia lashes out, angry that the Mother thinks she can decide that Lucia is trash and toss her aside. That anyone gets to decide her worth. Her arm strikes out as tears burn in her eyes. A wet, gurgling sound turns her attention.

Gabrielle's eyes go wide in shock, and red starts to bloom outwards from her chest. A long gash trails across her white dress.

Lucia's stomach drops. *No. No.* She didn't mean to do that. She thought… she thought she had no magisk.

Lucia rushes across the floor, sliding to her knees to cradle Gabrielle's body in her arms, blood dripping from the side of her sister's mouth.

"Gabrielle," Lucia chokes out, tears burning her eyes. Gabrielle stares up at Lucia, and gone is the hatred, leaving only her sister's lovely brown eyes. "I'm sorry, Gabrielle, it was an accident. I didn't mean to."

"I n— I never..." Gabrielle coughs. "I never blamed you for being like this, Lucia. You deserve everything. You are my sister, and I will love you always." Tears drip onto her sister's face. Gabrielle smiles. "You have power now. Use it wisely."

Lucia shakes her head. "No, no. It's not worth it, it isn't! Not if I don't have you. Gabrielle, I love you more than any gift; you are my sister." Lucia looks up at the Mother, who stares down at her with large, blank eyes. "Help her! Help my little sister!" she screams.

The Mother shakes her large head. "You are the one who did this. I've heard you over the years, the anger in your heart. The sadness. You said you'd do anything for this power."

"I didn't mean it. I take it back! You can have the power. Just give me my sister!"

"I am sorry. It's not my choice."

Lucia blinks through a cloud of tears, and the Mother is once more frozen in place. Hetan stands before her once more.

"Hetan?"

"You brought this on yourself. How does it feel, Lucia, to lose someone you most love?"

"Please, Hetan, I don't understand. I don't— I tried sending you a letter when I heard about your parents. I tried—"

"I don't want a letter from you!" he shouts, the floor shaking again as he slams down a white staff. "It would not have made me feel better to hear from the person who murdered them!"

Lucia's eyes widen in shock. Murder? "I didn't—" Lucia's eyes move slowly toward her mother who stands looking worried on the other side of the chasm. *Why does that sound so familiar?* Those words cause a nagging in the back of

Lucia's mind as a chill creeps up her spine. She looks down at her hands, which are covered in blood, but Gabrielle is no longer lying in her lap.

Lucia looks back toward her mother again. She stands slowly, walking toward the woman as she tries to push away the confusing cloud over her mind. That feeling she got this morning, that odd sense of familiarity, is back.

Hatsia looks scared as her daughter approaches, walking right over the giant crack in the floor without falling through.

It's all a lie, Lucia does have a gift. She remembers it now.

"Lucia, get away!" Hatsia screams. "I don't want you. I hate you and wish you were never born!"

Lucia grabs her mother's arm, her eyes clenching shut as she tries to hear the woman's thoughts. Nothing happens. All she sees is black, a blank emptiness.

Pulling back, Lucia looks up at her mother's empty face, then at the witches frozen in the pews. Her grandmother and Gabrielle, who was just bleeding out on the floor, are amongst them, dressed in black. They stare at her with emotionless eyes.

This isn't real. None of this is real.

Lucia remembers it... the gathering at the Dome, enrolling at Eirini, Adelaide. Her mother—her mother killed Hetan's parents.

"Wake up Lucia. Wake up!"

There's a tugging and an unnatural warmth that envelops her, and then Lucia is falling. She goes down, down, down, into that lake once more. She sees Adelaide as she reaches out, her arm outstretched toward the beautiful vampire. Adelaide's fingers slip through her grasp, and she is falling once more.

Lucia coughs and gasps, falling to her knees on the padded floor of the Noxidome as she tries to catch her breath. She feels like she's suffocating, and she's so nauseous she might just throw up.

When she gets her breathing under control and her chest no longer feels like it's going to crack open, Lucia blinks up at the audience who stares stunned at her.

Did she lose?

Lucia turns to look at the rest of the contestants beside her, but they're all still... their eyes are still closed. Lucia stands on shaky legs, her eyes wide in surprise.

"I passed," she whispers, as cheers break out around the room. She is the first one to finish the second trial. *She hasn't failed yet.*

Chapter Twenty
A Truth and a Lie

Lucia is nervous under her mother's gaze. The woman is looking at her, smiling, and Lucia has not had that in so long. It takes all of her composure to not jump around in giddy excitement.

"Before I have to leave, I want to show you something," Hatsia says. Her eyes flit over Lucia's head to Fabien who stands amongst his friends. The man nods in their direction and Lucia waves.

"I'm glad you and Fabien are getting along. You seem to be doing well here. It reminds me of when I went to Eirini."

Lucia's eyes widen as she turns back to her mother.

"You went to Eirini? I thought you hated it."

Hatsia shakes her head. "I do not hate this academy, though there are things I would like to change. I met your father here, you know."

Lucia knows her mother and father met in school, but she did not know that was at Eirini. That changes so many things in her mind. She wonders why her mother changed her mind about Eirini if she went here. If it wasn't for the Triune, she would have never let Lucia come.

"There can only be one winner of the Triune. As my firstborn, you carry the legacy of the Dol'Auclairs. You're the one who should become the Orbis Libra's vessel and inherit the power that comes with it as your grandmother did. Especially now, with how well you are doing, it would open many doors for you. It won't be easy; you are behind in your training, but I think Eirini can teach you much about your magisk that you couldn't learn back home."

Lucia is in such shock at her mother's words, it's as if she's a whole other person. When Lucia was young her mother wasn't always strict. Sometimes she was kind and did things all mothers do, doting on her daughters, but when Lucia neared the age when her magisk was meant to develop, things began to change. Is it really Lucia's fault her mother is the way she is now? Was it her own failure that created the strict, unhappy woman?

"I thought it would be best if you had someone here looking out for you, someone besides your sister, so Linae offered up Fabien and I think it was a good choice. He's a good man with a good head on his shoulders. You need someone who can help you. Some witches don't believe you're ready, and they would not have chosen you for the task if the Orbis Libra had not picked you. But I have no doubts you are willing to do anything to make this family proud. Am I wrong?"

Lucia hesitates, doubts flooding her mind as she looks into her mother's inquiring face. Can she do it? Can she do anything? She swallows the lump in her throat, thinking of all the secrets she is already keeping. In a way, she is already doing it—protecting the coven at all costs. Her eyes widen in panic when her mother turns to walk away.

"Come with me," she calls, and Lucia nods, scrambling to follow. "And your cloak, Lucia. It will be cold."

Lucia grabs her cloak from the chair it is draped over.

Mother and daughter stroll out of the auditorium and onto the quad. They pass between the witches' dorm and the Noxidome, heading out to the forest.

Lucia follows her mother on foot to the trail up the mountain, glad that she wore the boots she was given before the first task, enjoying the view and fresh air. She is confused, though, about where they're going.

Lucia is glad for her cloak because an icy wind blows through her skirts and whips her loose curls around her head. She's panting by the time they reach a short plateau near the middle of the mountain; the air thinner and it's colder. It's late afternoon now, the sun hidden behind the clouds. She can see her breath. She has never been this deep in the forest before.

"What is this?" Lucia looks up at the carving out of the side of the mountain, a woman sculpted from rock. The site is hidden from the academy far below, covered by tall trees. She wonders how her mother found this place.

The sculpted woman is on her knees, her large hands out before her like she's cradling something. Where her knuckles touch the ground, a cave opens; the woman's hair is made of vines and it hangs down to partially cover the entrance like she's trying to keep it hidden.

Hatsia stares at the sculpture fondly, a look Lucia has never seen on her mother before. She runs her fingers along the rough stone making up the fingers that dwarf hers like a parent to a child.

"When you were younger, your grandmother used to tell me stories about our homeland that were passed on from her mother, and her mother's mother before her, and on and on. She would tell me that Ashad Escana was the most beautiful place in the world. A place where everyone and everything lived in harmony. Every animal on this earth gathered there, drinking from the endless flowing rivers. The water was crystal clear. You could see straight down to the bottom, to all of the fish and marine life that lived below, and no barriers existed from land to sea to sky. And there was a great big tree with many species of fruit that everyone fed from, no one ever going hungry because the tree gave life and never went barren."

Lucia listens in awe, following her mother into the cavern. She hasn't heard many stories of As-Es. Not much of that history is passed on anymore. Hontaras has been the home of witches for so long now.

Hatsia calls fire to her palm using the cantus "ahi"—*fire* and lights the torch left in a sconce on the wall. Lucia gasps, her hand trailing the walls as petroglyphs are revealed to her, drawings along the cave wall depicting figures moving and fighting, animals dancing, and birds flying across the sky. As the light flickers across them, they truly look like they're alive.

Hatsia lights a brazier set upon a stone block in the center of the room. The iron basin fills with flames, illuminating the entire space in an orange glow. Hatsia continues, circling the room as Lucia's eyes hungrily devour the ancient drawings and symbols. Images of their home in Ashad Escana as Lucia had always been told and then images of coming here to Hontaras.

"As-Es was a paradise for God's chosen children. But as with all good things, there were those who coveted the tree and its land. They were greedy and pillaged As-Es, killing our people and creatures, ripping up earth to plunder the riches. Worst of all, they tried to dig up the great tree, killing the earth and all that relied on the tree for life. These barbarians took many families that belonged to As-Es, to use their 'gifts' to help them build a new home in another land. They wanted what we had in Ashad Escana. Peace and beauty. They were willing to take it by force. Only one family survived the brutal travel. Sisters. Deipara, the eldest, then Valeria and Noemi, and the youngest, Zarha. Unfortunately, Lupita died shortly after they landed. They were brought here as vassals of these men.

"Those four sisters were married off to the men and made to have their children. Their families became known as the Dol'Auclairs, the Colflars, the Sacrenladre, and the Devroues. The four great covens we know today."

"But how did they become witches? Did they possess magisk in As-Es?"

Hatsia shakes her head. "Not exactly. Not as it is today. They discovered magisk right here," she says, arms splayed wide. "When the eldest, Deipara, learned her youngest sister was going to be married off to one of their particularly brutal captors—the one who ruled this land, Agon Araneidae—Deipara came to this cave. They had often come up here to worship and pray, for the great tree of their homeland had been their grand deity, Ihrone. Deipara raced up to the mountain in the dead of night, lighting the fire in this sconce. She fell to her knees, feet bare and bloody, crying out to a deity she couldn't be sure still existed after it was cut down, let alone hear her cries so far from home. Desperate to save her sister, she prayed for Ihrone's help. The magisk of their land still lived on, through the sisters, and Deipara's wish was heard. All four sisters were given Gifts—the gift of mind, body, earth, and matter. Together, the sisters got together and created a ritual. One that allowed them to save Zahra and killed Agon, leader of the vampires, striking him dead with none the wiser."

Lucia is confused. *If Deipara killed Agon, why couldn't they kill the rest of the vampires and return home?* She has never heard any of this history before and wonders why it isn't common knowledge among the witches.

Hatsia turns away from the cave walls she was staring at to face Lucia. "I can hear your mind turning. No, that did not mean freedom for these women. The magisk required to kill Agon was great, and it was draining. None of them knew the cost of the magisk they had used or the conditions required to meet it. Great darkness and evil were born that night. It was a dark time. It wasn't until Deipara was able to capture and seal that magisk inside of herself that they could work to free themselves."

Hatsia's eyes harden, burning with anger in the glow of the firelight. Lucia watches her through the flames and is truly terrified.

"The vampires destroyed our homeland. Though the Araneidae is gone now, destroyed in the War of Mystics, many cults that were born from our enemies still live. They think we have forgotten what they did to us so many centuries ago, but we have not, nor will we ever. They wish to use the power of the Orbis Libra to reclaim their control over us and finish what they started so long ago, ruling over all of Hontaras. Lucia, you are descended from Deipara, our great

Mother. The vampires wish to see us as their subjects once more, able to feed and use us as they wish. You can help the covens make sure we stay free."

A rage wells inside Lucia. Anger at what was stolen from them, and pride at the legacy passed down to her. Her mother paints a beautiful picture of Lucia as a savior for her people. She wants to bring the witches to victory as her ancestor Deipara had.

Lucia is still in shock from the events of today as she lies on her bed staring blankly out of the window, memories of her test—Gabrielle dying in her arms, Adelaide dressed as the Priestess, Hetan accusing her of killing his parents—playing over in her mind.

On the walk she took with her mother, she learned so much, her head is still spinning. She doesn't know what to make of it all. What to make of Adelaide, descended from those enemy vampires, or the witches who have kept so many secrets? Lucia wants to believe her mother. To believe that the reasons for what she has done are just. To keep the freedom of the witches. But why Hetan's parents? Where do the wolves fit into all of this? There is still so much missing.

There's a knock on the door that startles Lucia from her musing. Is it Gabrielle? She hopes so. She wants to know what was so important she missed the trial and maybe talk with her about some of the things her mother said.

"Lord Fabien?" Lucia says in surprise as she opens the door. The witch leans across the door, a smirk on his face.

"Congratulations, Lucia, you've made it far." Fabien strides into the room, the door closing behind him. Lucia folds her arms over her chest, feeling a bit uneasy about him being here alone. It's not proper. "I was right about you. The covens have gone back and forth for years about whether you would be our salvation or downfall. They questioned if you were suitable to take your grandmother's place alongside countless Dol'Auclairs before you. My mother and I believed in you, and look at you now, in the final stage of the Triune."

Lucia nods, smoothly putting her hand behind her back when he tries to grab her hand. "Thank you," she says. "The Sea Serpents have been good friends to the Golden Griffin. I—and I'm sure my mother as well—appreciate it. You've gone out of your way to try and help me with my magisk, which you didn't have to do."

"Of course," Fabien says, striding forward. Lucia gasps, backing into the wall as he scoops up her hand in both of his. She stares wide-eyed as he kisses the back of her hand.

"Uh, should we wait for Gabrielle to be here to talk more, Fabien? I'm afraid this isn't appropriate."

Fabien lifts his head, looking down at Lucia with a fond smile that turns her stomach. "There's nothing improper about a man coming to congratulate his betrothed," he says, and Lucia's stomach drops at those words.

"Your—what?" she whispers, sure that her ears have deceived her.

"Your fiancé. You did speak to your mother this morning, didn't you?" he asks, looking as confused as Lucia.

Lucia's mind is spinning. She feels disoriented and like she might be sick. She spoke to her mother after the trial, about staying focused on her duties and practicing her cantus. About the importance of their legacy. But nothing about this. Nothing about him or *them*.

"It was made official at the coven meeting last night between our two families. She was supposed to tell you about the ongoing discussion, but I suppose you've been so busy," the man goes on. "The covens have decided that we are to be married. The negotiation has been in progress for weeks."

Lucia steps away as if she's been struck.

All of these weeks, she has been meeting up with Fabien, and he has been helping her with her cantus at her mother's request. That's the only reason Lucia took his offer of assistance. Was it all for this—so she would marry him?

"I... I need some fresh air," Lucia croaks, stumbling away from him, her white dress billowing in the breeze from the open window. "I—Please leave."

Lucia presses her palms to her stinging eyes, a lump gathering in her throat as she hears Fabien turn away.

"You're right, I should let you rest. It has been a long day. I will see you tomorrow, Lucia." The large, heavy door of Lucia's bedroom closes behind Fabien with a thud.

Alone, Lucia's back hits the wall as she tries to catch her breath.

The prophecy Lucia got from the Siren comes forth to her mind. She hasn't thought about it since that day, so much happening that overshadowed it. She thought it was silly, but now it is stuck in her mind.

Which of those options was Fabien? Or was he one at all?

She still remembers them like a poem she can't get out of her head: *Three loves but only one that is true. Your great love will bring loss, so be warned of the path you choose. If you choose wrong, your death might await. Or life in a cage, walking the trail of fate. But if you choose the last, another will grow to hate.*

Lucia collapses on her bedroom floor, her emotions flooding out in the privacy of her chamber—every emotion she has bottled up throughout the Triune, every expression of horror and anger she wished to show when Fabien revealed this curse of news so casually. As if this is something they've been plotting and whispering about behind her back. Which, in a way, it is. Her mother didn't even bother to tell her, even as she showed up to watch Lucia complete the second trial. *For her*—Lucia did it all for her and the covens!

The rising moon illuminates Lucia where she's sprawled on the floor. She pulls her knees up to her chest, fishing for the pearl within the confines of the small pouch in her dress, whispering, "Jiji, projice Hatsia" to activate the pre-canted charm. She holds the pearl in shaking hands, her chest heaving as she tries to steady her breathing so she can speak clearly.

"Hello?" Hatsia's voice trills over the line, and her cheery voice is like a shock down Lucia's spine.

"You—" She struggles to catch her breath. "How could you not tell me?"

Hatsia pauses the sounds of clinking silverware over the line. She must be having her tea and cake right now.

"What are you talking about, child?"

Lucia wheezes, "Don't act like you have no idea, Mama. I can't handle any more secrets." It feels like every word is a lie. Everything that her mother does and says.

Another pause. Her mother's voice softens into condescension. "Dear, you shouldn't get yourself so worked up."

Lucia hears faint voices in the background. Her mother must be entertaining company. She thuds her head back against the wall, eyes squeezing shut.

"You married me off without even asking me, Mother! How could you make such a huge decision for my life? An arranged marriage? I should get to decide who I love. I should get to decide who I spend my life with."

Lucia's heart is racing. She's never spoken to her mother like this. She's known all her life she was a tool for her mother and the coven, but this is the one part of her life that she always thought she'd have a choice in.

Despite her telling Adelaide she's afraid of love, Lucia always entertained the idea somewhere back in her mind that one day when she mastered her magisk and was coven head of the Golden Griffins, she would settle down and find someone.

At the thought of Adelaide, Lucia's heart beats even faster. Three loves. *Could the vampire be one of them? Is that blasphemous to even think?*

Lucia feels indescribable anguish at this moment, especially when her mother answers coolly:

"No one said anything about love, Lucia. Mrs. Devroue is an old friend, and the Sea Serpents are a well-respected coven with many more resources than us. We may be a distinguished family, but one cannot live on name alone. They can offer us many things we need right now, things that'll help your campaign against vampires. When you become Eidan, we'll need this connection to make certain... changes. You, my daughter, will take our coven, all of the covens, into the new generation of witches."

Tears burn in Lucia's eyes. She licks salt from her lips as tears track down her face. *Changes? A campaign against the vampires?* Lucia doesn't want any of that. She doesn't care about any of that.

"I don't want... *how could you?*" Lucia wheezes, her breath catching painfully in her throat.

Lucia can't breathe or even speak as her chest constricts painfully, pushing against her ribs. She has to climb onto her knees, her head dangling between her shoulders, to try and ease the pain. She is in a world of agony, her heart shattering into many little pieces, and the ribs in her chest feel near to breaking.

It feels like a heart attack.

At least, this is what she thinks one would feel like.

Lucia's pearl slips from her hand as her fingernails dig into the carpet. She presses her forehead to the ground, taking deep breaths to try and get her nerves under control. She hasn't felt this close to breaking down in years.

"Lucia!" Hatsia snaps, the orb blinking with the rise of her voice. The scathing words echo across the walls. "Control yourself. You are a smart girl, but you have no nerve. You are silly and prone to such childish fits. You are ill. You need a steady hand to guide you. You need Fabien as your husband and partner. If he was a woman, he'd be the one taking your place instead. Is that what you want? To end the ruling line of the Dol'Auclairs? Fabien is practical and calm, and you are only a girl. You may wait until after the Triune is over, but you will marry him," she hisses.

For a moment, Lucia's heart stops beating. After all these years, her mother is finally admitting it. Lucia is a failure and a disappointment to the Dol'Auclair line.

She wants to throw out that if anyone is sabotaging the Dol'Auclairs it is her mother, with her lies and the secret of what she did to Hetan's parents, but she bites her lip.

"Is that what Grandmother said?" Lucia asks, pain lacing her words. "You sound just like her right now."

The words her grandmother said the night of her first failed blooming play through Lucia's head. Words Lucia thought she buried deep inside.

You will be the downfall of the Dol'Auclairs.

"Yes, your grandmother thought it was best, Lucia. The Grand Elder. I wanted you to be able to choose who you marry. I didn't want you to have this life at all, I thought Gabrielle was more suited, but it is out of my hands. There is tradition. Your grandmother knows what's best for the family and our coven. You have to trust her judgment."

"How can she know what's best for my life!" Lucia shouts, tears burning down her face. "Soy u fun ke—*you should have told her no!* You should have told her she doesn't get to dictate what I do with my heart and my body."

"Lucia—"

"If you truly cared, you would have put me over her! You would have put me over her!" Lucia screams, all of her anger coming out like a tidal wave she can't hold back. Her mother has never defended her against her grandmother. She's never been the safe place Lucia needed. "Itoj mi. Itoj mi, Mama."—*Protect me, protect me.*

There's silence on the line as Lucia's heart breaks. Her last words, *protect me*, lingers between them like she whispered a forbidden cantus.

Hatsia sighs. "Lucia, you are hysterical right now. I can't talk to you when you're acting like this. Like a spoiled brat. Call me when you've stopped being so insane."

The line goes dead, the pearl fading to black.

Growing up, Hatsia was a harsh mother with a stinging hand, but she wasn't usually cruel with her words. She preferred silence as her poison. Maybe that's why Lucia was able to take it for so long. Now, the poison has nearly reached her heart and Lucia thinks she just might die.

"Agh!" Lucia shouts and launches the pearl across the room. It shatters against the wall, crumbling like dust.

Lucia spends a long time curled up on the floor, the glow of the moon shining down on her as she cries, ribs cracking and aching under her struggle for breath, all of the air sucked out of her lungs and the walls closing in on her.

It's so cold.

Lucia feels like she is drowning, and there's no land in sight.

Chapter Twenty-One

Sage Advice

It's a Friday night when Lucia's plan to avoid Adelaide comes to a head. She'd been avoiding her for a few weeks now—avoiding everyone, actually. She would go to class and then immediately back to her room.

She hasn't seen much of Gabrielle, nor has she sought her out. Her sister was acting wild, more so than usual, when Lucia had seen her last. She said she was "looking for the academy killer" which Lucia told her was a horrible idea.

Gabrielle said that she believed the killer was tied to the man who attacked Lucia outside of the Dome and that she couldn't drop it until she found the truth. She had an entire string of theories that were nothing more than coincidence. Lucia thinks the idea is ridiculous, but if it keeps her busy, she can have fun with that. It's distracting her at least.

Lucia knows what her sister would say if she told her about the engagement and her conversation with their mother—she should just quit and not give in to the coven's demands—but Lucia knows that is not the right option. *Or maybe she's afraid that Gabrielle would be right.*

So, Lucia has been hiding from everyone. She waits to eat until the canteen is empty and she can occupy her hidden bench alone. It's during one of these trips that Lucia's finally caught. It's midnight, and she's headed toward the steamed buns when an arm hooks around her waist. She gasps, pulled along by Adelaide to an empty hall.

"Okay, I'm done letting you be mad at me," Adelaide says. She's in a red leather outfit covered in lace in every place there would be bare skin, the top a deep V that goes nearly to her belly button. Lucia has to tear her eyes away to look up at the vampire's smug face.

"What?"

The vampire leans over Lucia, her arm resting on the wall above her. "You've been mad at me, and I get it. I was insufferable, that's why I let you have your space. But I'm not going to let you ignore me any longer. I kind of don't hate talking to you, Princess, and I've missed your voice."

Lucia just blinks up at her confusedly. She thought Adelaide was mad, but the whole time she was letting Lucia ignore her. It seems the vampire didn't care about Lucia's outburst at all. *It was all in her head.*

"O-okay. Did you want to work on our project?" Lucia asks. It's been a few weeks since they have, so they should finish soon or they will miss the deadline. Lucia has been so distracted she has neglected a lot of her schoolwork.

"Ahh, no. That's not exactly what I meant. Or, no, it's not at all what I meant. Come on, you're going out with me."

Adelaide takes Lucia's arm and weaves it into hers as she strides down the hall. Lucia struggles to keep up with the woman's long legs.

"Going where?" Lucia panics.

Lucia struggles against Adelaide's hold before giving in and letting herself be led through the academy building. She tries to hide her face in her hand when her stomach growls. Even if the vampire didn't have superior hearing, she'd have heard it.

"Are you hungry?"

Lucia hesitates. "I—I missed dinner."

"That just won't do," Adelaide sighs. "Gone for a few days, and the witch starts neglecting herself."

"I am not neglecting myself," Lucia scoffs. "And my 'not eating' has nothing to do with not talking to you."

"Ah, so you admit you were ignoring me."

Lucia splutters and the vampire just chuckles, leading her out to the front lawn.

They stride down the quad, which is thankfully empty, Lucia's hand still in Adelaide's as her shorter legs work to keep up.

"I have a nice place in the city I can take you."

"In the city?" Lucia shouts, and then quieter, "In the city?"

Adelaide raises a brow as Lucia wiggles her arm free. "Do you have a problem with that?"

"Well, uh—we aren't allowed to leave campus."

"Says who?"

"Says..." Lucia doesn't know. Her mother? The thought of the woman makes her scowl.

"Come on, Princess, you're not scared, are you? I promise I'll protect you from the humans." She winks. "Again."

"I'm not afraid of the humans." Lucia pouts, crossing her arms over her chest. What is she afraid of? That her mother will be mad, upset, or disappointed? Well, too late, because Lucia's the mad one. Besides, her mother already admitted Lucia was a mistake and a disappointment, so there's nothing to lose there. Maybe she should go to the city with Adelaide. Why can't she have fun for once? Make a decision on her own like an adult.

"Okay, I'll go with you, Adelaide. But if you're boring, I'm leaving straight away."

Adelaide throws her head back and laughs, a deep, genuine sound Lucia doesn't think she's heard from the vampire before. It leaves her a bit awed as the vampire's pale hair glows in the orange of the sunset, her beautiful tawny skin like gold in the light.

With all the talk of love, Lucia can't help but stare at Adelaide a little longer. A little harder. She doesn't have feelings for the vampire, so what is this feeling in her gut... the fast beating of her heart and sweaty palms. The vampire makes her nervous. Why? *Does Lucia find Adelaide physically attractive?* Beautiful even. *Could she be one of the three the Siren spoke of?* It sounds ridiculous to even think so Lucia pushes it away. Her admiration of the vampire is nothing other than the lustful lure of all vampires, a part of their dangerous seduction.

"Up you go, Princess, into the carriage."

Lucia blushes as Adelaide helps her up into the carriage, hands on her waist. She bats the woman away as she climbs in and scoots to the window. "No touching," she says, giving her best scolding look. The vampire doesn't even seem fazed by it as she slides in way too closely and bangs on the glass. "Calm down," Lucia says, grabbing Adelaide's arm. "The man will go in a moment, have patience. Were you raised in the stables?"

"The stables?" Adelaide raises an eyebrow. "Princess, it's sweet that you think many folk up in the wetlands have stables. Or that a vampire has much use for horses. That's countryside living."

The carriage begins moving, and Lucia doesn't respond. She hadn't thought about the difference in her and Adelaide's backgrounds too much. Her being from Swaydan, let alone being a vampire. There are a lot of customs, attitudes, and language that Lucia doesn't understand. She wants to know though. She finds it fascinating.

"What is it like in the south? What do you do? And what about your brother, Siphon? I haven't met him yet. Not really." Lucia has been curious about him since seeing him in Gabrielle's memory.

"You have a lot of questions."

"I do."

Adelaide smiles, sitting back with an arm over the seat and propping her feet up on the glass. Lucia restrains herself from admonishing the vampire.

"Well, I guess I'm obliged to answer them."

"Well, you don't have to if it's personal or—"

"Don't worry, Princess, I want to answer. If it'll settle the voices in that pretty head of yours."

The voices... For a moment she wonders if Adelaide somehow knows about her ability, and then she shakes the idea away. *It was probably a figure of speech.*

"Well, it's wet and humid, but it's always a party. For the vampires at least, we know how to have a good time. No offense, kuai-yuel, but you witches are boring."

Lucia can't take much offense, it's true.

"What do I do? Things I can't do here at this civilized establishment. Fight, fuck, drink—well, I do those things anyway, but Siphon scolds me for it. He's tough, but he's a major softie. Hell if I know where he gets it from. He's a quiet, sensitive soul, definitely out of place. But he's a good fighter and a leader, so the others let him be."

"Is that important to vampires? Being able to fight."

Adelaide's arm drops down over Lucia's shoulder as she looks down at her, their eyes holding. "What else is there?"

"I don't know," Lucia says, trying to steady her pounding heart. "Family, friends, passion for things like art and nature. I know you like poetry, and you seemed interested in those paintings your uncle did in the dorms. That's something else."

"I suppose."

"You suppose?"

Adelaide shrugs. "It's all just... passing the time."

Lucia doesn't agree, but she drops it. She supposes Adelaide has a lot of time seeing as she's nearly immortal. They sit in relative silence the rest of the way down the valley as Lucia watches the sights go by. The path down the mountainside is beautiful in the evening light. She ignores Adelaide's gaze on her. The vampire always seems to be watching her. What she's looking for, Lucia doesn't know.

Whether she finds it, Lucia's afraid to know.

"Have you never seen a market before?" Adelaide asks, smiling fondly as she watches Lucia run around looking at all the colorful buildings, face pressed against the windows. She has to pull the witch away when she stands in the middle of the road staring at strangers passing by and nearly gets hit by a car. "Okay, that's enough, Princess. I'm not going to come back to the academy with the Dol'Auclair heir's blood on my hands. I'm not that reckless."

When they were in Domeg, Lucia didn't get a chance to see the market, since she was shuffled off to the inn immediately, and it was a much smaller, less advanced human city.

"It's just... so fascinating," Lucia says in awe. She's seen technology before. The school has electricity, and the inn in Domeg did as well, but even lightbulbs are rare in Laesbury, where she's spent most of her life. Most of what Lucia knows is what she has read in books. She hasn't been to a big city like this before with huge, shiny buildings covered in hundreds of flashing lights. It looks like it has eaten ten Domegs.

"Hey, got any change?"

Lucia's eyes widen in horror as a man tries to reach for her, but Adelaide pulls her into her side, hissing at the man who jumps back in fear.

"Humans are scary." Lucia shudders as Adelaide leads her down the street, tucked under the vampire's arm. She feels safe there, knowing the vampire is stronger than a human.

"Don't worry, I'll protect you from the scary humans." Adelaide chuckles. Lucia pushes her away.

"Stop saying that, it's not funny." She pouts.

Adelaide tries to reassure Lucia she doesn't think it is, but it's hard to take her seriously as she can't even get the words out through her uncontrollable laughter.

"Humans have weapons and guns," Lucia says. She doesn't say what they are both thinking, the men who had busted into the inn back in Domeg looking for Lucia. She had mostly pushed it from her mind, but now that it's there, it reminds her of the man who attacked her outside of the Dome. As far as she knows, her mother hasn't learned anything about the man with the skull blade, and Gabrielle has been chasing dead leads.

"Oh, I know," Adelaide says, grabbing her hand and leading her into a small shop that smells like fresh dough and cheese.

Right. It's a known rumor that the Silver Spiders are weapons dealers. They're thought to be involved in a lot of shady underground work. It makes sense now, why she hadn't been frightened when those men had busted in during their breakfast. But Lucia has never gotten that vibe from Adelaide. The woman doesn't seem so terrifying.

"What is this place?" Lucia asks as they get up to the counter.

"It's a pizza shop. You can choose all of your toppings to make it just how you like it."

Lucia gasps. She's had the academy's pizza, which is on the top of her favorite human foods list, but she hasn't had it like this. There are so many things to choose from. Lucia takes a long time picking out what she wants, the line growing behind them. And when she tries to pay, Adelaide stops her, handing over the money and leading Lucia outside to a table on the deck. They have a beautiful nighttime view, and they're all alone out here.

"Why did you do that?" Lucia asks, picking up her pizza dripping with cheese and pepperoni and onions, olives, artichoke, mushrooms, and sweet chili. She chose too many toppings probably, but she was so excited. "I have money," she says, taking her first bite of the delicious treat.

"You don't have human money," Adelaide says, wiping sauce from the corner of Lucia's mouth. "They'd look at you funny if you pulled out a teirin."

Lucia reaches for a napkin, her face heating at the lingering touch of Adelaide's hand. She looks at the space in front of Adelaide, realizing she didn't get any food.

"I thought you said you could eat?" she asks. She hasn't ever seen Adelaide eat food.

"I can," Adelaide says, leaning back in her chair, her feet coming up off the ground. "But I don't need to very often. Food doesn't hold much pleasure for me."

"Then how did you know of this place? It's very good."

Adelaide drops the chair back down to the ground with a clink. "A friend of mine. He's a little shit, but he's cool. He loves eating, and he forces Cassius and Siphon to take him here at least once a day. Why they let a fledgling runt like him order them around, I don't understand."

"Maybe because they're friends?" Lucia offers, remembering the small vampire who trails Adelaide around. She still needs to ask about Cassius, but she doesn't want to ruin the mood. "That is the sort of thing you would do for a friend."

Adelaide laughs. "Maybe." Her eyes are trained on Lucia, straying to her lips.

"He's the one with the dual hair, right? The one who studied medicine?" It's still a bit odd to her, a vampire studying medicine.

"Mhm. Adakai. Kai, for short."

"He seems nice," Lucia says, finishing her slice of pizza. She only met the vampire once or twice, but he was sweet and seemed like one of the last people she expected Adelaide to be friends with. But it also kind of works. Opposites and all that. He seems a lot like Gabrielle, fitting himself in everywhere.

"He reminds me of you, actually," Adelaide says. "Except you don't act like you're hopped up on caffeine and sugar twenty-four hours of the day. Well, except for when you enter human cities."

"Hey!" Lucia says, shoving Adelaide again. The vampire doesn't budge, but Adelaide catches Lucia's hand, holding it in two of hers. Lucia's heart thumps painfully loud and she's sure the vampire can hear it.

It's peaceful. Lucia had forgotten how safe and comfortable she feels in the vampire's presence. She almost forgets why she'd been so adamant about pushing her away. Regardless of her betrothal to Fabien, they can still be friends.

Adelaide talks about all the things she's seen and done, the places she's gone all over Hontaras. She seems so much older than her twenty years. She's lived a more fulfilling twenty than Lucia has, and Lucia tries not to think about how much longer the vampire will live than her.

For Lucia, who has never left the north, it's all so fascinating, and she longs to hear every detail. She listens rapt, at their small table under the stars, her hand being warmed in Adelaide's.

She can picture traveling through the south, Adelaide showing her these new sights, taking her through her home. The illusion is almost too compelling.

It's dark when they finish eating, and they are walking the street when Lucia sees the shop. A small bookstore nestled amongst the other shops. It's too perfect. Lucia has been meaning to find a way to sneak out and come here. The Page Sage.

"Hey," Lucia says, pulling away from Adelaide. "I need to run into this shop, do you mind?"

Adelaide looks at the bookstore curiously. "I can go with you—"

"No! I, uh, I mean, I wanted to get something for my mother. She needs a book that they only sell here in the human city and it's sort of private."

Adelaide's face drops and Lucia's stomach twists at the sight. "Sure," Adelaide says, scuffing her heeled boot on the stone walkway. "I'll wait out here."

Lucia smiles in relief. "Thank you, I'll be real quick."

Lucia scurries off into the shop, a small bell ringing when she enters the cozy, warm place. The lights are dim and there is an eerie glow over the books, many shelves packed into the small shops and overflowing on the tables and chairs and even books stacked on the floor.

"Hele?" Lucia calls, squinting into the dim place as she maneuvers around the books, hoping the shop isn't already closed.

"Hello."

Lucia shrieks, caught off guard as the shopkeeper appears behind her. She tries to steady her racing heart as she turns to the man. He looks the same as he had at the second trial, except he's in a thick, cozy sweater, and a hat covers his bald head. Lucia wonders what he's doing living in a human city rather than one of the four rings. An ability like his would be very useful and well sought after.

"Can I help you find a book?" the man asks gruffly. His voice and face don't match his helpful words.

"I, uh, actually wanted to speak with you. You're Aamad, right? A friend of orun-kun Ekrul."

The mage looks Lucia over, eyes squinted. "I remember you," he says, turning and walking down one of the aisles. "You're one of the contestants for the Triune."

Lucia follows as the man shifts around, organizing the scattered stacks of books. "Yes, I am. That's one of the reasons I wanted to talk to you."

Aamad climbs up a ladder, squeezing books into the overflowing shelf. "This is about being a Sage, right?" Lucia's eyes widen. She stumbles back, nearly knocking over a stack of books. "Hey, watch it!"

"How did you know?"

Aamad gives her a pointed look. "Sage... mind. Remember?" He pokes his head. "I made that test for the second trial. The way you beat it seemed odd to me at the time. You were much quicker than the other contestants, and you didn't come out of it the same way. It should be a smooth, clean removal, but when you broke out, it was like my connection to you snapped. Like you forced your way out."

"Right..." Lucia hadn't thought of that, that he might have been aware of her ability at the time. "Can you... read my mind right now?" she asks nervously. What if he sees something she doesn't want him to? Something like the memories she got from her mother.

"No. I mean, I could, but I don't. My ability works best with touch, but also, I don't make a habit of reading people's minds. You're just easy to read, girl."

Lucia tries not to feel insulted by that. "Well, I wanted to ask your help. I've, uh... well, I've seen some things. Things I shouldn't have. I don't want that to happen again. I want to learn how to control it."

Aamad jumps down from the ladder with a thump and lands in front of Lucia. "Why don't you ask your coven? They should be helping you learn your gift. That's what the collective is for."

Lucia squirms, fiddling with her necklace. Aamad must sense her unease because he sighs and says, "This isn't an ability you can hope to master alone. It isn't going to be as easy as the other gifts, and sometimes it won't always feel like one. Tell me, girl, what happened when you used your gift before?"

Lucia keeps the details of what she heard out but tells him the situation surrounding each encounter. The man nods.

"Like me, it seems touch is a key factor, but also emotion."

"Emotion?"

"Yes, your ability is tied to your emotions, some sort of turmoil inside of you that is making it act out. You need to get that under control if you want to stop any more accidental sharings."

"Share? You mean I could also give memories to someone else?"

Aamad trails back to the front of the shop, dropping off a stack of books on the glass countertop. "You could. Again, every gift is different and so is every witch. I can't tell you how to control it, that's something you need to learn yourself. Gather your coven for a seance to ask the Mother for guidance, or find someone you trust to practice with. Do something before your gift gets out of your control."

Lucia nods, considering his words. The last thing she wants to do is tell her coven about her gift. If she accidentally shares what she knows it would be bad. Maybe she can just tell Gabrielle? Her sister always knows how to help, and Lucia feels bad she's been shutting her out. But she's also afraid of bringing her sister into this or making it her responsibility. Lucia has leaned on her a lot growing up, but she can't do that anymore. She needs to figure it out herself.

"Thank you for all your help," Lucia says, her eyes straying to the door where she can see Adelaide's blurry figure through the glass. She picks a book at random and pays for it, before heading back out to the vampire. Adelaide smiles at her, holding something out to her.

"What is that?"

"It's ice cream." Adelaide beams. "Try it."

The pair make the trip back up to the academy, and Lucia thinks the vampire will walk her back to her dorm but instead she says, "What do you say, little witch, up for one more adventure tonight?"

Lucia groans. This vampire is going to be the death of her. But at the thought of returning to the witches, where Fabien might be sitting in the common room for her to see, the thought is a little less appealing than spending more time with the vampire.

"Okay."

Chapter Twenty-Two

Servants of Chance

Walking into a den of vampires isn't as terrifying the second time. With Adelaide beside her, hands nearly touching, even the eyes that watch her arrival don't feel so harsh.

The common room lights are dim, and there are drinks and food across marble countertops. Lucia chooses to ignore the deep, red liquid in some of the cups and the vampires with a wolf or a witch over their lap. Feeding.

Adelaide greets a few people as she crosses the room, pulling her toward the staircase to head up to her room.

"And where are you off to?" a male voice says from the couch. Siphon.

Adelaide curses under her breath, her eyes closing briefly before she turns to face her brother. He pats the couch to the left of him. Kai is cozied up to Cassius's side. He beams when he sees them, waving at Lucia, who gives an awkward wave back.

"Come on," Cassius adds, eyes flickering from Lucia to Adelaide. "Join us for a minute. We want to get to know your friend, Adelaide."

Reluctantly, Adelaide pulls Lucia down onto the couch beside her. Siphon's face is blank, not giving away any of his emotions. Around campus, people speak of his cold, silent nature. There are many rumors surrounding him.

"Deal them in, Oliver," Cassius says to the vampire holding playing cards. He has slicked-back hair and a charming sort of face. The cards are made of brass, the rectangular pieces thin and tough, beautiful artwork etched into their faces and the backs stained red.

"Lucia doesn't know the rules," Adelaide says as Cassius mixes a white powder into his glass of what Lucia assumes to be spirits, the amber liquid seeming to burst into flame. He drinks the burning liquid, a sinister smile spreading across his lips.

"Oh, come on, it's not like you need super strength or speed to play cards."

Adelaide glares at him.

"I'm joking," he says.

At the same time, Siphon says, "I'll teach her."

Lucia lays a hand on Adelaide's thigh to calm her, and the vampire stiffens briefly under her touch. She's quick to pull it away.

"It's fine," Lucia says. "I like games."

Cassius smirks.

"The name is Servants of Chance," Siphon says, ignoring his friend. "These are the rules: Everyone starts with a hundred points, which are tracked by the dealer known as the Overseer. Oliver is the dealer. You can gain or lose points, and first to zero wins. Keep in mind we're vampires; this is a fast and intense game. We even have a special deck to keep them from tearing," he says, motioning to Oliver, who spreads the cards across the table.

There are ten cards, each with a beautiful image carved into it. Lucia stares at them intensely, making sure to memorize them.

"The cards have special meanings, most important, the Monarch, and for every time that no one can find it, the Overseer will lose twenty points. The Overseer will show everyone the card and then shuffle them very fast. You have to keep track of the Monarch and beat your opponents to the card. That's where the game can get violent. Reaching for the cards, you can get sliced and bruised. It's half of the fun. If you have the Monarch, you lose five points from your total or you can choose for someone to add five points to theirs."

Lucia looks at the Monarch. It's a woman sitting atop a curled dragon, between the curl of its tail and head. She wears a crown of blackthorns.

"Then you gain five points if you get the Jester by accident, mistaking it for the Monarch."

The Jester depicts a man lying on the ground, with long hair like a dark halo around his head. The Monarch stands over him, a foot on his chest and a sword plunged into his heart. Lucia shudders.

Cassius butts in. "Lastly, you can try for the secret card, which you will not be shown at the start of the round. It's the Double Agent. To get this card, you must take a risk. Without knowing where it is, you are using luck. Once you've chosen the card you think it might be, before you can look, you must yell, *Backstabber!*"

Lucia jumps at the outburst, grabbing Adelaide's hand.

"If it is the right card, you can choose to add ten points to any opponent. If it's the wrong card, you add ten to your own."

This card has two Jesters facing away from one another, a heart in the hand behind their back, and flowers held outward in front of them. *Lucia doesn't get why anyone would take the risk if they won't lose any points for it.*

Siphon says, "The other six cards are the Dwarf, the Troll, the Herd, the Maiden, the Nobleman, and the Ambassador. You neither gain nor lose points if you get those. Understood?"

Lucia is wide-eyed, trying to take in all of the information. Her heart is racing for some reason. She's never played any card games before, mostly board games with Gabrielle or the handmaidens back home. It sounds fun enough though and a bit dangerous.

Kai leans forward, looking apprehensive. "Are you sure she should play this game?" he asks Siphon. "She's a witch. The last time we played, someone got punched in the gut."

Cassius rolls his eyes at Kai. "Yeah, you're the one who punched someone in the gut, Adakai."

Kai looks sheepish at the admission.

"I'll be okay," Lucia says, taking a deep breath. "I can handle it. I'm not made of glass."

Adelaide sighs. "Okay. Anything goes, as long as you don't purposefully cause serious injury to anyone." She looks sternly around the group.

Lucia doesn't think Adelaide likes the idea of her playing, but she doesn't try to talk her out of it. Lucia's grateful. She doesn't think she could stand another person trying to tell her what to do right now, or what is best for her.

"Okay, I'm ready," Lucia says, leaning forward.

Cassius looks surprised that she hasn't run and tucked tail, and that makes Lucia's chest puff up with smug pride.

"How about we make it a little bit more interesting," he says. "Every time I get the Monarch, I can ask you one question."

"And if I get it?" Lucia says, quirking a brow.

The vampires *"Ooh."*

"If you get even one Monarch, I'll back off," he says cockily, his eyes flicking to Adelaide and then Siphon. "Is that okay?" he asks the older man, who nods. "There's no threat here, we just want to see what our Adelaide finds so interesting about you. Honestly, I'm getting tired of her following you around, complaining that she upset you and now you're not talking," he mocks, which earns a glare from Adelaide. "No offense, but I don't like witches. And I don't like Dol'Auclairs."

It's hard not to take offense that he doesn't like anything that she is, but Lucia is curious to find out that Adelaide has mentioned her. She peeks up at the vampire. *Does Adelaide like her that much?*

Lucia grins. She wants to prove to this vampire, and the rest of them, that she isn't just a witch, nor is she just a Dol'Auclair heir.

"Deal."

There are six players. Oliver, who's the Overseer, shows them the Monarch and slides it into the deck. "Try to keep up," he says.

Oliver shuffles so quickly that Lucia has a hard time seeing his hands move. When he finishes shuffling, he quickly lays the cards in a row on the table.

"Start!"

The vampires move so quickly that Lucia nearly doesn't see it. Her head spins as she looks around at the other players. Cassius sits there, proud, a card dangling between two fingers.

"Flip." He spins the card to face Lucia, the Monarch smiling right at her. "I'll give you a pass since it's the first round."

"What a saint," Adelaide mutters under her breath.

Now that she's prepared for the fast pace, Lucia can better make out the sight of multiple hands, but she isn't even sure which card is the Monarch. She sits there without a card once more.

Cassius asks his first question. "Have you killed anyone before?"

Lucia splutters. "Excuse me?"

"Have you. Ever taken. A life."

"No, I've never killed anyone. I've never hurt anyone either," she says, thrown off guard by the wild question.

"Would you?"

"Kill? No, of course not. Killing is wrong—*always*."

Cassius hums, his eyes flicking to Adelaide, something passing between them that Lucia can't parse. He doesn't seem too surprised by her answer. *Was that a test? What kind of question is that and what was he hoping to find by asking her?*

"Try to keep up," he says. "The goal is to actually attempt to get a card."

Lucia scowls, leaning forward to be prepared. Oliver shuffles and lays out the cards again.

"Keep it civil," Siphon warns.

"Start."

Lucia takes a chance and reaches in, aiming for the card the majority is, but she's a step behind. She groans as multiple fast hands strike hers, crushing it between them. They don't seem to be phased, but her knuckles are throbbing.

"Are you okay?" Adelaide asks, worry etched on her face. Lucia nods. She can't let them see her weakness.

The game goes on in a similar fashion, and Lucia is losing painfully. She has more than a hundred points now.

Kai gets the Monarch in the next two rounds and then Siphon does. The overseer gets twenty points when no one finds the Monarch on the fourth.

Lucia looks over at Adelaide, who has a wrinkle of worry between her brows. She doesn't seem to be trying to play the game at all, too worried about watching Lucia. But Lucia is distracted, not only by the game and Cassius's gloating but by a woman watching Adelaide across the table.

The vampire is playing with them, but she hasn't gotten or lost any points. She's spent more time sucking some human treat that makes her lips blue and staring at Adelaide with bedroom eyes. The vampire doesn't seem to have noticed, but Lucia has, and her blood is boiling. It's hard to concentrate.

"I'm getting bored with winning," Cassius gloats, flicking the Monarch back to Oliver. He's already in the lead, and Kai and Siphon are right behind him.

Kai wears a short black chiton with silver chains cinching his waist and black sleeves half up his arms. Besides being super quick, his strategy seems to be trying to distract Cassius by touching his arm or leg when Oliver is shuffling the cards and leaving his bare legs on display. Cassius is still doing well despite the distraction.

Lucia wishes everyone would just focus on the game. She is growing flustered by all of the blatant flirtings. Especially that which is directed at Adelaide. She was meant to be spending time with the woman today.

Lucia motions for Cassius to get on with his question. She has prepared herself for him to say something absurd again.

"Are you scared of us, Lucia? Do vampires make you shake in fear when you sleep at night, the thought of being bitten, your throat torn and sucked dry?"

Lucia looks over at Adelaide, who stiffens beside her. She looks at her face, red eyes, and small fangs which she hides now behind her lips.

At one point, vampires frightened her. The thought of entering their dorm even gave her chills. Lucia has heard every story there is about vampires. About them being bloodsucking daemons with skin like hellfire. That they're cursed to an eternity in tophet—*hell*. But she's never been afraid of Adelaide. Not once since she met her.

Lucia remembers her grandmother's terrifying face when she sentenced Abhain to an excruciating death and her mother's thoughts about Talulah's and Ukaih's death.

"No," she says. "I'm no more afraid of a vampire than I am of a witch."

There are a few snickers at that, as Lucia holds Cassius's gaze. She can see what he's trying to do now. He's trying to make a rift between her and Adelaide, putting the idea in her head that Adelaide is some sort of monster and therefore the two of them are *different*, and unable to be friends.

Kai *awwws* and Cassius scowls. "Oliver, shuffle the deck," he snaps.

For a while, Kai gets into the lead, and Lucia learns he is nicknamed Whirlwind for his quick reflexes.

Lucia is far behind, and not a single point has been taken from her total. She grows frustrated as Cassius gets the Monarch once again and takes back first place. The man seems to be exceptionally pleased with himself now, and Lucia starts to worry. She doesn't think Cassius would hurt her again, not physically at least. Adelaide assured her he wouldn't, though she is still uncomfortable with the vampire's lack of explanation for why he had attacked her before. The situation still leaves a sour taste in her mouth.

They're keeping something from her.

"Lucia, have you heard the rumors about Adelaide?" he asks, leaning back on the couch with his arm over the headrest. He holds her gaze. "She's quite a vixen. Likes to party... likes to... enjoy many pleasures." Adelaide growls, but he continues. "How does that make you feel? I know you witches are pious."

Lucia's face flames in mortification. She knows Adelaide has... partners. As Cassius said, there are many rumors about her around the school. She has seen herself, witches, wolves, and vampires alike throwing themselves all over the woman. The vampire's intimate life is none of her concern, but still, she tries not to think about it. It isn't her place; they're from two different cultures with different attitudes about that sort of thing.

Lucia shrinks in her seat. "It's none of my business," she says, breaking eye contact. She must look pathetic. The vampires can probably read on her face that she's lying if the beating of her heart didn't give it away. Lucia can try to deny it all she wants, but she cares. Instead, she says, "Adelaide's my friend. She can do what she likes."

Cassius chuckles. "You are an interesting little witch," he says. "I don't think I've had a conversation so long with one before. Not without wanting to rip their head off. You're exactly as I expected, and yet, nothing like I imagined."

"Oliver?" Lucia calls, not dignifying that with a response. He's trying to make her uncomfortable.

This time Lucia is agitated, riled up by Cassius's jesting. She reaches in quickly and sloppily, the feeling of a needle prick pinching her skin as she reaches for the card.

"Ow," Lucia hisses, her hand stinging. She sits there, hands out in front of her, blood welling at the tip of her finger. She was cut by one of the vampire's sharp nails.

Lucia sucks the blood away without even thinking, and when she looks up all eyes are on her.

"I'm so sorry," Kai says, trying to reach out to her. "I didn't mean to cut you."

"It's okay," she says, cheeks warming at the intense gaze on her. "It's just a small cut. See?" She shows it to him, the blood wiped away. Though it wells back up, it's only a shallow but long slice across her pointer finger. He looks relieved.

"Eep."

Lucia goes red when Adelaide grabs her hand, her eyes trained right on Cassius, whose fangs drop at the sight of her bringing Lucia's finger to her lips, sucking it into her mouth, hot like a volcanic cavern.

Blood rushes to Lucia's head so fast she feels dizzy, a tugging like a whirlpool in her gut making her throb down to her core. She has to pull her finger from Adelaide's mouth, wet with spit, as she tries to calm her heavy breathing.

Adelaide purrs, "Your blood tastes like sugar."

"T-thank you?" Lucia responds, breathless.

Cassius's eyes darken. "Again," he growls, his face like a storm. His two braids whip around as he turns to Oliver.

"You can do this," Adelaide whispers, her breath ghosting over Lucia's ear. "Don't let him get into your head. It's easy. It's not about going faster but making everything else slower."

Slower? That shouldn't make any sense, but it does. Lucia looks up at Adelaide, holding the woman's stare. She smiles.

Make the game slower...

Lucia racks her head for a cantus for that. Adelaide's hand rests on her thigh and she tenses, then quickly relaxes as the warmth seeps into her skin through the fabric. Though she doesn't have strength and speed, she isn't helpless. She does have abilities the vampires don't, even if she's not the best at them. She just has to be good enough to get this card.

This time, when the cards are shuffled, Lucia closes her eyes, focusing on Adelaide's touch rather than her discomfort or Cassius's judging eyes. Her breathing slows and there's a tightening in her gut as the noises of the room, the partying, and music and games happening across the common room vanish.

When Oliver says start, Lucia's eyes snap open and she whispers, "Ai lora." She can see the other players' movements like they're moving through jelly. Lucia feels her hand close around the cool metal. Her eyes fly wide in shock, looking down at the glimmering face between her fingers. The Monarch. She got the Monarch!

Lucia can only sit there in shock as Kai and another young vampire jump up, hooting. The boy gloats in his friend's face, and Lucia almost laughs as Cassius growls, pulling the smaller vampire down into his lap. He glares at Lucia over Kai's head.

"You cheated."

Lucia's smile drops. "I didn't cheat. You said there were no rules and seeing as you all use your strength and speed, it's equal."

"*Strength and speed*, not magisk tricks."

"If you want to go again, just ask."

"No. Lucia, you won the Monarch fairly," Adelaide says. "Cassius is just being a poor loser."

"She did win," Siphon agrees. Lucia nearly forgot he was there. He has been quiet the entire time, watching Lucia closely but not saying a word. She thinks he might have learned more about her in this short time than Cassius has without asking her a thing.

Cassius smirks. "The girl said she wants to go again. Let her prove herself and see if she can do that again. Oliver?"

Lucia takes a deep breath, trying not to let the vampire get to her. It's just a game, there's no harm. If she backs out, they won't respect her. If Lucia hopes to be Eidan one day, she'll have to deal with vampires like this. And with Adelaide at her side, for right now at least, Lucia doesn't worry.

Oliver deals the cards, but this time Lucia doesn't use her magisk. If Cassius doesn't want that, she'll just have to try harder to beat them without it even if it isn't fair. This time, when Lucia's hand goes out to reach for the card, a hand comes down not aiming for the Monarch, but for her. Lucia's hand opposite Cassius's is struck down by a fist.

Lucia cries out as Cassius snatches the winning card, and she pulls the arm to her chest, throbbing in pain. It feels like the woman who hit her was trying to break it.

"Foul!" Adelaide shouts. She flies out of her seat toward the woman and has the vampire's throat in her hands so fast that Lucia can't make sense of what is happening. The woman, despite her willingness to hurt Lucia, looks terrified as she's faced with Adelaide's rage. Lucia would be too. Watching the scene unfold, she is horrified.

Adelaide has the woman pinned to the ground, the same woman who had been eyeing her the entire match. She is pinned beneath Adelaide's knee in her gut. Adelaide's clawed fingers are choking the life out of the flailing woman, her red hair spilled out across the stone floor. A cup of red liquid Adelaide had knocked over when she jumped is pooling beneath her like a river of blood.

"It's okay," Lucia says, her heart beating so fast as she grabs Adelaide's arm, trying to pull her away from the trembling woman she has her teeth bared at. She is frightened by the murderous look on Adelaide's face.

"It is not okay! She could have hurt you."

The room is tense; no one seems to be moving. Adelaide in this state is a terrifying sight. One Lucia has never seen before. Swallowing the lump lodged in her throat she pushes through that fear and searches for the Adelaide she knows.

"It's a game," she says, her voice breaking with emotion. She nods to the woman who hurt her. "What she did isn't technically against the rules, not if we can't prove it was purposeful. And it's only a bruise." If anything, Lucia's lucky not to have more injuries by now, playing with vampires. "It was my choice to play, Adelaide. I'm fine."

The vampires won't respect Lucia if she lets Adelaide jump to her defense every time they touch her.

Lucia wraps her arms around Adelaide's middle, startling the vampire, who lets go of the woman's neck, which is littered with red-and-purple finger-shaped bruises. They begin to heal even as she pulls Adelaide back down to the couch, keeping herself pressed to Adelaide's side so she won't attack again.

"I'm good. I'm fine," Lucia says, breathing through the pain throbbing in her hand. It doesn't hurt as bad anymore with all the adrenaline pumping through her blood. Adelaide doesn't look happy about it, but she relaxes in Lucia's hold.

"Your question?" Lucia asks, facing Cassius head-on. Because this is obviously what he wanted. What he was willing to hurt her for. And she wants to distract Adelaide from the woman who has sunk into her seat like a scolded child.

"This one should be easy," he says, still looking smug. "And remember, don't lie." He doesn't care at all about the scene he just caused. Lucia knows that he was in on whatever just happened, though she can't prove it.

Lucia nods.

"Are you *engaged*?" The look on his face as he says those words, eyes flicking to Adelaide and back, is pure hostility.

The blood drains from Lucia's face, her confident glare dropping. She can feel Adelaide's eyes on her, but she doesn't want to meet the vampire's gaze. The atmosphere has shifted.

"I—" Lucia takes a deep breath, choking down the lump in her throat. She's sweating, all eyes on her. "Yes."

Silence descends on the room.

"It's an arranged marriage," she finds herself defending. "F-for my coven."

Lucia can feel Adelaide shift away from her and she wants to grab her and pull her close, but she doesn't. She looks up at Adelaide. The vampire is like a stone beside her, her face concealed as she turns away. Lucia can't tell what the woman is thinking. She didn't plan for her to learn of her engagement this way. It means nothing. There was nothing to tell.

She did not choose her engagement, or her betrothed. Like the card game, Lucia is just a servant of chance.

"One more round," Lucia says, teeth gritted. Cassius looks up at her in surprise. He didn't expect her to want to go again.

"Lucia—" Adelaide starts, but Lucia nods to Oliver. Looking hesitantly at Cassius, Oliver begins to deal another round.

This time, Lucia doesn't follow the Monarch. She doesn't reach into the pile of sharp claws as they go for it. Cassius looks at Lucia confusedly when he sits there with the winning card in his hand, wondering what was the point. Lucia doesn't meet his gaze. She takes a deep breath and closes her eyes, her hand hovering over the remaining cards. The room is silent as Lucia stops, her right hand atop a card in the middle. She yells, "Backstabber!"

Lucia opens her eyes when she doesn't hear a response. She is gaining many confused looks. Cassius, still unsure of her play, nudges Oliver who reaches for the card Lucia chose and flips it slowly. Lucia waits with bated breath.

"It's... the double agent," he says shocked.

Lucia grins, looking up to meet Cassius' eyes. She may not have lost any points, but she did add ten to his. That nullifies his win from finding the Monarch—two turns worth. *That in itself feels like a victory to her.*

Adelaide stands suddenly, pulling Lucia up with her. "This game is over. Lucia already passed your little test, Cassius." She looks down at Cassius, who leans back against the couch, arms crossed over his chest.

"Are we good?" Adelaide asks, looking toward her brother. He nods, motioning for them to leave, and Adelaide takes it.

"Oh, and Lucia," Cassius says when they begin to leave. He's a bit less smug than he'd been earlier. "Be careful. Adelaide has never been one to listen to reason, but you seem smart enough. This little dalliance with a vampire can only end one way. Not only will mother dearest not approve of this relationship, but your betrothed has some powerful friends too, and I don't think he'd be too happy with you, *or Adelaide* if he found out. Remember that."

Lucia stumbles along as Adelaide pulls her up the stairs to her room. Lucia worries her bottom lip, standing behind Adelaide as the door clicks shut behind them.

Lucia tries to speak, to tell Adelaide that she doesn't care for Fabien. She doesn't know why, but the vampire must know.

"I don't—"

The vampire turns quickly, pinning Lucia to the door. Lucia freezes, words cut off as a pair of lips crash into hers.

Chapter Twenty-Three
Kuai-Yuel

Is Lucia dreaming right now, or is Adelaide kissing her? Her lips feel numb, her back pressed into the cold door.

Adelaide is... *Adelaide is.*

Lucia leans forward into the kiss. Cassius's warning falls away as Adelaide's hand cradles the back of her neck, keeping their mouths interlocked. Lucia melts, meeting the lips in a sultry rhythm, just like they are dancing. It's a bit awkward and sloppy. She's never kissed anyone before, nothing but a peck with a childhood friend. But just like when they did the Malevoi, Lucia follows Adelaide's lead. There are no thoughts in her head, just the warmth of Adelaide's lips and the sound of their ragged breathing.

Adelaide pulls back, her face still close, breath warming Lucia's face.

"I had to do that."

Lucia stands there stunned, eyes still shut trying to hold on to this moment. Adelaide kissed her, and she kissed back. Worse, she liked it.

Three loves. Lucia can't deny it anymore, not with the way her heart is beating, squeezing painfully in her chest. Not with the way her body is reacting to Adelaide pressed against her: her nipples hard and pebbled, and warmth gathering between her thighs.

"We shouldn't have done that," Lucia whispers, her sense returning to her. Her face heats as shame fills her, remembering her grandmother's words of lusting vampires trying to lure her away from the Mother. She broke the Holum Actus, giving in to her desires before marriage. She's *engaged* to Fabien. Whether she likes it or not, it's true. She spent the entire day trying to fool herself, but that won't change.

"You like me," Adelaide says, wrapping an arm around Lucia's waist and pulling her close. "You can't deny it. I can hear it in the beating of your heart. I can smell it in your desire. You can't lie to me, Princess."

Lucia shakes her head, pulling away. Maybe it's true, but it's a mistake. "I can't, Adelaide, I am taken."

"You don't love him."

"I—" The prophecy hits her again. Words that are beginning to haunt her.

"I could," Lucia says.

"You don't."

"*I could*," she says stronger.

Adelaide growls, turning away. She paces back and forth, Lucia rooted in place as she watches helplessly. She has been trying to push them down, the growing feelings for Adelaide. Feelings that, if she's being honest, were there from their first dance at the gala. No, before that. Since Adelaide caught her from the tree. The vampire has just gotten under her skin.

"I'm sorry," Lucia says. "My love is political, just like my body. I don't get to think with my heart. I've never been allowed to. Don't you see, Adelaide? Unlike you, I was born in a cage. My entire life has been mapped out for me by fate's hands. You said to me once you wanted to be alive with me, but I'm not *living*. Being born a Dol'Auclair is a curse."

Adelaide turns burning red eyes on her. "Then break free, what's stopping you? Your family can't control you. Unlike you, I didn't get to choose my chains. You can decide if you walk your family's path."

The prophecy rings again—*walk the trail of fate.*

Could she choose something other than this?

"It's not that simple. I will be cursed, Adelaide. *Cursed*—if I disobey my family. The Mother is watching me, even now. I will never be free, don't you get that?" she growls, pulling at her curls. She's frustrated with everything. Angry at everyone. *It isn't fair.*

"Even if I wasn't promised to Fabien, I couldn't be with you."

"Because I'm a woman?"

"Because you're *dead.*"

Lucia's eyes widen as she sees the stung expression on the vampire's face. "I'm sorry, I didn't—*I don't mean that.* You're not dead." Lucia shakes her head, running her hands roughly through her curls in frustration. "Neither would work. We couldn't pass on the Dol'Auclair line. I'm the firstborn. There is so much pressure on me. And yes, they hate you're a vampire, they hate that you're a Skullkin, and they would hate everything about you. Vampire, woman, it doesn't matter. You aren't a witch, and you aren't a political advantage for my mother. We just... don't work."

Tears well in Lucia's eyes, her lips wobbling as the weight of everything crashes down on her. Adelaide sighs, her face morphing into sympathy as she crosses to Lucia, taking her hands.

"Okay, no more kissing. Just—*come here.*" Lucia lets Adelaide pull her over to the large bed.

"I don't understand," Lucia says. "What do you see in me?"

"You don't get it, do you?" Adelaide says, looking genuinely confused. "You don't see how beautiful you are." Adelaide's hands run up Lucia's stomach, around her hips. They trail down and cup the back of her thighs. "You're... magnificent. So damn irresistible."

Adelaide pulls Lucia down atop her, leaning back on the red silk sheets. Lucia's leg is between her parted thighs, hovering over her. Adelaide lies back and looks up at Lucia.

"And those eyes... so warm and kind. Sad eyes. You don't wish for anyone to feel the pain that you have."

Lucia pulls back, her face heating. She looks away from Adelaide's piercing gaze. "You can't have gotten all of that from my eyes," she huffs.

"No, not your eyes. But watching you. Listening. You don't think you're good, but you are, Lucia. You're so kind, like a real-life seraph without wings. And I know my moral compass is questionable most times, but I know a good person when I see one. You want to help people. I know it. You're a better person than I am, you've just been hurt so much."

Lucia's heart aches as if Adelaide reached into her chest and squeezed it. She buries her face in Adelaide's neck, tears wetting burning marbled skin as she lies atop the vampire.

"Adelaide—"

Lucia groans as she is pulled into another memory. This time it is Adelaide's. She tries to pull back, but it is no use, she's sucked into the other woman's mind:

"Siphon, you owe me big-time," Adelaide mutters, standing in the small, shoddy room she rented in an inn that's falling apart. Everything here is broken and dirty, and the room smells like stale air even with the window open.

Adelaide asked for a trip, and this is not what she meant. Here cleaning up Nikolay's mess. Some damn thieves raiding their warehouses and selling their weapons to hunters.

Damnit. She hates this shit.

She was thinking of Etryae where she can gamble in the fancy high-tech cities, or the beaches in east Swaydan, not some small town in the quiet, sleepy far north of Naprait. What is known as the "true north" is so close to those snooty Golden Griffin witches. Luckily, they don't leave their ivory towers often, so Adelaide hasn't had to worry about running into them.

Also, she has a little thing that is making her time here not a complete waste. A thing with fishnet stockings and short skirts.

Adelaide has had no luck finding her target. She was told a suspect was found fleeing this way, but he could be anywhere. Even using her charms, she hasn't had a single clue. No one knows anything about this guy. He's a ghost.

That, or someone is hiding him.

Apparently, he had some sort of skull blade. That only ticks Adelaide further because from the description it sounds a whole lot like hers. The one she gambled to Cassius. She knew she shouldn't have tried to take him in a fight. Cassius is good at games, but at least the ones out of the ring she has a chance of winning.

"You know what, I deserve a break." Adelaide pulls on her cloak and heads outside. She needs to find something fun to do in this lifeless town. Maybe something to drink.

She licks her fangs, a mischievous smile spreading across her lips. She hasn't had a good feed and fuck in too long. Everything is getting so boring.

Adelaide is eyeing up some cute human when she hears it—something in the back of her mind, slamming against her skull.

Is it... crying?

Adelaide doesn't realize that she has started to veer away from the woman draped beside the tavern door. She heads toward the forest, chasing that niggling in the back of her mind. Like she is being drawn somewhere, and she doesn't know why.

When she has walked a long time, almost in a trance, she hears a shout and takes off in a run. She comes across a clearing where a woman is falling from the sky.

Like fate...

There's an odd pressure in Lucia's chest as the vision warps, and she reaches out trying to grab ahold of something. A sharp pain splits her head as she transfers to another memory:

Adelaide walks into a lively warehouse, dropping her bags at the door.

She's glad to be back home in Swaydan. Loud, busy streets and the way the city feels alive. She's also glad to be off that train. It's the reason she doesn't travel much, having to take a train everywhere. "Ugh. They should have invented better travel methods by now."

"They have," Siphon scoffs beside her. "But you hate boats worse than trains. You'd also have to be squished in with a bunch of humans, which you also hate. At least in a train, you can request a private cabin."

"Whatever," she mutters.

The north is slow and quiet, like a graveyard. It is surrounded by trees and mountains. Adelaide prefers the busy cities and swamps of home. She made sure to get on the first train out, after the gala.

Their southern warehouse is underground, surrounded by massive gates. It's one of her favorites. She prefers it to Whoynia and even Etryae, though the east can be quite fun. All of the technology the humans developed up there makes the place a tech haven. It just reminds her of how backward the north is. The witches have a tight hold of that land, and they prefer living in the past. While she was there, she had to be on her best behavior. It was exhausting.

"This was a bust, just as I'd imagined it would be. It only created more work for me," Adelaide complains to Siphon, who also sets down his bags to be scooped up by some fledgling that'll bring it to their rooms in the lower levels. She smiles when he slips cool metal into her hand, tucking the weapon into the band of her leather pants.

"The calling of the Mystic Council would have happened whether you were there or here. Just be lucky you were nearby and didn't have to rush to Olympia. You wouldn't have had time to request your private accommodations."

Adelaide rolls her eyes. Siphon loves being a smug asshole.

The warehouse is a massive thing that goes deep underground into many different tunnels and has over a hundred different rooms of all manner. Currently, it's lively, some sort of rave raging in the other room. Adelaide can see the flashing lights, and the pounding bass nearly shakes the floor.

The party never ends.

"I swear Nikolay is torturing me at this point. Why the hell did he have to choose me for this Triune business? You're the golden boy, you'd have been better."

"The Orbis Libra is the one that chose you."

"So? Choose someone else. I don't want to go to that damn academy. Pull Cassius from the icy mountains, or wherever the fuck he is. Simple. You two are birds of a feather, anyway. And Nikolay's favorites."

"You know why, Adelaide," he says, pinning her with a look.

"Why, because we're his 'children'?" Just because he calls us that doesn't make it true. Besides, he calls all of us his children. Which, to be honest, is a bit weird. And incestual. Some of his children are..." She makes a crude motion. "If you know what I'm sayin'."

"Gross, Adelaide." She cackles, always happy to offend his traditional sensibilities. "You have to play nice while we're at Eirini Academy. There's a delicate peace—"

"Peace?" she says in disbelief, turning back to look at her brother. Though she doesn't consider Nikolay her father, she will always consider Siphon her brother. *Is that what Siphon is doing this all for? Peace.* Something so incredulous and fictitious it's a wonder anyone believes it. She shouldn't be too surprised her righteous brother would.

"Nikolay has worked hard to build the vampire's reputation back up from that of the past," Siphon says. "We're headed into a new age and the vampires can't be left behind."

"We're already being left behind." Adelaide throws her hands up in the air. Every day the witches work harder and harder to put vampires in the ground. Nikolay's riches are the only thing that keeps them from truly succeeding.

"And that's why we need to win the Triune. That's why I beg of you to take this seriously."

Adelaide drops down onto the couch, accepting the company of a woman who comes over, brushing up against her and baring her neck. *She's human.* They keep many in the warehouse for this purpose. Humans that like being blood bags.

Adelaide puts her feet up on the table, lounging back. She drapes the human over her lap, fangs extending at the sight of a pulsing vein. She looks up at Siphon, who's still hovering beside her. He adverts his eyes, looking uncomfortable.

She motions to another human nearby who's blushing and eyeing him from across the room. He shakes his head and Adelaide rolls her eyes.

"Politics don't breed peace," she says, her words coming out as a lisp around her fangs. "It's just a bunch of arrogant people leading the ignorant, and the ignorant leading the ignorant… People yell at each other across a table, pretending like they care what the other is saying or that they understand each other at all when really, they're trying to secure their own interests while giving up as little as possible. It's just a bunch of pretending. Treaties are make-believe borders that separate people who hate each other. What happens when people realize there's nothing more than pretty words holding them back? This world will be a bloodbath."

Adelaide sinks her teeth into the human, whose name she doesn't care to know. The woman moans, her head thrown back in ecstasy. Adelaide doesn't worry about being messy, she lets the blood run down the human's neck and past her own chin.

Though she doesn't have to drink blood as often as born vampires, she loves it anyway. The dirty deliciousness of it all. It's exhilarating.

"Join me, Siphon."

He backs up, shaking his head. His eyes flash red for a moment, but he pulls them back to green.

"I'm not hungry. I'm going to check on the gun shipment that just came in." He strides off quickly, disappearing around the hall.

The cults are involved in a lot of things, from the drug trade to gun production and selling. Humans come to them mostly, human gangs and businessmen. The vampires don't have much interest in it, nor the money.

The Spiders are extremely wealthy with jewels and treasure Nikolay's family has passed down, but they do it for connections. Offering the humans use of their warehouses and protection to manufacture their goods. It's great for making allies and getting information. The cults need it if they're going to keep the witches off their backs.

Though there are many cults, the vampires are like a hive mind. Everyone answers to Nikolay. He's basically the progenitor of vampires. Some even call him the king.

The witches have the human Mystic Enforcement Agency on the Spiders' necks at every turn. The vampires have had so much trouble with the nosy do-gooders that it's making Nikolay antsy. Giving the witches more power would just be asking to get crushed once and for all.

Adelaide has a bad feeling about what that means for her. She doesn't care too much about any of it. She just wants to drink blood and alcohol, have sex, and party. People, as well as alliances, are fake. *Why should she pretend they aren't? Why should she act like any of this matters?*

Her mind drifts to the witch... Lucia Dol'Auclair. Seeing her at the Dome took her breath away. She nearly revealed herself to the woman but held herself back.

She feels stupid for not realizing who she was. This is Adelaide's fault for never paying attention to these things. It's not like she didn't know the beauty was a witch. The pretty woman wouldn't stop mentioning it.

Besides, she was at the Golden Griffins barrier. So, yes, she knew the woman was a witch. She had that sweet smell they all have. That isn't the problem. Adelaide likes sweet things. She also likes fooling around with witches. There's something taboo and dirty about it. Also, they're secret freaks. But that wasn't what drew her to Lucia. There was this glow, an aura around her that Adelaide couldn't look away from.

She could have let the witch fall, but she isn't that cruel. She could have saved her and gone on her way. Something was urging her to help Lucia, demanding it, and Adelaide was too weak to refuse.

She grits her teeth, holding the human in her lap closer. She pulls her fangs out, licking at the wound. The human squirms in her lap, looking up at Adelaide with wide eyes, begging to be taken. Adelaide's heart drops. She no longer feels in the mood, thinking about Lucia.

The human's eyes are too blue, nothing like the big brown eyes of her witch.

She stands, pushing the human off her and onto the couch. The woman whines, but Adelaide only rolls her eyes and turns away. She wipes at the blood around her neck and mouth with her sleeve, thankful she's wearing black.

Now that she's full she wants to go downstairs and change and sleep in her own bed. The party will still be here when she gets back. It never ends.

"Delai!"

Adelaide turns at the sound of her nickname. Only one person calls her that. *Doll-ie.* Kai comes crashing into her, nearly bowling her over. She groans, already in a bad mood. He always does this. The fledgling vampire is always full of energy and ready to fight.

Adelaide amuses him.

The two scrap, knocking one another around the room with powerful kicks and hits that send each other flying across the room. Kai is scrappy and has sharp nails that always give her trouble. He's quick.

Kai throws Adelaide into the sofa, the wooden legs scraping against stone and nearly crashing it into the pool table on the other side of the room. She stands, spitting out blood. Damn, they'll have to get a new couch.

The feisty vampire jumps, wrapping his legs around Adelaide's waist from behind, biting into her shoulder. The little shit. *"Ow,"* Adelaide hisses, throwing him off her. His back hits the ground, but he's up quickly, springing from the floor. He just never stops.

This time, when he rushes her, Adelaide pulls her blade. He doesn't have time to react.

Slink!

"What the piss, Delai!" he yelps, grabbing his leg. Her spiderweb dagger sticks out of his leg.

She pulls the dagger from him and wipes it on her pant leg as she prods the small teeth marks on her collar. It's no longer bleeding, which is good. He didn't bite too deep, so it'll heal quickly. Nasty little thing.

She pats the blade on her leg. Bambi. He comes in handy when Adelaide isn't in the mood for a pissing contest. She doesn't like the biting, scratching stuff, and when she isn't in annoying, authoritarian territories, she keeps it on her at all times.

She's glad to be back home. She couldn't have used Bambi back in the north. They're real sticklers for this stuff. The witches have a huge monopoly on the land up there and they'd throw a fit to the Council. Only Mystic Enforcement officers can have weapons.

Nikolay let her pick a few weapons out of one of his shipments for her eighteenth birthday. He thought she would pick a gun, but she got two blades: her skull and Bambi. The guns are mostly for buying connections with the humans, and local Mystic Enforcement who look the other way for some of their greater crimes.

"You have to stop stabbing him," a deep voice rumbles from the shadows. It sounds like thunder as the man rolls the steel door shut cutting the main room off from the party raging on the other side. The room goes silent as the soundproofing mutes the noise.

Adelaide smirks, turning to see Cassius strut farther into the room, hands in his pockets. She wasn't expecting him home before her.

The insomniac vampire has glitter under his eyes and Adelaide wonders if he just got back from a club. It looks like it. She's jealous. All she got this week was betrayal. Siphon was moody and boring as usual, so he was no good company.

She shrugs. "I hate biting, and this little brat deserves it."

Kai pouts as Cassius pulls him up off the ground. The crybaby is always trying to bat his eyelashes at their superior. And it usually works too. She doesn't know why. He looks like a skunk to her, with a patch of blond down the front of his brown hair. He does have cute brown doe eyes. They have nothing on Lucia's, though. Her eyes were like magisk, shining a deep auburn in the sun.

"You're just jealous I can keep up with you now," Kai teases, hiding behind Cassius before she can retaliate.

Adelaide flips him off. "I would hope you can. Nikolay would be very upset if Siphon was slacking on your training, pup."

He growls. "Don't call me pup, I'm not a wolf."

"There, there, Adakai," Cassius says, patting his head. Kai snaps his teeth at the older boy, who just laughs in return, his untamable curls bouncing as he throws his head back. Kai wipes his bloody hands on his pants, taking more weight on his healing leg.

"What are you doing here, Cassius? I thought Nikolay sent you to the east for cleanup?" Adelaide says. She wishes she'd been on that trip instead. Though she doesn't like the snow or cold, cleanups usually mean she can use Bambi. And maybe torture a guy or two.

Only the ones who deserve it.

Cassius leans against the wall. "I was bored, and the people are no fun. They're modest, which is boring, and I was freezing my balls off. I left Linus and Titon there instead."

Adelaide raises an eyebrow. She doesn't believe that. *Cassius, bored?* No, he's always bored so that can't be it. He loves a challenge in the form of games and people, and when they don't give him that he gets moody and annoyed.

Cassius has been heading a group for months, chasing stolen goods. Someone has been hitting their supply recently, and the problem is only growing. For a while, it had mostly been contained to the west, but recently they have been seeing more thieves crop up all over the place. They haven't been able to find all of them, nor can they find a pattern. The thieves are like ghosts, and there doesn't seem to be anything connecting them.

"How was the north?" Cassius asks, taking up a pool cue. He motions to the other. Sighing, Adelaide joins him, racking the balls.

"How do you expect? I was surrounded by snooty witches."

Adelaide's mind wanders to a flustered princess in her formal dress, drenched in rain, nipples beading through her top. Adelaide bites her lip. Dammit. She can't get that witch out of her head.

Brown skin, big brown eyes, curves Adelaide just couldn't help herself from touching over layers of fabric and silk. Dancing with her was a dream.

"I call solids."

The room blinks into focus as Adelaide's pulled from her musings. She notices Cassius sunk five balls in his break shot. He looks smug about it too. The vampire is only passionate about two things. The first thing is winning.

The second is fashion; he's incredibly vain. Now he's in corduroy pants and a black lace top with puffy sleeves. The two solo strands of hair on either side of his face, which hang much longer than the rest of his afro, are decorated in silver ring clasps.

Adelaide looks over at Kai, who's stuck to Cassius's side while the senior vampire leans over the table trying to line up his shot. The fledgling is shouting things to try and distract him. Cassius keeps batting him away. Adelaide shakes her head. *They're clueless.*

"Have you talked to Nikolay since you've been back?" Adelaide asks, trying to sound nonchalant. She knows there's more to his early trip home than he's letting on.

Cassius looks up at her.

The dual-haired baby vampire pouts now the attention isn't on him. He comes around the table, tugging on her arm. She ignores him. It's the only way to punish him, to not give him attention. And it's fun making him pout. He's a spoiled little brat, the fledgling, completely ignoring the order of ranks here. Worse, they let him.

"Why? Are you still fighting with your father?"

"He's not my father," Adelaide growls. She hates when people call Nikolay her "father." He's a man who raised her, sure, but that doesn't make him a father.

Cassius smirks, putting his hands up like he's warding off an angry child. "I did talk to him. The Orbis Libra is up for grabs, chi? Well, it's no surprise Nikolay wants it. This is an opportunity for the vampires that we won't likely get again. One we've been searching for a long time. Both to keep power out of the hands of the witches and to gain more magisk ourselves. If we control the magisk, we won't have to worry about Enforcers or the Caput Trium hanging over our shoulders again. We can expand further and reclaim the land that was once ours."

He lines up his shot, sinking the eight ball in the corner pocket and securing his win. He racks his cue stick, turning to pour a drink from the bar.

"Yeah, and Siphon can do that. I'll wave and watch from the sidelines."

Cassius shakes his head. "Sorry, not happening."

"Why not?"

"Because you were chosen. And the Master wants it to be you."

Adelaide drops her pool cue. "Me? Why? He should know this is the absolute last thing I want to do, and it's the perfect thing for Siphon."

"He already has plans for Siphon, don't worry." He throws back the entire glass of alcohol, the strongest they have. It was made by a very skilled witch. Cassius shrugs. "He thinks you're the one to do this. Nikolay has a plan, and I don't question it. Don't worry, you won't be alone. Kai and I are coming with you."

Adelaide shakes her head. *No. No, it can't be. Nikolay, the bastard.*

"Pack your bags, re-borns, we're headed to Eirini."

Lucia gasps as she is dropped back out of Adelaide's memories. She's a bit dizzy, reeling from all of the information she just gathered. Adelaide too was smitten from their first meeting. It wasn't just her...

Lucia's heart aches. Because no matter what she feels for the vampire or vice versa, nothing can happen between them. It isn't possible. She might be Adelaide's fate but Adelaide isn't hers—Fabien is. And she can't veer off that track.

Adelaide rubs Lucia's back and lets her cry. She doesn't say anything at all as Lucia falls apart and cries for everything. For her family, for her heart, and the ridiculous engagement she was forced into. Lucia never wanted any of this. And she thought it was enough. She thought she could go along with it all and it would be fine. But she isn't fine.

"It's okay. It's okay, kuai-yuel."

As Lucia touches the vampire skin to skin, crying in her arms, Adelaide's thoughts flow into her mind and it only makes her sob harder.

Kuai-yuel—my moon.

Chapter Twenty-Four
Flying Amongst Stars

All eyes are on Lucia as she sways down the aisle. The temple is packed, lit by a thousand candles. When she gets to the end, she stands before the Priestess, eyes straying to her sister, who stands beside her. Her sister slowly unties the robe that has been covering her all evening. She's wrapped in only a thin, white chemise. It's nearly see-through, leaving no barrier between her and the ancestors.

Lucia is nervous. This will be her first time communing with her ancestors, waiting to receive her divine message. The Mother has called for her at last.

It's an awkward event with the tension still lingering between her and her mother, but Lucia is excited nonetheless. *She's finally being accepted.*

Gabrielle tilts Lucia's head back, pouring peppermint oil over her hairline, dripping down into her curls and face. She then binds lilac and lavender around Lucia's wrist and throat; her hair is pulled up with a crown of feathers like Griffins' wings.

Gabrielle kisses Lucia's cheek and whispers, "Don't be scared," before letting go of her hand. Lucia nods, briefly touching the flaming moon that still sits around her throat.

On bare, shaky feet, Lucia approaches the Priestess. Her hand dips into a bowl of coal, and she applies the fine black powder with a thumb down the center of Lucia's forehead, on her temples, and smears it across her lips, where the oil fell. All the while, she chants, "Awo baban o al."—*Enter in dreams, ancestors.*

The lights flicker.

Lucia kneels on a cushion, coal applied to the bottom of her feet and up-turned palms, and a blindfold is secured over her eyes. She's then guided up and into a large tub filled with ice. She shudders as she steps in, slowly lowering to sit.

Gabrielle's hands return, situating Lucia with her neck supported by the rim of the tub, as the Priestess continues calling on the ancestors beyond. When the candles go out all at once, even with the blindfold on, Lucia is the only one who can see.

Lucia feels an odd but familiar warmth before her eyes are flying open and she's gasping for breath. She's on her hands and knees in an ocean, yet the water only goes to her elbows; it's the same ocean she has visited many times now. *This is the ancestor realm?* She's been here before, at the Dome and during the second trial.

Lucia stands slowly, staring up at the big, beautiful sky that only seems to grow more beautiful every time she visits. The sky is a richer purple and pink, and there are more stars in the sky. She turns, wondering whether she should walk around looking for the ancestor who's come to speak with her. She's nervous, afraid that none will show, or that the ancestor will have no wisdom or guidance for her.

"Lucia, so we meet at last." A feminine voice echoes around Lucia.

She searches all around, startled when she turns back the way she'd been before and sees it: a large Griffin that towers above her. It has the head and wings of an eagle and the body of a lion. Lucia's eyes grow wide. *It's the Golden Griffin of her coven.*

"Who are you?" Lucia shouts up at it. Its large head lowers toward her and she nearly stumbles back in shock.

"I am who you pray to, child."

"Who I—" Lucia's eyes grow wide in wonder.

"Mother," she gasps, quickly dropping to her knees before the divine deity. "I am honored that you came to speak to me. But... why?" She has never visited anyone's spirit walk before. Not that Lucia has heard of.

"Why not?" The Griffin circles Lucia, its large head bumping her back. "Stand, child."

Lucia obeys, standing slowly, still so in shock that the Mother is standing before her.

"B-because I have disobeyed you and your rules." Her kiss with Adelaide pops into her mind. "And because you were angry with me. You didn't give me a gift until well past my first blooming."

"I ask nothing of you child, therefore you cannot disobey me."

"But—"

"And who is to say when blooming is? Not all gifts are meant to come at the same time."

Lucia's eyes widen in shock. *The Mother isn't angry with her or planning to punish her coven for her sins. None of this makes sense.*

Lucia turns quickly, the water splashing around her as she spins to face the large Griffin.

"But why did you give this gift to me now?" she wonders. "I don't mean to be ungrateful for such a powerful gift, but the power of the Sage—the ability to see into minds—has been causing me nothing but problems. I don't know what to do about what I can see."

"Seeing isn't your problem, Lucia, it's that you're not seeing hard enough. You see what is only on the surface."

"I don't understand."

The Mother stands, stretching her large wings. Lucia is nearly knocked over by the gust of wind. "I am not able to stay long, but I wanted to see you."

Lucia shakes her head in disbelief. *She's leaving already? It shouldn't be this quick.*

"Wait—I just now got my magisk, I don't know how to control it."

"You have much to learn and so little time, child. Magisk is not something you gain; you are born with it. If you have not unlocked your magisk until now, it isn't because it was missing, it's because you had yet to find it."

Lucia's head is spinning. *Find it? What does she mean? None of the Mother's words are making sense.*

"Can you help me?" Lucia shouts. "What do I need to do?"

"Love. It isn't just the joining of two bodies, but of two minds. Love is the key to everything, Lucia." The Mother takes off, pushing from the ground and into the air. Lucia stares up at the sky as she circles above, the waves from the Mother's take-off battering her legs. The voice echoes, *"Maybe you can do what I was unable to do.* Love will set you free. But *beware* love is also blinding and can lead to dangerous things."

Lucia gasps, jerking upright, water and ice splashing over the side of the tub. The candles flicker back to life as she pulls the blindfold from her eyes.

No, no! She didn't get her path; the Mother told her nothing. Another cryptic love prophecy. What is she supposed to do now?

Lucia looks up as her mother approaches and helps her out of the bath, her teeth chattering from the cold. Gabrielle wraps a towel around her. The entire coven is watching, waiting to hear how it went.

Is she supposed to love her mother... Fabien... or could she possibly mean... Red eyes flash into Lucia's mind. *Who is she meant to love?*

"You were down so quick," Hastia says, shocked. "What did they say to you?" Lucia grimaces, pulling the towel tighter around herself.

"Ah, ah," the Priestess says. "You're not meant to share your walk. That's between Lucia and the ancestors. Her message is for no one else's ears."

"It was good," Lucia lies, glad that she's unable to tell anyone what was said to her. "I spoke to Great-Grandmother Leilan, and I feel much clearer on my path now."

The night is brisk but refreshing as Lucia arrives back at campus, cooling her heated skin. She walks barefoot across campus, to her dorm, still in a haze from the ceremony and confused by what the Mother said. So much of it contradicted what Lucia had grown up believing.

"Go on inside, Gabrielle, I think I'm going to stay out in the fresh air for a bit," Lucia says. Gabrielle gives her a worried look, her hand halfway to the door.

"Are you sure?"

Lucia nods.

"I—" Gabrielle's face drops and she leans back against the door. "I know we haven't talked much since we've been here. Not as much as we did back home. There's *so much* I need to tell you. I just... can't yet. But we're good, right?"

Lucia nods, smiling fondly at her little sister. There's a lot she needs to say, so much she thinks she might explode. But she can't even make sense of half of it in her own head let alone drag Gabrielle into it.

"I'm good, Gabrielle. And I agree. We need to have a chat soon, just the two of us."

Gabrielle laughs, opening the door. "Looking forward to it."

When Gabrielle's inside Lucia lets out a big sigh. She's shivering, still cold from the ice bath though she is dry now, with only a thin cloak over her white dress.

"Look at you."

Lucia turns, jumping at the sound of Adelaide's voice. Her beautiful Adelaide. She presses her hand to still her beating heart.

"Come," Adelaide says, holding out her hand. Warmth blooms in their touch. Lucia pushes close to the vampire as they walk across the lawn, confused when she's led past the dorms and into the surrounding woods.

"Where are we going?" Lucia asks, faltering when she spots an old, black barbed gate surrounding a small hill. Tombstones are standing like sentinels against the purple of the setting sun. *There's a cemetery back here?*

Adelaide pulls Lucia along. Noticing her hesitation, she says "Eirini's legacy. Vampires and witches who fought on this land during the War of Clans were buried there," she says. "This school was a combat zone before it was a school, for one of the most brutal of battles. Supposedly, a pair that's buried here took their last breath beside where the main building is now. It was a temple back then. A witch and a vampire, they both died at the other's hand."

Lucia feels a chill pass through her. She hasn't learned that in Mystic History. She knew Eirini wasn't always an academy, it was once a temple, but she didn't know it was an active battleground. She grips Adelaide's hand tighter. It should probably make her scared to be walking alone with the vampire, but she feels nothing but safe.

Lucia begins feeling tired by the time they reach their destination, a clearing deep in the forest. Her weary eyes widen in awe at the sight. A tall, beautiful treehouse lit by ahinre—*firebugs*—which glow a dazzling orange and yellow like flames.

Adelaide is agile. She helps Lucia up the branches and into the small single room, the moon shining into the square, paneless window bordered by winding branches. There's an odd warmth here, hot air blown up from the ground.

"This has been here for a while," Adelaide says. "Siphon told me about it. He found it in his first year at Eirini." She runs her finger over the etching in the trunk. *Olympia,* with a heart beside it. It's an odd thing to carve into a tree, the name of the city.

Lucia pulls off her cloak feeling a bit warm, and sits back on her hands, staring up at the beautiful ahinre, their tiny whispers like a song.

"I heard that your brother came to Eirini years ago," Lucia says, fishing for more information on the man her sister is spending time with. "That he was only here a year before he dropped out. Um... that he was engaged to a woman at the time, and she just disappeared."

Adelaide raises an eyebrow, sitting opposite Lucia in the small room, their feet interlocking.

"Is that your way of asking if he hurt her?"

Lucia blanches. "No, no," she says, shaking her head. "I wasn't— I didn't—"

"What happened with Virenna is his story to tell. I don't even know everything," Adelaide says. Her red nails trace up Lucia's leg.

"I trust you," Lucia says.

"You shouldn't."

Lucia catches Adelaide's wandering hand, interlocking it with her own. The Siren told Lucia of true love, and again the Mother told her her path was love. Lucia still doesn't understand it, but she isn't going to keep ignoring the signs. Lucia was afraid of this thing between them, not because she didn't *like* love but because she was afraid no one would ever love her. Her mother never did. Neither did her grandmother. But maybe she doesn't have to be afraid everyone will hurt her.

"I do trust you."

Adelaide smiles, and the pair just stare at each other for a few minutes. Lucia feels completely relaxed in a way she didn't even feel just earlier with her coven.

"Come here," Adelaide says, patting the space beside her. Lucia's eyebrows furrow, but she comes to sit beside the vampire, smiling dopily as she turns her face up to look the much taller woman in the eyes. "You said you were struggling with your magisk, shi?"

Lucia nods. "Yes, why?"

"Well, I was thinking I could help you," Adelaide says with a mischievous twinkle in her eyes that makes Lucia nervous. She crosses her arms over her chest.

"And how pray tell are you going to do that? You can't do magisk."

"No, but as someone who does a lot of fighting, I know about training. Specifically, training the body for things that are difficult or unpleasant. And it seems to me that for some reason your body sees your magisk as something unpleasant. Given your nightmares, I can imagine why."

Lucia swallows, her heart beating fast as she considers Adelaide's proposal.

"Okay. Help me."

A large grin overtakes Adelaide's face. Lucia squeaks in surprise when Adelaide's arms wrap around her waist, and she's leaned back against the vampire's chest. Lucia is all too aware she is only in a short, thin dress. There aren't many layers between her and the vampire in leather pants and a white button-up undone at the top. A spider chain hangs from her neck, and the warmth from Adelaide's skin makes the metal spider sear into Lucia's shoulder like a brand.

Adelaide's arms wrap around Lucia's middle causing her stomach to swoop. Her lips are at Lucia's ear.

"One thing I know about training is most people learn by earning rewards—some by pain, but I don't think you're the type. You like pleasure."

Lucia shivers in Adelaide's hold. The vampire lifts her arms, hands gripping her smaller ones.

"Another important thing in training is clearing your mind. I think you have way too many thoughts running through that beautiful head, witch, and I need to quiet it so that you can focus on my words and your magisk."

Fingers trace over Lucia's sensitive palms, tuning the delicate nerves. Lucia's nipples peak, poking through her thin dress as hot breath bathes the back of her neck. How she is going to concentrate through this, she doesn't know. A fire she only feels around Adelaide is burning through her. Her breathing is already ragged, and they haven't even started.

"Imagine your magisk running through you, Lucia. What I know of witches is you have to say a houzuz—"*curse*. Lucia cringes at the slur. "—or else your magisk won't work. Words, intention, execution. So, I want you to think of something easy to try first, okay?"

Lucia nods. *Something easy.* Lucia racks her brain for a neno-grade cantus. Something she would have learned in lower academy if she'd had use of her magisk then.

"Okay, uh, give me something I can do a L'Paeru on. I'll place it across the room and try to get it to come to me."

Adelaide takes off her spider chain and drops it in Lucia's hand. Lucia stares at the eight-legged creature, silver and studded with beautiful gems. She places it in the space where she had been sitting across the room before, and it sparkles under the glow of the ahinre flying above.

She comes back to Adelaide and focuses her attention on the chain. "Awa nib." She holds her hands out toward the necklace to draw it in, but it doesn't move. She tries again. "Awa nib... gabru." *Come here, necklace.*

The night is silent save for the twittering of ahinre as Lucia waits for something to happen, but after an awkward amount of time has passed, she feels defeated.

"Hey, don't get down on yourself," Adelaide says softly, lifting Lucia's chin to look up at her. Her hand caresses Lucia's face, a finger trailing down her cheek to her neck. "You've done it before. You used your magisk at the first trial and during Servants of Chance."

Lucia huffs, shaking her head. "Those were flukes. I was in distress or feeling intense pressure. Maybe you're wrong, maybe I need the pain to ignite my magisk. Maybe I should go back to training with Fabien. It worked when he—"

Lucia is startled by the deep, furious growl beside her, rumbling through her back. Adelaide's eyes burn red, teeth bared.

"He's the one who hurt you—bruised you—that day?" she asks through fangs.

Lucia's eyes widen in shock and fear for Fabien. "He was just trying to help—"

"He's the one you're *marrying*? A man who would lift his hand to you?"

"He didn't touch me, it was the—*it was just a training thing.* You should understand, you said fighting and pain are how vampires earn respect."

"You're not a vampire, Lucia, and though I haven't known you long, I already know you don't learn by fear or pain, or even pride. I think that's the problem, none of these witches, your family or friends, truly know you at all."

Adelaide's hand trails up Lucia's stomach, fingers brushing over her nipple. Lucia gasps, lurching forward in the vampire's tight grasp at the heat that burns through her at the light touch. "You need gentleness, you need patience," Adelaide whispers, her fingers continuing to softly explore. Lucia squirms in her grasp, unable to speak at the intense, unfamiliar pleasure.

"Ad-Adelaide," she moans. Adelaide kisses the side of Lucia's neck, but her hands go still. Lucia struggles to catch her breath, eyes tearing and body aching from the loss.

Lucia's breath is ragged. Her mind is torn, but she doesn't move away from Adelaide or ask her to remove her hands.

"I don't know how to do this," Lucia says, her voice shaking as she tries to focus back on the task at hand and not the intense craving Adelaide grew in her. "I couldn't even do cantus as a kid when little baabs were doing accidental magisk they repeated from parents and family."

Adelaide is quiet for a moment before saying, "Then do that."

"Do what?" Lucia questions.

"Do the same cantus a baby would do. If you skipped that step as a child, then maybe that's the problem. Your body isn't strong enough to hold the magisk or cantus. Like in fighting, you have to build your muscles, and that's something you do slowly, building up the weight over time. I wouldn't jump in as a fledgling and try to fight Siphon or Cassius, that would be suicide. Only Adakai is that stupid."

Lucia's eyes widen as the genius of Adelaide's words hits her. She forgets how smart the vampire is because she doesn't put in much effort in class, but when she does speak it's always intelligent.

Lucia crawls over to the necklace and places the chain in her palm. Closing her eyes, she whispers, "Olef, olef, olef." *Float.* It's one of the first cantus most children do.

She hears Adelaide's gasp and opens her eyes to see the necklace hovering over her hand. A grin stretches across her face as she beams at Adelaide, bounding back over to the vampire on her knees in the low room and throwing her arms around her.

"I did it! My magisk did what I wanted to without any effort," she cries gleefully. She never thought it was something she'd be able to do. Without pain or fear or pressure, she got her magisk to work for her. It was an easy cantus, but still, it was progress.

Adelaide laughs, squeezing her tight. When she lets her go, she says, "Come on, now, let's do that a few more times. I'm sure you can."

Lucia happily sits back in the vampire's lap, getting comfortable as she focuses on the glittering spider. "Olef." The chain lifts from her palm. She does it a few more times, lifting it higher and then dropping it back in her hand to do it again. Each time, it does so without struggle and Lucia grows giddier.

"Now let's try something else," Adelaide says, fingers dancing over Lucia's ribs. Lucia squishes the vampire under her wide hips, but Adelaide doesn't seem to be complaining.

Lucia thinks of another, a common and terrifying one all young witches learn. Setting down the chain, she stares at her empty palm. "Ahi."

A small flame flickers in her palm. Even though she already got the last one successfully, she's so surprised by her success that she nearly headbutts Adelaide, shaking out her hand at the sight of the fire in her palm. It's only a small and barely warm fire, but it startles her nonetheless.

When Lucia kneels in front of Adelaide, eyes wide as she stares at the vampire, she bursts out laughing at her own foolishness. The vampire joins her and the two of them break out in a fit of laughter, Lucia on her side, tears streaming down her face. Lucia sighs, sitting up and wiping her tears. She hasn't laughed that hard in a while.

Adelaide comes closer, drawing Lucia in with one hand at the small of her back and the other behind her neck, fingers digging into the curls at her nape. Lucia gasps as the vampire tugs them a bit, pulling back her head to meet her eyes. They're closer, really close, breath mingling.

"Is this okay?" Adelaide whispers, heat against Lucia's lips. She's sweating because of the warm air inside the tree house and the way Adelaide's touch has her temperature rising. Her body is still aroused. The ache between her legs has her whining.

"Yes," Lucia says against the vampire's lips, leaning in to bridge the gap between them. She dives in with all passion and no finesse. The vampire chuckles and Lucia pulls back. "Are you laughing at me?" She pouts.

Adelaide shakes her head, but there's still a smile on her face. "No, I—just, like this—" Adelaide guides Lucia's head with a hand in her hair, gasping as the vampire devours her lips.

Adelaide growls when Lucia tentatively licks at her lips. "Keep doing that, and I'm going to devour you, little witch."

Adelaide's hand wanders up her bare thigh making Lucia's knees shake. Thin, strong fingers caress her most sensitive place through the thin fabric. Lucia shudders, lips pulling off of Adelaide's as she curls in toward the vampire, her head finding refuge against the vampire's neck as slick gathers in the silk fabric, wet soaking her frilly bloomers.

"*Ah*—Adelaide," she moans, hiding in the curtain of the vampire's short hair, lips at the tan neck. She can't keep her hips from moving, chasing that feeling of pleasure. She never imagined anything could feel as good as Adelaide's hands do. She feels both unhinged and ashamed, a wonton whore her mother would shame if she could see her.

"That's it, kuai-yuel, take what you need."

Lucia cries out, biting into Adelaide's neck as if she were a vampire herself, her hips moving quicker with the help of the vampire's arm around her back. Now that she knows what the word means—*my moon*—something stirs in her chest and gut when she hears it roll off the vampire's lips. Lucia doesn't even like sweets, but the saccharine words are like the best medicine on Adelaide's tongue. Lucia dives in, panting against the vampire's mouth as she kisses her wetly, a great pleasure building in her gut.

"Adelaide, I'm gonna—"

"Cum for me, sweetheart."

With those words a thread snaps like the awonok e kadara—*strings of destiny*—and she gasps, shuddering against Adelaide as a flood of warmth gathers between her thighs, wetting Adelaide's fingers through the fabric. Adelaide strokes her through it, kissing her forehead and petting her curls as Lucia nestles into her chest, breathing heavily as her heartbeat settles.

Lucia has no words, eyes closed as her head lies against Adelaide's shoulder. She feels a twist of shame coil in her gut and tries to remind herself of the Mother's words during her spirit walk. *I ask nothing of you, therefore you can't disappoint me.* Lucia's own family's and coven's faces pop into her mind—the whispering and the judgment like on the day Lucia failed to bloom—Mia wasn't lying when she said it was different for firstborns. Even a kiss out of wedlock would cause her great humiliation back home. Never mind the fact she is promised to another.

"Hey, laeomenz—*what is wrong?*" Adelaide asks as Lucia pulls away. She rubs her hands up and down Lucia's arms, looking worried as she sees the shifting expression of sorrow on the witch's face. Lucia shakes her head.

"It's nothing," she says, her voice cracking. Adelaide pulls her to her chest.

"I didn't overstep, did I?" Adelaide asks warily, concern filling her tone. "I didn't—"

"No, no," Lucia assures. "You did nothing wrong. It's just a bit overwhelming is all. I'm not used to— I've never—" Lucia knows that Adelaide is very experienced. This is probably nothing to her. But to Lucia, it is a lot. It's everything. And she doesn't know how to put that into words.

Adelaide kisses her cheek. "I get it, it's okay. Just let me hold you, *shi*?" Lucia nods and Adelaide holds her tight. After a while, when Lucia is beginning to drift off, she feels herself being lifted in the vampire's arms. She blinks her eyes open wearily, waking as Adelaide takes her through the trees to a small river and sits her on a large boulder.

Lucia yawns as Adelaide removes her dress and soiled undergarments, folding and stuffing them into her leather trousers. Then, she lays Lucia in the river, which must be run by the same heat that warms the tree house because it's warmer than Lucia expects, like bathwater or the place in Lucia's dreams she keeps visiting.

Lucia is silent as Adelaide washes her down, cleaning the slick that has gone sticky and dry between her legs. Lucia shivers, not because she's cold, but at Adelaide's careful attention to her body. Once she's clean, Adelaide puts her back in the dress without the undergarments she stole and brings Lucia to the treehouse to lie atop her discarded cloak. Lucia settles on her side, Adelaide against her back. She reaches out to wrap the vampire's hand around her. Tears gather in her eyes, and she feels silly for being so emotional.

"I'm sorry, I probably seem like a mess to you," Lucia says, her voice thick with emotion.

"Why would you say that?" Adelaide whispers.

"Just, I know you've done this before. This probably doesn't mean anything to you, but—"

"Lucia." Adelaide stops her, winding their fingers together. "I can feel everything. My senses are heightened as a vampire. The sound of your racing heart, the smell of your arousal... the grooves of your palm against my stomach, your fingerprint etched into my skin. I feel it all. It isn't *nothing*, and it is anything but familiar to me. Everything about you and what you make me feel is so new."

Lucia laughs to keep from crying, her heart squeezed in a fist so tight she thinks it might burst. She curls herself further into Adelaide's body.

"Thank you," Lucia whispers. "For helping me. For so long I have felt lost. Like the woman in that poem, I was a stranger within my own family, driven to the sidelines because I'm different. I've never felt like I belong anywhere. And it's weird because you and I are so different. We should be more different than two people can be, and yet I feel so complete when I'm with you. Like I belong."

Adelaide is quiet behind Lucia for a while, and she begins to wonder if the vampire fell asleep. Finally, she feels fingers in her hair, brushing over her curls.

"I get it. Maybe that's why from the beginning I've felt so drawn to you. I put on a tough facade but the truth is, I've had to work to be seen by my cult as strong. Unlike the others at the top—Cassius, Siphon—I'm not a born vampire. I was made into this, and I didn't have a choice."

Lucia tries to turn, but Adelaide holds her in place. She can feel the vampire shaking behind her. It's barely noticeable, but Lucia feels it. She's in tune to every part of Adelaide's body.

"What do you mean changed?" Lucia questions, her heart beating quicker.

Adelaide answers her with silence again. The only sound is of Lucia's heavy breathing and the thump of her heart.

"You wonder why some of us struggle, it's because we're hungry. There isn't enough food for everyone; we have vices that help curb the hunger, but that doesn't make it go away. And because of that, we are angry, even violent. We are always on edge. And the ones who can eat don't. They've been conditioned their entire lives by people—people like yours, the witches, the wolves—to believe they are monsters. My own brother has fallen for it. Believing that vile rhetoric about himself. No matter how hard I try he won't listen to me, and I understand why. I can never fully understand what he has gone through."

Lucia brings Adelaide's hand up to her lips and places a kiss on her knuckles, trying to give the vampire the same support she has shown her.

"There are many secrets we vampires keep from the witches. From everyone. And one of those is that *not all vampires are born*. There's actually a small, select few of the original bloodline. The Araneidae."

Lucia is stiff in Adelaide's arms, letting the information sink in. She's in shock, her mouth opening and closing as she tries to find the right words.

"And what were you before you were turned? Human?"

Adelaide lays a kiss on Lucia's neck. "I think that's enough information for the night, little one," she says. "Just remember this information I'm sharing with you is—"

"Secret. Of course. I wouldn't tell a soul." Lucia swallows the lump in her throat. "And your vices? Sex, parties..."

"They were. But it was never enough, I was still always so angry. Lately, the only vice that has been able to tame me is you."

Lucia nods but can't speak. She closes her eyes and tries to go to sleep as Adelaide hums, settling against her back. But Lucia is wide awake now, mind racing and body humming with energy. This was a huge thing for Adelaide to entrust her with. Lucia worries about what would be done with the information if anyone else found out. If her mother found out...

This is the exact kind of information the woman would want from her.

Chapter Twenty-Five

The Balance of Fates

"*For Lucia of the Golden Griffin coven, by your humble Caput Trium.*" Lucia reads the note for the last Triune challenge. "*A war of words to test your true beliefs. Let the people decide whose hearts they seek. The three contestants will hold a debate to convince the people they would be best suited for the Orbis Libra. Those strong in heart and conviction have a fragment of what it takes to be Eidan, and not be swayed by darkness. The one able to persuade the masses will be crowned our winner and gain the dark power of the magisk core.*"

Lucia shivers at the thought of carrying all of that power. She doesn't know how her grandmother did it for so long.

The sound of crinkling wrappers has Lucia turning to see Gabrielle slipping all the chocolates and strawberry sweets from her basket. Again.

"I never knew you were such a fan of sweets," Lucia says, raising an eyebrow. Her sister doesn't dislike sweet treats, but she's never been as food obsessed as Lucia, so this new habit is confusing.

Gabrielle blushes. "They're not for me," she says sweetly. "I have a friend... who has a huge sweet tooth."

"Ah. And you're buying this friend with"—she looks at the wrapping behind Gabrielle's back—"strawberry sticks and tarts." Her sister shrugs. "Why don't you make sweets for them?"

"You know I can't cook, n loray."—*on my life*. Gabrielle snorts. "I'm trying to get on their good side, not poison them."

It's true, Gabrielle is a horrid cook. She nearly burned the kitchen at the estate when Mika let her practice once. He never let her again. "Anyway, I can't make anything edible with Mallei, but... I can make clothes!" She lifts the hem of her pink robe and shows off a near copy of Lucia's boots she was sent for the first trial. "They're... a little sloppy, but that's because I'm still practicing. I'll get them perfected soon," Gabrielle says with an excited squeal.

Lucia rolls her eyes. "So anyway, about my last trial. I think that's a little more pressing than fashion."

"Nothing is more pressing than fashion. Besides, it's only a debate. That's the easiest one yet."

Lucia gives her a deadpan look. "Je pak, Gabrielle."—*Be serious*. "Public speaking is one of my worst qualities. I might have a panic attack right on stage and embarrass myself in front of the entire council."

Gabrielle's smile drops. "Right. We have a lot of work ahead of us. But don't worry! Professor Gabrielle is here!"

Lucia and Gabrielle spend the next few days after class meeting up to work on Lucia's speech. Her mother sent her the points she wants to be emphasized during the trial, but that's only half of the battle.

Caught up in classes and growing nervous for the end of the competition, Lucia also forgot to ask her sister about the things she's been getting up to while they've been parted. She knows her sister has been hanging out with Siphon, she just doesn't know why it's a secret. Gabrielle has never been shy about sharing her crushes before. Maybe for the same reasons Lucia hasn't told her about Adelaide, who she has been spending more and more time with.

"Lucia, it's very simple," Gabrielle groans. "You just have to memorize these lines. Mother wrote it all down for you."

Lucia hums as Gabrielle works through another knot in her hair, the movement relaxing as her sister combs out her curls, the small wooden teeth scratching her scalp pleasantly.

There's a scroll in front of her that her mother sent, and old family journals dating back to before the War of Mystics that she wants Lucia to use in her debate. The history and pride of their family name and notes about the power and influence the covens have over the other two Mystic families.

The problem is, Lucia doesn't want to say any of it. It's condescending and boastful, speaking of vampires and wolves as if they're less than the witches. Those aren't words Lucia feels comfortable saying, nor ideas she wants to associate with. Especially after what Adelaide told her, she doesn't want to spread a hateful ideology that has hurt Adelaide's brother and other vampires.

"Why don't you say it then, Gabrielle? I will practice a *quen-grade* Iruji cantus so that you can go up for me, or maybe we'll do an Oporaa, and you can just switch places with me permanently!" Lucia jokes. It's only half joking though because Lucia is terrified. About speaking, and the growing pressure of competition.

The closer she gets to the end, the more she realizes just how different her life will be if she wins the Triune. Becoming Eidan is a big and dangerous responsibility. A lifetime commitment she wouldn't be able to back out of. Her grandmother served until her body gave out and she was at death's door. She never took breaks and barely came home to see her family. Now she is old and fragile, and the only hope she has is Lucia, the coven runt, to take her place. *What would that mean for her and Adelaide...?*

"Sure." Gabrielle laughs. "I don't think there's a magisk grade high enough that'll allow me to body swap you permanently, and even if there were, no offense, Lucia, but I wouldn't want it. You're cute, ebe sisi—mi sisi."—*big sister—my sister.* She squishes Lucia's face between her palms. "But I'm damn beautiful."

Lucia blushes, batting her sister's hand away. Gabrielle pops her with the comb.

"Now come on! Back to work. Mother will chew you out if you choke on stage and embarrass her. And as your lovely instructor, I will too."

Lucia loses track of time and ends up spending the next two hours studying with Gabrielle. She's exhausted by the time they finish, and Gabrielle doesn't even return to her room. The pair curl up under the covers, arms entwined and breath mingling as they did as children, and on nights Lucia had nightmares and Gabrielle would climb into her bed.

Lucia finds time in the mornings before her first class to exercise the tools Adelaide taught her, doing small, easy cantus in repetition until she tires. She has been slowly building that up until she can do a cantus with higher and higher difficulty.

"Lady Lucia."

Lucia jumps, hidden away in her booth with her untouched breakfast in front of her. She had been so carried away, summoning her spoon the short distance to her hand, that she had forgotten where she was. Gabrielle never showed up for breakfast this morning, so she decided to practice her magisk instead.

"Hele, Lord Fabien," Lucia says breathlessly. She's wary as the man sits across from her, sliding his pudding over to her. She has been avoiding him, and up until now, it has been working.

"It's koklemu—chocolate lemon. I know it's your favorite," he says.

"Takke'," Lucia says, grabbing it slowly. It is her favorite. Gabrielle made it for her as a child to cheer her up when she was sad, or her mother disciplined her.

Lucia doesn't even like sweets, but Gabrielle does, and making them for Lucia was an excuse to get some. She had first made it on Lucia's eleventh birthday, the night after she overheard her mother and grandmother arguing in the sitting room about Lucia's lack of magisk. Her mother hadn't even come down and given her a "happy birthday" the next morning but Gabrielle had.

Gabrielle's koklemu had been awful, but Lucia felt too bad to tell her so, and the gesture had cheered her up, regardless. It warms her heart as she takes a bite of the—much better than Gabrielle's—pudding. It's a bit sour which keeps it from being overpowered by sweetness.

"I know things have been a bit odd in the past weeks," Fabien says, "but you are going to—*may the Mother bless us*—be the Eidan soon. And when that happens you will be much busier than now. We should, as betrothed, spend time together and get to know one another on a deeper level. So maybe start by calling each other my lady and my lord. And... join me tonight for Dai Gemus."

Lucia's face heats. Dai Gemus is a romantic day to attend the temple with a guest. It's the day of the spirit and celebrations. People also often refer to it as Ifidai—*the day of love*. Witches are said to become enlightened or find their soulmates on Dai Gemus.

"I don't know why that is necessary. I assume you've spoken to my mother, this is a political marriage. There's no need for us to get any closer."

Fabien sighs, grabbing Lucia's hand before she can move it away.

"Don't be like that, Lucia. This may be political, but we are not strangers. There's no reason this should be painful for either of us. The least we can do is get to know one another better."

Lucia hesitates in her response, not wanting to be difficult. Fabien hasn't exactly done anything to her, he's as wrapped up in this as she is. But she wishes they didn't have to pretend this was anything other than what it is.

"I... yes."

Lucia can't exactly say no if he's insisting. It would be rude, and if it got back to her mother, the covens would have a fit. She's meant to be meeting with Adelaide tonight to study, but they'll have to push it back a bit.

Lucia sits in the front row of her Mystic Theory class, bored as Professor Doyle goes on about an author and scholar who predicted the end times. He was a witch and was only a boy during the War of Mystics.

Lucia isn't too interested. She's mumbling cantus under her breath, imagining what she's going to practice later, and replaying the night she spent with Adelaide in the tree house. She's all too aware of the vampire behind her, the woman's gaze burning into her back as she remembers the feel of the vampire's hands on her.

"In this passage, Louis Dupont talks of his fear for the future and an impending war worse than the last. He opens his journal cryptically, with the line: *The balance of fates isn't always split even. Sometimes, things tip into an order of odds. When that happens, Mother helps those who live long enough to see it; to the fall of mankind and Mystics everywhere.*"

Doyle snaps the book shut, strolling down the aisles between desks, her strong fragrance from spending after-class hours in the gardens following her across the room.

"Assuming you all did the assigned reading, can you tell me what Mr. Dupont believed about the three Mystic races? Their origin of purpose."

Lucia startles at the tome coming down on her desk. She turns from where she'd been peeking back at Adelaide. Snickers break out behind her making her blush and stumble over her words.

"Miss Dol'Auclair, can you tell me what Dupont believed the purpose of the witches was?"

Lucia looks up at the woman, glasses hanging at the tip of her nose. She tries to remember where in the lesson they were and whether she had gotten to finish her reading for the class amidst all her other work. "D-DuPont theorized the Mystics to be mortal beings created with *divine* purpose. He believed a deity, or supreme being of justice and impartiality, made witches to be the creators of life."

Professor Doyle nods, her eyes lingering disapprovingly on Lucia for a few seconds more. She was probably hoping to catch Lucia off guard. Luckily Lucia knows her witch history.

The woman is a bit prickly for someone who spends so much time with plants. Lucia had expected her to be more motherly.

"Good. Dupont had a lot of theories about the origins of Mystics. He believed the three Mystic clans to represent balance, the scales of fate. He's also the one who coined the term "Orbis Libra" for the magisk core and he believed there were two, one yet to be known, and that without the magisk cores—light and dark, opposites—our world would plunge into eternal darkness, and daemons from below and seraph from the sky would descend onto earth in a deadly battle. He thought Earth lay at the medial between Zien and Tophet, acting as a barrier for much more wicked things. Very eerie stuff, he was quite paranoid. Now, can anyone tell me what he wrote about the part vampires and werewolves play?"

Blythe proudly raises their hand. Beaur snickers at their eagerness, and they kick him under the desk, causing him to grunt in pain.

"Yes, Kanoska?"

"Well, Louis believed—"

"Formality, *Kanoska*," the professor says sternly.

Beaur laughs once more, earning himself a disapproving stare from the professor.

"Mister Dupont," Blythe corrects through gritted teeth, "says vampires are guardians who protect humankind from their fatal sins. But, his findings contradict many scholars who see vampires as bringers of death, as well as the witches' own belief in the Mother."

"A theory that seems much more fitting," Beaur snickers.

"Mister Kanoska," Doyle snaps, shutting the disrupting wolf up. The older woman turns back to Blythe, the veins throbbing at her temple.

"And what of werewolves?"

"Werewolves are the balance, thought to be made in the image of the great deity Dai. They are the intermediary, or links, between life and death—witch and vampire. Where witches and vampires are feminine and the masculine, wolves are either both at once or neither, genderless."

Professor Doyle claps once, gathering everyone's attention. "Good. Now, everyone, turn to page sixty-four in your textbooks."

"That was awesome," Beaur says, sidling up to Lucia as they leave class. "Professor Doyle caught you eye-banging that vampire chick."

Lucia covers her flaming cheeks with her textbook. "I was not—"

"Don't call her a chick!" Blythe growls, bashing him over the head. "You're around humans *too much.*" They turn around, heads swiveling back and forth. "Did we forget Boen again?"

"Ow, Blythe, did you use your wolf for that hit?" Beaur grumbles, rubbing his head.

"Azueme is the daughter of a mafia overlord," Blythe says, pulling Boen forward. He hadn't been left behind, only swallowed up in the crowd leaving class. "She can kill you if she wants. Boen and I would probably never find the pieces. They are *bringers of death,* you know."

"That's a theory," Beaur says, despite being the one to agree in class. "Mystic *Theory* remember?"

Blythe hits him again.

Lucia uses their distracted arguing to slip away. She gets around the corner, and then *fwoop*! Her world spins as she's grabbed and spun into an empty classroom.

Once she's regained equilibrium, she glares up at Adelaide, who is smirking down at her, hands sitting proudly on her hips. Lucia rolls her eyes, moving to walk past the vampire, but Adelaide is in her way, backing her into a desk. Lucia finds herself up on the desk, Adelaide between her spread thighs. Like a flame, heat travels up the back of Lucia's neck.

"What are you—" Adelaide's hands caress the outside of her thick, silk-covered thighs, hands going up to her waist. She speaks in Lucia's ear.

"I just wanted to see you before tonight. I was thinking about the last trial of the Triune, and I felt bad that I'll have to destroy you onstage." Her hands grip tighter, Lucia's back arching toward the vampire's body. Her breath catches in her throat.

"Funny you think I'll let you destroy me," she gasps.

Adelaide quirks a brow, lips trailing her vulnerable, exposed neck. "Won't you?"

Lucia lays a hand on Adelaide's chest, holding her back as she steadies her heart and disoriented mind.

She gets why her mother insists she stays so covered up because every touch of Adelaide's skin upon her flesh burns. Here she sits atop a desk in an abandoned class, shivering under a vampire's gaze. The scandal.

"Maybe you should spend less time trying to defile the competition," Lucia whispers, sliding from the desk, "and more time practicing." She winks, striding toward the door. "Also, we'll have to push tonight back a few hours. Ma ru lai."—*See you later.*

Lucia gets through the rest of her classes with much difficulty. Her mind is in a million other places, and between her legs burns for the vampire's touch. She's even antsy while she practices her Triune speech with Gabrielle who seems to be just as unfocused.

Then she spends time at the temple with Fabien, their interaction is stilted. Fabien tries to make conversation but Lucia doesn't have much to say to the mage. She gives her dance to the Mother atop the altar. A dance that was influenced by her times dancing with Adelaide.

It is uncomfortable for Lucia, knowing Fabien is watching her do a dance that was in part only meant for the vampire's eyes, and more so when he praises her for her dancing, with what she might believe to be an adoring twinkle in his eyes. It only deepens the guilt in her gut knowing what she did and the feelings she has for the vampire while she's meant to be his betrothed. He has been true to her, and she has not been to him.

It isn't fair to either of them. She doesn't want this. She isn't sure what he wants, or if his feeling for her are his own, but he has gone along with it either way. Conspired with both of their mothers to spring this betrothal on her.

Lucia rushes through her goodbyes with Fabien, trying to ignore the dejection in his eyes as she bursts out of the witches' dorms, scurrying across the lawn to meet Adelaide. They're going to be studying in her room tonight since it's so late and they're very far behind on their project for Mystic History.

"Tama hei," a strained voice calls out, causing Lucia to turn, nearly stumbling as she comes to a stop. *Hetan.*

"Hele, Hetan," Lucia says rushed, a tight smile on her lips. Something seems off about Hetan. His hands are deep in his pockets, and his face is a bit pale. He looks antsy. "Do you have some time to talk? I was thinking we could go up to the canteen and—"

"I have somewhere to be," Lucia says, feeling guilty when she cuts him off. She bounces on her feet, eager to go see Adelaide.

"Well, it's just that I wanted to—"

"I promise," she says, squeezing his arms, "we can meet up tomorrow after the debate. I have an hour free before Magisk Relations and it will be just you and me. You'll have my undivided attention."

Hetan hesitates, looking like he might push, but he sighs, his chest deflating. "Yeah, Lucia," he says with a small smile. "That sounds wonderful."

Feeling so guilty, since she has been too busy lately to make time for Hetan, Lucia hugs her friend, only able to wrap her arms halfway around his large torso.

"I'll see you tomorrow!" she shouts over her shoulder, rushing to the vampire dorms.

"...we were naive, two lovers planning to end the war and bring our clans together. It was the War of Clans, a long and brutal war. Witches were enslaved by vampires at that time—forced to feed them and kept from using magisk. The

werewolves refused to choose a side, so witches turned to the humans—populating rapidly, their numbers growing vast and their technology frightening..."

Lucia is only half listening. Wrapped up on Adelaide's comfortable bed, her exhaustion hit her full force and she began to drift off as the vampire's soothing voice lulled her to sleep.

It had been page after page of poems and waxing poetic about Corseia's beauty and her caring heart. But then she gets to the war and Lucia jolts awake.

Lucia is entranced as she listens to Giuseppe's recount of that time. Lucia knew things were bad in the Isobuta period, she's read about it and heard stories before, but hearing it like this is horrifying.

It's not just history, it was Giuseppe's and Corseia's lives.

"Witches, alongside humans who also lived under the threat of the vampires, turned against them, fighting for their freedom. Despite being from a prominent cult at the time known as Araneidae, I didn't agree with my family's ideals. They had control across Hontaras and many other cults were loyal to them.

When I met Corseia, who was a passionate and powerful witch, my life was changed. Rather than sit by and quietly disapprove, I decided to help her change reality. Corseia didn't want revenge, or a cycle of death and violence as the covens demanded, but for us all to live in harmony.

That was the cause of her demise."

Adelaide looks up at Lucia as her eyelids flutter, a smile on her lips as she turns back to the page to read the last passage.

"In the days before his death, as the journal nears the last pages, Giuseppe wrote:

She is beauty and life. She is my only salvation for I have done much wrong in my life and sat by in the face of many evils. My pen and brush are the only ways I can honor her, as my family won't respond to my attempts to end the war. Corseia is better than me in many ways, her magisk is wild and fearsome. It is like a storm in her rage. She will end this war. I have full confidence that if anyone can end this hatred, it's her.

I met her younger sister, a sweet and timid girl who, though agreeing with Corseia, feared standing against their family. She looked up to Corseia as if she were a deity, likening her to the goddess Mirza, a wise and brave olympian. I thought that was fitting. My Corseia—my Olympia."

Lucia yawns as Adelaide flips the page, her eyes drooping.

"You aren't paying attention, are you?" Adelaide says, coming over to stand beside the bed. Lucia is laid out on Adelaide's bed, her eyes drifting closed. The week is catching up to her, the lack of sleep with late nights studying at the canteen and exhausting her magisk.

"Sorry," Lucia mumbles, yawning and stretching out as the vampire sits beside her. "It's fascinating, but I'm so tired." She looks up at Adelaide, who looks exhausted as well. Maybe it's the competition. It seems to be getting to all of them.

Concerned, Lucia sits up, running her finger under Adelaide's eyes. The thin, pale skin looks purple, and the veins are more pronounced than usual.

"Are you okay?" Lucia asks, her hand tracing down Adelaide's face. Even her red eyes look duller. "Have you not been sleeping—or do vampires sleep? Is that a foolish question?" She tries to remember if she has seen Adelaide sleep. She has a bed but...

Adelaide cups Lucia's hand in hers. "I'm fine, and yes, I sleep. Not much but I only need a fraction of what you do."

"Then why do you look ill?"

"I'm a little hungry."

Lucia's eyebrows furrow. "Oh, why didn't you say so? We can head to the canteen and—"

Adelaide chuckles. "You're cute, Princess, but that isn't the type of food I meant."

Lucia's mouth drops open. "*O-oh* you meant... blood." Lucia gulps. She forgets sometimes that Adelaide drinks blood. Feeds off people. The thought has her pulse ticking, and she doesn't miss the way the vampire's eyes track the movement in her throat.

"Why haven't you eaten?" Lucia asks breathlessly, squirming on the bed at the thought of Adelaide's lips on her skin. "You said that you had no shame. That you enjoyed indulging in, uh... blood. Are there no volunteers? I don't know how it works. You don't kill people. You—they—"

"Lucia. No, I don't... well, I don't kill when I feed. I take willing—very willing—participants. I just haven't had a hunger for any of my usual snacks lately."

Lucia nods, but she truly doesn't understand. *How long can a vampire go without blood?* She feels like Adelaide is keeping something from her, but she doesn't question it. When Adelaide comes in for a kiss on the lips, Lucia wraps her arms around the woman's neck to keep her there. She has been craving her lips all day.

Fire ignites where their lips meet, wet and firm. Lucia feels breathless and lightheaded, her skin tingling where they touch. The vampire steals her every breath.

In a rush of speed, she finds herself on her back on the bed, Adelaide looming over her. Her heart nearly beats out of her chest as her adrenaline spikes. The vampire makes her feel cornered, like a cat and mouse. Except she likes where she is at.

"I missed you," Adelaide says, and Lucia nods eagerly in agreement.

"I'm sorry I came so late. I was with my Lord Fabien—"

Adelaide's finger comes to her lips. "Don't speak his name in this room, Princess. Especially when you're underneath me." Lucia nods, gasping when Adelaide devours her lips once more.

Lucia squeals when Adelaide pulls away, hands sweeping under her thick thighs. The vampire pulls Lucia's legs around her hips, hands rucking up her dress. Lucia is embarrassed by how many layers there are. She's wearing netted stockings under her silk dress and knee-high socks Gabrielle made for her with her Mallei.

"I can help—"

Adelaide grabs her hands when she moves to pull down the stockings, pressing them into the mattress above her head.

"Don't touch. I've been dreaming about peeling off all of these ridiculous layers. *I'm going to enjoy unwrapping you.*"

Lucia keeps her arms where Adelaide placed them, eyes rolling up as the vampire's sharp nails caress her round hips. They run up and down her calves, rolling down the socks and tossing them off the bed. She moves to the stockings next, taking her time, trailing her nails down them to leave tears.

"Please," Lucia whispers. Her body feels like it might burn up, the place between her legs aching for... something. Anything. It feels like madness. Lucia wonders if this is the evil her mother always warned her about. Because she likes it a lot.

Adelaide comes back up, kissing her numb. Her lips feel bruised, the vampire's tongue stroking the roof of her mouth. She leans up, following the taste.

"It's okay, darling. I'm not finished with you yet."

Warm hands pull the stockings the rest of the way off, cooler than the usual burning hot. It leaves her shivering as Adelaide strokes her inner thighs, stroking her soft belly.

"Lower," Lucia whines, trying to move Adelaide's hands down to her soaked bloomers, her dress and slip hitched around her hips. She's never been so wet before. Never so needy. She's never craved anything like she craves Adelaide's touch.

"*Oh,*" she gasps, as lips come to her neck. A wet tongue licks up her throat, sucking on her collar as hands tease the band of her underclothes right below her navel, trying to arch into the sensation. Teeth scrape at her neck, and she truly moans.

"Careful, darling, the walls hear everything."

Lucia's cheeks burn remembering the sensitive ears downstairs. The thought of people hearing her. *Of Cassius...*

A shameful thrill goes through her at the thought. She knows Adelaide is only playing with her—the vampire dorm rooms are soundproofed because of their sensitive hearing—but the thought is still fascinating.

"Ahh!" Teeth bite into Lucia's lips as long fingers stroke her core. She's not sure when Adelaide removed the many rings, but strong fingers dip into her wet folds and a deep growl vibrates her neck as the vampire's teeth sink further.

"Ah, ah, ah," she moans. Lucia spasms, body unsure if she should press away from the fingers stroking up and down, up and down, insistently, so fast she's trembling, or from the sharp, pleasurable sting of teeth. Instead, she rocks in rhythm with the fingers, trying to get them deeper.

"Ah, Adelaide, Adelaide, ah, please, more, please."

Adelaide looks down at deep brown skin broken with a sheen of sweat, warm brown eyes clenched shut in pleasure. She smiles as if Lucia's moans and begging are music to her ears.

"So wet for me," she whispers, licking up the shallow bites she left. Adelaide doesn't have to do much; Lucia was already on the edge before she even touched her. Speeding her hand just a little faster, slick juices running down her wrist, Adelaide moves up just a tad, pressing right...

"Ahhh!" She grins as Lucia comes undone underneath her, hands digging into her shoulders and legs clamping around her waist as she lightly rubs the little button that's making Lucia see stars.

Lucia whines, her voice like bells, panting and dripping wet down her thighs as she shakes through her orgasm. "Ah, ah. I'm—" The tears prickling in her eyes are like a dream as she collapses into the deep red covers beneath her.

Adelaide slows her hand, fingers soothing shaking thighs, which fall open in exhaustion. Lucia blinks up at red eyes as the vampire brings her hand to her lips, tasting the sweetness.

"You're going to be the death of me."

THE BALANCE OF FATES

In Adelaide's arms, even the thought of the last trial tomorrow is only a small worry in the back of Lucia's mind.

Chapter Twenty-Six

The Ties of Death and Love

Lucia's hands shake as she buttons her dress. *Today is the last trial.* She still has no idea what she's going to do. There will be so many people there, and they'll all be watching her. Her, Adelaide, and Hetan.

Lucia is closing her door behind her, ready to make her way to the auditorium when she nearly bumps into a figure shaking beside her door. The woman's head is down, her black hair curtained over her face. She's trembling and Lucia can hear sniffling.

"Mia?" Lucia questions, ducking to see the woman's face. "Are you crying?"

Mia finally lifts her head and there are wet trails down her cheeks. Her round face is pinched in sadness. Lucia wants to take the woman into her arms, but she hesitates. She looks around the hall hoping to find someone. Gabrielle or Caitlyn, maybe. They'd be better at this than her.

"Are you okay?" Lucia asks. "Is there someone I can get for you?"

Mia shakes her head. She takes a deep breath and pushes her hair back.

"I'm sorry Lucia, this is embarrassing," Mia whispers. "I know we aren't really close, but you're the only one I can talk to about this—being the firstborn and all. Gabrielle wouldn't understand."

Lucia nods, moving off to the side of the hall as a group of girls pass. She wonders if they're heading to the auditorium and tries not to get anxious about being late. She needs to focus on Mia right now.

"It's okay," Lucia says. "Whatever it is, I'll try my best to help you."

Mia leans back against the wall. She worries her bottom lip between her teeth. "It sounds very silly now, but Caitlyn and I got into a fight."

"That's not silly," Lucia says, trying to comfort her. You guys are pretty close."

"*Very*. We've never been in a fight before. Not like this. But it seems like arguing is all we do nowadays. She doesn't get it—the stress I'm under. She's suddenly acting like coven hierarchy is nonsensical. *Like it's evil or something*. I don't get her. She's been acting so odd lately—always busy, brushing me off, snapping at the smallest things. She used to be so easygoing. I loved that she didn't care about anything, money or appearances and the like. I felt like she was the only person who saw me, and not what I had. Now she hates me for those same things."

"I—" Lucia searches for a response. She doesn't know what to say. Growing up, she didn't have friends, she was isolated by all of her peers. Hetan had been that for her before they were separated, but they were only kids then and things aren't as easy now because of the secret she holds and the responsibilities they both carry.

The closest she can think of is Adelaide. Adelaide is the first person to really *see* Lucia. But they're not friends, they're... well, Lucia isn't quite sure. They're *more*.

Lucia tries again. "If Caitlyn is truly your friend then it will work out. When someone *gets* you, that will never fade. It's meant to be. You've just got to give it some time and I bet everything will work out in the end. Caitlyn is a sweet girl, I'm sure whatever it is she's going through, she wishes she could talk to you about it. When she's ready she will."

Mia smiles, pushing off of the wall to stand straight.

"You're right. Every time we fight, we always make up in the end. Takke Lucia."

Lucia nods, feeling much lighter after having been able to help someone.

"Of course. You can always come to me if you need anything. A friend of Gabrielle's is a friend of mine."

Mia leaves, rushing off to her room and Lucia goes the other way, heading off with her head held high.

Lucia turns to Ekrul as he enters the stage. They're in the auditorium of the academy building, the room more packed than any of the other trials had been. Even the Caput Trium is present, front row, for the debate.

The auditorium is buzzing with excitement and energy, witches lining the walls to record the last trial with an abasleg—*memory charm*—so that the Mystics unable to attend can still watch the three contestants' speeches.

"Thank you, everyone, who was able to make it today," the orun-kun says, his voice echoing in the crowd's heads, quieting the room. "Today is a special day, the last of the Triune before you all decide who among these three young Mystics will become the Orbis Libra's vessel. Unlike the other three tests, these results will not be immediate. There will be a week until the final results so that we can gather everyone's votes. Another gala will be hosted at the Hallow Tower, at which the results will be read and the Orbis Libra bestowed on the winner."

Lucia takes a deep breath, her nerves all over the place. She's too scared to look into the audience and find her mother's eyes, shaking as she stands between Adelaide and Hetan. She's still unsure what she is going to say. She knows what she *should* say, but what she should and what would be easiest are not the same.

"I'm joined by the finalists, Azueme Skullkin, Lucia Dol'Auclair, and Hetan Anoki. Let me give you all a rundown of the rules. I will ask some questions and you will speak in whatever way you think encapsulates the type of leader you will be. Then I will give you each a chance to address one another. Understand?"

The three stand at podiums facing the audience. They nod. Lucia is nervous, wiping her sweaty palms against her dress. She isn't sure if the room is hot, or if it is just her. Hetan and Adelaide seem unaffected by this heat, listening intently to the orun-kun.

Lucia can't help but notice every movement in the audience, every draw of breath and whispered conversation. Her eyes lock onto the pair of vampires in the front room leaning close to pass secrets as Ekrul speaks.

"First question, starting from Miss Skullkin, down to Mr. Anoki. What do you think the biggest issue plaguing Mystic society is, currently?"

Adelaide gives a toothy smile. Lucia doesn't notice any nerves, no shake of her steady hands as she lays them atop the podium and meets the eyes of everyone in the audience, her quick gaze flitting back and forth.

"I think the biggest issue is an inflated sense of self. I speak to everyone who disagrees with our current state of leadership. Those who sit in the light judging the rest of us down below, don't belong where to be where they are. I'll be frank, the witches aren't as strong as they believe themselves to be, or convince everyone else that they are. They've gotten themselves where they are with false smiles and promises of peace."

Adelaide looks at the row of witches at the front of the audience. "*Lies and manipulation.* The Grand Elder was a powerful witch, and she has kept us subjugated for a long time, but with her moving on, we don't have to fear. There is no other her equal. There needs to be a new order of hierarchy."

Lucia's heart is beating fast. She tries to meet Adelaide's eyes, but the vampire isn't looking at her, and Lucia can't tell if that is intentional. *Maybe this is as hard for her as it is for Lucia. Maybe she is more affected than she seems.*

Lucia isn't surprised by Adelaide's words, the vampire has made her dislike of the witches known, but listening to her lover bash her people onstage is difficult, even though Adelaide warned her she would be harsh.

"Thank you for your thoughts," Ekrul says. "Miss Dol'Auclair?"

Lucia tears her gaze from Adelaide, gritting her teeth in a pained smile as she tries to remember the bogy's question. Her eyes focus on the short creatures glimmering scales as she focuses her thoughts. She has to separate *this Adelaide*—the one competing against her in the Triune—from the one whose lips she has kissed and whispered her secrets to. They are not the same. Adelaide isn't holding anything back and neither should she. She has to stick to what she practiced.

Lucia remembers the books worth of information her mother sent her that she poured over with Gabrielle and straightens her shoulders as she says, "I think the issue lies not with the systems or authorities of power, but with too many opinions. It's difficult to navigate the avenues in which we go about maintaining peace and order when everyone's arguing about who should be the one to do it. You can't focus on the people while you're trying to tiptoe around the feelings of those who wish to stifle your progress. The witches don't have the time to placate the petty trepidations of people holding onto past grievances. We must look to the future, not the past. Because if we were to look back, we would remember what Hontaras looked like under a different rule."

Lucia struggles not to look at the vampire beside her once more, as Ekrul gives the floor to Hetan. She can feel Adelaide's eyes on her now. She isn't trying to look away anymore.

Lucia tries to stay focused, ignoring the echoed grumblings of vampires in the audience and the laughter from the witches. It twists her stomach to hear that laughter, and she can picture the smug faces that accompany their words, the same looks that have been directed at her for years, telling her she wasn't good enough to be considered one of them.

"Leaning away from the broader terms of law and order," Hetan says, "my concern with our current society resides with the people. I speak for the clans when I say these are scary times. Even scarier than anyone is making them out to be. We wolves don't care about the Orbis Libra or who's going to lead us, we're focused on maintaining our lives and the lives of our families. Beyond the hunger problem and growing animosity among neighbors, werewolves are at the lowest recorded population in history and steadily declining. People are being killed, but it was noted first among the wolves. I have sat in on many meetings within different clans, not just here in Naprait, but across Hontaras. My people are going missing and dying, but no one is looking into it."

Lucia is shocked by Hetan's words. Most of what he's saying is news to her. She tries not to let her shock show as she peeks over at him. His wide shoulders are held back, his chest puffed out as he stands as a pillar of strength. He looks older somehow, speaking with such conviction, his words echoing the stone walls. He looks like his uncle, commanding the room. Everyone is held in rapt attention, Lucia included.

"Here on campus, we've had two deaths that have no justice, which is unheard of since this land became an academy, and yet no one is looking into it. And if you think that is bad it is even worse outside of these walls. Many Mystics are being found dead, specifically in the borders around the north and east. Mystics and other magisk creatures have no voice, or anyone to fight for them. No one seems to care about a few voiceless Mystics and magisk creatures, but I do. My parents were killed, and I never found justice for them. They were the head of the wolves—the chief and her mate—and yet no one knows what happened to them, or why they had to die. That's why I want to be that voice. I want to be the Eidan for change."

Lucia's heart is pounding as Hetan's words stick in her mind. Lucia never realized this was his motivation for becoming Eidan. He never seemed particularly worried about the competition, helping her any chance he got. She thought like her, he wanted the magisk because it was what his people wanted for him.

That he was doing it because he was *chosen*. She hadn't put much consideration into her aspirations for the Orbis Libra's power. She knew that no matter what she wanted to use the magisk for, it was out of her control. Her coven and her mother would guide her through her reign. She would do as the Eidans before her.

Lucia looks over at Adelaide, hating the space between them. Hating that she can't go over and grab the vampire's hand. She wants change too. She wants peace between the three Mystic families just as Corseia and Guiseppe had, and she has repeated over and over that that was her goal. *But, what has she done toward that end?* She has no plan in place. She has no idea what she's doing.

"Okay, I'll give you three the floor," Ekrul communicates, stepping back slowly with his short legs. "I'll be here only to mediate and make sure things stay civil."

Adelaide grins, leaning toward Lucia, who has to work to keep her heart from leaping out of her chest. She feels like she's being undressed on stage, each layer peeled back as the vampire's eyes rake her up and down.

Focus, Lucia. This isn't about Adelaide and her right now, it's about the competition.

"You feel pride in your witches," Adelaide says, and Lucia tries not to think of all the things she's told the vampire. *Would Adelaide be low enough to use those things against her?* Lucia shakes her head feeling stupid for even thinking such a thing.

"Yes, I do."

"What would it take for you to lose that optimism?"

"If they were to break the values they uphold or the civil law, I couldn't stand by that. But that's unlikely, the Dol'Auclairs are one of the original witch families, and we helped shape Hontaras and the Mystics in it. There was no peace before my ancestor Deipara Dol'Auclair brought us together."

THE BALANCE OF FATES

Lucia tries not to let her eyes stray to her mother. It feels wrong standing up here and lying. The witches aren't perfect, but no one is. And they shouldn't be blamed for her mother's mistake.

"I would argue the vampires live much longer. We've had as much if not more of a hand in that. My *father*, Nikolay Skullkin, fought in the War of Mystics. Also, I think you've been misled about the part witches played during the war. They were not on the side of justice. On the contrary, they were one of the main factors in the incitement of the war. A war that saw many witches, vampires, and wolves dead."

"The witches were the ones who called for peace," Lucia argues, her face hot. She scrambles to remember all that she has learned in these few short weeks. "In the battle of Olympia, right here in this very town, upon the grounds of which Eirini Academy of Mystics was built, my ancestors risked their lives and died bringing about the end to the war and saving countless lives."

"My—"

"If I can interject, this is a three-way debate," Hetan calls, meeting Adelaide's annoyed glare. "The vampires are cowards. You have such long lives, but is that at the assistance of those you feed from, or because you've chosen on many occasions to shirk your duty to help your fellow Mystics and instead flee underground in pursuit of business, money, and greed?"

Adelaide's eyes squint, her arms crossed over her chest. "The vampires help when they see it necessary and when they find value in doing so. Protect the majority at the cost of a few." She shifts toward Hetan, pointing a finger at him. "I believe this debate is between the Pri—Lucia and me. I find no value in your input seeing as you stand no chance of having the strength to lead our great Mystic population. You are weak, and as you said, you are leading your people to extinction. I won't allow the rest of us to sink with you."

Hetan growls, his face sprouting fur, and he tries to leap over his podium toward Adelaide, who rises to the challenge as she meets him with fangs bared. Before the two can clash, a barrier erects between them as the Magisk Creatures professor positioned off to the side of the stage uses her ability. Ekrul shuffles forward as quickly as he can.

"Enough!" Ekrul shouts, his voice ringing in Lucia's ears. She winces. *"Anoki,"* he scolds, waiting as the werewolf takes a few deep breaths. "Any more of that and you will be thrown out. Do you think you can keep yourself together? The both of you." He looks back and forth between Hetan and Adelaide. Hetan looks ashamed, but the vampire is grinning madly.

Hetan takes a few more deep breaths and then nods. "I'm sorry for my outburst, orun-kun. It won't happen again." Lucia watches her friend and is worried for him. It's nearing the full moon. It's becoming harder for him to control himself, and Adelaide's baiting isn't helping. Lucia hates seeing them fight and has to remind herself it isn't personal. It's a competition.

"Okay, continue. Don't make me stop this debate again."

The fabricated stone breaks and crumbles away and Gael steps back.

Lucia folds her hands, her heart still racing as she speaks not to her competitors, but to the audience. Her voice is a bit shaky, still affected by her friend's outburst.

"The requirements of Eidan, to successfully take hold of that power, you need two things. A strong will and high magisk control. I will admit that my magisk still needs work, and I'm getting stronger every day. I aspire to be as great as my grandmother and the witches before me. I will do *anything* to that end."

Lucia's hands shake as the second trial flashes through her mind, Gabrielle's bloody body in her lap. She takes a deep breath, trying to push all of that away, focusing on the speech her mother gave her.

"As Eidan, one of us will become a vessel for the magisk core, and our feelings will be feeding it, be that good or bad. I say, who of us three do those of you believe have the qualities you're seeking in someone who'll hold such responsibility? My life has always belonged to my people, the witches. I am no stranger to sacrifice as my grandmother before me and will do so for all Mystics, giving up my life and freedom to protect yours. In that way, I am already a vessel."

THE BALANCE OF FATES

The three contestants are escorted backstage as they stop for a small break. Lucia walks to Adelaide, hoping to speak to her before they go back onstage, but the vampire is headed straight toward Cassius, who is standing by the door in his fishnet top and silver pants, his eyes flaring red. She looks very serious. Lucia watches worriedly as they begin whispering, and Adelaide follows him out the back door.

Lucia is jittery, her heart beating quicker. Her adrenaline is still pumping from her anxiety in front of the crowd, made worse by not believing the things she said out there.

Changing course, Lucia heads over to Hetan, but the wolf walks right past her to stand in the corner.

"Hetan, are you okay?" she asks. He had barely looked at her throughout the trial, and he didn't address her once. She thought he was trying to stay focused for the trial, but maybe it was more than that.

Hetan grits his teeth, turning his face away. He finally turns back to her, standing there awkwardly. His voice is low when he says, "You couldn't speak yesterday because you were busy? Busy hanging out with that vampire," he growls, nodding his head to the door Adelaide exited.

Is he mad that she hung out with Adelaide?

"I— Yes. We have a project to work on together."

"All night?"

Lucia blanches. "Were you following me?" she asks, wondering why it's any of his business who she hangs out with. She thought this had to do with the competition, but no, it is personal.

"I wasn't following you," Hetan says, pushing off the wall and getting close. Lucia takes a step back. "I was making sure you were okay. You've been spending a lot of time with her lately. I've seen you, coming and going from those bloodsuckers' dorms, and the triplets say that you and the Skullkin brat have been close in class."

"You don't need to protect me. I'm fine."

"Are you? All of these murders going around campus and not one of them has been a vampire. That isn't suspicious to you at all?"

Lucia swallows the lump in her throat, her fists clenching at her sides. "That has nothing to do with Adelaide."

"And how would you know?" he asks. "Because you're *'friends,'* and she said so? Do you believe everything that bloodsucker says?"

"That's none of your business, Hetan," Lucia says, offended that her friend has been keeping tabs on her and who she hangs out with. He sounds like Fabien. She knows they haven't seen each other much. He is busy going back and forth from campus and visiting with his uncle and her with *everything else,* but if he wants to spend more time with her, he could just ask. What he can't do is tell her who her friends should be.

"Is it your fiancés business?" he asks. "That's another thing you've failed to update me on. Congratulations, I guess."

Lucia's mouth drops open. She hadn't even thought of that. She hadn't wanted to tell anyone. Adelaide only found out because of Cassius's pettiness. Gabrielle doesn't even know yet. Lucia was waiting for the official announcement of their engagement so she wouldn't have to tell her sister herself.

"I'm sorry I didn't tell you," Lucia snaps. "I didn't think you had to know everything about me. What about the missing wolves and everything you've been going through? I thought we were friends, yet you never told me any of that."

Hetan scoffs. "You've been pretty busy. Besides, both my uncle and I have gone to your grandmother about the deaths of my people, but it seems despite the treaty, the Grand Elder didn't find much alarm or urgency for 'a few' dead wolves. But you can bet your mother has been vocal about that *single* witch's death."

Lucia grits her teeth, taking a deep breath to calm herself. She can't deal with this right now; she needs to focus on the trial. Lucia turns to walk away, but Hetan stops her, turning her with a hand on her arm.

"You're walking away again? Going to that vampire?"

"Hetan, just stop."

"Why? Do you *like her*? Do you have feelings for one of them, Lucia?"

One of them.

Lucia turns her hard eyes on her friend. She remembers the night at the bonfire when Hetan almost kissed her. *Is that why he's doing this?* "Why? Do you think I should like *you*? We're friends, Hetan, nothing more. We had one kiss when we were ten and that is it. So, don't think you have any right to question me or my heart."

Lucia storms away to be alone. She has so many thoughts rushing through her head yet she can't grab hold of any of them. Her mind is a storm until they are called back onstage. Adelaide slips back in right on time, and Lucia has no chance to speak to the vampire as they are led one after another. The crowd quiets for the final part of the last trial.

There is heavy tension. From Adelaide's conversation with Cassius, and Lucia's and Hetan's argument. Guilt weighs on Lucia for her harsh words. She wasn't listening to what her friend was saying. She was so angry and so bitten with guilt that she lashed out. Now she feels like the worst person, and she can hardly concentrate on the orun-kun's words.

"Adelaide, if you wish to start."

Adelaide steps up to the podium, her hip cocked and a smirk pressed firmly on her lips. The lines of her body are rigid, her mouth tight, but only Lucia can see through the relaxed act. *Something is wrong.* She wishes she knew what she talked about with Cassius. She wishes they were alone right now so that Lucia can be in her arms.

"As you all know, this will be the first opportunity anyone other than a witch has had to vie for Eidan. We don't know what effects that will have on the winner. Every witch who has held the Orbis Libra has been affected in different and wholly unusual ways and I garner that for a wolf or vampire, it will be the same. But whatever powers I would gain as Eidan, I can guarantee it would not be so devastating as the power the Grand Elder wielded with it. No one should have that much unchecked power again. I want to address the gross imbalance of power between the three Mystics, as it is no secret the witches run things in Hontaras—"

Lucia tries to stay composed and remember that they're competing as Adelaide continues to trash the witches and wolves, but it's hard to stay silent even when she knows some of the things she's saying are right. It makes it no easier. There's a bitterness in Adelaide's words now that wasn't there even before. Whatever happened during their break has made Adelaide angry and Lucia is anxious, wringing her hands as she wonders what it could be.

Lucia tries to stay angry at Hetan, but as Adelaide speaks, her mind drifts to her friend. He's right about the witches too. Lucia can try to ignore it all she wants, but they have been complicit in the problems plaguing Mystics. Lucia just doesn't know what she's supposed to do about it. What *can* she do? Would it be too extreme to suggest that witches just aren't meant to control the Orbis Libra at all… to step back and let someone more deserving take it? Lucia's eyes stray to Hetan. So strong and tough, yet also so gentle. A point between two places—the fulcrum in a scale. Even Louis Dupont wrote he thought of the wolves as balance and unity.

"I would like to ask Mr. Anoki a few questions about something I think he failed to mention in his previous discussions. That is finance. He wants to help the wolves financially. *The starving families.* I'm curious how he plans to visit and distribute resources across rural Hontaras?"

Hetan clears his throat. He looks tired and nervous, which Lucia hadn't noticed before. His hands tap agitatedly across the table.

"With the power, I'd have as the magisk vessel, I could revitalize many rural and border towns that have become barren. I could make them thrive. We could produce so much more food and—"

"What after that? Labor, distribution… these people will need to be paid. They have families to feed as well. As far as I'm aware, your clan relies on government funding through the M.E.A. to feed and support yourselves. You're bankrupt, indebted to *the humans*. You can't even help yourself, running back and forth from school to that shitty clan of yours to try and hold it all together."

"Language," Ekrul warns. "Keep it civil." Adelaide doesn't even have the decency to look sorry as Hetan splutters, trying to rub some sort of response together.

Lucia feels pain as she watches the anger fill his eyes. Her head spins as she listens to Hetan talk. They never really spoke of the problems the wolves were having. Their conversations stayed away from those rougher, deep subjects. *Is it true? Are the clans starving?* Her eyes flit to her mother who sits beside Madam Devroue, heads bent as they whisper. *What are the witches doing about this?* she wonders. *Are they doing anything at all?*

Lucia is deep in her head as Ekrul calls her to speak. Her face burns as she stares out at the audience who wait for her to say something.

This entire time Adelaide has been attacking Hetan, all Lucia can think is—*it's not his fault*. The problems with the wolves are the failure of the witches. As are the problems for the vampires. It's all the witches, they've been the ones in power. Lucia's grandmother was the Eidan for nearly a century. Yet, the vampires and wolves are fighting, and for what...

"I—uh—" Lucia's eyes go to her mother who sits primly in the audience with a smug smile on her face. Madam Devroue is beside her. Lucia's heart races, thinking about the speech she has been practicing about how amazing the witches are. About how much they have helped since the War of Mystics. *But what about Hetan's parents? What about the starving, dying wolves and the vampires in hiding, going crazy from the lack of blood, and the blood shame?*

Lucia closes her eyes. Her chest is so tight she can barely breathe. It feels like the walls are closing in on her. She tries to block out the audience and thoughts of her family to say what's really on her mind.

What does *she* want to say?

"As Eidan, I want to unite the Mystics. I-If I become Eidan. Because I'm not sure I should be."

The room is silent as everyone stares at Lucia. She's sweating, her hands and voice shaking.

"And I don't mean the unity we have now. I don't think we've united at all, actually. To be united we'd have to understand one another, and it has been made painfully clear to me since I've gotten to Eirini that we do not. Not even me; I thought I knew everything, and I realized I didn't know anything. About my fellow Mystics, or life. I have been so painfully sheltered my entire life. And what kind of leader knows nothing of the world they're trying to change? *To fix.* I—I thought that I had been through things and experienced pain, but I realize that even my suffering was a privilege. It exists inside a bubble that extends no further than myself. I have not faced the system's abuse and persecution that the vampires or the wolves have undergone. I couldn't even see that it was happening. And for that I am sorry."

Lucia moves closer to the mic, which screeches with feedback. She ignores the rising of angry voices, people whispering all over the room. She needs to get this out. She has to say it all. She doesn't care about the looks people are giving her, or what they might be saying. She just doesn't care anymore.

"I recently read a journal about two people who were killed for loving each other, and for wanting better for Mystics. We can't point a finger at the wolves for needing help from humans, because we made that necessary. We haven't been helping each other. None of us. Even this school, which is supposed to be progressive for having us all on one campus, has separate dorms for vampires and witches, and wolves. Every day there is fighting, always fighting amongst one another. Except, not always... because I've also seen love."

Her eyes stray to Adelaide, who stands watching her with rapt attention. The vampire smiles, red eyes burning into Lucia, who finds the strength to go on, even as her mother seethes in the audience.

"I have seen love on this campus, and friendship. I know it is possible. If we just break out of these ideas we have of one another in our heads and just... listen."

Lucia has a sort of out-of-body experience as she goes on about the things she learned and the ways she wants to help all Mystics and unite the three families. When she is finished, the room is silent, but she refuses to feel shame about wanting peace. She knows it won't be easy, but she'll do whatever it takes. Just like Corseia and Giuseppe tried to do. And if that means not having her as the Orbis Libra's vessel, then she is fine with that.

After a moment, the crowd erupts into noise, and Lucia is frozen as she watches fighting break out amongst witches and vampires, and wolves, an uproar caused by her words. The teachers rush forward, escorting the contestants offstage as they move to control the crowd, and Lucia's head is spinning as both a roar of outrage and applause follow her.

Lucia's heart races as she looks up at Hetan and Adelaide. She smiles at her friend who returns it warily, that familiar warmth coming back to his eyes. She nearly collapses in relief.

Adelaide makes her way toward Lucia and Lucia moves to meet her right as the door bursts open and her mother storms in, lightning in her eyes.

"Lucia, come here now."

Lucia's bedroom door slams closed, and she is left facing her mother's anger.

"Mother, I—"

"What in the Mother's name, was that out there, Lucia?" her mother shouts. "You spit on the name of your grandmother, curse the Dol'Auclair name. Do you have no shame, no respect for your heritage, to trash the witches while propping up the enemy?"

Lucia's eyes flash with anger. "That is the problem!" she shouts back. "*The enemy,* that is all I ever hear. But they are not our enemies, not the wolves or the vampires. We are! We are our own enemy, Mother. You, my mother, the one who gave me life, were my first bully. You are the one who made me hate myself and made me feel like I was not worthy of love or respect."

"This is madness, Lucia. You are *sick*. Sick!"

"Stop saying that! I am not sick, Mother, I am hurt. I am deeply hurt by the way you treat me. Like I am not your daughter, but a pawn for the coven. It took meeting Adelaide to realize my worth. To realize who I truly am beneath all of the brainwashing and lies."

Lucia looks into her mother's eyes, lips wobbling and tears blocking her vision. She wipes at them angrily, trying to see the woman, hoping to find some sort of warmth or comfort. She does not.

Her mother's eyes are hardened by years of delusion and brainwashing. Hatsia's lips are pursed, her face twisted with disgust.

"*Adelaide*," she says like a curse. "That Skullkin vampire, that's what you call her?"

Lucia swallows the lump in her throat, taking a step back toward her bed. She hadn't meant to mention the woman, but now she can see the wheels turning in her mother's head.

"Fabien told me about this vampire you've been spending so much time with. He's been worried about you. Worried that she cast her enchantment on you. I thought he was mistaken, that you couldn't possibly be that weak, not my daughter. To let a vampire get her hooks in you."

"She didn't—"

"What was it?" Hatsia yells, charging at Lucia. She wraps Lucia tight in her bonds, vines tying her hands and feet together, holding her just above the floor. "What was it that she said or did? Did you forsake your virtue for this daemon? Abandon all morality and honor to lie under vampire scum!"

Hatsia's anger is like a whip, her hand stinging Lucia's cheek and the vines pulling her down so she must look her mother in the eye. In those eyes, Lucia does not see her mother. She sees a stranger. And it pains Lucia at that moment to realize that the stranger *is* her mother. Lucia has never truly known her mother at all.

"I—" Lucia's voice wobbles as she struggles to speak through her pain and heartbreak. "I have done *everything* for you, Mother. Everything. All I have ever wanted is your love. For you to be proud of me. But it will never be enough."

Tears fall down Lucia's face, wetting the binds that hold her.

"I will never be enough, no matter how hard I try. And I love you, Mother, but I will not become you. I will not become what Grandmother made of you. Nor what the covens demanded. I would rather be with vampire scum than be with you and be unloved. I will not take the mantle of Orbis Libra, and I will not walk the path of fate you have set for me. I refuse. If you do not agree, then strike me dead here or set me free. Either way, I will be done with you."

Hatsia looks horrified. The woman stands there for a few moments, not even looking at Lucia as she gathers her thoughts. Hatsia's face slowly rearranges to one of cool indifference. Her usual detached stare.

Through gritted teeth, the woman says, "You will come to see things differently one day. You are still like a child."

Lucia only turns away.

Lucia is numb. She sits on her bed staring at Caitlyn who shakes with nerves from where she stands in front of the door. Her mother left the woman to guard her so she wouldn't run. She said that she would come back after Lucia had calmed down and once she talked down Madam Devroue, who was shaking mad at the thought that Lucia might have broken the betrothal, *which she has.* A betrothal she had never asked for in the first place.

Lucia clenches her fist in the folds of her dress. Her mother thinks she will change her mind, but she will not. She meant every word.

"I'm sorry," Caitlyn says softly. "Your mother paid me to make sure you don't leave this room."

Lucia snorts, rolling her eyes, something she got from Adelaide. "You're doing this for money? That's all it takes to buy your morality?"

Lucia has always liked Caitlyn, but she is angry. The woman would fall at her mother's feet for *money*. Keep Lucia locked up like a prisoner. Lucia could try to use an enchantment on the woman, she has been getting better at her cantus, but she worries Caitlyn still might be more advanced than she is at magisk, so she doesn't want it to come to a cantus fight.

Also, the witch is an Augure, she's a lot stronger than Lucia. And she doesn't want to get into a physical fight with her sister's friend either way—*the sister who is missing from her side once again*. Lucia tries not to feel bitter about it. She was in her sister's head, she knows Gabrielle needs her space, and to not be rushing to her older sister's aid, but it still stings.

"A little cash?" Caitlyn scoffs, her head hitting back against the door. "That wolf was right, you know *nothing*. I don't know how they expect you to be Eidan when you're this unaware! You can't just sit here and try to act all good now. Like you *actually* care."

Lucia's brows scrunch, confused why the younger witch thinks *she's* the one in the right here when Lucia is the one being held against her will.

"What is that supposed to mean? Are you mad that I'm trying? I'm *trying* to do better here, what do you want from me?"

"No, I—" Caitlyn rubs her temples. "It means you're oblivious, Lucia. You don't see anything even if it's right in front of you! If it doesn't affect you and your narrow view, you're ignorant. That's the privilege of being a Dol'Auclair I guess."

"*Privilege*? The Starlights are also a main family of the four major covens. And, unlike me, you got a gift on your first blooming. This entire time, the whole competition, everyone doubted me. No one, not even I, thought I'd get this far. I admit I have not been blameless in this mess, but you too uphold the covens' values even now, even after all of the things you said to me before. There is pressure on me that you couldn't even comprehend, so the last person I need a lecture from is *you*. Just earlier Mia was upset—she was losing it, because of something you did. So don't paint yourself as perfect."

"Do *not* speak about Mia," Caitlyn snaps, her face contorting into anger for a split second.

Lucia is taken aback by the reaction, watching as the younger woman reigns herself back in.

Caitlyn sighs, shaking her head. She stands straighter, moving closer to Lucia. "I might be one of the four, but the Coflars are not like the rest of you. We have always been looked down on and mocked for living in poverty in Whonyia and having a relationship with humans. Do you know what's in Whonyia? Nothing. We are fighting to survive out there. Like Hetan, we have had to rely on humans. At the mercy and kindness of the Mystic Enforcement Agency. Your grandmother and all the rest of you have turned a blind eye to everyone else. You were spouting on and on about how witches have failed the wolves and the vampires, and yet you fail to see all of the damage they have done to their own. That is all I care about. You're right, Lucia, I do care. I care about the legacy of the witches and our values, which your own family continues to stomp on every day!"

Lucia swallows the lump in her throat, collapsing back on the bed. She feels chastised once again, made to feel small by even this young witch. *Has she been that oblivious?*

"I'm sorry," Lucia says, defeated. "You're... *you're right*, I don't know what you've gone through. I just... that's why I want to help. That's what I'm trying to do. I'm trying to learn, and I just keep messing up!" Lucia groans, frustrated with herself and her ignorance as she pulls at her hair, the curls tangling in her fingers. "And Adelaide... well, I just wanted *one thing*." A tear drips down her cheek. "Just one thing that was mine."

There's silence between the two women, Caitlyn against the door, and Lucia slumped down on the bed picking at the threads until her fingers are sore. She looks up when there's movement. Caitlyn is moving away from the door. The woman gestures with her head.

"Go. I'll cover for you if your mother returns."

Lucia is confused by the witch's change of heart. "What— How?"

"Don't worry about it. Just go see your vampire."

A tentative smile spreads across Lucia's face as she stands, moving toward the door. Caitlyn makes no move to stop her. "Thank you," she says, taking the woman's hands in hers. "Thank you. And I promise, if it's the last thing I do, I'll try my best to make things right. For your family and many others."

Lucia rushes across the academy grounds to find Adelaide. All she can think of is the vampire.

Without a thought or worry, Lucia bursts through the front door of the vampire dorms and looks around frantically. Her cheeks are warm from running and her hair is a bit wild. She spots Adelaide brawling with Kai. She turns at Lucia's noisy arrival.

Adelaide doesn't speak as she crosses the room, throwing the younger vampire aside to take Lucia's hand and rush Lucia up to her room. She closes the door and pins Lucia against it, attacking her lips before she can say a word.

"You shouldn't be here right now," Adelaide says against her lips.

"Why?"

"The others, they're mad about the trial. Tensions are high, the vampires need to let off some steam. Drinking, partying... fighting. It will be chaos here tonight."

"Well, I needed to see you. I needed—I needed to be with you."

Adelaide groans, diving in for another breathtaking kiss.

"Do you need to let off some steam?" Lucia asks. She begins undoing the knot on her cloak, giving the vampire a sultry look under her lashes. "Because I can think of a way I can help you."

Adelaide is panting hard, her fangs extended and her eyes red. "You're not playing fair, little witch," she says.

Lucia smirks, pushing the vampire back to the bed. "You're right. *I'm mean.*"

Adelaide falls against the sheets and Lucia is over her, licking a path up her neck. "Let me taste you," she whispers. "And tell you exactly what you mean to me."

"Are you sure about this?" Adelaide asks, her hands gripping Lucia's hips. "Your mother—"

"I don't care about my mother. This isn't about her."

Adelaide nods reluctantly and Lucia feels relief rush through her at the dangerous gleam that comes into the vampire's eyes. *Good.* She doesn't know why the vampire suddenly cared about what her mother might think, she doesn't even like the witches, but she's glad those thoughts have fled Adelaide's mind.

After baring herself, Lucia undresses Adelaide too. Her hands shake with every piece of cloth she removes until tan skin is all she sees. She blushes at the sight, despite all of the naughty thoughts she has had of the vampire.

Lucia is shaking with both excitement and nerves as Adelaide watches her, moving in first to take the woman's lips, an action she is most familiar with. The vampire meets her passionately, grabbing Lucia's hips, but Lucia removes Adelaide's hands.

"Ah—ah. No touching."

Adelaide groans, lying back, and Lucia laughs. Her fingers trail up Adelaide's stomach, which jumps at her touch, her fingertips burning across the flesh.

Lucia nips at Adelaide's neck, tasting the skin, and slowly moves down toward Adelaide's naked breasts. She whispers across the vampire's skin, "I love your fire and passion. I love your strength and how protective you are over the things you care about."

She sucks a nipple into her mouth and Adelaide moves against her, arching into the wet suction. Her hand moves down Adelaide's thigh.

"I am jealous of you. Your beauty, eyes, and skin are like an open flame. Long, graceful legs like a gazelle."

Lucia's fingers cup Adelaide's sex. The vampire is watching her like a predator watches prey, with thin, sharp fangs descending below her lip.

"You are so free," Lucia whispers, her fingers moving slowly across wet lips. "I don't know if I'm envious of your freedom, or if I want to join you and run away from everything."

"Yes," Adelaide growls. "Yes, run away with me."

In a flash, Lucia finds herself on her back. She gasps as the vampire's mouth latches over her neck, baring herself to the woman and putting herself at her lover's mercy. Adelaide could do anything to her right now.

Anything.

"Can I?" Adelaide rumbles against her throat, panting like she is out of breath and dying of thirst. Lucia's pulse thrums under the vampire's lips, fangs scratching over her skin.

Lucia's heartbeat rages like a storm as she nods, her chest heaving as she lies vulnerable and so terrified. Not of Adelaide, but of the weight of the moment and the depth of the emotion she feels right now for *her vampire*. Her fingers grip Adelaide's shoulders.

"Do it."

Twin pinpricks sting Lucia's neck as Adelaide indulges in her hot blood, groaning and falling heavy against Lucia as if she is drunk on the taste of her. Lucia feels warm and her head fuzzy as an indescribable pleasure fills her body and she is swept away with Adelaide.

Lucia lies naked in the crook of Adelaide's arm. They're both laughing, breathing hard, kissing sloppy and lazily in the afterglow of their lovemaking. *This is what Lucia needed.* She doesn't want to think of Hetan or her mother, or any of that. Except... the burden has weighed too heavy on her. And as Caitlyn pointed out, Lucia was too narrow-sighted. Aamad said she needed to find someone she trusts. She trusts Adelaide.

"I need to tell you something," Lucia says quietly, almost hoping the vampire won't hear her. Her head is still spinning a bit from the high of their activities, but she is clear on what she needs to do.

"You can tell me anything."

"It's— I know you don't like the witches already and this won't help. But I need someone to talk to. It's been eating me up."

Adelaide shifts so that they're facing each other on the bed. She takes Lucia's hands and kisses her knuckles.

"You know those welts healing on my back right now, do you know what they're from?"

Lucia shakes her head. She assumed maybe it was from her fight with Adakai. The boy is scrappy and has sharp little claws. He also looks like a biter.

"That was from Cassius."

"You fought Cassius?" Lucia gasps. "I thought you said—"

"No, I didn't fight him," she says. "It was a punishment. A punishment for seeing you."

"I—I don't understand. Have you been hurt *every time* you see me?"

Adelaide doesn't answer the question. She says, "Nikolay wasn't happy about the last trial, or finding out that I've been seeing you. None of them are. They don't think I tried hard enough—or was hard enough on you—during the debate. You're right, vampires hate your family. I don't particularly like them either. For the way, they've treated you, but also what they've done my people. But I do care about you so much, Lucia. And I would never betray you. Not on my undead life."

Tears gather in Lucia's eyes and she squeezes Adelaide's hand tighter.

"I don't—I don't know what to do. My mother has done something terrible. Many things, probably, but she killed Hetan's parents. I can't tell him, because he would hate me and seek retribution against my mother. I—I hate her, but I don't want her dead. Or for my entire coven to pay for her actions. I know I should tell the truth, but I'm selfish because I'm afraid of what he'd do to her... to us... to me. And I'm just scared."

"Hey," Adelaide says, catching Lucia's tear. "You don't hate your mother."

"I do."

Adelaide shakes her head. "You don't, Lucia. Because I know you and I know how big your heart is. You can't help it; she is still your mother."

Lucia drops her head on Adelaide's shoulder feeling defeated. She should hate her mother. She really should. But maybe Adelaide is right, and Lucia hates it.

"You may not hate her, but I do. I will never forgive her for what she has done to you, nor any of your coven." The vampire's hand runs up and down Lucia's back soothingly. "I'll be here for you. No matter what choice you make. If I have to fight off every one of the cults, or the clans, or even your family then I'll do that. For you."

Lucia squeezes her eyes shut tight, pain lacing through her. Adelaide thinks too highly of her. She thinks Lucia is so *good*. Lucia doesn't deserve that, not when she has been lying to someone she cares about. She knows what she must do. No matter how much it hurts, or what it will cost, she has to tell Hetan the truth. It is only the right thing to do. And she thinks she can do it if she has Adelaide beside her.

Lucia gives Adelaide a watery smile, feeling lighter now that she knows. "You're not afraid of anything," Lucia whispers. "I envy that too."

Adelaide shakes her head. "I am. I *am* scared. The vampires hate that we're together, they've made that perfectly clear. I'm scared, not that we can't or shouldn't be together, not about what I feel for you. But I'm afraid one day you'll no longer love me."

Lucia freezes, her eyes going wide as her heart patters wildly in her chest. "I—I—"

"You love me," Adelaide says with conviction. "You must. There's no way I can feel so strongly for you as I do—feverish and without breath—for you with your beating heart and cool skin and passionate kisses, like you feel *everything*, to not feel the same."

Lucia breathes heavily, too afraid to say a word. Her mind is spinning at the words *I love you*.

"I'm afraid that you'll realize the truth—that I'm undead and *some other thing* and this impossible love you feel for me will be cut, like my ties to this life. Death has always mocked me. But to take not only my life but also take you? I would wish I was dead for real."

Lucia cups Adelaide's face in hers, and though the vampire can't cry, Lucia can feel she is. She says, "Dead or not, it doesn't matter. Even in death, I'll love you. My heart is too big not to, right? Why would I be given this depth of feeling if not to love, even after life? I am Lucia Dol'Auclair, a witch born to love a vampire. If anything is cruel, it's that I cannot join you in this life after death. Or maybe it's that you will continue to love me, into your long eternity without me. We may not be able to be together forever, but I can give you this, Adelaide S kullkin—"

Lucia's lips come to Adelaide's ear, whispering slowly, quietly, pouring her heart into the words.

"I... love... you."

Chapter Twenty-Seven

Descent to Madness

"Cassius?"

Lucia wakes to the sound of Adelaide's voice. She's cursing, a piece of plastic at her ear—a human device she uses like a sphaera. Lucia groans when she feels the vampire sit up quickly, pulling on her leather pants.

"Where are you going?" Lucia croaks, rolling over to squint up at her. Adelaide leans over the bed and kisses her temple. She hums happily.

"Go back to sleep, kuai-yuel, I'll be back quickly."

"Are you sure?"

"Promise. Sleep."

Lucia turns back over, snuggling into the thick, warm blankets as the door closes behind Adelaide.

It feels like not much time has passed when Lucia awakens again to the sound of shuffling and banging like someone is walking into things across the room.

"Adelaide, is that you?" Lucia mumbles, blinking out in the dark room. A chill falls over her as she gasps, her eyes widening at the figure standing above her.

Lucia falls out of bed with a pained thud, a crazed Siphon looming across from her. He seems out of it, muttering to himself. He doesn't even seem to notice her.

"S-Siphon?" she asks, standing with the bed between them. "Are you okay?"

"Blood," he croaks. Lucia presses her hand to the marks Adelaide left on her neck.

"Do you need your sister? Should I get—" Lucia moves to skirt around him, but his eyes snap to her, freezing her in place. They look frightening. They look like Cassius's the night he attacked her, crazed and murderous.

"Blood. Please, just... *a little blood.*"

The moonlight from the window hits Siphon when he moves toward Lucia, highlighting his face. His skin is deathly pale and ashen. His mouth is covered in red, and so are his hands. *Did he—*

Siphon lunges for her.

"Sunpa fila!" Lucia shouts, arm shooting out toward the lunging vampire. With a flash, Siphon goes flying back into the wall, seizing from the shock burst. Lucia doesn't have time to celebrate the successful odua-grade Itoju, but she uses the distraction to go racing past Siphon, her heart pounding in fear as she throws open the door.

Since the last vampire attack, Lucia had learned a few protection cantus. She hadn't been able to use them, but she thought they would be good to know. Now she's glad for the oversight. It wasn't very powerful, especially not against a vampire, but it was all she was able to manage.

Lucia hesitates for only a moment. *Should she try for downstairs?* Adelaide's room is on the top floor. Lucia would have no escape in the stairwell, and the chance she can outrun a vampire is none.

In a split-second decision, she runs for the balcony at the end of the hall, which leads to the bridge. She's near the door when Siphon comes barreling behind her. She tries to shock him again, but he's expecting it, dodging out of the way. It gives her enough time to get to the door as he crashes messily into the wall. Missing is the grace and poise with which he usually moves.

Barrelling through the door, Lucia is out on the bridge that separates the vampire's dorms from the werewolves.'

"Rasin!" Lucia shouts, and the door seals behind her, and she can hear a crash as Siphon runs into it.

It's freezing, the cold is like a shock to Lucia who is still in her nightgown, only a thin chemise covering her. Lucia sprints across the long bridge, lungs burning and arms swinging fast. She can see her breath in the icy air before her and hears the *thump, thump* as Siphon comes crashing through the seal.

Dais Tofet, he's that strong? Lucia curses. He's on her in a flash, knocking her hard to the stone. Her head hits the ground painfully.

It's hard for her to think properly to come up with a cantus. Lucia feels dizzy.

"Ap—" she wheezes for breath trying to get a cantus out. One she has never even attempted before. "Apamorha!"

A strong armor is erected over Lucia, so when Siphon's strong fist comes down to hit her, it knocks her breath but isn't fatal. She rolls out of dodge of his next attack, jumping to her feet.

Lucia's dizzy and stumbles, weighed down by the armor. When the vampire comes at her now, he barrels right at her, and she doesn't have time to move. They go crashing into the side of the bridge.

Crack! The stone crumbles beneath her, and they both go over the side. The wind rushes past her as she falls almost in slow motion, staring up at the high moon, her arms outstretched as if to catch herself. There's nothing to grab.

"Iba as!"

Lucia is thankful for her Magisk Skill lessons as her landing is softened. She bounces, rolling across the ground. She groans, her entire body aching. Though it was a better landing than if she'd hit the ground normally, the impact still knocks the breath out of her and rattles her bones.

THE BALANCE OF FATES

Lucia has just enough time to stumble to her feet, then Siphon recovers and charges at her once more. She's taken such a beating she can barely move, the high-grade cantus zapping what little energy she had.

All she has is the dented armor she erected. She can only raise her arms to let the metal take the brunt of the hits, though she can still feel the bruising every time he makes contact.

"Siphon," Lucia wheezes, seeing no hint of humanity behind crazed blood-red eyes. "Please, this isn't you. You're not a killer." She bends over, coughing up blood. She doesn't know Siphon beyond her sister's memories and the way Adelaide talks about her brother, but she doesn't believe this is something he would do. He stepped in to save her when Cassius attacked.

"I have to," Siphon hisses, awareness flickering behind his eyes for only a moment. "I have to—*Olympia*."

Lucia screams as Siphon grabs her, his teeth sinking into her neck. She feels faint, the light wavering behind her eyes as they grow heavier.

Lucia wonders if this is how she dies. *Does her life end here?*

Lucia's eyes droop, her body going limp in Siphon's arms. She stares up at the bright, full moon.

What would Adelaide think? Would she be disappointed in her, upset she was so weak? Would she blame her brother? Her arms push weakly at the feeding vampire. *I want to be alive with you,* Adelaide had whispered in her ear weeks ago.

She can't—she's not ready to die.

Lucia stares up at the sky, those stone creatures looming above like guardians, silhouettes against the moon. They stare down at Lucia, held in Siphon's arms, her throat between the vampire's powerful jaw. When she first saw them, she had been terrified, their beady eyes looking into her, but now they look almost protective. She stares at long, bat-like wings and pointed claws.

With the last of Lucia's strength, she calls out a single cantus, her voice cracking on the word. "*Ji ed'okuta!*"

As Lucia lets her eyes flutter closed, exhausted and losing blood, all she hears is the sound of cracking stone. The noise is like crackling thunder, a large, dark figure swooping down from above as her eyes drift close.

Lucia groans as she wakes, her body aching and her neck stiff.

"Hey, careful, don't move around too much," Gabrielle says.

Lucia's head snaps over to Gabrielle beside her, sitting on the end of the bed. She begins to smile until she sees it. Her sister looks distraught, with dark circles around her eyes, messy hair, and a wrinkled dress.

Lucia has never seen her sister look so lifeless like she hasn't slept in days. The memory of Lucia's attack hits her, her hand flying to her throat, which is covered in Iwsan leaves. They burn, which means that they're working, healing Siphon's bite.

"W-what happened? Where's Siphon—*Adelaide?*" Lucia asks her sister.

Gabrielle seems to look even sadder, her gaze turning down to the bed where she's fiddling with the thin sheet covering Lucia's body. Lucia didn't think that was possible, she hates the sight of it.

"No. He wasn't—" Lucia can't help but think of the worse, her hand covering her mouth as the blanket slips down her shoulders.

"Not yet," Gabrielle says, her fingers stilling where they're tangled in sterile white cloth. "But it's only a matter of time. There's going to be a trial. And Adelaide... *Lucia*, she was taken too."

"What?" Lucia whispers, her eyes opened wide. "What do you mean, *they took her?*" Lucia can't believe her ears. Her nose twitches from the burning smell of the medicinal leaves and she begins rising from the bed without thought. She has no clue where she's going, but it's wherever Adelaide is.

Gabrielle pushes her back to the cot.

"You need to rest, just stay down."

THE BALANCE OF FATES

Lucia shakes her head. She's still a bit dizzy and her vision blurs from the fast movement. *How could her sister be asking that of her at a time like this? Doesn't she understand?*

"What happened, Gabrielle? Tell me."

"Okay," Gabrielle says, holding Lucia back. Lucia plops down, watching her sister intently as she hangs her head. "Give me a moment."

Whatever it is that happened seems to be taking a toll on her. Gabrielle usually never takes anything seriously. She is always bubbly and fun—*Lucia's opposite*. Right now, Lucia thinks they look a lot more like sisters.

Lucia waits impatiently while Gabrielle gathers herself. Her fingers drum on her leg as thoughts of Adelaide flit through her mind until finally, Gabrielle looks up at her.

"You were attacked right next to the wolves' dorms. Hetan, he—he's the one who found you. You were on the ground, with barely any breath in your lungs and Siphon was caught beneath a stone statue. One of the ones that loom above the vampire's dorms. If he hadn't found you, you would have bled out."

"Okay, and?" Lucia says. She can barely focus on how that makes her feel, too worried about Adelaide.

She nearly died out there. Siphon had bitten her, tore into her neck. *She was bleeding out.* Her hand goes to her bandaged neck, brushing over the slimy leaves.

"And he freaked out. He was so beside himself. So much so that he called for Fabien and told him what happened, and the Sea Serpents and the wolves went for Siphon. As your betrothed, it's within Fabien's rights to have Siphon apprehended. But Adelaide and her two friends were not happy about it. They fought."

Lucia's heart races, palms sweating as she listens to Gabrielle's retelling of events while she was passed out. *Adelaide fought Hetan and Fabien?* Her heart clenches painfully. *She should have been there. She should have...*

She can picture it. Adelaide, Cassius, and Kai faced off against the wolves and witches. Flashing red eyes and pointed teeth.

"Adelaide injured Hetan, slicing him across the face. She hurt a lot of people, trying to get to Siphon. But, they were outnumbered. In the end, they took her too."

This time Lucia does jump up, and Gabrielle doesn't stop her as she anxiously begins gathering her things. Her slippers are on the floor and a clean dress is sitting on an empty cot. The one she had been wearing must have been torn up and filthy.

Lucia is frazzled, her nerves a mess as she begins thinking about Adelaide, locked up in some cell. Is she on campus? Did they take her somewhere else?

The thought of her vampire being confined in one of the dungeons back in Laesbury, or worse, beneath the Dome, has her blood turning to ice. She shivers at the thought.

Is she okay? Are they treating her right? *Have they...* she shakes the thought away.

"I have to go—I have to—"

"Lucia, calm down," Gabrielle pleads, moving to get in her path. "She didn't kill anyone, so her punishment won't be as harsh as Siphon's."

"But, I'm fine. Siphon didn't kill me."

Gabrielle's face drops and Lucia's stomach sinks lower. She does not like that look.

"Before he attacked you, he... that's why Adelaide wasn't there when you were attacked. They found the body of his first victim. They were planning to cover it up, it seems. When Fabien found out, he was going off, spouting his belief that Siphon was the one behind all of the killings. Things don't look good for him. *For either of them.* I think they might... they might..." She's unable to finish her sentence.

Lucia shakes her head, anger filling her again. It seems like that's all she has felt lately. Angry. Nothing is fair. The vampires aren't bad people. Adelaide isn't a monster.

"Why—Why weren't you here, Gabrielle?" Lucia can't help but lash out, her sister's face morphing into one of guilt as Lucia loses it. She watches, wide-eyed as Lucia pulls at her hair, her voice breaking. "I *needed* you."

"I'm sorry."

Gabrielle's face falls and Lucia is struck by the devastating look on her sister's face, and her next words shrivel in her throat. It's enough to have her stop in her tracks. Taking a deep breath, Lucia sits back down, pulling Gabrielle down with her. She pulls her sister's head to her chest, the quick beating of her heart slowing under Gabrielle's ear.

"No, no. I shouldn't have said that."

Lucia's voice is still raw from Siphon's attack, rough and low as she apologizes for her outburst. This isn't Gabrielle's fault. None of it is. It's *Lucia's*.

Gabrielle has always been there for her, so it's unfair to blame her. She saw Gabrielle's memory; she knows her sister likes the vampire, and yet here she is once again only thinking of herself. Not thinking about how Gabrielle is feeling about all of this.

Caitlyn's words about Lucia not seeing anything outside of her bubble weighs even heavier on her. She knows nothing about what Gabrielle has been going through. She has been so focused on herself since she has gotten to Eirini and tried to push her sister away for her protection that she didn't see what was right in front of her.

"You really love her, don't you?" Gabrielle asks. She pulls back, smiling as she cups Lucia's face in her hands. "You love Adelaide."

Lucia pauses for a moment as if to deny it. Then Adelaide's lovely face pops into her head, and Lucia knows she can't keep lying to her sister. If there's anyone who would understand, it's her. But only if Lucia is brave enough to let her in.

Lucia pushes her face further into her sister's warm palm. Her shoulders drop as the weight lifts from them.

"I do. I love her so much, Gab. It's crazy because we haven't known each other long, but I—"

Lucia goes rigid. She curses as she's pulled into another memory, a stabbing pain shooting through her head.

Lucia watches through her sister's eyes, an event only less than a day prior:

Gabrielle is in shock, frozen at the side of the tub. The thick, cloying smell of smoke chokes her as she sits in the crumbling building she followed Siphon to, mostly bare aside a few stray items—a couch, a broken radio lying on the floor, trash—to what she's witnessing now.

She hears footsteps, Adelaide approaching. She called Cassius with the phone she bought from Blythe, asking him to send Adelaide here. She knows the vampire was busy, but this is more important.

Adelaide freezes beside her in shock at the sight and Gabrielle wants to look away but she stays strong.

Siphon sits before her in an abandoned tub, his body charred. If Gabrielle had gotten here any later, he would have been gone now. But she had been here, and she used a cantus to douse him with water.

Gabrielle is a sight kneeling beside Adelaide, with a dark head full of bubble braids and a garish bright pink top covered in hearts, tears tracking down her face as she clutches Siphon's hand.

Siphon's face is red and peeling, his expression one of utter pain.

"You need to leave, Gabrielle," Adelaide croaks. Her eyes don't leave her brothers, wide in horror.

Gabrielle's head snaps up. "I can't," she says, her throat thick with tears. "I have to—"

"Now!" The vampire's voice is frightening, and for a moment she nearly buckles under the command. She hesitates, not wanting to let go of Siphon's hand, but the look on Adelaide's face changes her mind. *If it was Lucia sitting in this tub*—If it were her sister, she would be losing it too.

Gabrielle slowly drops her hold on Siphon, standing on shaky feet. When Adelaide's storming, blood-red eyes don't leave him, she turns and runs. Except, instead of leaving as she should, she crouches down behind a crumbled block of wall. Adelaide is so focused on her brother that she doesn't even notice her lurking. *She should leave,* this is a private moment, but she is too afraid that if she does he will disappear.

She shakes where she hides across the room, the memory of when she had first walked into the abandoned warehouse burned behind her eyelids. The smell of burning flesh is sour in her nose.

Adelaide collapses to her knees, hands quickly patting at the dying flames across her brother's body.

"Who did this to you, Siphon? Who—"

"No," Siphon croaks, eyes opening slowly. "No, Adelaide."

He's collapsed there like a broken puppet, laid awkwardly against the porcelain. Adelaide's eyes stray to his ring which lies on the floor beside the tub, the silver spider decorated with emerald gemstones sitting amongst scratched wood and dark ash.

"How could... *Why?*" Adelaide says. Her voice sounds hollow as it echoes the large, barren room.

The place is dark with a broken light fixture swinging above and cobwebs hanging from every surface. Gabrielle can't help but think that the crumbling building looks more alive than the pair of siblings.

"Don't tell me you did this yourself, Siphon."

Siphon closes his eyes again like it's too painful to keep them open.

"I didn't want you to see this. I left a note."

He points. The movement looks painful as he gestures to the folded note amongst the dust at the legs of the tub. "I figured Cassius would find it and—"

"And what!" Adelaide screams. "Do you think he doesn't love you, too? We all do. I don't want a damn note. I need you, Siphon. Do you think I can do an eternity without you?"

Adelaide tries slipping the ring back onto his finger, but he bats it away, his head lolling to the side. "You won't die," she says. "You aren't going to die."

She puts her arm to his mouth pressing hard. He tries to turn his head. "Drink!" she yells. "Drink, then you will start to heal."

He's thin, his face gaunt. Much paler and ashen than usual. He's been starving himself. Gabrielle doesn't know how she didn't notice before, but it's obvious now. He probably hasn't been eating for a while.

Siphon shakes his head.

"I won't drink blood anymore," he says. *"I can't.* You'll be so much happier when I'm gone. Watching me only causes you pain. I don't want this life for you. I never wanted you to be changed. I wanted you to live a normal life. Maybe... maybe my death can bring you that."

Adelaide shakes her head frantically, tears pouring down.

"You're not happy here," he says. "The only reason you stick around is for me. Go. Go and do whatever you want. Be free."

"I am. I'm fine, Siphon. It's you I'm worried about. You have so much to live for. Someone told me life doesn't have to end after death. Neither does yours. Please, Siphon, please. I need you; you can't leave me. I have so much to tell you. I—I met a girl. She's so beautiful. And kind, *very kind*. Better than me. I know I never take anything seriously, but I truly, *truly* love her."

Siphon smiles slowly. "The witch?"

Adelaide nods.

"You deserve to be happy, Adelaide. You deserve love. I hope you can keep it."

Adelaide shakes her head violently, a wave of anger rising in her. "Live! If you can't live for yourself anymore, then live for me. At least for now, until I can show you how beautiful the world still is. *Until you believe it too."*

THE BALANCE OF FATES

Gabrielle's heart breaks as the siblings stare at one another for a painful few seconds that feel like forever. Siphon stares into Adelaide's eyes, the passion and sincerity she holds there. He slowly reaches for her arm, and she helps, lifting it to his lips.

Gabrielle lets out a painful breath as his teeth sink into his sister's flesh. She had tried feeding him her blood, and he refused.

Adelaide grits her teeth at the pain, the burns slowly starting to heal on his face and the hand holding Adelaide's arm. Adelaide collapses against the tub, both from blood loss and relief, handing him the ring, which he slips back on.

Gabrielle slumps back against the wall, closing her eyes as she tries to still her rapidly beating heart, adrenaline still pumping fast from when she first found Siphon burning alive. Her heart had shattered at the sight.

"You shouldn't have saved me," Siphon whispers. Gabrielle almost doesn't hear the words.

"Don't say that," Adelaide growls.

"We're cursed, Az. When I said I didn't want this for you, I meant it. We're cursed. It's only getting worse for me. At first, it was gradual, these moments of madness, but now with every attack, there are fewer moments between of lucidity. All I see when I close my eyes is her. *My Virenna.* Even then, it wasn't as bad as this. I'm losing pieces of myself. Of my memory. Things aren't making sense."

Adelaide's heart clenches. She shakes her head. "I don't understand. None of that is happening to me."

"It's like pieces of time are missing. And I'm scared. Being what we are... the curse of living so long..." He sighs, the action seems almost painful. "We were designed to hurt people to prolong our own lives. It had to come at a cost."

Adelaide clings to her brother's hand.

"Then we'll find another way. We'll find a way to help you, no matter the cost. You will know peace, you will know love again, as I have. No matter how long it takes."

Siphon sighs. "Then I hope for your sake, we do."

Gabrielle gasps, pulling away from Lucia, her eyes widening. Lucia reels from the memories, trying to put them all together.

Pieces of time missing... things not making sense... Lucia can't figure it out.

"Wha—what did you just do?"

Lucia stares at her sister in shock, her eyes filled with tears at the memory and the pain she felt through Gabrielle. That's why she was gone from the trial. She must have been with Siphon. It must have also been why Adelaide left. Except, she never said anything...

"I am so sorry," Lucia says, wrapping her arms around her sister again. "I am so sorry you went through that and I wasn't there. I—I should have been there. You should have told me."

"You... saw that?" Gabrielle asks warily, looking shocked and awed as if she can't believe it. "Lucia, you have a gift?"

Lucia nods, biting her lip in worry, not knowing how her sister will take the news. Or finding out Lucia has kept it from her. To her surprise, Gabrielle isn't mad. She begins laughing. She throws her head back, giddy with joy.

"Oh. Lucia, that's amazing!" she says. "Why would you keep that from me? Why haven't you told anyone?"

At the look on Lucia's face, her smile drops.

"What? Lucia... what did you see?"

Silence fills the room for a few minutes while Lucia tries to gather her nerves. Her shoulders slump as she collapses against Gabrielle's side, an action she hasn't done in so long. Gabrielle has always been her rock and her safe place to fall. The realization hits her that she can't keep hiding the truth, trying to protect Gabrielle. Gabrielle has always been so strong. Stronger than Lucia.

So, Lucia tells her everything. From the very first vision she had. When she's done, Gabrielle shakes her head, tears welling in her eyes.

"I'm so sorry, Luc. I'm sorry you've had to carry that. You shouldn't have kept that from me. I could have helped you."

Lucia gives a watery laugh at the irony. "It's okay. You've been protecting me our whole lives. It's not your job anymore. It never should have been."

"No, no I haven't. I couldn't even find the killer. I was so sure they were targeting you too. I found the skull dagger, which I found out belonged to Adelaide. Except she lost the blade to Cassius in a fight, and then Cassius gave it to Adakai as a present. And, well, as clumsy as he is, he misplaced it, and then Blythe, the scavenger they are, found it and took it for themself. Except Blythe said they lost it too. That's where I drew a dead end. *That stupid dagger*. I should have been here for you, but I was on a wild goose hunt with Siphon. Maybe I was just fooling myself so I could spend time with him..."

Gabrielle groans, running her hand down her face. She pushes back her curls and takes a deep breath. "I was trying to find a way to help you, but I should have just trusted myself and our bond. Caitlyn said it would be best to give you space and let you—"

Lucia smiles, laying a hand on her sister's shoulder to stop her rambling. "I don't care about the dagger, Gabrielle."

Gabrielle shakes her head. "No, no, it's not just that. I haven't done nearly enough, nor will I ever be able to make up for your childhood. I never stuck up for you growing up. Mother kept you alone, trapped in the house. She put all of these huge responsibilities on you, and I did nothing. I went to parties, had friends, and I got to live my life while you were suffering. All I ever did was pick up the pieces after you were already broken."

"It's okay, Gab. You were young, you didn't know."

"But I did!"

Gabrielle takes Lucia's hands, holding them in hers.

"When I was maybe twelve, I had woken one night because I couldn't sleep and wanted to get some lavender milk. I found Mom crouched on the floor in the living room. The rug was pulled back, and a piece of the floor was pulled out. There was a little cubby there. She had a scrap of a scarf in her hands, and she looked so distraught. When she noticed me, I thought she would yell and be angry, but she pulled me to her by my hand, and we just stayed there for a bit, my head against her chest. Mother was always so focused on you, so I was so excited she was embracing me. That soured a bit when she started talking about you. She was vague, but she was going on about how you reminded her of an aunt she had. She said she called her Olympia. I don't know, I thought it was an odd nickname. She said sometimes she could see her in your eyes. She showed me that necklace—"

Gabrielle pulls it out from the white smock the healer put her in.

"She said she kept little things of her aunt's because they reminded her of her grandmother. How she was before she became Eidan and lost her sister. That Grandmother was so distraught by her sister's death that it drove her to the bitter woman she is now."

Gabrielle laughs her face brightening for a moment.

"Mother actually said that. She called the Grand Elder bitter. She said sometimes it's hard to even look at you, that you were the image—in mind and body—of her aunt, and she found herself blaming you for the childhood she had with her mother. That's where I got this charm. During my blooming, I pictured it in its place in the cubby under the stairs and it came to me. I thought it was fitting that you have it."

That was a summoning? Lucia had always thought Gabrielle forged it.

Lucia pulls the necklace over her head. A piece of a great aunt she never knew. She holds the warm golden charm in her hands, running her fingers atop the flames it has flames coming from the top of the moon. She rubs her thumb over the face, a small smile gracing her lips despite the melancholy memory. The thought that she is like any of her ancestors makes her feel warm. She has always felt like an outsider.

"Wait, you said she was called Olympia?" Lucia asks confusedly.

Gabrielle nods. Lucia remembers last night, the words Siphon had spoken when he attacked her. He had called her by that name.

"Whoa," Gabrielle gasps, looking at where Lucia absently rubs the charm, jumping back as the necklace begins to glow. Lucia drops it to the floor in shock, backing away from it. *What the—*

The necklace pops open, the face lifting as if there is some invisible seal there. Inside is a small scrap of paper folded many times over itself. Curious, she reaches to pick it up. Gabrielle comes to look over her shoulder.

"Read it, read it!" Gabrielle says impatiently.

"Okay, relax, I will."

Heart beating loud in her ears, she reads Corseia's letter:

"A meeting of two people isn't the joining of two bodies but of two minds. Meeting Guiseppe was one such collision.

I'm not sure if anyone will ever see this. But the love I feel is too great to fade into oblivion. I must try as I can to keep our story alive.

When I fell in love with him, it wasn't like a witch falling in love with a vampire. It was two souls coming together at last. But the covens didn't see it that way, nor did the vampires. They killed him and tore him from me. They ripped out my soul and left my mind with the greatest torment.

I know they're coming for me next. I won't give them a chance. They won't have my half of him too.

No matter if the coven burns all my things, rips down his art, and strikes dead anyone who knew us, I will not let them forget him. He will not fade into oblivion. As Eidan, I will tip the balance of fates.

I curse the Araneidae and all the cults. When the blood runs dry and their throats ache, may they lose their hearts and their minds, descending into madness that will reveal to the world how wicked they are. They started this curse and brought the witches to this place of fear and anger.

In the future, they will be the ones the world brings to its knees."

"What does that mean?" Gabrielle asks, "Who's Guiseppe?" Lucia isn't listening. Her mind is spinning. Some of the pieces begin falling into place.

May they lose their hearts and their minds, descending into madness...

"It was her. It was Corseia who started this madness. She cursed Siphon and Cassius, and all vampires."

No. No, no, no. Lucia shakes her head in disbelief. The words of the Griffin during her walk with the ancestors come to her mind once more as she reads over the letter again, her eyes scanning the page over and over.

The joining of bodies and minds. The Mother had said that to her during her ceremony with the ancestors. At least, she thought it was, but it wasn't the Mother at all... It was Olympia—*Corseia.*

Lucia thought the necklace was Gabrielle's creation, but it was a summoning. *An item that belonged to Corseia.* Since Lucia wore it when she went into that tub for her spirit walk, it must have worked as a conduit and linked her to Corseia. *But why did Corseia pretend to be the Mother? What was the purpose? It makes no sense to Lucia.*

Lucia stands from the bed once more, wincing as she tugs at her injuries. Gabrielle tries to help her, but she shakes her off. *She can help Siphon and the vampires.* She just needs to explain what is going on.

The letter says Corseia was Eidan, which still has Lucia's mind spinning. She had never heard of this before. To her knowledge, Sonya Mitsu had the Orbis Libra before her grandmother. But if it's true then they can use it to help the vampires!

"Where is everyone?" Lucia asks, just now realizing it's eerily quiet. She expected her mother would be here with a lecture.

"Everyone is gone for the gala," Gabrielle says. "Mother went to in case you were chosen as Eidan. The winner is supposed to become the vessel tonight, but they decided if you were chosen they'd wait until you were healed."

Lucia's eyes widen as she realizes how long she was out.

"I need to get there right now."

Lucia is a mess when she bursts into the Hallow Tower. She is in a thin black robe she threw over her smock, lightheaded, and her heart racing. She got here as soon as she could. She still aches from the attack and is bruised, with a bandage on her neck. Her curls are plastered to her head from the heavy rain, a storm brewing outside just like the last time she was here.

People stare as Lucia cuts through the crowd, shaking from the cold, water trailing the floor behind her as she scans the room for her mother. She finds the woman in the corner with Madam Devroue, a glass of wine in her hand. Lucia rushes to them.

"Mother, I need to speak to you."

Hatsia turns quickly, eyes widening when she sees her daughter.

"Lucia? What do you think you're doing here looking like that? You should be in bed."

Lucia shakes her head. "It's important, Mother. It's about the murders—"

"We know, Lucia. We have apprehended the vampire who is doing it. We'll get the truth out of him about whether he had any help. I'm sure that sister of his is guilty too. That's why you should have listened to me when I told you they were no good. Maybe now you've learned."

Hatsia takes Lucia by the shoulders and begins steering her toward the door. "Now, you will take my carriage. Not back to Eirini, but back to Laesbury. We have a lot to discuss when I get home."

Lucia shakes off her mother's hand. "You're not listening to me. It wasn't Siphon's fault. He—"

Lucia gasps as her mother's arm tightens on hers, her vines coming out and wrapping painfully around her. Her voice is low by Lucia's ear, seething as she hisses, "You have the nerve to defend them here? After what they did!"

Lucia's heart beats fast as she stares up at her mother's fury. She feels like a kid again, being scolded by the woman. She had been so terrified then, afraid to even speak when her mother was angry.

"Y-you don't understand," Lucia says. "They were cursed and—"

Slap.

Lucia's head snaps to the side as her mother's hand comes down on it. Her heart squeezes in her chest, tears stinging in her eyes.

People are watching.

Hatsia speaks low so only Lucia can hear her over the music. "I don't want to hear another word about those vampires out of your mouth, do you understand me? I spent the night convincing my friend to forgive you for breaking your vow to Fabien, only to find another one of our people *dead*. All the while you're off whoring yourself to some bloodsucking daemon. Now, I will forgive you for falling for their seduction because I know you are weak. But you will never embarrass me like that again. You will marry Fabien and you will shut up and do as I tell you."

Lucia's blood boils, and the chills stop as she burns with rage. She stares up at her mother with hard, teary eyes.

"No."

"Excuse me?" Hatsia says, pulling back to look at Lucia.

"No, I will not marry Fabien and I will not listen to another word you say. *Let me go.*"

Lucia's eyes flash blue at her command, and she wrenches her arm away from her mother's stunned grasp as the vines drop limply to the ground, disobeying her mother's influence.

"Lucia, you—"

"I no longer belong to you Mother. I am not your puppet. I know things about you that you do not want to get out." Lucia grabs her mother's wrist, the memories flooding into Hatsia—the memory of Lucia learning the truth. Lucia gets something in return. A vision of her mother approaching hunters, paying those humans to kill Talulah and Ukaih. *So it's true.* There's no denying it now, her mother did have Hetan's parents killed.

Hatsia shakes her head in disbelief, eyes wide as she takes a step back.

"Lucia—"

THE BALANCE OF FATES

Lucia turns and flees. She can't even think about what she had just done—she had given *someone else* memories.

Lucia needs to find Hetan. She has to talk to him right away, and finally tell him the truth. Their conversation is long past due.

Snow falls outside of the large windows, the first snow at the end of the autumn season, and a voice sounds over the noise of the partying crowd as the music lowers.

"And now for what you have all come for. The announcement of the next Eidan, the vessel of the Orbis Libra."

Hetan.

Lucia spots her friend across the room, head held high as he stares up at the stage waiting for the announcement. Lucia moves quickly, pushing through people as she makes her way toward him. She isn't paying attention when she bumps into someone, her pulse beating quickly, and her eyes trained on him.

"Sor—"

Lucia gasps, eyes glazing a hazy blue as memories flow through her once more. She's in Caitlyn's memories, just flashes of faces and places moving quickly like a picture book. Snapshots that turn darker and darker. When Lucia pulls herself away, she stares at the woman in horror. The sweet, unassuming young witch.

"It was you... you—you're the killer—"

There was another Sage involved in this. *That's why Gabrielle couldn't find the killer.* Caitlyn is a Sage. She must have been using the ability to make herself appear as an Augure. She would have to be very skilled in her ability to do such a thing. She was using it to mess with people's minds. And Siphon, the vampire so weak from lack of blood, is more susceptible to this mind control. It only accelerated the curse Corseia placed on him.

Caitlyn's face morphs from confusion to panic as she realizes Lucia has figured her out, putting together the truth of Lucia's ability. Lucia stumbles back, ice in her veins as she stares at the woman behind the murders at Eirini. She killed so many innocent people.

Caitlyn is quick though, recovering, and Lucia is still frozen in shock.

"You're the one who sent the man with the skull dagger after me," Lucia says through a tight throat, her voice only a whisper.

"I did."

Caitlyn smirks, her face morphing into something unrecognizable. Nothing like the sweet, humble woman she has known her to be. "When I visited the Crimson Ash clan earlier this year, I found it. I recognized it immediately as belonging to your Adelaide, *that filthy Silver Spider*. I was hoping you'd figure it out, but strangely enough, you didn't care about the murders at all."

Lucia's mouth opens and closes like a fish, guilt burning through her veins.

"I—I— that's not true. I did. I cared. I just—"

"It's fine," Caitlyn chuckles, slinking closer to Lucia where she stands frozen on the ballroom floor, the witch spinning her in what would look like a dance to an outsider. "I wouldn't expect a spoiled little *Princess* like you to care about a few measly lives. And Gabrielle, sheesh. She was the worst detective."

Lucia is held rooted in place by Caitlyn's words, helpless as the woman circles her. Lucia tries to make this make sense in her mind, but she's coming back blank every time. This whole time Caitlyn was right under her nose, and she hadn't noticed. So absorbed in herself—the competition, her ability, *Adelaide*. Everyone was right, she is selfish. She's no different than her mother who she scorned.

Lucia is so caught up in Caitlyn's web she doesn't notice the woman reaching into the folds of the cape draped over her shoulders. She is trapped in her own mind, unsure of whether it is the other Sage's doing or her own. She barely feels it when the dagger slides into her gut, piercing through her flesh like churned butter.

Lucia stares wide-eyed at Caitlyn as her hands come to her stomach, sticky warmth beneath her hands as her mouth opens and closes, no sound coming out.

THE BALANCE OF FATES

The room is packed, and everyone is focused on the stage. They don't notice as Caitlyn whispers, "I'm sorry, Lucia," and slips away, disappearing into the crowd.

Lucia stumbles, falling into the people in front of her.

"Hey, watch it, witch—" the vampire falters, nose twitching as he smells the blood. Lucia's vision is white, dizzy as she falls to the ground.

"And the winner of the Triune, our next Eidan—*Lucia Dol'Auclair!*"

A storm brews outside, snow falling in a flurry of white as a scream pierces the Hallow Tower. A crowd gathers around Lucia's crumpled body, a pool of blood staining the white marble floor.

Acknowledgments

Thank you so much for reading The Balance of Fates (my labor of love) all the way to the end, and I hope you enjoyed it as much as I loved writing it. If you could leave a review and let me know what you thought that would mean the world! If you want to say hi, email me rrwrites@raquelraelynn.com I can't wait to hear from you.

    I want to thank the pioneers of self-publishing for allowing me and others with marginalized voices to be able to tell our stories and highlight those that are often invisible within traditional writing spaces, without having to change, dim, or prove our stories and stories about people who look like us matter. I am also grateful for social media and the impact it has had on publishing and the amazing readers who champion these spaces and give voices to smaller and unknown writers and have loved the madness writers have created within their stories as I have all my life. Thank you for loving and sharing stories like mine and making this dream possible.

About Author

Raquel Raelynn Simpson is a Black-American writer, born and raised in Washington state, and "The Balance of Fates" is her debut novel. She is the second youngest of ten siblings, a twin, and the proud aunt of many wonderful nieces and nephews. Growing up, Raquel was surrounded by teachers and authors that stoked her love of writing. Teachers are the unsung heroes who have inspired and pushed her to follow her passions, work hard, and believe she could do anything so long as she has the hunger to learn and grow. Through the books she read, Raquel found a home and escape to different worlds when she felt alone. Now, as an adult, Raquel is passionate about writing romance and fantasy books that all people can see themselves in. Her mission is to create books that people can get lost in and find a place to belong when they feel alone, just as she did.

Made in the USA
Las Vegas, NV
17 August 2023